GROUND LIONS

Lou Campanozzi

This novel is a work of fiction. Names, characters, places, and incidents are either products of the author's imagination or are used fictitiously. Any resemblance to actual persons (living or dead), events, or locales is entirely coincidental.

The publisher would like to thank Geoffrey Lister for his photograph "Rochester Skyline", courtesy of Rochester Photography.

....

Campanozzi, Lou.
    Ground lions / by Lou Campanozzi. -- 2nd ed.
    p. cm.
    ISBN 1-58943-019-0

    1. Police--New York--Fiction. 2. Rochester (N.Y.)--Fiction.
3. Buffalo (N.Y.)--Fiction. 4. Mystery fiction. I. Title.

PS3553.A43935G76 2001   813.6
                    QBI01-701269

AMERICANA PUBLISHING, INC.

This book is dedicated in loving memory to Major Anthony Fantigrossi, who, before his untimely death, had been the Rochester Police Department's Chief of Detectives. He was a man's man and a cop's cop. If he was alive today, and Lieutenant Mike Amato was a real person, they would have been great friends.

Major, this one's for you.

Prologue

The young boy, clutching the well-worn fabric of his mother's long, wool dress between the thumb and forefinger of his right hand, stepped off the train. His attention was not focused on the noisy, amoebic crowd that seemed to flow around him every which way. He seemed unaware of the unintelligible language spoken and even shouted by the members of the crowd. Nor was he vaguely aware of the short, stout man strutting in a rapid gait who was now approaching his mother.

The only stimuli to enter the world of Antonio Amato were the white snowflakes that drifted effortlessly from the gray sky above, falling on his worn sweater and on the tip of his extended tongue. This was his first experience with crystals from heaven. He had not seen these sky crystals in all of his nine years in Valledolmo, Sicily. The sky crystals had not been present in the cold February air of Ellis Island. It was only as the train slipped past Syracuse and picked up speed for the last leg of the long journey to Rochester, New York, that Antonio was confronted by this strange phenomenon of the New World.

The portly man, who walked with more importance than was his to claim, tipped his hat to Antonio's mother as they exchanged greetings. It was then that Antonio shifted his attention to the stranger.

"Antonio," his mother said in Sicilian as she cupped his chin in her hand. "This is your father."

"*Buon' giorno, Papa,*" the boy said as he let go of his mother's dress and looked into the man's face. The boy searched for features that matched the ones his memory had stored in his head. There were none. Seven years was a long time to hold such memories, Antonio rationalized. Even so, he admonished his faulted memory; one should surely remember his own father. Nonetheless, Antonio offered a pleasant smile behind rosy cheeks, which did much to conceal the mental scolding he was giving himself.

Bending over at his ample belly, Francesco Amato lowered himself closer to the level of the lean boy. Placing a beefy, calloused hand on his son's shoulder, the older man looked into Antonio's dark eyes as if looking for something beyond the eyes of youth. Taking a breath, Francesco began to speak to his son without emotion.

In the same Sicilian dialect spoken by all the people Antonio had known in the Old World, the father said to his child, "This is America, my son. Here there are many opportunities for one who works hard and works long hours. But here, there is no room for foolishness! Here you must walk the edge of the knife and be honest in all of your affairs. You must never bring dishonor to the name of your father."

"*Si, Papa,*" Antonio acknowledged as he lowered his head.

"I have been busy looking for work for you so that you will be able to start your life here in a prosperous way. Come," Francesco said ceremoniously, taking his wife's elbow in his left hand and placing his right hand on his son's shoulder, steering him away from the train. "I will find your suitcase. Move quickly, now. Time is not wasted in America!"

Although he could not understand why, Antonio longed to return the firm grasp of his father's hand with a hug. Perhaps the desire was based in the bonds of family that were not erased by the passing of years. Perhaps it was even strengthened by the rigors World War I had forced on the family as Antonio's father sought his fortune in America. Regardless of the need, the boy knew he would not, *could not*, embrace his father; such things were not done. Emotions, and love was major emotion among them, were something private. They were not revealed to the eyes of strangers, especially not to the *Americani*.

As his father retrieved the family's three suitcases, Antonio shifted his gaze to the young boy — surely younger than himself — who hawked the news of 1921 America to all who passed. He was sure it was a job he could do, that is, once he could speak a few words of the strange language. He thought it to be a good plan. However, his father had made other arrangements.

Before the bells announced the advent of noon at the parish church, Saint Francis of Assisi, young Antonio stood near his father in the center of Victorio Ruggeri's barbershop. The deal was made with a handshake and sealed with a shot of colorless, licorice-scented anisette. Antonio Amato was to be at the shop every day within minutes of leaving school, all day when school was not in session, and to stay until closing. Antonio would be an apprentice barber and would sweep the floor, lather men's faces for shaving, sharpen razors, and, most important of all, he would stand outside the barbershop during any of his free time. Once at his station at the front of the shop, he would be required to knock on the window if a policeman appeared. For these duties, he would be paid two cents every day and a nickel on Saturdays.

Walking back along the streets that he was sure he would never come to know, Antonio asked his father why one of his duties required him to warn Signore Ruggeri about the arrival of the police.

"These are not things for your concern, my son," Francesco said with finality. "Signore Ruggeri is a hard working man. But, there are some things that are not for the government to know about. Just do your duty well and do not shame me."

Antonio Amato would learn the lessons of duty and hard work, and they would be the foundation of his success. He would pass the lessons on to his son, Michael, and they would become Michael's hindrance.

The incongruity of not shaming his father, while acting as a lookout for a bookie, was lost on the boy. This was one of the strange ways of Sicily. And, he accepted it without question.

1

Tuesday Night: Victims and Friends

On this hot, muggy night in the waning days of summer, I had no way of knowing that by the end of the week the clearly defined lines which separated my friends from my enemies would be an elusive, fuzzy shadow. I was raised with strong beliefs about loyalty, and it would be a very cold day in hell before I hurt a friend or allowed an enemy into my heart. However, life is filled with strange twists of fate, and fate would see Thursday emerge as a very cold day in hell. By Sunday morning, hell would freeze over.

One thing the cop business taught me over the years is that friends and enemies are connected or separated only by the thin lines of their beliefs and values. If the beliefs are shared, the two people are friends. If the beliefs differ, the two are enemies. However, this case changed my thinking regarding that philosophy. What I learned from this murder could fill a bookcase. I walked away with one basic lesson after the four days and nights this case lasted: It isn't the beliefs and values that separate people; it is the mere *perception* of those beliefs and values that create friends and enemies.

Such was the situation with Danny Martin and me. He was the bad guy. I was the good guy. That's what I perceived, and that's what separated us.

Danny Martin grew up just five houses from my family home. When he was born, I was a senior in high school, and by the time I got back from 'Nam he was out of diapers and finding his way beyond the Martin yard.

When I was a rookie cop, I worked the midnight-to-eight shift. I still smile, even now, when I remember Danny running up to me as I dragged my butt up the steps to my parents' home. The kid would get up on his tiptoes, grab the police whistle swinging from my gun belt, and blow it until I finally gave in and agreed to play catch for ten minutes. With all that background going for us, Danny and I should have stayed friends, *compadres*, buddies. However, our ideologies separated us and threw our worlds apart.

By the time Danny was eighteen, I was a Sergeant working in the Vice Squad. And him? Well, he was hanging out with a group of wiseguys that were leading him to no good. In the old neighborhood, people depended on their friends, so it wasn't out of the norm when Mrs. Martin asked my mother if I would talk to Danny. After listening to my mother and reassuring her, I made it a point to grab the kid and spend a little time with him. It was easy to see, even for a hardhead like me, that Danny was growing up to be an angry young man. He was angry about his old man getting killed in a car accident, angry about growing up in a neighborhood that was definitely going downhill fast, angry about God not listening, and angry about life in general.

I listened, I talked, and I remembered. His words had been my words when I was breaking into this manhood thing. I really don't know why I was so angry as a teenager. Maybe it was just the thing that puberty and hormones do to you. Maybe it was the neighborhood. Maybe it stemmed from assuming that life "out there" beyond the neighborhood promised nothing better than the lives my parents were living. Although I didn't understand my own anger, I understood Danny Martin's anger.

After more than a few talks and walks, Danny casually announced he was joining the Marines. I like to think it was my manly wisdom that got to him, but maybe he was just tired of listening to me bending his ear.

"It's my ticket out, Mike," he said. "The way I figure it, I can quit the gang with some honor and get away for a couple of years. By the time I get out, I can move away from here. Maybe do like you did and join the force." I told him I thought it was a good plan. In fact, it was the same one I had used.

Danny Martin seemed to be a pretty good Marine. Even though my critics — and God knows there are enough of them — would tell you I'm a heartless guy that is void of anything resembling sentimental feelings, I beamed inside the first time I saw the kid in his dress blues. I have to tell you, at the time I was pretty proud of for having steered Danny in the right direction. However, when his enlistment was up, Danny never made the jump into the Department. Although I picked up an application for him and talked to one of the Department's recruiters about what a good catch Danny would be, the kid just disappeared a few months after his discharge. The rumor mill said he was either in drug rehabilitation or doing a little time down state for an assault beef. I don't know which was true, and by that time I stopped caring. It was a good lesson that reaffirmed my earlier convictions to keep my nose out of other peoples' business.

The next time I ran into Danny he was hanging around his old crew and becoming a fixture at one of the mob joints. I tried talking to the kid, but he turned a deaf ear to my mini-lectures about growing up and not bringing disgrace on his family's name. Finally, I decided to let him throw away his life if that was what he wanted. If he wanted to grow up to be a dirt bag, a mob wanna-be, that was his business. We bumped into one another now and again, but our conversations were terse. My mom asked me to talk to him again, but I refused. I explained to my mother that Danny was wasted and I couldn't reach the kid. "He likes being with the *ruffiani* now, Ma. He don't have time for me," I explained.

About two or three years after that, Mrs. Martin died. At the risk of being called a romantic, I have to say I suspect she died of a broken heart. The only positive moves her son had made in his life were serving his country honorably and marrying Kathy Conte, a good kid from the old neighborhood. One could only hope that Danny's wife would be spared the sorrow and humiliation suffered by her mother-in-law. It was a good thought to keep; but, the truth be known, I would have laid eight-to-one odds against the possibility.

* * *

At ten o'clock on a hot, humid Tuesday night in August, I was standing with a couple of other cops behind Aquinas Institute, a Catholic high school on Dewey Avenue, looking down at Danny Martin's body. A bullet had put a neat, almost secretive wound in his back, just inside the left shoulder blade. A second shot entered a little higher and more to the center. A third shot, probably for the sake of insurance, was destined for the back of the victim's head. However, the round ended up passing through the right side of the neck. By the amount of thick, liver-red blood around and under the body, it was apparent Danny Martin had bled to death with his heart pumping away until the veins were dry.

Although I had originally been mad about being called away from a rare, albeit enjoyable dinner with my ex-wife, Diane, my rage built considerably when the uniformed Sergeant told me the victim's name. Maybe I didn't like what Danny had become, but I still felt the rage over the fact that someone had killed a person I once called "friend."

The homicide scene was located in one of Rochester's better neighborhoods, not the type of place where the mob carried on its nefarious business transactions. In recent years, many of the large homes of the area had been cut up into apartments, but it was still an area where middle-income families lived quiet, middle-income lives.

Aquinas Institute was one of the oldest Catholic High Schools in the city. For four or five decades, it remained strictly a boys school; but, back around the late '70s or early '80s, the archdiocese decided that it was economically feasible to allow the boys to mingle with the girls. The parking lot where we now stood was at the rear of the school. Beyond that was a football practice field and farther west was the large, wood-frame residence that housed the priests of the congregation of Saint Basil who taught at the school.

I crouched down at the left side of my victim and ran my hand over the body's shoulders and sides, ostensibly feeling for a weapon, but perhaps more truthfully, saying good-bye to the boy who had blown my police whistle a lifetime ago.

The victim was face down with his hands resting by his sides, the backs of them pressing against the driveway's asphalt. Other than the three bullet wounds, there were no visible signs of him taking a beating or having been assaulted in any way. Apparently, the mob had a beef with the victim and muscled him into a situation where he was forced or tricked into a car, and then brought here to be executed. The victim obviously had little time or inclination to fight off his killer or killers. If it was done in true mob fashion, the intended target had been blindsided by the abduction or trickery. Without suspicion, the kid had probably accompanied a couple of the cowardly mugs on some non-existent errand, was then tricked into getting out of the car, and with no warning, had two shots pumped into his back. Probably after he fell, the third shot was fired.

As I stood up and let the kinks in my knees work themselves into a tolerable discomfort, I caught myself wearing a sardonic grimace. Here I was looking down at a human being that had been a part of my life, a kid I knew and worried about, and I had already removed any personal link between the two of us. I had been kneeling down next to the body of Danny Martin, my little buddy from way back when, yet all my mental notes were about a thing called a "victim".

It was a habit that had served me well over the past twenty-plus years of digging around dead bodies. After my first few murder calls, I learned not to think of a homicide victim as being a man or woman. No, that was too personal. The simple word "man" brought to mind connotations of son, husband, or brother. A couple of sleepless nights had taught me that a cop had to learn to separate himself from such nuances. "Victim" was a better word. It was a cold, clinical word, a word without association to anyone in my personal world.

Danny Martin had made the switch from neighborhood kid to victim the minute the first bullet entered his body. When his heart stopped beating, the change became permanent. From now on, in all of my reports, in each of my conversations, and in my testimony — if it came to that — he would be "the victim". It would be neater that way. Neater for me. Neater for my mind.

Bobby St. John and Frank Donovan, the on-call team of detectives, had arrived at the scene a few minutes before me. Standing near the body, I took a second to watch the two detectives methodically work the crowd as they looked for witnesses. Finally, I approached Donovan, who was in the process of interviewing the first cop to arrive on the scene.

Francis Patrick Donovan is a big man who carries his two hundred thirty pounds somewhat comfortably on his six-foot one-inch frame. We have a few demographic differences between us. The big Irishman has almost ten years' seniority on my forty-eight years of life and about five more years on the job. He was my subordinate in the Department's hierarchy of rank, but as an investigator, I had to consider him my superior. Those differences aside, our love for the job and years of working together bound us together in a strong friendship.

"So what have you got, Frank?"

"Not too much yet, Boss. Bobby's checking the crowd to see what, if anything, they know or will admit to knowing. Officer

Ross was first on the scene. He heard shots while he was doing a report across the street. He followed the sound, came over here to where he thought the sound came from, and found the victim."

"Lieutenant," the young cop acknowledged as he touched the brim of his cap in a snappy salute.

"Relax, kid," I said. "We don't get too formal in front of dead victims." Ross smiled at my remark as I asked him to repeat what he had been telling Donovan.

"I just finished a simple assault, a domestic, a couple of blocks up the street. I came down here near the high school, you know, to find a hole where I could do the report. I stopped over there under the street light," Ross said as he pointed to the side street directly opposite the south end of the school. "That's when I hear a 'crack, crack' then a pause, and a third 'crack'. I'm no expert on this Lieutenant, but I'm saying to myself, 'Those have got to be gunshots!' I pulled away from the curb, made a right-hand turn onto Dewey Avenue, drove down a block past the high school, and I see nothing. So then I hooked a U-turn and pulled into the driveway there on the north side of the school. I scanned the parking lot with the spotlight and that's when I saw a big hump of something here on the edge of the parking lot. I came over here, and it's only when I got right up next to it that I see the hump is the victim."

"You see any cars? Any people?"

"I think a car pulled out of the south driveway, way over there on the other side of the school, as I came in from this side, but I can't be sure. I mean, I didn't see any lights or anything. I just heard the motor and it sounded like it was heading away from me."

"Did you handle anything around here, Ross?" Frank Donovan asked.

"Yeah, sure," he admitted eagerly. "I rolled the guy over on his side to see how bad he was bleeding, you know, how bad he was. Other than that, I don't think I touched anything. I just

went back to the car and called for an ambulance on the double
… bosses, detectives, technicians, all that stuff."

I was impressed with the young copper who appeared to have
his stuff together. His report was complete, yet concise, without
a lot of ambiguous phrases that left plenty of room for
questions.

"Do you think he was dead when you got here?" I asked.

"No way, Lieutenant. But by the time I got back from asking
for assistance, I'm pretty sure he was dead. At least, he wasn't
talking any more by then."

Frank Donovan and I exchanged a quick 'Did-you-just-hear-
what-I-just-heard?' look.

"He talked to you, Officer?" I asked the kid-cop.

Ross nodded before his lips began to move. "I asked him
what happened, and he just said something about being weak,
and about a locker check or something like that, and he was
asking for his wife."

"A locker?" Donovan beat me to the question.

"He just said he knew he was dying and getting weak. Then he
said, 'locker.' He paused a little to get some air, because he was
really gurgling by that time, and then he said, 'ask wife to give'
and then nothing."

"Okay," I interrupted. "Here's what I want you to do, Ross. I
want you to get off somewhere quiet and I want you to write out
exactly what this guy said. Verbatim! Word for word. Don't add
anything and don't leave anything out. You think about it, okay?
You think about it and you write it down in your time book.
Okay? You got that? Don't edit the words, and don't try to make
sense of it. Just put it down exactly as it was said. Okay?"

"Yeah, okay Lieutenant, but my Sergeant wants me to start the
reports like five minutes ago. The Lieutenant is on him about the
fact I might have to go into some overtime if I don't jump on it
right now."

"Forget about the overtime, and for now you can forget about
the report," I said emphatically. "You just do as I asked and I'll

talk to your bosses." I saw the look on the kid's face and realized I had scared the hell out of him. "I'm not upset with you, Ross. You did a great job here, kid. I just get so fed up at these dippy bosses who can't get their bookkeeping minds into a crime fighting mode." Patting the kid on the left shoulder I repeated, "Nice job."

Donovan and I huddled with Bobby St. John and shared our information with the younger detective. He briefed us about a neighbor seeing a dark, full-sized car leaving the parking lot's south side right after the guy heard gunshots.

"That agrees with the motor sound Ross heard," Donovan acknowledged. "How long after the shots did the citizen hear the car?"

Bobby St. John was a no-nonsense Detective who did his job right. I watched as he pulled out his spiral pad and flipped to the page that summarized his notes in neat shorthand. "He says it was a little while, like maybe thirty or forty-five seconds after the last shot, but definitely less than a minute."

Officer Ross interrupted our conversation by asking if we wanted his boots for evidence. When the expression on my face quizzed him, he added, "I tracked a lot of the victim's blood around, Lieutenant. I got another old pair of boots in my locker at the section office. I can use them for a few days if I have to."

Donovan took the kid aside and made arrangements to get his boots photographed and processed for future reference.

"The kid's pretty sharp," I remarked to Bobby St. John.

"He'd better be. I recruited the little brother from the 'hood. He better fly straight or I'll kick his skinny little black ass from here to tomorrow," the trim detective said with a wink.

"You made out better than I did," I said as I jutted my chin toward the victim.

St. John's eyebrows turned down and in toward the bridge of his nose, and I realized he had no idea what I was talking about.

"I tried to recruit that one," I said, pointing at the body. "It was a long time ago. As you can see, it didn't work out."

Changing the subject, Detective St. John pointed his thumb over his shoulder at the rectory. "Do you have any idea what that is, Lute?"

"It's where the priests who teach here live. We should probably get someone over there to check it out. One of them may have seen something or at least heard something."

I was going to volunteer to check it out; but, officially, the homicide belonged to Donovan and St. John. They would work out who would do the interviews with the priests. Besides, my motivation for volunteering was based on avoiding the chore ahead of me.

My team stayed at the scene to square things with Ross' Sergeant and make sure things got done right before they headed for the Detective Bureau. While they handled that end, I braced myself for the unglamorous job of telling Kathy Martin the news that would probably shatter her life. In my convoluted thinking, I hoped that she would be glad her mob-hopping husband was dead. Deep inside I knew that was just a hope, and life was seldom supported by hope. The fact is, I would much rather go into a raging bar fight without a backup than make a notification of death. There is no easy way, no nice way, and no gentle way to tell a wife, mother, father, or husband that death had called unexpectedly and ripped a part of their life out of their heart.

Over the radio, I had the Records Division check out Daniel Albert Martin's rap sheet. When they gave me his most recent address, I pointed the car south and then west to Rochester's suburban community of Gates, New York. Twenty minutes later I pulled into the neighborhood of small Cape Cod style homes that had ample and nicely manicured front lawns. After a few miscues, I found the street, took a deep breath, and let the car slide silently into the driveway.

The house was dark, which gave me little comfort. My weaker side suggested the death notification could wait until morning, but my cop side made a stronger argument for doing the deed and getting the job done right. Kathy Martin needed to be told that her life had irrevocably been changed. I rationalized that the sooner she begins the grieving process, the sooner it will be over. In reality, I was going there to develop leads, to further the investigation, and to gain some insights about the victim and his lifestyle. That was it, pure and simple. It was as mercenary as one could be, but it was the truth.

A minute or two after I tapped the doorbell, Kathy Martin made her way to the door and pulled back the curtain. She stiffened at the sight of my badge and ID card pressed to the glass, and then fumbled through the process of rolling back the dead bolt and uncoupling a small chain lock.

My last memories of the woman were of a skinny, awkward pre-teen. Now, as I stepped into her home, I was caught off guard by how attractive the woman was, even when awakened from a sound sleep. She was small, almost tiny, with black hair that came down to her neck. Her uncombed hair framed a face that had no make up and needed none.

I began introducing myself, but she stopped me by saying, "I know who you are, Mike. You're Mike Amato, from the old neighborhood." The words were spoken without any bias, but with a hint of suspicion. "Is Danny in trouble?"

"Hi, Kathy. May I come in? We need to talk." My words were meant to be casual and without a hint of the trouble I was about to bring to her young life. They didn't do the job.

"Is he hurt?"

I blurted out the words that the years had taught me would never be said gently. "He's been shot, Kathy. He's dead."

The sound began deep in her throat, pushed up slowly, then developed into a strained rumble that began as a moan and ended up as a muffled cry. The cry was cupped under the slender fingers of her hands that formed a tent over her nose and mouth. Draping my arm over her shoulders, I guided her to the couch. I found myself hating Danny Martin for doing this to his wife, for making me the messenger of death once again, and for befriending violent scum who did this thing to him, to her, to us.

Between the young widow's sobs, I managed to extract the name of her sister. I looked up the number in a telephone book that rested on a ledge near the kitchen phone. Contacting Phyllis Conte, I gave her the news. The conversation was short, maybe less than ten seconds. She said she was on the way, and then the phone went dead.

I gave Kathy the message that her older sister was on the way to be in order to be with her. Then we engaged in a conversation of stunted sentences.

"Are there any children?"

"No. Danny wants to wait."

"Is there anyone else I can call?"

"No, I don't think so."

"Your mom, dad?"

"They're both gone, Mike. They passed away."

Her fingers were pressed together on her lap, as if in prayer, as her head rolled slowly from side to side. I decided it was best to let her cry a little before I pushed for information. However, she soon broke the silence.

"Why, Mike?" she asked. "Who did this to us?"

"We don't know why yet, and we don't know who." Silence, sliced only by her short, deep moans, filled the room again. Rather than listen to the haunting sounds of moaning, I covered the semi-silence with words. I hoped the words would bring her some comfort. I feared they would not.

"It was quick, Kathy. He didn't suffer. We have some leads and we'll have more information for you in a few days. You don't worry about that, okay? We'll get who did it." The sentences were lies, but I figured they were lies she wanted to hear.

The young woman finally gave in to the emotional beating she had been given. She slowly slumped over to her left side and when her head rested on the arm of the sofa, Kathy pulled a small pillow to her face and let the tears flow.

I left Kathy Martin to her agony and scanned the kitchen for a coffeepot, grounds, and a filter. The three items were lined up like soldiers next to the powdered cream and a bowl of sugar on the counter near the sink.

The brown water had just made its way through the grounds and filter when the sound of tires rolling across the fine, crushed gravel of the driveway announced the arrival of Kathy's sister. I opened the door as Phyllis Conte reached for it. The older, taller sibling entered the house and went past me without a word. The two sisters did the things that families do best in a time of crisis. They embraced tightly and leaned on one another.

Leaving them alone to seek the comfort they needed, I returned to the kitchen to await the coffee. Finally, the appliance offered up the gurgling sound that coffeepots make when they are through with their business. I found three mugs in the cupboard above the counter where the lined up coffee ingredients still stood at attention. My thoughts strayed to looking for a bottle of sambuca or anisette, but the need was fought successfully and I opted for sugar and cream. As I sat alone in the kitchen running over the questions that needed to be asked, the older sister walked in.

"I took the liberty of making some coffee," I said with an apologetic smile. "Somehow, I don't how, it usually helps in times like these."

"You're Mike Amato, aren't you?" Phyllis asked after she picked up one of the coffee mugs and sipped.

"Yeah, right."

"Do you remember us?" she asked almost suspiciously

"Sure I do. Your dad worked for Gleason's. He was kind of a short, chunky guy. Your mom made the best *frattata* in the entire neighborhood. There's only one place in the city that can even come close to making potatoes, eggs, sausage, and peppers taste like your mother made them taste." Having passed what I suspected was a test of my memory, I opted for a bit of humility.

"I'm surprised you remember me," I offered with a smile. Now it was my turn to take a sip.

"We all remember you, Mike," Phyllis said as she made a slight toasting gesture with her cup. "Lieutenant Mike Amato, right? You're a Lieutenant now, right? Or is it Captain or Chief by now?"

"Lieutenant," I confirmed as I looked into the attractive doe-like eyes of the woman who was about a dozen years my junior.

"You were one of the few who made it out of there and did something with your life. Not like Danny, that no-good —" She let the nasty word hang unsaid. "I knew he would break her heart by either getting busted and humiliating her or by getting killed. I tried to tell her Mike, but she wouldn't listen. She saw something in that rat the rest of us never saw."

I let the woman's steam go by without any reaction. She needed to vent. When it appeared that she had blown an appropriate amount of anger at her dead brother-in-law, it was time to move the case along. "I need to talk to her, Phyllis."

"Not now. No way! She's just quieted down."

She shifted the conversation to what-have-you-been-doing-with-your-life questions. I summed up the past 20-some-odd years with three words. "Marriage, divorce, work."

As she recalled her jobs, marriage, and divorce, my mind roamed back to Phyllis Conte with her baby sister, Kathy, in her arms. At the time Phyllis was about fifteen or sixteen years old, I was about twenty-three, maybe twenty-five. It seemed like a big age difference back then. Now, over coffee and a kitchen table, the age difference didn't seem to be such a great void.

"It's funny," Phyllis said after a fresh sip of coffee. "All of us kids remember the other one's parents. I remember your dad, too. His name was Tony, but he liked to be called by the old way, right, Mike? He liked to be called Antonio. Am I right?"

"You're right," I said with a nod, wondering why we were making small talk while I had a homicide to investigate. "He liked all the old ways. He was funny about that."

The conversation stumbled over other remembrances and then stalled. Pushing myself up from the table and excusing myself, I moved toward the living room.

"She'll be out for at least a couple of hours, Mike," Phyllis said from behind me. "I gave her some Valium. By now she's out like a light. Let her rest. You can talk to her tomorrow."

Only then did it dawn on me why we had been tripping down memory lane. Phyllis had locked me up with chitchat so her sister could slip into la-la land.

"That was dirty, Phyllis," I said as I wagged a scolding finger at her.

"She's my kid sister, Mike. I'm supposed to take care of her. You know that. Besides, she doesn't know anything about Danny's business. He came and went as he pleased and she never knew where he was going, how long he would be gone, or what he was doing."

Contrary to my natural inclination to be irritated by the fact that she just scammed me out of talking to my first lead, I smiled and let it slide. For the next few minutes we made small talk and then exchanged friendly good-byes. Leaving her my card, I asked her to call me when Kathy was feeling well enough to talk. Driving back to the Public Safety Building, I had to admonish myself for allowing the long legs of Phyllis Conte to enter my thoughts when my mind and focus needed to be on Danny Martin and his killer.

It was after two in the morning when I finally made it back to the Detective Bureau. Frank Donovan allowed me time to fill my coffee cup. It was some raunchy coffee that was lousy when it had been fresh some nine or ten hours earlier and the re-warming did nothing to help the flavor. To cover the musty, burned taste of the brew, I topped it off with a shot-and-a-half of sambuca. When that didn't help, I grabbed an eighteen-hour-old donut from the box that was perched on top of a row of file cabinets. Frank then started the rundown of activities at the scene. Basically, it got down to no runs, no hits, and — as far as we knew — no errors.

"The crime scene is clean of anything besides the obvious stuff," he said, easing his ample body into a chair next to my desk. "The civilian witness, if you want to call him that, can only say he saw a car, 'a fairly large, dark car,' pulling out of the parking lot less than a minute after he heard what sounded like gunshots. The next thing he sees is Ross' headlights pulling into the parking lot from the opposite side of the parking area. When he sees it's a cop there, he goes over to see what's going on. Bobby and I covered the rectory, and the couple of priests we talked to didn't hear or see anything. They're going to pass the word to the other guys in the morning over breakfast. If they have anything, they'll call us. Either Bobby or I will go back and see them later today."

"Medical Examiner?" I asked.

"Confirms our observation of three shots into the victim. He doesn't think any one of the shots would have been a fatal one, but all together they led to Martin bleeding to death." Donovan lifted the bottle of sambuca. After giving me another shot of it, he poured a stiff shot into his own cup of nasty tasting coffee.

"Other marks?"

"The M.E. wasn't too forthcoming with the particulars on this, Boss, but he says there seems to be some pre-mortem marks around the neck. He says he needs to get the body in a better light to look at it more closely. For the meantime, it looks like there is a very minor scratch around the front of the neck, right around the Adam's apple area. It could be from an attempt to strangle the victim, a scratch he got in a struggle, or even a scratch from the victim himself that was made when he scratched at a pimple or something. The ghouls were kind of vague about the whole thing. You know, not too sure, just kind of guessing."

"When's the autopsy scheduled?"

"He says our guy is batting second or third in the morning line-up. If St. John or I don't make it, I'll ask Paskell or Verno to cover the event."

"Did you guys hit the mob joints?"

"We were going to, but a team from Vice was on the road. They drove by the scene right after you ran the records check on the victim, and they heard who it was. Much to our surprise, they volunteered to do the snoop and scoop routine."

"Come on, Frank," I moaned. "You know better than that! We'll never hear from them again."

"I got it covered, Boss," Donovan said soothingly. "I just rattled them on the radio. They're coming up here within the half hour to give us a briefing."

"What've we got in the form of reports from the scene?"

Donovan walked to his desk, retrieved a folder, and presented it proudly. "From your lips to my ears!"

With a replenished cup of coffee from a fresh pot that had been made by Detective St. John, I browsed through the reports. There was the usual cryptic scribbling on the Crime Scene Technician's Report that told me a lot of work had produced nothing of great importance. The Crime Report was a fairly decent summation of what happened. I already knew most of the information, so I went looking for something new. I skimmed the opening verbiage of Officer Lester Ross' report and focused on his account of the short conversation he had with the victim. I read it out loud in a low whisper so I would get the real sense of the neatly printed words.

"The victim (V) stated, in sum and substance, that he felt very weak, and when Reporting Officer (RO) asked V who had hurt him, V said something that was partially unintelligible followed by the words 'locker' and 'wife'. In an effort to secure a dying declaration, RO asked V if he knew he was dying, and V said that he was feeling feeble. V then went silent, and RO believes at that time V expired."

I re-read the entire report out loud and then read it a third time. It was good, concise, to the point, and clear. But, something was wrong with it. True, the grammar and punctuation needed some work in order to make it acceptable to Sister Mary Grace's standards, but that didn't concern me. As cop reports go, it was a pretty good piece of prose, but still, the "sum and substance" portion bothered me.

Needle Nose Crandall, Officer Ross' Lieutenant, presented himself at my door just as I lifted the phone from the cradle to call the budget conscious supervisor.

"I need a word with you, Lieutenant," Crandall said as he crossed the threshold.

"And, I need a word with Officer Ross," I responded. "Can you get him up here post haste?"

"He's gone for the evening. I can't afford the overtime.. That's what I need to see you about," he said officially. "You have no authority to command my officers, and you're way off base when you countermand one of my Sergeants, who is doing an admirable job of supervising the personnel in the field."

My eyes never left the skinny, freckled, eagle-beaked twerp that was obviously masquerading as a cop when he should have been working as a pencil-necked computer geek at Kodak. I got up, slowly closed the door separating my office from the Squad Room, and continued to look over the specimen of modern policing that was so attractive to our recent city administrators, yet so utterly rejected by any real street cop. I took a threatening step toward this offensive, emaciated, college-bred MBA in a cop's uniform, with every intention of making him feel unwanted.

"First things first, Lieutenant Crandall, and that is, you don't walk into my office and even hint at chewing me out in front of my men. Secondly, I don't give a wind-blown fart about your overtime budget. I have a dead citizen out there and tomorrow, next week, next year, or when you're on your handball court sipping spring water out of a plastic bottle, I'm the one who will be responsible for solving that case. Tonight while you were sharpening your pencil and going over your balance sheets like you were a CEO managing a candy factory, I was talking to the victim's widow, and I am here to tell you that she, as well as me, is somewhat unconcerned about your fiduciary problems."

"You, you have no right, no right at all..." stammered Needle Nose.

"Now, the third point I would like to make," I said facing him nose to needle-nose, "is that your Officer Ross is a witness to a homicide. He had a conversation with the victim before the victim went toes-up. You may call me old-fashioned, but I am very interested in that conversation. It is very crucial to our investigation, and I need to discuss that conversation with Officer Ross."

"You have his report!" the young Lieutenant snapped with indignation. "I personally saw to that!"

"Which brings me to my next point. If you had any experience at all with the street side of police work, a side that you appear to be too apprehensive and shaky to concern yourself with as you hide behind your desk playing boy-wonder manager, you would appreciate the fact that only so much can be captured in a police report. The real nuances, the substance of what was seen, done, and heard, can only be gleaned from a face-to-face interview with the witness."

"You...you're trying to intimidate me and...and I don't care for it one bit!"

"And you are very perceptive, my little cohort. You should be intimidated because you messed up tonight. In fact, you messed up bad! In your eager-beaver attempt to suck up to those who you think will be pleased by your frugal money management, you have violated at least a half-dozen General Orders of our glorious Rochester Police Department. Those orders are concerned with the handling of a criminal investigation, securing witnesses, crime scene management, and personnel management."

"Well, I didn't…that was not my intent, I assure you."

Checkmate! I had the needle-nose against the ropes. I hit him where he lives: right in the rulebook.

"Now, my suggestion to you," I said in a gentler tone, "if you care to take my suggestion, is that you reach out for Officer Ross, you get him in here, and you have him avail himself to the detectives who are handling this case." I brushed some non-existent lint off the little man's right shoulder and added, just for giggles, "Of course, if you feel duty-bound not to take my suggestion, I will be duty-bound to make that part of my report."

Neil Crandall didn't like doing what I had suggested, but he was weak enough to do it. I offered him my hand and apologized if I had offended him in anyway. He accepted the apology graciously, but he wasn't dumb enough to believe it was a real apology. It was simply a vehicle for him to save face. I knew it and more importantly, he knew I knew it.

With Crandall out of the way, Donovan took meal orders from St. John and me, and then headed for Nick Tahou's to get us our standard late-night homicide dinner. White hot dogs smothered in Greek sauce, onions, and mustard was the standard fare during an all night session such as this was surely to become. Four extra white hots were added to the order to make sure we had enough for the Vice cops who were on their way to meet up with us.

When Frank Donovan returned to the office, the two Vice Squad Detectives were briefing Bobby St. John and me. As we unwrapped our dinner and began to eat, the room was filled with the odor of the Bratwurst-like white hot dogs and the secret ingredients of Nick Tahou's sauce. Between bites and swipes of napkins, the vice cops filled us in with their early morning observations. The long and short of it was that all the mob hangouts were running business as usual. The normal assortment of cars and people that were expected to be around were where they were supposed to be.

"When you look at it on the surface," Detective Gil Cruz said as he wiped some mustard off the corner of his mouth, "everything is pretty normal. All the usual dipshits are dipping in their dipping spots just like they always dip."

"Why do I get the feeling there's a 'but' coming up?" St. John asked.

"*But,*" Cruz intoned with a broad smile. "The Old Man is out and about and that, my dear associates, is not the norm."

The "Old Man" referred to by Cruz needed no explanation or description for any Rochester cop who had any idea about what was happening on the local crime scene. Vincent Alberto Ruggeri was the head of the local mob and had held the position since I was breaking in my first pair of uniform pants. Although he was now in his 70's, the nickname had been tagged on him almost fifty years earlier. His penchant for doing things the old way, for keeping his local crew in check, and for speaking the old Sicilian dialect, had earned him the nickname he wore like a badge of honor.

"What's the norm?" Donovan asked.

"The norm is that the Old Man goes home to mama about eight, maybe nine o'clock just about every night," Cruz said as his younger, silent partner nodded in agreement. "Once in a great while he might be at one of the joints if there's a high stakes game, or the goons from Buffalo or Toronto are in town, or something of importance like that. Other than those infrequent times, he's in the old homestead before ten o'clock every night."

"Give me the Reader's Digest version," I said after I swallowed the last bite of pork hot dog. "Where did you see him? Doing what? With who? When?"

"Carson and I made a sweep of all the places right after we left the stiff. When we made our first swing of the major hangouts everything was kosher. We decided to take another sweep and when we got to the Bay Street hangout, the Old Man pulled up. As usual, "Twist" Tortero was driving him, but they drove past the place first. It was kind of like they were looking around before they went in. Anyway, they make a second drive around the joint like they were expecting someone to show up, and then they park out front for a few minutes. Twist is looking here, there, and everywhere while the Old Man just sits in the back seat. After a couple of minutes the Old Man taps Tortero on the shoulder and both of them get out of the car and go in the place. All the while, they're both looking over their shoulders."

"And theeeeen?" Donovan asked in a drone voice.

"Then, the Old Man goes inside with Twist still standing outside by the front door." Cruz raised his eyebrows, obviously enjoying his narration more than Donovan was enjoying it. "The next thing we know, the place empties out. Fifteen, maybe twenty people stroll out of the joint and they all mill around. Ten minutes later the Old Man comes out and the place goes back to business as usual. Tortero and the Old Man drive off and we follow them to the Old Man's house. The Old Man goes in and goes nighty-night. End of story."

"Write it up for me," I said as I slid off Donovan's desk. "Run the report by your boss in the morning and tell him I need to have it up here immediately and without it going through the normal channels. If he has any heartburn with that, tell him to call me."

When the Vice cops left, Donovan told me that Lt. Crandall had called to say he was sorry but he couldn't locate Officer Ross.

"He could be stringing us along, but he sounded like he really had tried to nail down the kid," Donovan editorialized. "Crandall says Ross was pretty angry about being pulled off the job. Ross supposedly told Crandall something about getting lost for the next couple of days, which are his normal days off."

I nodded at the information. A much younger Mike Amato would have done the same thing. I totally understood the frustration felt by the young cop.

An hour later, a false dawn was peeking up on Rochester's east side as I headed to my apartment for a shower and a change of clothes. On the way, I tried to sort out the mob's reaction to the killing of Danny Martin. The Ruggeri family had a long history with my family. Now, well into his seventh decade of life, Vincent Ruggeri was Rochester's version of the Mafia Don. In reality, Rochester's organized crime group was actually only a part of the Buffalo, New York family, and what Ruggeri headed up locally was a crew, a sub-part of the family. Still, the Old Man had an impressive organization of gambling joints, loan sharks, drug distribution, and various other nefarious activities to manage for the Buffalo mob. With all those problems, why was he breaking his routine tonight and going out after he had already left the office, so to speak, for the day? Was he checking on the success of the hit? Perhaps it was an unauthorized hit, and he was checking on what the hell was happening in his organization.

In the shower, I mulled over the many things that needed to get done in order to get the investigation going.

What was the deal with the marks on Danny Martin's neck? Why was the Old Man out and about? Why was he so weird in going into one of his own joints? Word for word, what did Danny tell Ross? Could Kathy Martin add anything to this puzzle? Had Phyllis Conte been merely friendly or was she perhaps hitting on me just a little?

In the midst of all the questions there emerged a feeling of excitement, a burst of exhilaration that comes with a fresh case and a new hunt. "Man, I love this!" I said to the showerhead.

Instantly, I felt guilty about my exclamation. A person I knew had been killed. His wife was suffering and was now a young widow. As a cop, my first duty was to prevent crime. Failing in that primary endeavor, my job was to solve the crime and bring the offender to justice. I had no clues or significant leads, only a lot of questions. However, I couldn't deny it, there was a certain thrill about a new homicide, a fresh case.

The next twenty-four hours were going to slow that exhilaration, and in forty-eight hours it would be dead and replaced with new, less positive emotions.

2

Wednesday Morning:
Old Friends and New Bosses

It's been said that upstate New York has only two seasons: winter and construction. Rochester, just about sixty miles east of Buffalo, personifies that observation. Located on the shores of Lake Ontario, just about 50-some-odd miles south of Toronto, Canada, the city has one constant weather factor that can be predicted day in and day out: high humidity. On this thirteenth day of August, the town was in its construction mode, so it took more time than usual to make the trip from my place in the northwest suburbs to the Public Safety Building. It's a trip I usually enjoy making, whether I'm coming home or going to work. Although there's a certain amount of peace and comfort offered by living in the suburbs, it's the city that ignites my pilot light. It's there, in the middle of neighborhoods and downtown traffic, that I come alive.

Based on my limited traveling, I have to guess Rochester is typical of most of the larger urban areas located in the northeast corner of the country. The city is home for about a quarter of a million people, but another half million or so souls are spread out in the suburban towns and villages that surround the metropolitan hub. During the day, the city swells when over a hundred thousand additional bodies rush in to provide the labor force for Kodak, Xerox, Bausch and Lomb, General Motors, and a couple of hundred smaller companies.

In spite of its size and industry, there's a little bit of a small town feeling about this town. Our citizens have divided themselves into two broad categories. A Rochesterian is either a West-sider or an East-sider. From there, the citizen's identity is narrowed down to the neighborhood that spawned the soul. When asked, "So, where ya from?", names such as Corn Hill, Bay-Goodman, Dutch Town, Charlotte, 19th Ward, Swillburg, or about twenty-five other neighborhood names may be offered to the inquirer. These are names that mean nothing to anyone who was not born and raised in this particular corner of the earth. However, to those who are from those neighborhoods, the locations remain a part of their heart and soul.

Beginning before the Roaring Twenty's and lasting right up through the early 1980's, the mere mention of the neighborhood in which you lived spoke volumes about you, your ethnic origin, religion, annual income, social standing, and your propensity for speaking ill of any of those factors.

The city has changed quite a bit in my eight-eight years. The change has not simply been a matter of witnessing the racial and ethnic makeup of neighborhoods re-configuring themselves as they evolved during a half-century. That evolution had been going on for 200 years. In fact, it was the change which had breathed life into the town. The evolution I speak of is the change in the town's self-image and pride. Starting back in the early 1980's and lasting right up to now, Rochester began to give up on itself, and it sometimes looked like the old broad would simply call it quits and die. It sometimes seems to me that the city has stopped evolving, and I fear it will simply cease to exist. The buildings and streets will still be there, and people will move through those streets and buildings, but the heart and soul of the city, the flavor of the city, may be dying.

On some optimistic days I think Rochester is making a comeback. Maybe, at my age, I'm simply hoping it's on the comeback trail. Downtown had recently stretched a hand out of its apparent grave and began to revitalize. Some of the old neighborhoods have begun to celebrate their diversity instead of their homogeneity. So, there seems to be some life breathed back into the old lady, and it looks like she's enjoying making the come back.

That's what makes my line of work so interesting: things change! Today is not going to be like yesterday, and tomorrow will not resemble today. I love the unexpected!

Those were my thoughts as I drove to work on the warm, sunny morning following Danny Martin's homicide. I didn't know it at the time, but the day was going to give me a fill of the unexpected.

The first fluctuation in the norm came as I neared the cop shop. I had left my apartment, fought my way around most of the orange barrels and construction equipment that marked the roadway digs, repaving, and bridge repairs, and was just approaching the exit for the Public Safety Building, when I suddenly exited the Inner Loop, crossed over the top of the expressway that serves the central city, and headed back to the suburbs. If anyone knew that I had just fought my way through all the construction to get into the city, and now was heading right back into it the maze of detours again, they would have thought I flipped. However, it was something my gut told me I had to do.

Picking up the radio mike, I interrupted Detective Verno who was already in the squad room hunting and pecking at a computer keyboard in a frantic attempt to catch up on reports. I let him know that I would be going to the victim's home before coming to the office. He acknowledged the transmission and came back with two messages. First, as long as I was heading that way, I was to notify the victim's wife that Detective Frank Donovan would be by to get her about ten o'clock a.m. in order to bring her to the ME's Office and officially identify the body.

Secondly, although the Major had already been briefed, he wanted my body in his office as soon as I got to the building.

Majors were all alike. They always want everything done as-soon-as. For now, I thought to myself, screw the Major. I had my own agenda regarding things that had to be done.

I got off the I-490 Expressway at Lyell Avenue, where the mundane small businesses of the city drift into the mundane small businesses of the suburban town of Gates, New York. Already feeling the clamminess of ninety-five percent humidity in the relatively cool seventy-eight degree morning, I settled on the fact that this was going to be one of those sweaty, two shirt days.

Without really paying attention, my unit found its way to the Martin residence — a home filled with emotional relatives, pots of coffee, and trays of cookies. For each of the minority cultures that make up my city's majority, food is the one constant that sees people through celebrations of happiness, as well as through the rituals of suffering. By this time of the morning, the telephone network of aunts, uncles, cousins, and in-laws had been active for many hours, and had spread word of Kathy Martin's grief. Without requests or orders, the women headed to their respective kitchens and independently, without a word of collaboration, begin to prepare what would collectively become a banquet of breads, soups, meats, sauces, pastas, and pastries. The food was prepared, placed in containers, and transported to the home of the grieving member. Once in the home that had been visited by death, the assortment of food was assembled on tables. The widow would not have to lift a finger in order to care for and nourish the steady flow of relatives and friends who would drift in and out over the next few days, each offering small words and gestures of comfort.

Danny Martin had made a home for his family on a quiet street that was barely wide enough for two cars to pass each other side-by-side. It was one of the post World War II developments where entire neighborhoods sprang up within a week's time. Now the homes were considered "starter homes" for young families to purchase as they struggled to build escrow and move on to larger, newer homes, farther out in more distant suburbs. While parking the unmarked cop car on the street in front of the Martin residence, I counted eight cars in and around the driveway. I made my way to the side door of what had been a relatively happy home until about eight hours earlier when I had broken the news that the occupant had been personally touched by the violence of the world.

The doorbell was answered by a guy who was built like a fire hydrant. In fact, if you put a yellow raincoat on this jerk and stood him on a street corner, the odds were eight to five the Fire Department would hook up hoses to the bloke. He gave me a scowl along with what was supposed to be a threatening look as he asked me who I was. It was obvious he was not a family member I cared to impress, so I flashed the tin at him, pressed it to his forehead, and didn't give him the courtesy of asking who he was. Phyllis Conte came to the rescue by welcoming me into the house and introducing me to an assortment of cousins, aunts, uncles, and friends. The fire hydrant was left out of the round of introductions, so I figured he was a mob representative dispatched as an emissary for the Old Man, and one who was not really known or welcomed by Danny Martin's family.

Phyllis took me through the small crowd of relatives, down a short hall, and to her sister. Kathy Martin was curled into a fetal position on the bed that she had shared with her husband for the last six years. I gently parked myself on the edge of the bed and spoke to her in a whisper that I hoped was comforting, as I updated her on a case that really hadn't progressed. She gripped my hand and I took the moment of faith to tell her Donovan would be by to chauffeur her to the Medical Examiner's Office so she could identify Danny. Naturally, this news did not sit well with her. It never does.

"Is it really necessary, Mike?" she pleaded. "I mean, you know him. You could do it, couldn't you?"

"It has to be family, Kathy. I know it's hard," I said as I patted her hand that lay lifeless at her side. "I hate to make you do it, but it has to be done."

The thought of looking at her husband in the morgue brought more sobs from the frail-looking woman. Making the excuse that there were a couple of things I needed to attend to, I got up from the bed and offered my sympathy along with my need to leave. Besides, now was a good enough time to pop the question I needed to ask.

I started to leave the room when I stopped, turned around and asked, almost as an afterthought, "By the way, Kathy, did Danny use a locker anywhere around town to, you know, maybe store some things, some stuff?"

"Locker? What do you mean, 'locker'?" the red-eyed, woman asked.

"I really don't know," I answered honestly. "It's just something that came up. It could be a foot locker, a locker at the bus station, maybe one of those rental storage units, or something like that."

When she was unable to provide an answer, I pushed a few more questions at her about where Danny said he was going before he left the house the night before, but Kathy was of little help. Her semi-audible sobs were interrupted by seconds of silent staring. It was obvious she had been medicated and for the time being would not be able to contribute anything of value to the case.

With a tissue pressed to the underside of her nose, Kathy Martin shook her head in the negative when I asked again about the locker. I crouched down next to her and told her I wouldn't be bothering her anymore and offered to go through her sister if anything came up. I had my hand on the doorknob when she stopped me with a few words that made no sense.

"Mike," I heard her cry-worn throat whisper. "He really admired you. He wanted to be just like you. It might sound stupid, but you were kind of his hero."

Without words to say, I simply smiled at her, offered a clumsy wave with my fingers, and left her to her sadness. Phyllis followed me out, and we both went into the kitchen to get cups of coffee before adjourning to the driveway. Passing from the bedroom to the kitchen, I shared words of condolences and greetings with the senior members of the Conte and Martinelli families who had joined together in this time of need. Some of the Martinelli clan had held on to the Old World family name, while some had Americanized it the way that Danny's grandfather had done. It was a move that was frowned upon by some, but it was necessary in order to make one's way into the doors of Kodak and some of the other Rochester industries that did not see the wisdom of hiring Italians before, during, and following the World War II years.

While I renewed some very old neighborhood acquaintances, I was aware of the hydrant-shaped goon watching me. Each time I looked up, he looked away. Although he tried to look disinterested in my actions, I had the strange feeling he was noting my every move and each person to whom I spoke.

"Who's the short, gorilla with the gold chains hiding in his chest hairs?" I asked as I pointed my coffee cup in the direction of the human fireplug.

"He says his name is Tony and that he was some friend of Danny's. I told him I wasn't in the mood to have any of Danny's so-called friends around, but he didn't take the hint. Now he's playing doorman for us."

We made idle conversation about the old neighborhood, who was doing what with their lives, the passing of our parents, and the twist and turns of life. Phyllis said she would remain with Kathy until well after the funeral. I complimented her for being a good sister.

Excusing myself for a minute, I made my way to the goon at the door. I offered my hand to him, and when he took it, I pulled him close to me.

"Listen to me, you turd," I said with a smile, so the others in the room would not be concerned about my private conversation with the hood. "The family doesn't want you here, so I suggest you leave. If you don't leave, I'm going to make a call. As a result of that call, I *will* learn that you have an outstanding warrant. Learning that you have a warrant, I'm going to have you busted, and once you're in a cell, I'm going to see to it that the paperwork gets lost. So, for your good and for my happiness, why don't you just pack it in and leave. Tell the Old Man the family doesn't want his stink around here."

He gave me a look that told me how pleased he would be to read my obituary someday, but he left without a word. With that matter out of the way, I returned to Phyllis.

"What's this about a locker, Mike?" Phyllis asked as she looked at me with blue-hazel eyes that were very attractive, even as they attempted to squint out the morning sun that leaked in through the white lace curtains over the kitchen window. She had gentle, smiling eyes that were very much like my ex-wife's. The thought passed through my mind that many divorced men are attracted to women who look and act like their former wives. I wondered if that was why I was attracted to Phyllis.

"It's just something that came up," I shrugged. "Probably nothing."

After I drained my coffee, Phyllis' hand covered mine as she took the cup from me and we shared an awkward smile over her clumsiness. "If you were his hero, he sure had a lousy way of showing it, huh, Mike?"

"That's what I was thinking. But, then again, I'm not the kind of guy who makes a pretty good hero for anyone."

"Well, you were always one of mine," she said as she went on tiptoe and brushed a light kiss across my right cheek.

I found myself wanting to linger there with Phyllis in the morning sun. There was something about her that made me want to be with her, to talk with her, to share thoughts that I had not shared with others. Maybe it was because ours was a relationship that was a throwback to earlier times, easier times, and happier times. I wanted to stay, but I didn't. Personal needs aside, there was a job that needed my attention and my time.

Back in the car, I pointed the vehicle east and made for the center of the city. Along the way, I changed course for the second time that morning and ended up passing through the old neighborhood. The heat and humidity made the ride an uncomfortable one, but the truth of the matter was, the side trip was not one of pleasure. It was one of necessity.

To anyone who had not lived in the neighborhood, Prospect, Troup and Atkinson Streets carried no meaning. Suffice it to say they are streets and alleyways similar to ones found in the old, run-down sections of any large city. Here is where our memories and histories are anchored. The lives of the Conte, Martinelli, and Amato families, along with a couple of hundred other families, are chronicled in these narrow streets and clapboard homes. These streets and street corners, the two-story, wood-frame houses, the light poles, and the vacant lots, were the cradles of what we were to become. For me and for many others who had also moved on, this is the place where memories lived.

On this particular morning, I thought it strange that we never saw the neighborhood as a haven, a sanctuary from the rest of the word. Some tried to leave the haven quickly; others found leaving painful and had to be pulled away from it. Some had fled far, while others had kept near. The truth of the matter was that we may have left the neighborhood, but it never left us.

Back then, in the '50s, sociologists would have labeled the entire area as a neighborhood in transition, one that was transitioning from being home for the Eastern Europeans to the homes of Western Europeans, and later from Western Europeans to the Africans, and from the Africans to the Caribbeans. Today, it would probably be labeled a ghetto, a ghetto in transition from homes to vacant buildings, from vibrant life to stagnant aging. They could call it what they wanted, whatever fit the terminology of the day's government grants, but to us it was *us*!

I pulled the car and myself away from the vacant lot that had once been the Amato home and headed for the business of the day. If homicides were to be solved, what we did during the first forty-eight hours was crucial. Mistakes made now and opportunities missed during these infancy hours of the killing could never be recaptured. The thought led me to shake my head and admonish myself for taking a trip down memory lane when I needed to keep my focus on the job at hand. It was the second or third time in the past twelve hours that I had to remind myself to stay focused.

Over the last couple of blocks I prepared for the necessary meeting with my boss. It's probably fairly well known that I don't care for bosses — even if I am one — because most of them eventually forget where they came from. They get their stripes, bars, and oak leaves, and then forget what it was like on the streets. They forget about being human. Their memories become clouded with visions of the next step up the ladder and they begin to ignore the people below them while trying to impress those up above. Lt. Neil Crandall, Officer Ross' boss, was a great example of my theory. My boss, Major Ken "Skip" Winston, appeared to be an exception. He was no Charlie Novitski, the former boss of Detectives, but Winston was still okay in my book. He demanded a lot from his Detectives, but he also stood up for us.

Ken Winston was junior to me in seniority, but outranked me by two steps. He worked patrol as an Officer before earning his Sergeant's stripes and going into the Tactical Unit. The Tac Unit is always in the middle of the hot calls, and it was there, as part of a stakeout team, that Winston grabbed a bullet during an aborted drugstore robbery. His nickname was not the product of liberal, yuppie words; rather, it was earned from the manner in which he got shot.

The robber, a fifteen-year-old gang-banger, had panicked when Winston announced, rather loudly, that he was a cop. The kid, in his anxiety attack, fired a shot at Winston from his automatic. The bullet skipped off of the counter, hit a cash register, then split in two, with the larger fragment entering Winston's right forearm. It was what we call a "cheapie" wound, which means it was a minor, bleeding injury without a lot of pain and suffering. Even so, it was still good enough to earn the injured cop a Departmental Purple Heart. After learning exactly how he had been shot, Winston protested, "The punk skip shot me!" Hence, Kenneth George Winston became forever known as "Skip" Winston.

While he was recuperating, Winston was sent to the Detective Bureau where he showed some flair for crime analysis. Consequently, when Skip made Lieutenant he was assigned to head the Checks and Fraud Unit. He soon had the reputation of being a no-nonsense type of boss who demanded perfection and made himself an example of the standard he expected from the cops in his squad.

Along the way, Skip Winston, because he is black, drew some heat from both sides of the racial fence. Some white cops dismissed him as just another Affirmative Action skater who was being moved up the chain of command so the politicians could show him off to the black voters. Because he worked hard to get ahead, earned a bachelor's degree, and wouldn't buckle to the pressures exerted by exploiters, he was considered by blacks to be an Uncle Tom. It was no surprise to him that those accusations came from those *he* considered to be the real Affirmative Action skaters.

When he became Captain Winston, Skip's reputation was severely wounded. He was sent to command the Internal Affairs Division of the Department. The very nature of the assignment made all who were sent to the unit suspect in the mind of every other cop. Winston took the hits in stride and continued doing what he had always done. He moved full steam ahead and called the shots the way he saw them. I heard a few war stories about times when he went to the mat with an assortment of Chiefs in favor of some street copper that was in the right, even though special interest groups were demanding their pound of flesh. On the other hand, Skip Winston had cost about a half-dozen guys their jobs, but I truly don't believe any of them are missed.

After being a Captain for about two years, Winston was promoted to Major and slipped into some hush-hush administrative job. When Charlie Novitski moved on, Major Winston took over as the Commanding Officer of the Criminal Investigations Division.

Personally, I always liked the guy. He was a gutsy cop. Regardless of the characteristics others measured him by, such as his color, education, and past assignments, he had the one thing I always looked for: guts! When he took over as the CID Commander, he cleaned house and got rid of some of the dead wood. It was rumored my ass was going to be the next one out the door, but a year and half after his leadership began I still headed up the Violent Crimes Squad.

About a month into his leadership, Skip Winston told me he lived by two simple rules.

"It gets down to this, Lieutenant," he said across the desk. "As a manager, one has to pick the right people to do the job, and then stay the hell out of their way while they do it. Second, you always let people know exactly where they stand. If you do well, I'll let you know. If you screw up, you're out of here! In other words, I'll give you your rope, but I'll hold you accountable for the results."

Based on the way he conducted himself over the past eighteen months, I found him to be a man of his word. There were some minor signs that he had some political ambitions, but if that was the case, he didn't let it interfere with the job he was doing.

On this particular morning, I knocked on the frame of his office door at about nine-thirty. Looking up at me, he waved me in, glanced at his watch, and invited me to sit down. I began the briefing by explaining why I was late. He accepted it with a little nod that told me silently but clearly, "Okay, but don't think you can make a habit out of making your own hours."

I gave a full-blown briefing about the scene, the body, the nature of the wounds, the follow-up at Martin's house, and the Vice Squad's observations. He nodded now and again, jotted down a couple of notes, and let me run through the entire chain of events.

"What's next?" Winston asked.

"Well, we have to see the wife again and spend some time with her in order to get some answers. We need background on this guy, like who he had as friends, enemies, and associates, where he spent his time, if he had a girlfriend, and what he did for laughs. We need to get a better handle on what he did last night and what he told her before he left the house, that is, if he was even home. Stuff like that. And, we need the autopsy report to see what the ghouls came up with. There are some marks on his neck, and we need to get a handle on that. Then it's going to be time to hit the streets and harass mob friends."

"What's that going to do for us? I mean, you really don't expect to get any information from those goons, do you?"

"Directly? No. They won't tell us squat, but it's good to shake the trees. This killing has all the markings of a mob hit. We need to see the reactions, who is where, and what they're doing. I got a guy or two that I can talk to, so I want to reach out for them and try to get a private meeting with them later on."

Winston scanned my face for a second, maybe two, before saying, "I understand you and the victim have some history."

"Same neighborhood, but he was almost twenty years younger than me. I hardly knew him even though his mother and mine were fairly close." The remarks were meant to sound casual, so as to deny any closeness that may have existed between the Amatos and the Martins. "The kid grew up without a father for most of his life. As far as I could see, he was headed for trouble from the time he hit his teens. His mother wanted me to talk to him, but it was a waste of time. Martin eventually joined the service; I think it was the Marines. Anyway, when he got out, he drifted right back into his old ways and old friends. I haven't even seen him for years."

I intentionally played down the early-life relationship I had with the victim. The Department didn't like detectives investigating crimes when the victim or the suspect was a friend of the cop. Quite truthfully, there was little that Danny Martin and I shared in common that could be labeled as a friendship. But, if the bosses knew I had an interest in Danny Martin, I would get pulled off the case. There was no way I wanted that to happen. I had to have this case. *I* had to solve it.

"It's not going to get in the way is it?" the Major asked. "I mean the family stuff and all that."

"No problem on this side, boss. Our folks are dead and gone, and as far as I'm concerned he was just another mooch wanna-be."

"Is there any indication from Vice or the Organized Crime Bureau that Martin was a made man in the mob?" Winston asked.

"There's no chance of that," I answered with a smile. "There's no way he got made a mob soldier. He never moved in those circles. If you want, we'll run it past the OCB guys, but the kid was just a wanna-be."

Winston nodded, tapped his pencil, and nodded again. "Okay for now. You go ahead and catch up with what's happening. I'll go brief the Chief. Is there anything he needs to know? Any special ramifications?"

"Not for right now. I would like to get some continued cooperation from the Vice Squad and the Organized Crime cops. They were great last night, but I'm going to need to see some of their information. If the boss can clear that path, I would appreciate it."

"I'll mention it and see what I can do," Winston said, making another note. "You think this will blossom into a bigger problem?"

"Not really. Martin was strictly low-level. There's no inkling that it's going to lead to any internal war. If he was tight with the Old Man there might be some retaliation, but there's no sign of that right now," I ventured. "The only thing is ..."

"Is what?" Winston interrupted, not wanting any loose ends or possibilities hanging out there in the unknown to come back and bite him in the ass.

"The Old Man came out last night after the hit. The Vice Detectives thought it was a little unusual."

"What do you make out of Ruggeri's moves last night?" Winston asked after scanning the notes he had taken during my briefing.

"It looks like he went back in to see what was going on. He probably got a call about Martin being found dead and he possibly wanted to go in, you know, to make sure his plate was clean. Every so often these things flare up. He may have been worried a feud was building, and he probably wanted to nip it in the bud."

"Get on the OC guys and see if they can pick up some info," Winston said. "I don't like the Old Man breaking his routine. It doesn't fit."

"I'll reach out for a guy I know. He might be able to shed some light on it.

"See if you can get a feeling for the motive," the boss suggested, as if speaking to himself.

"My guess is that he yanked someone's chain, short-changed another mutt, or got caught playing hide-the-salami with somebody else's wife. You know, something like that."

"Hide the salami, huh? Get the hell out of here, Ace," Skip Winston commanded with a grin. "You and I both have work to do."

I strolled down the hall of the Detective Bureau and into the Squad Room. Paskell and Verno were there catching up on reports from past cases. I was forced to grin seeing them type reports by means of the typical detective's two-fingered, look-and-leap method of typing.

"What's going on?" I asked as I picked up a stack of reports from the beat up plastic in-basket on the front edge of my gray, metal government-issue desk.

"We're nailing down the reports on the Vetter Street homicide from last week. Donovan is on his way back from the Martin house. He called in to say he already scooped up the wife for identification at the M.E.'s dungeon. As we expected, the victim is who we thought he was. Bobby St. John just went down to pull some records. He got an anonymous call saying the victim was a snitch and that's why he got snuffed. Bobby said he'd be back in a few minutes."

"Any idea who made the call?" I asked.

"Not really. Bobby says it sounded like a nut, some wacko citizen trying to play cops and robbers."

Coffee was the next thing on my agenda. I lifted what appeared to be the fresher of the two glass pots off of one of the hotplates and poured some of it into my coffee mug. I plopped down at my desk and began reading reports. It was time for me to fit in some of the administrative work that I was being paid a supposedly handsome salary to do, which drove me absolutely mad. I made my way through the mid-year summary of the budget. It was two months overdue in leaving my desk, so I put my initials on it without bothering to pour over the numbers. Next on my list of exciting things to do were the personnel evaluations. I hated the task. I figured every one of my guys was top notch, or else they wouldn't be working on homicides. When the phone rang, I welcomed the break.

"Amato," I droned into the mouthpiece.

"Lieutenant, this is the Major. The Chief would like you to come up to his office and meet with us post haste."

"On the way," I responded and then dropped the phone into the cradle. This was not a good sign.

Conversations with the Chief are a rare event for someone at my mid-management level on the totem pole. That was especially true with this guy, Chief Matthew John Murphy, a retired FBI transplant who had taken over our fair Department. In the eleven months since he had been brought in "to straighten out the Department," which was a political colloquialism for doing things the politicians' way instead of the cop way, I hadn't seen much of the guy and hadn't really formed an opinion about him. In fact, since he had come in as the top cop, I had only talked to him once, and that was at his swearing-in ceremony.

Murphy is a tall, lean man who looks and acts like he could hold his own in a boxing ring or in a boardroom. His trim, big-boned build provided the former impression, and his neat, impeccable appearance in eight-hundred-dollar suits provided the latter. He hadn't messed with me in any way during his tenure, so I didn't have any complaints about the job that he was doing. On the flipside, I did have two concerns about him and his ability to lead *my* Department. The first concern was that he was a Fed, a Feeb. There aren't too many local cops, myself included, who have much love or any admiration for the FBI. The Feds aren't real cops who do real police work, and I wondered how he was going to run a real police department when he had never done real cop stuff himself. The second concern was centered in the reality that the FBI — the "Famous But Inept" — worked in small groups that were focused on specialized crime problems.

With the Feds, they don't break wind without getting the okay from the U.S. Attorney. In an urban police department, you're winging it every day of the week. Due to the fact that the Rochester Police Department has about 700 sworn cops who handle every type of crime known to mankind, I wondered what experience Chief Murphy had in handling the reins of such a large, multi-faceted organization without the entire Department of Justice backing him up.

In any event, Matt Murphy left my Detectives and me alone to do our work, and that's all I cared about.

My concerns aside, I obeyed the instructions. A boring 30-second elevator ride in a box that holds the smells of too many arrests and too many sick and filthy suspects, provided my transportation from the dirty, tiled hallways of the fourth floor's Detective Bureau to the bright and airy, carpeted sixth floor halls of the Rochester Police Department's Administrative Offices.

The Chief's aide, Sergeant Pete Polson, announced my arrival into his telephone-intercom. Two minutes later a buzzer on the Sergeant's desk sounded and the sad-faced man managed a weak grin with his permission, "Chief Murphy will see you now, Lieutenant".

I had been to the Office of Chief of Police on several other occasions, when other men, who came and left with an average two-year frequency, had occupied it. I knew the room was spacious with a large, built-in bookcase behind the occupant's oversized desk. Matt Murphy now made his imprint on the office. As I scanned the workstation of the man who was our leader, I was dismayed by some of the things I saw. The light blue walls to the left of the desk were filled with photographs of Matt Murphy engaged in handshake poses with every FBI Director from the time of J. Edgar Hoover to the present. The wall on the other side of the room was adorned with a large rendition of the circular Federal Bureau of Investigation emblem and an assortment of Bureau memorabilia, cartoons, and awards. Nothing that noted the man's affiliation with the Rochester Police Department was visible in the entire chamber. I instantly took this as a bad omen. My feet were now planted in the office of a man who did not perceive any allegiance to my agency, the agency he had been chosen to lead.

Upon seeing me, Chief Matthew Murphy stood and came around the desk with his right hand extended. "Thanks for coming up so quickly, Lieutenant," he said with a warm smile as he pumped my hand once. Taking the lead from his gesture, I sat in a rather comfortable chair that was padded and covered in leather. Next to me was Major Skip Winston in a similar chair. He was wearing a look that gave me no indication of his mood or the reason I was being summoned to the Department's palace.

The Chief's comment was obviously meant to mellow my ambivalence toward this retired Fed and I accepted it with a quick smile and a short nod. Chief "Matt the Chat" Murphy, as he was known in the field, moved back to his side of the massive, dark, polished wood desk. I surveyed his athletic frame that had my five feet and ten inches topped by at least three or four inches. Murphy obviously was one of those jogger freaks I dodge every time I need to get somewhere in a hurry, and his smooth movements hinted that he had probably earned a black belt somewhere in his past.

"Let's chat a bit about what's going on with this latest killing," he said as he stacked thick reports. If an orderly desk is the sign of a neat person, as some suggest, then Murphy was the original neat freak. The pens, calendar holder, pencils, desk set, and envelope opener all matched. Each was at a functional, easily accessible place on the desk. I didn't want to distract myself from the pending conversation, but a quick look around the room sent the distinct message that the man was organized, clever, and professional.

It was widely rumored that Murphy opened every conversation with, "Let's chat." Based on his opening statement, I allowed myself an inner smile and acknowledged to myself that the Chief's nickname was well earned. However, not knowing what he wanted or why I had been summoned, I sat still and gave the man my full attention. It was his chat, so I thought it would be wise to allow him to make the first move.

"First, I want to say that I am really pleased by the work I see coming out of your shop, Lieutenant. I've seen some of the cases your people have worked on and, I want to say their work is first rate. I am truly impressed."

I nodded while keeping a tight, flight attendant smile pasted on my mug. I thought to myself how nice it would be if he ever got the urge to go slumming and take the elevator down a couple of floors to tell the guys down there what he had just told me.

"Now we've got our hands full with this Martin killing." He waited to see if I would ask why *we* had *our* hands full. When my question wasn't forthcoming, he continued. "I've asked Major Winston if he can spare your full attention to this case. He tells me that he can do that. Consequently, I would like to have you handle this case personally. I'll provide you with any support and assistance I'm able to give."

Was this guy telling me he wanted my Detectives off the case? If that was the case, the waters had to be tested.

"I assure you every homicide we handle gets my attention, supervision, and assistance, Chief."

"That's obvious, Lieutenant, but more than that, I would like to see you and you alone handle this Martin thing." There was a pause. When he saw the question furrow in my wrinkled brow he added, "There are some serious and sensitive issues here. I need to have one point man on this thing so we can minimize the people who are handling the information."

I interpreted that to mean two things. One, he didn't trust my guys, and two, whoever handled the "sensitive" information was going to be under a microscope to see if they leaked anything to anyone. I verbalized my first concern.

"You and your men are trusted without question, Lieutenant. I apologize if I sent any message to the contrary. However, this is a special case and it needs special handling. That's why we're having this chat."

"Why?" I asked.

"Why are we chatting?" Matt the Chat asked, wondering if I had missed his point.

"Why is this case so special? Danny Martin was a nobody, a hanger-on, a street thug, a wanna-be. Don't get me wrong, Chief," I explained with hands held up at shoulder-level and palms facing him in a signal that I was surrendering to his higher rank. "I'm not arguing with you or refusing. I'll do exactly as you request, but I'm obviously missing something here."

Murphy looked at Winston and then back at me. "What I'm telling you needs to stay within this room. Understood?"

"Understood," I confirmed.

"The Bureau has been very interested in Mr. Martin for quite some time," Matt Murphy said as he looked at me without so much as a blink of an eyelid. The words were not emphatic, but the look was!

"As far as I know, the *Detective* Bureau was never very interested in Martin, Chief," I said in a dead serious tone. If he was referring to his former employer, I wanted him to put it on the table in plain English. I wanted him to understand that when a city cops says "the Bureau," he's referring to the Detective Bureau and not the damn FBI. When I didn't get a speedy reply, I continued, "Not until he got killed anyway. Of course, those of us in our Detective Bureau became very interested in him. Those of us in the Violent Crimes Unit take every homicide seriously and we become very interested in all of them."

The Chief picked up a wood-grain fountain pen and ran his forefinger and thumb from the center out to the ends of it. It was a move that took less than a second, but it was a long enough pause to send the message he understood my point. He thought I was pushing the insubordination envelope. The move also placed emphasis on what he was about to say.

"I was referring to the Federal Bureau of Investigation, the other 'Bureau'," Murphy said with a feigned apologetic smile that told me he didn't think my sense of humor was so funny. Now the tip of the pen was pointing at me.

"Oh!" I acknowledged with some hint of surprise. I knew exactly what he meant! The boys in *The Bureau* always referred to themselves that way, as if there weren't any other bureaus known to modern man. *The Bureau* was said with the same reverence reserved for Jesus Christ. I just wanted Matt the Chat to remember he was on the other side now, and we had our own vocabulary to which he had better become accustomed. "May I inquire as to why those guys were interested in Martin?"

"Again," he cautioned as he leaned forward and placed his elbows on the desk, "this is highly confidential and is not to leave the room."

"I understand," I said, leaning forward and putting my elbows on my knees, mirroring his private chat position. I had already let him know I wasn't impressed with his Fed background. Now it was time to back off. It was important that Matt Murphy saw me as a confederate. Thus, it was crucial he saw much of my behavior as being similar to his.

"Due to the fact that he had some valuable information, Mr. Martin was about to become a protected witness. The Bureau — ah, the FBI, that is," he said with a quick, exaggerated smile, "was about to make Martin the subject of a federal grand jury investigation." The last sentence was meant to put me at ease about my strange assignment as a sole investigator on a mob-related homicide.

I nodded as if I was really as stupid as he seemingly thought I was. There was an uncomfortable minute of silence before Winston thanked Murphy for providing us with the background information. With the charade out of the way, the Major stood up, I rose, and the Chief came to his feet. There was a round of handshakes. Murphy thanked us and we thanked him. After the polite exchange, my boss and I were subtly guided to the office door.

Winston and I walked in silence as we made our way to the bank of elevators. Once in the elevator and alone, Winston shook his head and said, "You had to bust the guy's chops, didn't you?"

I smiled, but held my silence. When the doors opened, I followed the Major to the coffeepot in the anteroom of his office. We both filled our cups in continued silence and then I followed my boss into his office. Tossing my notebook on his worktable I asked, "Okay now, give me the straight scoop on this thing. What the hell is going on, Major?"

"Mike, you got what I got. I think the guy's leveling with us. What you heard him say is exactly what he told me before you got there."

"Boss, what we got up there was garbage! Martin wasn't about to be some frigging federal witness."

"What makes you so sure? You know something I don't know?"

"Look, I'm a little goofy, yes. A little nuts? Okay. But I am not stupid! Danny Martin was a nothing, a zero, zip. He wasn't in a position to know what was going on with Ruggeri's people. I don't give a lot of credit to our so-called Intelligence Unit guys, but they probably know more about what was going on than Martin ever knew."

"Come on, Mike, the guy was always around as a hanger-on, just like you said. He saw things, heard stuff, and knew people. He probably had thousands of little tidbits the Feds would love to know."

"Okay, okay, for the sake of argument, I'll give you that," I conceded. "I don't agree with you, but I'll give you the point. So then, tell me this one thing. If Danny Martin had a 'thousand tidbits' like you say, why would he roll over and talk to the Feds?"

That got Skip Winston's attention. He looked at me sideways, mulling the point over in his mind.

Pushing the attack, I added, "Take a look at his record. He had three minor arrests in six years and all of them ended up getting the kid a couple of bucks in fines. The last bust he took was almost two years ago! Why does he suddenly get the inclination to testify against his buddies? The only time these scumbags go to the other side is when they need a hand with some heavy-duty court action. See what I mean?"

Winston stood behind his desk and nodded to what I was saying. "I hear what you're saying, Mike, but still, there must be something. Maybe they were filling his pockets with coin. Maybe they were squeezing his family. You know the way the Feds work. They could have had him on a wire or something and used it to pressure him."

"Yeah, and maybe Chelsea Clinton will win a beauty pageant some day, too!"

* * *

I went back to my office and picked up my messages. One was from Phyllis Conte, asking me to call her. All the others were routine. Skipping the routine stuff, I placed the call to Kathy Martin's house. An elderly aunt picked up the phone and told me in a frail voice that Phyllis had gone to the grocery store to get some things. That being a bust, I made a second call to a person that could open up this case for me. That also was a bust. Next, I picked up a portable radio and called a meeting with Donovan and St. John.

A half-hour later the three of us gathered at a little sub shop and bakery over on Lyell Avenue. The smells of warm bread and aging Italian meats and cheeses were a welcome relief from the hot, humid smells coming up from the city streets. Once finished with my customary salami-and-sharp-provolone sub, I could shoot right out to the Martin house and meet up with Phyllis and Kathy. While we waited for our order, I briefed the team on the events that took place in Chief Murphy's inner sanctum.

Neither Donovan nor St. John took my instructions too warmly when I told them I'd be taking over the case. I assured them they had done nothing wrong, and I was only taking the action based on a direct order from "up above." It still didn't set well. I felt confident they picked up on the fact that I wasn't too happy about the order, so they didn't push me for any details. Just as I worked my way through the fat sub roll, Bobby St. John volunteered to work with me on the case and do anything he could to help out. Frankie Donovan, through a mouth full of pastrami, gave a "ditto." Both commented it might be fun to watch the boss work for a living. I flipped them off with the finger and smiled. Both men slid their lunch bills to me with broader smiles.

While leaving the deli, I used the cell phone to call the Martin household again and learned that Phyllis was back, but Kathy was napping. The kid deserved the rest, but I decided to head out there anyway. In the seven minutes it took to drive to the Martin home, I had done enough reasoning to know something spooky was going on with this case. Danny Martin couldn't have attracted the FBI with a red cape and a flare. There was something buried in this sandbox that I couldn't feel or see, but I could sure smell it!

I didn't like the fact that Matt the Chat had taken a personal interest in this case. I wasn't at all happy about the possible connection of the FBI with my murder investigation. I surely didn't understand why the Chief had seen fit to make me the sole investigator on the case. And, I sure as hell didn't like being fed some cock-and-bull story about Danny Martin becoming a Federal witness.

If Murphy was feeding me a crock — and I felt sure he was — the natural question was why he was doing it. Was I being set up? Was I being tested to see if I would obey, or to see if I was competent enough to handle a case on my own?

I sensed something buried deep. It would take the rest of the day to dig it out, maybe longer. However, by then I would find myself wishing I had left it buried.

3

Wednesday Afternoon:
Revelations and Lies

A buddy of mine once said that the difference between small towns and suburbs is that in the suburbs people sit on patios behind the house, and in small towns people sit on porches in front of the house. Fredonia, New York, is a front-porch town.

A small farming community in western New York, the Village of Fredonia is situated at the base of vine-covered rolling hills overlooking the southern shores of Lake Erie. The hills provide a channel for the warm air of the lake to rise up during the ebbing weeks of summer. The extended warmth offers a little extra precious time for grapes on seemingly endless miles of vines to ripen into fat, purple grapes that become the wines, jellies, and juices that find their way into grocery and liquor stores throughout the country. It's a quiet town of families who count their time there in generations rather than years. The most violent acts experienced in this community of large homes and narrow streets are those that take place on the football field at the annual high school game between Fredonia and neighboring town Dunkirk. However, over the years, so many of Fredonia's young adults married so many of Dunkirk's young adults that even the yearly football game is marked with friendship. It has become a ritual at each of those high-spirited games, that during half time, spouses yield to each other and switch sides of the field for the last half of the game. That's why it was so surprising that a major lead in the violent killing of Danny Martin came from the peaceful, rolling hills hamlet of Fredonia. As I finished lunch in Rochester, important events were transpiring there.

* * *

Christina Polshak hugged her mother-in-law and then kissed her two small children good-bye. She walked stoically from the gray farmhouse on Lakeview Street at the western fringe of the town, and placed a small suitcase in the trunk of the family car. She then positioned herself behind the steering wheel. Backing out of the driveway, Chrisy blew a kiss to her children and gave one last look and smile at the large, gray house with its long front porch. It was a porch built for the placement of rocking chairs and two-seater swings suspended from the ceiling. From that favorite spot, the young mother and her family enjoyed many cool summer evenings.

The home had been a part of her husband's family history for three generations. Since Chrisy's marriage to George Polshak, she was proud to be a part of the home and the history that went with it. With her foot off the gas pedal, the slender woman allowed the family station wagon to glide forward down the steep hill of Lakeview Street, past rows of grapevines and the old packing plant, and onto Eagle Street. In less than four minutes she had passed many of the town's large, two- and three-story homes that had raised so many children. Those generations of children had fought the nation's wars, raised the country's crops, and in the last generation, had begun to abandon the village in favor of bigger cities and more active lifestyles.

Chrisy parked her car on Main Street, directly in front of the Erie Federal Bank. Entering the fort-like building, she smiled greetings to the tellers, all of whom she knew by first names, and went directly to her safe deposit box. In the privacy of a small room made available by the bank, the young mother withdrew an envelope. She then took a moment to gather herself, and wiped a tear that ran down her right cheek. Once composed, she walked out of the bank, passing the three tellers once again, and said her good-byes to each of them by name.

Mrs. Polshak drove the length of Main Street, turned left, and then made the right hand turn leading to the tollbooths and the entrance to the New York State Thruway. Slipping the toll ticket into the sun visor over her head, she began driving east, past the grapevines that extended all the way to the town of Silver Creek. The purpose of the trip caused tears to flow down her cheeks once again, but she drew a deep breath and steeled herself for the journey and the task at hand. She knew it was important that she made the trip, but she had no idea of the valuable information contained in the envelope she carried in her purse.

* * *

When Phyllis opened the door, I greeted her with, "How's it going?" Unfortunately, the words were out before I realized how dumb the question was under the circumstances. I was once again surprised by how rattled I became when I was around the woman.

"It's a little rough, Mike," she responded with a sigh as she pulled the door open and gestured for me to enter. "We had to go to the coroner's place this morning, and this afternoon we have an appointment with the undertaker to go through all that stuff."

As she walked to the stove to pour a cup of coffee, I couldn't help but again notice Phyllis' long legs that rose from her bare feet and disappeared under the thin cotton dress. She talked of funeral arrangements and about Kathy not wanting a drawn out, three-day viewing at the funeral parlor. As she turned, I could see she was braless, and I found myself wondering why I had paid so little attention to this woman when we were growing up.

"Danny's brother, Anthony, is coming in from California as soon as he can get a flight. His sister, Chrisy, is driving in this afternoon from some town on the other side of Buffalo. So, anyway, with the autopsy and all, it looks like we won't have Danny laid out until tomorrow. Since Kathy wants to have a two-day showing, we'll have the services and burial on Saturday."

I waved off the plate of *cannoli* Phyllis extended and opted for a long *wandi* that dripped with honey. I told myself the sweetened, white cheese filling of the *cannoli* pastry tube was too fattening when compared to the long, slender, deep fried and honey-covered pastry of the *wandi*.

"I got a message you wanted to see me," I managed to say before I was forced to use the tip of my tongue to apprehend some honey that was attempting an escape from one end of the pastry. "What's that about?"

"Kathy's been asking for you, Mike. She says she needs to talk to you in private. She won't even tell me what it's all about."

"I'm not going to be able to tell her much, Phyllis."

"I know. In fact, I told her that, but she's insistent. She's in the shower now. You two can talk here, outside, or wherever she wants. I'll make myself scarce if you two want to talk in here." Phyllis pointed to the pastries. "*Manga!*" she commanded in the manner of our mothers. Because of our shared history, I anticipated the next questioned before it was uttered. "What's the matter? You on a diet?"

Not wanting to appear rude, or so I told myself, I reached for the *cannoli* I had eluded earlier. I took a bite and tried to keep most of the flaky, crumbling tube-like shell from falling all over the floor as Phyllis requested a favor of me.

"You're going to have to talk some sense to her, Mike. She's saying things, weird things about Danny being a cop and working for the FBI. Stuff like that."

"What?" I sputtered, sending cheese filling and pastry crumbs flying.

"She keeps telling me 'You'll see, you'll see!' But, I think she's trying to make him into something he definitely wasn't."

Phyllis elaborated on why she suspected Kathy was fantasizing and trying to remember her husband in a better image than the one in which he had lived.

"Or," she went on, "it's very possible Danny had been scamming Kathy with stories about being a cop. More than one husband has gotten his wife to believe he lived adventures he truly never experienced," Phyllis lectured as she pointed a wooden spoon in my direction.

What intrigued me was the fact that this was the second time in a matter of hours that Danny Martin had been connected with the FBI. First it was Chief Murphy had skirted the subject in an ambiguous reference to Danny Martin being an informant. Now it came form Phyllis, by way of Kathy.

"Let it go," I commented casually. "If that's what gets her through the night, let it be."

Our conversation drifted back to a time two decades earlier. As we talked, visions of younger years played in the corners of my mind...visions of teenagers talking, eating, and sipping soft drinks while crammed with friends into a booth at Critic's Soda Fountain. Those were nicer, simpler times. Back then, we were kids united by the commonality of who we were, rather than divided as we now are by what we had become.

When Kathy Martin walked into the kitchen I stood and embraced her with a gentle hug. Once again I was surprised by how small and dainty she was. Even now, freshly scrubbed, with a small amount of make-up on her face, she looked drained and used-up. She was wearing an orange summer dress with a non-descript pattern. White sandals were strapped to her small feet.

Her clothes gave an appearance of a young mother going grocery shopping. Her face, however, gave a totally different appearance. It was the face a woman who had lost half of her being and couldn't comprehend it.

"Can we walk, Mike? Do you have time?"

"I'll make the time," was my answer. Then added, "I could use a walk." I noticed that Phyllis had disappeared from the room.

We left the modest home, turned left at the sidewalk, and walked in silence past the other small, Cape Cod-style homes that blossomed in the neighborhood. The street was absent of children and noise. It was as if Kathy Martin and I occupied a private world.

Kathy finally spoke after we strolled passed three homes. "You asked about a locker, Mike. Can you tell me why?"

"Danny mentioned something to someone about a locker, and I was, you know, wondering if maybe he had something stashed away that might give us a lead, a little something about why he was attacked."

"It came to me this morning. I know what he might have meant."

I remained silent as we walked. I wanted to let her drift deeper into the conversation at her own pace, without me tossing questions at her.

"This morning after we went to see Danny, you know, the body." Having trouble bringing the words from her brain to her lips, she stopped and took a deep breath before continuing. "We were coming back home and Phyllis asked me if we had a safe deposit box or safety deposit box, whatever you call it." Kathy began to take slow steps again. "She said if we had anything in it, we better get it because the government sometimes puts a lock or something like that on the contents of the box, you know, until the will, the estate, and all that is settled."

"Uh huh," I muttered somewhat less than eloquently.

"I felt so, so, I don't know, kind of greedy doing it, Mike. I really didn't want to, but, you know, I've only got less than a hundred bucks in the checking account right now." She looked to me for understanding or approval. I didn't know which she sought, so I simply nodded. "Anyway," she continued, "we went to the bank and I withdrew the $690 we had in our savings, and then I went through the safe deposit box."

"Did you find something about a locker in there, Kathy?"

"No, Mike," she answered in a you-just-don't-get-it tone of voice. "That *is* the locker!"

With my eyes, I questioned what she meant by her last statement.

"Danny could never think of the words 'safe deposit box' so he would always say things like, 'We had better put this policy in the...the...the, you know, Kathy, in the locker at the bank.' It was just a, what do you call it, a mental block with him. He called the safe deposit box the locker at the bank!"

I digested the information for a few seconds before popping the hundred-dollar question. "So, if you don't mind me asking, would you tell me what was in the box?"

"There was the usual stuff people keep there, Mike. Our insurance papers, some small pieces of jewelry my mother left me, some stock certificates from a company that's probably out of business by now, and a little money."

"Anything else, Kathy? Any scraps of papers, notebooks, names, addresses, that sort of stuff?"

"Nothing like that at all, Mike."

"I don't mean to get personal, Kathy, but do you mind telling me how much money we're talking about here?"

"You won't have to tell, will you?"

"Tell who?"

"The government, the IRS."

"Forget about them! I don't even tell them how much money I have. Why would I tell them about yours?"

"It was $350, Mike. Two hundred-dollar bills and three fifties."

"That's it?"

"Well, that and some old silver dollars, about five or six of them. I think they were his dad's. Danny kept them for sentimental reasons."

I smiled and hugged Kathy Martin's shoulders with my left arm. "It'll be our little secret, Kathy," I chuckled.

We walked in silence for a minute or two and looped our way around a corner up to a busy cross street. Without any discussion, we turned around and took our time casually walking the two blocks back to what had been her home. Now it was nothing more than a house filled with pastries and sad memories. The friendship side of me argued that I should let this peaceful moment exist without interruption. However, the cop side of me had too many questions.

"About the stocks, Kathy," I mentioned casually. "What company issued the stocks, and how many shares are we talking about?"

"It was a hundred shares for some tool company, Mike. Danny's cousin gave him a tip about the company a few years back. I think they eventually went out of business."

"What makes you say that?"

"Danny and Richie, that's his cousin on his father's side, were talking about a year ago, and Danny was kidding Richie that he owed us two-hundred dollars for what we lost, and Richie said he lost a lot more than that."

I made a mental note to get the name of the company after we got back to the house.

"Do you know what Danny was into?" my cop side asked. "I mean, do you know what he was up to? Was he in any trouble? Facing some problems?"

"Everything between us, if that's what you mean, was good, Mike. As far as his work, well, he never talked about that."

"Never? Not at all?"

"One time, when we first got married, he sat me down and gave me the basics of what he was into. He said it would be best if we never discussed it again. Danny felt I was better off not knowing what he was doing."

"Did you ever get any ideas about what he was up to?"

"Gee, Mike! You probably have a better idea about that than I do!" she exclaimed.

I let the assumption go for a minute. Every citizen thinks every cop knows everything that's going on in town. I didn't want to tell her I wasn't interested in mob dealings, with the exception of those dealings that led to stiffs being deposited around town.

"Did Danny ever say he was afraid about being pulled into court? You know what I mean? Maybe something like he was concerned he was going to have to go to court and testify about some of the people he was hanging around with?"

"He knew he might have to do it someday, Mike, but it was like no big deal to him."

"Really, Kath? That didn't seem to bother him? He wasn't concerned about that in any way?" I couldn't fathom that Danny, or anyone else for that matter, could be blasé about having to spill his guts about friends and associates to a federal grand jury and then have to uproot his family to enter the witness protection gig.

"That didn't seem to bother him, Mike," she said, looking directly at me. "It was just in the past couple of months he started getting tired of it all. He wanted out, wanted, you know, to lead a normal life. Then, a few weeks ago, he told me that it was all coming together and maybe in a month or two he would be done with the entire mob stuff and we would be able to lead a normal life. He was really looking forward to it, Mike."

Something was definitely something wrong with this picture! One does not walk into the mob, hang around with all the mopes for a few years, and then simply walk away with a friendly "Have a nice day, guys!"

Now it was me who looked directly at Kathy. "Did he say anything about when this thing was all over that you guys might have to move? You know, like going into the witness protection program or something of that nature?"

Kathy was face to face with me and it was clear she was looking at me in an effort to comprehend this foreign language I was speaking.

"My goodness, Mike! What the heck was Danny into? Why would we have to move?"

"Kathy," I said in a matter-of-fact tone that suggested she wake up to reality, "Danny's little friends aren't exactly Boy Scouts, you know. He hung with a pretty rough crowd. If he told you it was all coming to a head, that he was going to be testifying in court, and he was going to be over and done with it, I would guess you two would have to leave here. See what I mean?"

"He never said that, or hinted at that, or anything else, Mike. He loved the job. He just couldn't wait for this part of it to end so he could be normal. You know what I mean? He wanted to do regular stuff on the job. Maybe even get to work for you some day."

"On the job?" I quizzed with some unintended sarcasm slipping through. "Work for me?" This was not making any sense at all. "After all the stuff he got into, he wanted to be a cop?"

Kathy didn't even complete the step she was taking when she stopped dead in her tracks. Her eyes became large. "Mike, are you telling me you don't know Danny was a cop?" The expression on my face asked the questions and gave my answer. Kathy read my face and repeated slower and clearer, "Danny was a cop, Mike. He was working undercover." Then her eyes narrowed. "You didn't know that? You didn't know they killed a cop?"

The words "You're kidding me" slipped out of my mouth. "What do you mean, 'a cop'? Do you mean he was an informant?"

"Mike," she implored with her voice and eyes, "Danny was a police officer, a regular cop, a Rochester cop."

"Are you sure?" I asked. We were now facing each other with only inches between us and speaking in whispers as if someone would overhear us.

The words, remembrance of how I had looked at and treated Danny the last few times I saw him, made it seem as if someone had drawn all the air, every muscle, and every bone from my body. I stood motionless, drained and unable to resolve that which I had believed to be true with the new information that Kathy was giving me. All I could do was ask, "Are you sure?"

"You really didn't know, Mike, did you? The Chief, the FBI guys, they never even told you that you were investigating a cop's murder? How could they do that?"

"Are you sure?" I asked again. "A Rochester cop or a Fed cop?"

"A Rochester cop. I'm sure, Mike. A city cop, just like you. If you don't believe me, I've got the proof at the house."

After a short silence, I began to move again in short, slow steps. I had to sort this thing out in my mind, and — due to a personal quirk — I could only do that if I was moving.

"Kathy," my voice said, still in a half whisper. "There's no way Danny could have been a cop. I've taught Homicide Investigations and Crime Scene Management to every recruit class for the past seven or eight years. Danny was never in any one of those classes."

Kathy gripped the crook of my right arm with her left hand and brought me to a halt. "Mike, I'm telling you he was a cop!" she insisted. "They sent him to some academy out of town. He's been working undercover all this time. Really! He really has!"

"If he ..." I started to say, but was cut off.

"I'll prove it to you, Mike. When we get back to the house I'll show you proof."

Standing motionless and holding each other's hands in an effort to support and stabilizing each other, we searched for truth and understanding in each other's eyes. By the look on

Kathy's face, I could only surmise that she felt as sorry for me as I felt for her.

"I didn't know," I whispered weakly in an apology that offered more to Danny who was dead and gone than to his wife standing in front of me.

We started our slow walk again and Kathy suddenly spit the words, "The bastards!"

"The bastards!" I agreed.

As we walked back to the house in silence, my mind went into overdrive. Was this the real reason I was asked to handle this case alone? Was good old Matt the Chat worried about the word of *Officer* Daniel Martin leaking out onto the streets and into the locker rooms of the Department? What else hadn't I been told? What other secrets were there? People owed me some answers, and I was going to get those answers.

As we approached the side of the Kathy's home, I stopped her with my hand on her right shoulder.

"Kathy, I know this is going to be hard, but I want you to sit on this information for the time being. I don't know what's going on or why the information about Danny possibly being a cop is being withheld from me. However, there must be more to this. I need your word that you'll keep this information under wraps for now. Okay? Promise me?"

She nodded and said, "Yes," then added, "but I already told Phyllis."

"I know, Kathy. She told me, but she says she doesn't believe it. But you've been hanging onto this secret for so long now, just hang on a little while longer."

"I want him to have a cop's funeral, Mike," she said firmly. "They owe him that much. They do owe him that much, don't they?"

"Yes, they sure do," I agreed. "I give you my word. I'll jump on it as soon as I get back to the office."

She was one hundred percent right. The Department owed Danny Martin a decent funeral, and I was going to see he got it. I was also going to see to it that I got some straight answers!

Before leaving Kathy, she and I went into her home. When we entered, Phyllis smiled at us, and quietly went out to the back yard. As Kathy requested, I waited in the kitchen while she went into her bedroom to dig out some stuff.

When she returned, she placed an accordion-type file folder on the kitchen table and told me to look inside it.

I slipped the large rubber band off the folder and spilled the contents out onto the table. On top of the pile was a Rochester Police Department badge. Under it was a Police Officer Certification issued to Daniel Martin by the State of New York almost six years earlier. There were also six neat bundles of rectangular paper. Each bundle contained one year's accumulation of pay stubs, and each one I looked at had been issued by YBA Industries. My face never twitched, but I had to smile in my mind when I saw the name of the company on the bundled pay stubs. The smallest bundle covered the present year, right up to the Department's last pay period. I did some quick calculations in my head, and didn't think it was a coincidence that the gross pay was equal to what a cop with Danny's tenure would be earning.

I had seen enough to convince me, but I still wanted to test the young widow's story.

"If Danny was working for the Rochester Police Department, Kathy, why are his checks from this YBA company?"

"Danny told me a long time ago that YBA was a fictitious company. I think he called it a dummy company. He said his pay was set up that way so no one, not even people in the personnel offices, would know he was employed by the city."

Her answer was right on the money!

* * *

I left Kathy Martin's home at 2:00 p.m. It took over two hours to make the twenty-minute trip from suburban Gates downtown Rochester. The fact of the matter is I do my best thinking when I'm driving, and I needed the time to do exactly that.

I felt like stomping into the Public Safety Building and demanding Skip Winston and Matt Murphy tell me — as they say in court — the truth, the whole truth, and nothing but the truth. However, I had the good sense to fight the impulse. What I needed to do was keep Major Winston and the Chief at bay for a few hours while I reasoned things out. If I went in there now, half-cocked, I would give the bosses too much time to maneuver and have their little meetings behind closed doors to discuss what to do with me. I needed to hit them hard with the information, but I needed to hit them late in the day, when they were in a hurry to go home and wouldn't have a lot of excuses for taking my information and then putting me off. Making use of the time, I went looking for a guy I had to see about this case. He was nowhere to be found.

I used the cell phone to call Major Winston and tell him I would be delayed. Naturally, he wanted to know what was going on.

"I just stumbled onto something that presents a major problem for us, but it might get us moving on this thing, Major," I said in such a cryptic manner that even I hardly understood what I was saying. "Give me an hour and I'll be in with it."

My boss acknowledged the message and wanted to ask more, but knew it would be imprudent to discuss leads over the phone that had the potential of being monitored by every assignment editor and half the journalists in four counties.

"Oh, by the way, Major," I added as if it was an afterthought, "The Chief will want to be in on this, so you might want to ask him to standby."

I needed to absorb and dissect the information that Kathy Martin had dropped on me. Before I went into a meeting with Winston and Murphy, I had to decipher what was merely plausible and what was fact. One or both of the men had lied to me this morning. To me, it didn't matter which one was the liar. The only germane issue was that I had been told lies. Matt Murphy had thrown out a story about Danny going to the Grand Jury, but he had not said one word about the kid being an undercover cop. Why did he feel it was necessary to keep that information from me? Maybe the man had grown so accustomed to keeping secrets while he was with the FBI, that he thought he could keep this item a secret. Well, the time was fast approaching when I would have to tell him that his secret had leaked.

Before I went on the attack, I had to be sure of my position. There's an outside chance, I reasoned in my mind, that Kathy had been scammed by her husband. Based on what she had shown me, she could be right on the money and Danny Martin had actually been a mole we planted in the mob. And still, another plausible plot existed in the scenario that Danny had deceived his wife into believing he wasn't really a street monkey, but instead, a Serpico-type cop, living the life of a spy.

Considering both possibilities, I figured the latter one to be the most probable. After all, if Danny Martin actually had joined the Department, he would have had to go through the Regional Law Enforcement Academy and I would have seen him, or heard about him being in a recruit class. Danny must have been running a scam on his old lady! That was the only explanation that seemed real.

On the other side of the coin was the reality of what Kathy had shown me and told me. She had a badge and an identification card that looked real enough. She had canceled checks from a company I knew to be a dummy company the Department used to cover some of its operations. I never heard of the Department sending a recruit to another police department's academy to get rained and certified, but I guessed it was a possibility.

My mind didn't know what it wanted to believe. If Danny Martin was a cop, then I was a jerk for having denied him my friendship all these years. If he was not a cop, then he was the jerk for getting caught up with those animals in the mob. The latter thought gave me little consolation. Even though it could make me feel better about myself, it made me feel bad for Danny. There was only one way I could settle my internal argument. I had to learn what was really going on. In order to do that, I must go into Matt Murphy's lair. I knew that *how* I went into that den would be crucial. If I went in with my mouth blazing, I would be shot down in flames and would get nowhere. If my approach was too meek, I would be subjected to more lies. In order to find out what was really going on, I would have to play the scene just right.

Kathy had raised the issue and had shown me the evidence. Now I had to test the evidence in order to determine what was truth and what was fantasy. The widow was holding the evidence. My bosses were holding the truth. If I played it right, I would get my answers.

4

Wednesday Evening:
Truth, Evasive Truth

It was almost five o'clock p.m. when my temper cooled and I pointed the car in the direction of the Public Safety Building. I parked the car in my assigned spot on the lower level of the PSB garage and went straight to Major Winston's office. Having only a few facts to work with, I expected to receive a song-and-dance routine from the Department's inner circle. If they suspected how little I knew, they would attempt to force me into justifying my case. In reality, however, I had neither the inclination nor the temperament for those games.

My history with the Department had taught me that the best attack was to fight innuendoes with assumptions that were stated as facts and to confront stalling tactics with aggression that demands action. Over the years, I had run the gambit in battles with the brass and that had earned me a well-deserved reputation as a hardhead who was not considered a team player. I knew I had to jump in and act like I knew every facet of what was going on, even though I didn't have a very clear picture regarding who was telling the truth.

Although I had planned on using a hint of tact in my approach, I had to garner Winston's attention. Having never been accused of being a cop with a lot of class, I led into the conversation with, "Do you want to tell me what's *really* going on in this case, Major?"

Skip Winston looked at me coolly as he eased his swivel chair back slowly. The notable creak in the chair's mechanics was drowned out by my boss' voice. "Would you like to rephrase that question, Lieutenant? Possibly with a slight hint of respect?"

"Why wasn't I told Danny Martin was a Rochester cop?"

"What?" Skip Winston asked me in the same manner and with the same expression I had presented to Kathy Martin a few hours earlier.

"I just found out Danny Martin was a cop. I need to know why I wasn't given that information."

"First of all, I don't have the slightest idea what you're babbling about. Secondly, you back off a little, Mister Amato. And third, where did you latch on to this piece of *alleged* information?"

It looked like he was telling the truth. Consequently, it was time to take it down a notch. "I didn't mean to be offensive, Major, but I'm mad! I've been kept in the dark on this thing. It's hurting the case, and to be perfectly frank, I don't like it."

Major Winston extended his right hand, palm down and pressed the air below it a few times in a gentle, slow motion. I took the signal to heart, sucked in a little air, and slowed down.

"I had a conversation with the victim's wife. She told me Danny was undercover for us. She's got some stuff at her house that makes me believe her." I plopped myself down on one of two chairs positioned at the visitor's side of Winston's desk, stretching my legs out and lacing my fingers together across my stomach. If he wanted me to be cool, it was my intent to act cool about the entire matter.

"I don't think it's 'alleged' at all," I added with a degree of smugness. "As a matter of fact, based on the evidence I've seen already, I'm willing to bet my retirement on it being true." I allowed him to mull over that information for a full thirty seconds before continuing. "As I said, I'm being kept in the dark on this case, and I would really like to know why that's being done."

Skip Winston remained silent as he chewed on his lower lip and narrowed his eyes. At first blush, someone who didn't know him would think he was angry. However, it was my guess that he was intrigued and mystified by the information that was being dumped in his lap. Keeping an eye on me, he picked up the phone and then hesitated. Appearing to think better of it, he set the handset back into the cradle. I tried to read the guy but couldn't tell if he was stalling me because I was right and he didn't know what to say, or if he was trying to determine if I was slightly — or possibly totally — nuts.

Finally he said, "You go do some things you have to attend to and give me some time to get in to see the Chief. When I have answers, I'll reach out for you. Fair enough?"

"Fair enough," I said, rising to my feet.

"Lieutenant!" Winston called out firmly as I turned to leave his office. "Don't you ever come in here and pull that on-the-attack act again and expect to walk out of here without Departmental charges pasted all over your ass!" He paused for impact and then asked with an icy stare, "Got it?"

"Got it, Boss," I acknowledged with a casual salute and a smile. His reaction to my insubordination told me a lot. If Winston had previously known the information I had just laid on him, he wouldn't have been so aggressive in dealing with me. Based on what had now transpired in his office, I had to believe that if I had been lied to about Martin, obviously Winston had also been kept out of the loop.

Before heading out of the building to kill some time, I stopped to make two calls. One was to my former wife, Diane. Last night, while Danny Martin was in the process of being killed, Diane and I had been in the middle of a dinner that I had hoped would lead to some talk about reconciliation. The meal ended abruptly when I received the cell phone call ordering me to the homicide scene. As I hurriedly left money for the bill on the table, I assured her we would meet tonight.

"Sorry, hon, but I need to put off meeting with you tonight," I now apologized over the telephone.

"The job?" she asked dryly, without any anger.

"The job," I conceded with some chagrin.

"Some things never change, do they, Michael?"

"This one is different, Diane. It's a special case with some personal ties."

"They're all special," she commented with a hint of disappointment. When I didn't touch the line, she added, "Is this the same Danny Martin you know from your old neighborhood?"

I paused for a second, wondering how she knew the victim's name.

When I asked, Diane gave me a one of those wife-type responses. "They have a new thing now, Michael. It's called 'the radio,' and on the radio they have news programs." The sardonic tweak was a classic trait of Diane

"What are they saying?" I asked.

"Just that his body was found behind Aquinas and you guys suspect foul play," she commented casually. Then she asked, "Is he?"

I was lost in a thousand different thoughts. "Is he what?" I questioned.

"Is he the kid you knew from your old neighborhood?"

"Yeah," I responded solemnly.

"I'm sorry, Michael. I know you wished better things for him."

Again I was silent. Diane never ceased to amaze me with how much she knew about my private thoughts. When I failed to respond, she said, "Call me when you get the chance, and don't forget, it's still your turn to buy. Have a good night, Michael. Good-bye."

Diane and I had a relationship that seemed to work fairly well, as long as we weren't married to each other. Although we separated more than ten years earlier — the divorce came five years later, after several attempts at reconciliation — we had begun meeting for dinner every month or so over the past couple of years. However, as often as not, I had to cancel the appointment at the last minute. Diane's suspicions aside, I actually looked forward to the quiet dinners and easy talk, even though I dreaded the lecture about always putting the job before everything else in my life.

It would take a book to explain why Diane and I split. Suffice it to say the break up resulted from two main factors: one was me, the other was the job. Diane said she had watched me evolve from a "sweet, caring guy into a calloused, filthy-mouthed cynic." Her opinion of police work wasn't all that lofty either. The two of us could never come to terms with an agreeable definition of "too much work." When I had sobered up long enough to realize how much I missed Diane in my life, it was too late to reconcile. However, through some twists and turns of fate, we had been able to pick up a couple of the pieces of our former life and were now able to enjoy a pleasant, albeit infrequent, evening together. In an effort to regain a relationship with her, I had backed off the drinking quite a bit and was working hard to clean up my language. I was doing fairly well at both efforts most of the time.

Diane has a gentle sort of smile that seldom blossoms into a full-blown laugh. The smile lives there in the corners of her mouth and her face is framed by soft-falling hair, whose color is somewhere between light brown and dark blond. During our infrequent dinners together, the smile often grew as we renewed our friendship and she noted my progress in winning the struggle to avoid swearing. Now, I am quite proud to say it's rare to hear the former trench mouth of Lt. Mike Amato utter even one syllable of profanity. On the other hand, I figure that swearing in Italian doesn't really count if there is no one around who understands it.

Modifying my language was relatively easy. Taking a fresh look at humanity was more difficult. And, changing the way I work has been impossible. The last time we met for lunch, Diane commented, "One-and-a-half out of three isn't too bad. It's not all that good, but it's not too bad!"

Having made the most difficult call first, I started on the second phone call.

"Yo!" I said into the mouthpiece when Fast Eddy picked up the line. "I need to meet up with you."

"I ain't got nothin' to tell you about this thing you got," Eddy said, in an obvious reference to Martin's murder.

"We still need to talk," I persisted.

"When?"

"Tonight. After dark. Let's say, about nine?"

"Nine's good. Where?"

"Water Street okay with you?"

"Water Street at nine," he confirmed. The phone went dead.

I hadn't been away from the PSB for an hour when the call came in for me to report immediately to the Chief's office. The request made me smile, and at the same time it angered me. Obviously, Kathy Martin had the straight scoop about Danny being on the job. Why else would Murphy want to see me "immediately"? If my information sucked, he would have told Winston to tell me I was all wet. On the other hand, if my information was on the money, Matt would want to chat. To do that, he would need to see me personally so as to question me about what the victim's wife knew, what she had said, and most importantly, who else knew what she had already told me.

I met up with Major Winston at his office. Together we jogged up the two floors of stairs from the Detective Bureau on the fourth floor to the Department's puzzle palace on the sixth floor.

At that time of the evening there was no one in the Chief's outer office, so Skip knocked lightly on the door leading to Chief Matthew Murphy's inner sanctum. After a minute or so, the athletic form of the former FBI agent opened the door and invited us in.

I was struck by a thought as I took a second look at the Chief's inner sanctum. If one is impressed by the trappings of furniture, I guess you could say Matt the Chat's office was impressive. I don't really know if the desk, chairs, couch, two end tables and coffee table were Louis XIV or Joe the Ninth. I'm not one who knows such things. All I do know is that the Detective Bureau Offices are decorated in something akin to an Early Depression or Late Garage Sale motif, and Matt Murphy's office was definitely several steps above those grades.

"I understand we need to chat, Lieutenant," Chief Murphy said.

"Oh, yeah," I responded flippantly. "We *do* need to chat, Chief."

"About?" he inquired with a look of innocence.

"About what I heard and saw."

"So, what is it that you've heard and seen?" he asked as he glanced to Ken Winston who was seated on my right.

"What I heard was Daniel Martin was a sworn member of the Rochester Police Department. Not an informant, a snitch, a crook, or a mob guy, but an honest to goodness, badge-carrying, crime fighting, true blue copper."

"And, ah, what is it you saw?" he asked. Murphy's voice was smooth and even, but his eyes darted from Winston to me and from me to the pencil he rolled back and forth across the desk.

He was obviously uneasy with the information I brought to him. I wanted to make him more nervous. "Is what I heard true, Chief?"

"I am neither able to confirm or deny that at this time, Lieutenant," Matt Murphy said in true-to-form FBI parlance. "Now then, what did you see?"

"Well, that right there tells me my information is correct," I commented confidently and added a couple of exaggerated nods of my head.

My observation and charade made Matt the Chat repeat the question a little louder and a little more emphatic.

"I saw the badge, state certification, and ID card he was issued a few years back," I responded as I looked defiantly at the man. "Of course, that was before your time. I also saw his paycheck stubs that have, by the way, been issued since your time with the Department. I saw they're from YBA Industries in bi-monthly amounts that, coincidentally, equal what a cop with five years on the job would be making."

Murphy's shoulders shrugged as he asked, "So what does that mean?" Looking to Winston he asked, "Do you see a link there, Major Winston? I surely don't. Someone has a badge that may be purchased at any uniform store and some paychecks from some company. Where's the connection? If there's a connection here, I don't see it."

"Chief, with all due respect," I moaned, "I was born in the morning, but I wasn't born *this* morning. Please don't treat me like a frigging idiot."

Matt Murphy looked at me with the slightest tinge of anger. "You'll need to explain that last remark, Lieutenant."

"YBA Industries does not exist. It's a scam, a phony company. The YBA Corporation has a long list of sister companies and divisions. The list includes YBA Landscaping, YBA Consultants, YBA Construction, YBA Photographic Equipment, and probably by now, YBA Computer Services. YBA has offices in Los Angeles, Denver, Albuquerque, New Orleans, Orlando, Pittsburgh, New York City, Detroit, and, if memory serves me correctly, Toronto, Canada. It has one actual address, and that is a Post Office Box in the Town of Pittsford, which is just about ten miles from here." I paused to see if I was getting through. Judging by the tapping of Murphy's pen on the desk pad, I assumed I was doing fine in the endeavor.

"The fact of the matter is this," I continued. "YBA Corporation and all the YBA components don't own a stick of furniture, they haven't got one square inch of office space, they don't make anything, and they don't provide any services. The entire outfit doesn't have one single employee. The entire operation is a hoax; a dummy company that is set up to provide cover for cops working undercover. If the copper is supposed to be a laborer, he is given the YBA Landscaping cover. If he's working high priced call girls and supposed to be an executive then he gets to work for YBA Consulting Services or YBA Corporation's home office." I paused and asked, "Do you want to know more?"

"There's more?" the not so chatty Matt Murphy asked casually.

"Okay," I said with a deep sigh of resignation. "The name YBA was thought up back around 1984, maybe 1985. Two old-time, ball-breaking narcs by the names of Joe Carnarro and Dutch Sensabaugh came up with the name one afternoon while they were having lunch at Roncone's. There was also, by the way, a third Detective with them. Anyway, Joey and Dutch thought it might be cute to name the front company YBA. The initials stand for 'You're Busted, Asshole.' " Again I paused. Then added, just for a kicker, "They were having tripe for lunch. I know because I was the third guy at the table!"

The last part was a lie. I hadn't really been there when Sensabaugh and Carnarro came up with the name. However, I knew the story was true because Dutch told me about it several times.

Winston was getting uptight and I sensed it was not so much in relation to my sarcasm as it was due to the information he was hearing for the first time. He was most assuredly coming to the realization that he had a guy working on the homicide of a cop and the guy, namely me, knew he was getting a snow job.

"What's the deal here, Chief?" the Major asked directly. He then modified it with a qualifier. "That is, if you are able to go into it, of course."

The Chief folded his arms across his chest and looked down at his wingtip shoes, where he spent almost a full minute in thought. Looking back up at my boss he said, "The deal is that there is something very sensitive going on and I am not at liberty to discuss it at this point in time."

"But, Chief," Winston said, but he was waved off by his boss, who was obviously trying to decide a course of action.

"I am ordering both of you to sit on this information for tonight," the Chief said evenly, without any emotion. "We will meet here first thing tomorrow, say about seven-thirty, and we'll discuss it then." He looked at both of us and asked, "Do I have your word you will remain totally silent on this matter, gentlemen?"

"Absolutely," Winston said.

"Ditto. I'll look forward to it," I said and hoped Murphy could sense the chill in my voice. "There is one other matter," I added.

"What's that?" the Chief of Police asked.

"The victim's wife wants a police funeral for him with full honors."

"That may not be possible," he said with a tone of annoyance.

"But, we will discuss it tomorrow," I suggested in a tone that let him know I was as serious as death.

"And why is that?" Murphy asked as he looked to Major Winston for some help in shutting me up.

"Because she's going to the press with the story tomorrow afternoon," I lied.

"She ... she can't do that," Murphy insisted.

Getting up from my chair and walking toward the door leading from his office, I told the Chief over my shoulder, "I don't think we can stop her!"

* * *

I left the confines of the cop shop with the intention of grabbing a sandwich and some fries over at Margaret Tannous' Golden Diner. I really wasn't in the mood for her teasing and light laugh, but I needed to be around someplace where I felt comfortable, some place with real friends. Margaret's was indeed that kind of place. The joint sat over on the city's west side about half way up Thurston Road, a local shopping district of small shops and hard working people. It was a comfortable restaurant with comfortable smells that hinted you weren't going to have your fanciest meal, but you were going to have a good meal.

"Lieutenant," she greeted me loudly.

"*Sitto!*" I exclaimed just as loud, holding my arms wide for the embrace that was forthcoming. Although her daughter had not, as of this time, presented her with a grandchild, the woman loved being called "grandmother" in her native tongue.

The warm, crushing hug from the little Lebanese woman brought a grunt from my belly and a smile to my face. Her firm, steady push on the small of my back as she ordered, "Sit down, Mister Big Shot," was her way of showing me to a table. The old woman reminded me of my mother and, like my mother, Margaret could read me. Knowing I needed to be left alone, she shooed her daughter away from me when the young, dark Lebanese girl tried to start a conversation.

Clapping her hands together Margaret ordered her daughter, Carol, "Go! Leave the Lieutenant alone. He needs time to eat in peace." Then, turning back to me as she wiped her hands on her trademark apron, she advised, "I have meatloaf, mashed potatoes, and gravy for you tonight, Lieutenant."

"Nah," I protested, "I'll just have a sandwich, *Sitto.* I still have work to do, and I just wanted to grab a fast bite."

"Go on!" she exclaimed. "You need a meal, not a sandwich. The meatloaf is better for you."

"I know you're probably right, but really, I just want a sandwich, maybe roast beef, and some french fries."

"You sure?" she asked, with a hint of disappointment in her eyes.

"I'm sure," I replied.

Waiting for the sandwich to arrive, my thoughts drifted to how good a scotch and water would taste right now. Another part of my brain reminded the drink-craving part of my gray matter that I had been away from hard liquor for almost six months and now was not a good time to go on a binge. To busy myself, I checked my watch and calculated it was seventy-seven minutes before I had to meet with Ed Cavaluso.

My mind drifted to Margaret and her apron. It was the apron that I had seen on my grandmother, mother, aunts, and all the other older women in my life. The apron with small, multi-colored flowers went around the back of the neck and covered the bust, as well as the stomach and upper legs, almost down to the knees. Margaret Tannous would not wear one of the plain white aprons supplied by the restaurant laundry companies. As everything else in her life, it had to be an apron that linked her to the old ways, the comfortable ways of life.

My mind shifted gears and began to replay and analyze the day's events.

If Danny Martin had been a cop, and obviously — according to Matt Murphy's reactions — he was, he had to have been inserted into the undercover role five, maybe six years ago. He probably started his work shortly after he got out of the Marines. I doubted the Department would throw a guy into deep cover without getting him trained and certified. Consequently, it followed that while he allegedly was out of town at some type of rehab center, he was really going through some police academy, just as Kathy had said. Danny Martin was probably sent to some academy like the State Police Academy down in Albany, or a Police Academy in Buffalo, or even New York City.

I had worked undercover during a stint in narcotics and knew it was a real struggle to play the role for real, while keeping in mind who you really are. Deep cover must be a hundred times more difficult, I reasoned. When a cop "went deep," as the saying goes, he never went near Headquarters. In his deep cover assignment, the cop lived the assumed role twenty-four hours a

day, every day of the week. There were a lot of horror stories
about coppers that worked deep cover and how they had a hard
time keeping straight on who they were really were, as opposed
to who they pretended to be. There were also the war stories
about cops in deep cover who began to identify more with
crooks than they did with the cops. There were other stories
about those who blew their brains out after the case was over
because they felt they had snitched out their "friends" who,
incidentally, were really the crooks they had been working so
hard to bust.

If Danny had gone deep five or six years ago, without the
experience of being around other cops, without the opportunity
of having a reality check now and then, without the benefit of
having friends to lean on and talk to about what he was going
through, he had to eventually become a basket case.

I found myself wondering who Danny Martin's contact was.
As a part of his job, he had to periodically meet with a contact
cop to let the Department know what was going on. The contact
cop would also have the duty of maintaining Danny's mental
health and well-being. If the contact cop was strong, Danny
would have a better chance of making it out of deep cover with
his wits and values. On the other hand, if the contact was weak
or insensitive to the kid's needs, Danny would end up getting
milked for the information, used like a whore, and then screwed
by the Department once he "came out". Without the support
system around him, the odds were that he wouldn't come out of
the assignment with all of his marbles, especially after being in it
for six years.

The most chilling part of the entire thing was that *The Bureau*
was involved in this plot. It was a sure thing that when Murphy
delayed "confirming or denying," it was because he had to talk
to someone about the situation. My bet was that he was
probably sitting over at the Federal Building with his former
cohorts asking, "What the heck do we do now?" If it was strictly

an RPD production, he could have called the shots. Obviously, that was not the case.

The lie I had told Murphy about Kathy Martin going to the press with the story of her husband's undercover life had rattled the Chief. That brought a smile to my otherwise drab mug. It was a lie that would make him work hard to insure Danny Martin got something out of the shafting he had already gotten from the City of Rochester.

A second, stronger smile came to my face when Carol Tannous, Margaret's busty, attractive daughter, slipped the plate with meatloaf, mashed potatoes, and gravy in front of me with the instructions, "Momma said for you to enjoy the meatloaf."

It would have been useless for me to tell her that I had not ordered the meatloaf. *Sitto* knew meatloaf was the best thing for me; therefore, I was going to have the meatloaf.

My fork dug into the meal as my mind shifted back to Police Officer Danny Martin. I wondered what support and guidance he had gotten during his years undercover. In my head, I ran through the list of cops working in the Vice Squad over the past couple of years. Although there were many that would have been very good for Martin's mental well-being, there were others who were not so hot. There were a lot of questions to be settled when we met with Murphy in the morning, but for now I had to be satisfied with searching for the right answers.

I hate being wrong. On the other hand, sometimes I really hate being right. One thing I knew for sure after chatting with good old Matt Murphy was that I was right about Danny Martin being a cop.

I finished the meal, wiped the remnants of gravy off my chin, and asked myself one more question: why was the Department, and whoever they were in bed with, still keeping Danny's true identity a secret? If he was dead, then the investigation was dead! If the people he was working against killed him, the Department would want to confirm Martin was a cop and let the guilty parties squirm into making some stupid mistakes. Besides, dead cops were great for politicians. If they couldn't get some votes by messing over a cop, the politicos sure as hell could garner a little positive publicity by pretending to cry over one. If Danny Martin's cop role had to be kept secret, then evidently there was at least one more shoe to drop. There had to be more going on with the investigation Danny was involved with. There was more action about to take place.

I paid the check, gave *Sitto* Tannous another hug and was given a peck on the cheek by Carol. After agreeing that I would stop working so long and so hard and would come by more often, I made for the door. As I walked to the car, a rather unsettling thought went through my head. If Danny was dead because of what he knew, and the Chief believes other people are still in danger of what Martin was digging up, then it was just plain common sense that the cop who was looking for Danny's murderer was probably pretty high on the hit list also! In other words, if Martin got bumped off because of what he knew, then the killer would probably also want to whack the cop who found out why Danny got killed.

"God!" I exclaimed with a smile as I checked my rear view mirror. "You have got to be a real frigging nut in order to enjoy this job."

* * *

In the past few years, the city's leaders had done a pretty fair job of bringing some attractive, safe areas back to Rochester. As for me, I still liked the old parks and walking paths. Cobbs Hill was one of those places.

Situated on the southeastern edge of the city, Cobbs Hill rises up above the rest of the Genesee Valley and offers a nice view of my town. From up there you can't see the pimples, scars, and blemishes on the old lady. In fact, from that vantage point she looks like a classy matron at peace with herself and her surroundings.

Way back when, probably in the 1920s or maybe during the Great Depression, the center portion of Cobbs Hill was dug out and the resulting crater was lined with cement to become the city's reservoir. The path around the water was probably a good half-mile or so in circumference, and it was a nice place for those who tended to enjoy jogging or a quiet walk.

The sun was just kissing the western horizon when I drove up to the top of Cobbs Hill. Even though the habit of arriving early for these types of meetings had almost gotten me snuffed in the Killing Cards Case, it was a habit I was reluctant to break. I liked to see the surroundings before I met with an informant. Surprises are not good things, especially when a snitch is involved.

Not being one who is inclined toward jogging or walking, I used the convenience of my car to make the loop around the reservoir, back down the hill to Monroe Avenue, and up the hill once more. Once the car was parked, I removed the tie that had been hanging loosely around my neck, and, on second thought, chucked the wrinkled, white shirt that had been beaten badly by the day's warm temperatures and extremely high humidity. Walking a few steps to enjoy the gentle breeze that was rising up the hill, I picked out a bench and sat down to wait for Eddy Cavaluso.

Cavaluso and I went back over twenty years. I was a rookie cop and he was already a better than average thief. I got lucky a couple of times and bent some rules a few other times in order to finally arrest "Fast Eddy." The nickname was a well-earned moniker that recognized his ability to do his thievery in a quick, in-and-out manner. It also came from the fact that as a construction foreman, he could get his crew to clean up a project faster than any other crew. Of course, if the mob wanted the job slowed down, Eddy could arrange that too.

He took his busts like a gentleman; often laughing at me good-naturedly and apologizing for making me do so much paperwork when the case was going to go nowhere. A couple of times I had to turn him loose, and Eddy Cavaluso would pat me on the back with one of his ham-sized hands and say with a deep laugh, "Better luck next time, kid!"

Anyway, to make a long story short, Eddy and I kept bumping into one another, and we got to be friendly adversaries. A decade ago, when a relative of Eddy's got caught up in a shooting, Eddy made arrangements for the kid to surrender himself to me. His explanation for the favor was, "He's gonna be picked up sooner or later, Amato, so forget about it, I might as well make sure you're the guy that picks him up! I know you won't do the kid wrong."

During those years as I was making rank in the Department, Eddy Cavaluso was rising in the local mob organization. Although I can't really say Cavaluso was what you might call an "informant," I will say he was a guy who would give me hints or maybe a word of advice if I were sniffing around the wrong tree.

Fast Eddy Cavaluso was now the number-two or -three man — depending on who you listened to — in the local mob scene. His sixty-seven years of life and fifty-seven years of crime had made him a cautious man. Whenever we met, which was probably only two or three times a year, Eddy would insist on using phones he felt were safe. Even on a safe phone, we would use a code for where we were to meet. I guess cops are just as kinky and paranoid as crooks, so I too felt uncomfortable with loose words over telephones — be they the Department's phones or the mob's phones.

Cobbs Hill was the "Water Street" we had talked about on the phone. I found myself wondering how many Internal Affairs cops — if they had indeed monitored the call — were staked out along Water Street in the middle of Downtown Rochester, about three or four miles west of the reservoir, waiting to see me and a mob guy meeting.

It was probably five or ten after nine when I saw Cavaluso's Lincoln pull into a parking spot about twenty yards from where I sat. His arthritis must have been kicking up again, because it took him a little time to push and lift his bulky frame out of the car. The next thing I saw brought a smile to my lips. Following Eddy out of the car was a little white dog with perky ears and a stiff, skyward-pointed tail. I watched with satisfied amusement as the Mafioso mobster, looking very much like the grandfather he was many times over, led the dog from tree to tree to tree, encouraging him, "Go ahead, boy. Do your duty!" The way I saw it, the dog was not in great need of any encouragement to take a leak. He seemed to be highly motivated on his own to mark every tree, bush, and rock within striking distance of the length of the leash.

As the old man walked away from me to take a look at what and who was around, I glanced in the other direction with the same objective. When Eddy approached me, I stood and shook his muscular hand. Perhaps arthritis had attacked his back and legs, but it had not hampered his grip. "Who's the mutt, Eddy?" I asked with a grin.

"Don't bust my chops, Mike. This here is Max, the best friend I got," my appointment said as the dog's nose kicked into high speed and he circled my pant leg going about a hundred sniffs a second.

Not being a dog kind of guy, I just shrugged.

"He was my wife's." Then, making an abbreviated sign of the cross, added, "God rest her soul. When she passed away I was going to give him to my nephew, but, hey, forget about it! She loved this little guy. I took a liking to him and now, well, now he's the best friend, maybe the only real friend, I got. I mean that!"

"I believe you, Eddy," I said with a couple of quick short nods of my head. "I heard about your loss," I said in reference to his wife who had passed away about six months earlier. "I offer you my sincerest sympathy."

"I appreciate that, Mike, I really do. Regardless of our different situations, I know it comes from the heart. And, I appreciated the sentiments in your card."

"It truly does," I commented with a nod. "I'm only sorry I wasn't able to come to the funeral home, you know, to pay my respects in person."

"Forget about it!" he proclaimed with a wave of his right hand. "The damn Feds were all over the place. They would have snapped a dozen pictures of you and me together." With a shrug he added, " I understand these things."

We sat in silence for a minute as two joggers passed within ten yards of us. The broad was kind of cute and when she looked my way, I flashed her a little smile, only then to realize she was looking at Eddy's companion, Max.

"So, I guess this is about the Martin kid," Eddy said.

"Right."

"Forget about it! It's not our thing, Mike," he said as he looked off into the distance.

"It's not?"

"No, it's not."

Again we sat in silence. I needed to ask him why I should believe that, but I couldn't phrase the question that way.

"I was at the scene, Eddy. It sure looked like a hit to me."

"Hey, don't get me wrong, Mike. I ain't saying he didn't get whacked by one of our friends. I'm just saying it wasn't an ordered hit. If yous guys think it was an authorized hit, forget about it!"

"So, from you're perspective, what do you think?" I asked, switching gears.

"Maybe you should talk to a little dolly by the name of Dee Dee. She's a hostess, a stripper, or whatever they call it, over at Tommy Thornton's place."

"Why would I want to talk to her?" I asked as I stubbed out another cigarette with the toe of my shoe.

"From what I hear, Martin had a case of the hots for her, a situation that was not too well received by her old man." Eddy waited to see if I bought the proposal, then added, "That's what I hear, anyway."

Again we sat in silence as the older man scratched the little white dog's ears.

After a full minute or so of silence, Eddy Cavaluso asked me, "You know what we called Martin?"

"His nickname?"

"Yeah. We called him 'Gabby.' Gabby Martin."

"You guys sure have a liking for nicknames, Eddy," I said as I pushed the dog's nose away from his attempt to inhale my right shoe through his overactive nose.

"Yeah, we sure do, *Ace!*" he said with a grin, reminding me that cops, myself included, also were fairly liberal with the use of nicknames.

"So, how did he earn the name?" I asked as I used a wet finger to chalk one up for Eddy in the evening air.

"He was always talking and always asking questions." There was a pause, then he threw in, "Questions, questions. Too many questions. Forget about it!"

"So what are you telling me, Eddy?" I asked right out. "Are you saying he got whacked because he asked too many questions?"

"Don't bust my balls, Mike! I'm telling you what you probably already know. This Martin kid was a snitch. No one trusted him. He was too much of a *ficcanaso*, a busybody."

"A snitch? Snitch to who?"

"You didn't know that?" he asked after he turned to look at me face to face with a serious look of astonishment.

In a day, maybe two, it was going to be all over the news that Danny Martin was a cop. I couldn't tell Cavaluso that fact right now. On the other hand, once the news was out, Eddy would think I had been playing him for a fool as we sat on the park bench and I said nothing about the subject. Then our relationship would be dead. I had to make a decision on how to answer his question. I opted to tell him a half-truth rather than a full lie.

"There are some things they're keeping from me, Eddy. I can sense it. The fact is, I know it! But, truth be known, if Martin was a snitch, I'm not aware of it. I swear to God! No one has told me he was a snitch or whatever."

"If that's what you're telling me, Mike, then I'll accept it. All I know is two things. One, some things he was told by my people were, well, they were made up things, but those made up things came back to us. And, two, since they found Martin's body, there's been a lot of Feds snooping around." Then he repeated, "A hell of a lot of Feds."

"Maybe he was a snitch to the Feds, Eddy," I offered. "If he was one of ours, I never knew about it. I swear to you, I never knew it!"

"You don't care too much for dogs, do you, Mike?"

The question was so far out of context that it surprised me. "I just don't have time for them, Eddy,"

"You see this little guy here? He's what you call a West Highland Terrier. A Westie, some people call them. He's as loyal as they come. This little guy will follow you through a hundred miles of snow and cold just so he can sleep at your feet at night. Loyal. He don't ask me for nothing. He just gives. Loyal. When Sara passed away, God rest her soul, I neglected this dog. Ignored him. That didn't matter to him. Forget about it! Every time I sat down, he sat down right next to me. One time, right after the funeral, I forgot to feed him for two days. For two friggin' days the dog didn't eat, Mike! You would think he would get mad at me, maybe bite me or run away. Forget about it! No way! He knew I was all messed up in the head. He still sat right by me. Finally, when I remembered to feed him, I got his bowl of food and set it down for him to eat. You know what he did? He didn't gobble it down. He licked my hand first! The dog was damn near starving, and he stopped to lick my hand." Eddy stopped his story to look me in the eyes again and then he added, "Loyal!"

I nodded in agreement as I tried to decipher if the parable of
the hungry mutt had been told to remind me that he expected a
certain degree of loyalty from me. Or, was he telling me Danny
Martin was no great loss because he wasn't loyal to his mob
buddies. I decided to ask.

"So what are you telling me, Eddy? You telling me that Martin
was snuffed because he was a snitch, that he had no loyalty, but
it wasn't an ordered hit? What are you telling me? I don't get it."

"I'm telling you that, and I'm also telling you to be straight
with me, Mike. You know things you ain't telling me. That's
okay. I know you can't tell me some of the things you know, just
like I can't always tell you some things I know. That's okay.
That's the agreement we got, Mike. We respect that we can sit
and talk and maybe help out one another now and then, but we
can't betray our own people. That's fine. The only thing I ask is
that you just tell me right out, 'Eddy, I can't say anything about
that matter.' I'm telling you: Don't lie to me."

I could have protested my innocence, but it would have just
made matters worse. So, instead of repeating my earlier half-
truth, I simply said, "I apologize, Eddy."

"Besides, you shouldn't be too broken up over the loss of this
Martin kid, Mike."

"Why do you say that?" I asked as I tried to decipher if he
knew I was, "broken up" by the death, or if he was using the
term as a figure of speech.

"Gabby was real interested in getting one of yous guys, Mike.
He was always asking who was a cop, what a cop was doing
hanging around, and who was being paid off. Things like that. I
don't mean he was out to shoot or kill one of your *compadres*, but
I think he would have ratted out one of yous guys if he thought
a cop was on the take or something. I'm telling you, the kid was
no good! If you think he's some kind of loss, forget about it!
Don't lose no sleep over this thing, Mike."

I tried to decide if I should tell Eddy that Danny's death was a
loss to me. If I kept it from him it would be another sign I

wasn't being up front in my dealings with him. My decision, in
the seconds it takes to make such decisions, was to tell him.

"I knew the kid, Eddy. He was from the old neighborhood.
His mother and mine were pretty good friends. The fact of the
matter is that I tried to get him to join the Department, but…" I
left the sentence unfinished.

Cavaluso pulled his upper body back and looked at me with a
look of sadness and surprise all mingled together in a face that
had known too much sadness and too many surprises.

The thought struck me that this friendly adversary of mine
was more appreciative of my past relationship with the Martin
kid than were my own superiors.

"I'm sorry, my friend," he said as he patted my left leg with his
right hand. "Now it's me that needs to ask your forgiveness.
Believe me, I meant no disrespect to you."

"I understand, Eddy," I said and acknowledged with a nod.
Then I added, "It may be hard to believe, but what I told you
was true. He was a friend from long, long ago, but still, I knew
nothing of him being an informant. In fact, the only times I've
seen him was when he was hanging around one of your joints."

Again Eddy Cavaluso patted my leg and then, with some
effort, the older man stood up and immediately upon him doing
so, Max got up from his prone position. The dog looked up to
his master and it looked as if the two of them smiled at each
other.

"Take care, my friend," Eddy Cavaluso instructed as he
offered his right hand.

I gripped his hand firmly and was again surprised by the
power in his old, calloused hands.

As we shook, he told me, "If you're thinking the kid got
whacked because we knew he was a snitch, forget about it. We
used the kid, Mike. The things he was told were bullshit things.
We were using him to mess with yous guys," he said with a tinge
of a smile. "Forget about it! He wasn't killed by us for that."

I watched with some sadness as my alleged antagonist walked to his car. He may have been my enemy by merely being on the other side of the legal fence, but we were still friends in so far as we shared ideologies about fairness, respect, and loyalty. The sadness I felt for the older man turned to a smile when I saw the dog jump into the car. Then, after Eddy had finally gotten his back and legs in the vehicle, the loyal mutt put a big, sloppy lick on the old man's face. And the old face looked happy.

Evidently, the loss of his wife had taken its toll on the man because I could not remember having seen him this sad.

I killed another hour or so trying to locate Dee Dee, but it was obviously her night off. Rather than spin my wheels anymore that particular night, I decided to pack it in and head for my apartment.

Sitting alone in the dark, I let the night breeze blow in from the open window, and breathed it deep into my lungs. Artie Shaw, Benny Goodman, and the Dorsey Bothers provided background music for my thoughts. Tomorrow was another day; one I couldn't wait for, yet, one I didn't want to see arrive.

The case was over twenty-four hours old and it was already into a stall. Nothing was coming up straight. Danny, the mob wanna-be, was actually Danny the cop. The obvious hit was perhaps not a hit at all. Then there was also the matter about Martin having been placed in the mob to get the goods on them; instead, they were using the kid to give us false goods. And, on top of everything else, it could be a jealous husband had nailed the victim.

Call it intuition, experience, whatever, but I fully expected to be taken off the case when the morning came. Matt Murphy needed time to meet with someone before he was going to be willing to share any more information with Skip Winston and me. Based on what Eddy Cavaluso had just told me, the "somebody" that the Chief needed to talk to was the FBI. After all, Eddy had said there had been a lot of Feds around after Martin got whacked. Knowing that, my assumption was that in

the morning I would be told in no uncertain terms that I was off
the case and that the FBI would handle it. Oh, I knew I would
argue and throw a temper tantrum and tell them it was a state
case, not a federal case, but it would be to no avail. They were
going to take the case from me and give it to a bunch of
Washington wimps who couldn't find their way out of a phone
booth.

I went to sleep with thoughts about an old man whose life was
nearing its end, walking with a spunky little white dog who
adored him. It was yet another odd picture in this case filled with
odd, mismatched pictures.

The Department or *The Bureau* might want to take me off the
case, but there was no way I was going to take me off the case.
This was my case. Danny was my victim. I owed this one to him.

5

Thursday Morning: Changing Partners

If I had known Thursday was going to be one of the longest days of my life, I would have waited a little longer to begin it. I guess it was the anticipation of wanting to hear what Matt the Chat had to say about Danny Martin that kept me awake most of the night, then got me up before sunrise and brought me to the office shortly after six in the morning.

My in-basket was full; so, after getting the coffee pot started, I banged out a quick memo to Winston regarding my meeting with a confidential informant the night before. Once I poured a cup of coffee that helped kick-start the day, I pulled a stack of reports, envelopes, and messages out of the plastic tray on the corner of my desk.

The first thing to grab my attention was the Medical Examiner's preliminary autopsy report on our most recent victim. According to the M.E., none of the three gunshot wounds suffered by Martin had, in and of itself, been fatal. However, collectively they had torn through enough organs, bone, and blood pipelines to send his body into shock and permit him to bleed to death in less than five minutes. Bobby St. John's report re-enacted Officer Ross' moves on the night of the murder. The total time lapse of Ross moving from his original spot when he heard the gunshots to the area where he found Martin's body, asking questions of the dying victim, going over to the patrol car to call for assistance, and heading back to the body, took less than four minutes. It was totally consistent with the Medical Examiner's findings.

Setting the report aside for a moment, I made a note to myself to get Martin's personal property released to his wife as soon as possible. A wallet, thirty-seven dollars, a typical junior-mobster wanna-be pinkie ring, and a drugstore watch were all physical property by which Kathy Martin would have to remember her husband. It wasn't much, but it was hers now, and it might bring her some minor comfort in the weeks and months to come.

I read the M.E.'s observations regarding the body and scanned over the usual height and weight stuff. Next, came the description of the wounds, the damage the three bullets had caused, and the effect of the projectiles on the victim's internal organs. The drawing of the body drew my attention. Each wound on the body was indicated with a small symbol to indicate the location and type of wound. A tiny circle marked the locations of the bullet wounds, abrasions were shaded areas, and a thin line denoted scratches or cuts.

The drawing of the victim's back showed three small circles. The drawing that represented the front of the body showed no circles, which indicated none of the bullets exited the body. However, on the front of the body there was a short, thin line drawn right about at the middle of the neck, roughly across the Adam's apple area. I flipped back to the narrative portion of the report and got down to where it read, "victim's anterior neck bears a thin, abrasion-like wound, horizontally positioned, approximately one-and-one-half inches long, which is minor in nature. It does not bear any foreign matter which may lead to the disclosure of the origin of the wound."

Now what the heck does that mean? Did Danny's killer try to strangle him? Was this horizontal abrasion the result of someone's thumbnail as they tried to choke the victim? Was he perhaps approached from the rear as the killer tried to strangle him with some type of ligature, and failing that, shot Martin in the back?

I pulled out the envelope containing crime scene photos and scanned them for one that would show the scratch. Finally I found one. Looking at the photo with a small magnifying glass, I could see the wound was so thin that a rope or anything of that nature could not, in all likelihood, have caused it. In order to clear up what the scratch indicated, the head ghoul at the Medical Examiner's office would have to be personally interviewed.

One of the fifteen messages that had accumulated for me was to call either Phyllis or Kathy at my earliest convenience. The message was taken around midnight while I was trying to run down the elusive Dee Dee. I figured my call to them could wait another hour or so, just in case either or both of them were finally getting some sleep.

As a number of reports were receiving my superficial review and scribbled initials, there was a knock on the doorframe of my office, and I looked up to see a tired looking Officer Lester Ross standing at the threshold.

"Lieutenant Crandall got a hold of me and told me to see you post haste, Lieutenant."

"Come on in, Ross," I said, waving him forward with my right hand. "How's it going?"

"I guess I screwed up the other night by leaving without clearing it with you," he said in a boyish voice. "I just, you know, figured that as long as my boss was accusing me of milking the overtime, that I would go ahead and leave like he told me to."

I smiled at the kid and then chuckled. "I know the feeling, Ross. My experience has taught me that the best way to deal with a stupid order is to follow it!"

"It was immature of me, Lieutenant."

"Your boss was just trying to do his job the way he'd been told to do it. Don't be too hard on him and don't be too hard on yourself."

"It won't happen again," he said. "I can assure you of that."

"Yes it will," I contradicted. "Just don't let it happen to me! Okay?"

"So, what did you want to see me about?" he asked, anxious to move to a fresh subject.

"Your reports were good, kid, very good. The only thing I need to know is specifically what the victim said to you."

"Like I said in my reports, I got up next to him, you know, crouched down, and he was face down, but trying to roll over. I asked him what happened, but he just coughed up some blood and started choking. He looked to be in bad shape, Lieutenant, so I asked him if he knew he was dying." The young copper looked down at the floor for a split second as he admitted, "That was hard to do. It seemed so cold to ask him that, but you know, I was trying to get a dying declaration, and in order for it to be admissible in court, the victim has to believe he's dying. You have to ask that."

"I know," I reassured.

"Anyway, he says to tell his wife he loves her and then he says something about a locker. Then I ask him who messed him up and he just said he was real weak. Then he repeated the part about the locker."

"Okay, Ross. Good. That's all in your report. However, in your report, you wrote that he said, 'in sum and substance' something about him feeling feeble. That's okay for the jury and District Attorney, but for a slow guy like me, I want you to tell me, as well as you remember, exactly what he said. Exactly! Word for word, syllable for syllable. Okay?"

"That's not a problem, Lieutenant," the kid said as he reached into his right breast pocket, pulled out a small notebook and flipped through a half dozen pages before finding what the page he wanted.

"I asked him, the victim, what happened and he said, 'Wife, love her, tell.' I know that don't make any sense, but I got the idea of it and that's exactly what he said. Word for word."

I could have kissed the kid! A cop who took notes! Praise God! Maybe there was some hope for the Rochester Police Department. "Go on," I said calmly.

"Then I asked him, 'Do you know you're dying?' He answered back, 'Locker.' I asked him the same question again, and he said the same thing. 'Locker.' I figured it was a nickname for some one or something like that. He started to hack a lot then, so I went for the main question, and asked him who shot him. That's when he said he was weak, only he didn't say it that way. He started to say, 'feeble.' "

"Feeble?" I asked. "Feeble? What kind of word is that for a street guy to use? Feeble? That's something some blue-haired, old lady would say, not a street mutt. Are you sure about that, Ross? Feeble?"

"You got to understand, Lieutenant, his words were all garbled and, you know, like when you got a mouth full of water and you try to talk. That's the way Martin was. A lot of what he tried to say was mixed in with all the blood he was bringing up."

"But did he say that exactly? Did he say, 'I'm feeble'?"

"Well, Lieutenant, I guess that's what he was trying to say. Actually he just said the first part."

"The first part?"

"Feeb."

"Feeb?" I repeated in a question.

"Feeb," Ross confirmed.

Just then, the phone rang. It was Major Winston relaying the message that our meeting with the Chief was going to be delayed, as per the Chief, until nine o'clock a.m. That was fine with me!

Getting back to Ross, I told him I wanted his notebook as evidence.

"But, Sir," he protested at the unusual request. "I have, ah, you know, stuff, other stuff, in my notes."

"Look, I don't care about how many chicks you have rated in the back of your book, but I need those notes, Ross. Number all the pages in sequence, if you haven't already done that, and just tear out the pages I want. Initial each of the pages, date them and put them in an evidence envelope for me."

"Okay," he relinquished. "If you say so, Lute."

"And," I said as I stood and leaned forward. "Not a word of this to anyone. That's an order! Got it?"

"But, if I'm handling evidence, then I'll need to make a report."

"Yes, you will. In fact, you will sit down right now and make out that report. Part of that report will be that I am ordering you not to tell anyone about this. That will cover your butt if your butt ever needs covering. Then, Officer Ross, you will hand the report to me. I will sign the report and give you a copy of it, but you will not show it to anyone. Keep it for your own protection. Then you will forget all about it and this conversation. Understand?"

"I, ah, I guess I understand, Lieutenant." He nodded his head in the affirmative, but his furrowed forehead said he questioned what was going on.

A half-hour later I had Ross' report, the notebook pages, and the evidence report all locked up in my desk. It was now time to see Skip Winston and see what was happening on his end.

"I don't know what to tell you, Amato," the Major said. "The Chief called here from parts unknown at about seven-twenty. He said that he was tied up with some people and that we should hang loose until about nine."

"He's meeting with his Fed buddies, huh?"

"Could be, but I don't know that for sure."

"If you were a betting man, Major, where would your money be?"

"My money would be on the very good possibility that Murphy is at the Federal Building as we speak, having cookies and milk with the Senior Agent in Charge and a couple of other Feebs, and they are deciding how much or how little to tell us when we meet."

His choice of words in referring to the boys at *The Bureau* chilled me. However I tried not to let it show when I said, "I'll take a piece of that bet, but I think the SAC is tea, herbal tea," I said, and then turned around to head back to the homicide squad room.

I traded a couple of early morning barbs with each of the teams as they reported for duty. We then briefed each other on the status of the cases each team was carrying. I glossed over my meeting with "an informant" the night before, but did not mention Officer Ross' notes. With the morning ritual completed, I grabbed a bagel and some fresh coffee, and once inside my office, closed the door to the rest of the world. It was time to do some thinking.

If Danny Martin, Officer Daniel Martin, had been trying to give us leads during the last few seconds of his life, he had done a fairly cryptic job of it. The locker he had mentioned was probably a reference to his safe deposit box or someone's safe deposit box. That hope had gone nowhere. If he meant to tell us about some other locker, well, that was like looking for the proverbial needle in the haystack. In addition to the train station, two bus stations, and the airport, there had to be four or five hundred, maybe a lot more, lockers spread out through the city. Then, throw in the private lockers one could rent, lockers at health clubs, and a few hundred lockers in some of our public buildings. Without exaggeration, it would take a year to check out all of them. Even if he was referring to a safe deposit box, it didn't necessarily have to be the family box. It was possible and plausible that Danny had gone out and gotten his own safe deposit box under his name — or some fictitious name — at some bank other than the one he and Kathy used. That had to be checked out, but where the hell does one start?

There was also the matter of, "Feeb." He had said it in relation to Ross' question, "Who shot you?" The young cop had done a good job under the circumstances. He kept his head together and sequenced the questions appropriately; first, confirming the victim knew he was dying, and secondly, going for the name of the killer.

Our courts liked things done neatly like that. To the toga-robed woman with the blindfold and scales, the information wasn't as important as the process that was followed. We are, after all, a nation whose legal system is interested in process and format more so than truth. In America, the courts aren't interested in the fact that Person A killed Person B. No, no! What *is* important to our black-robed judiciary is, "How did you *find out* that Person A killed Person B?" Truth took it in the shorts, but the process and the procedures were sacrosanct.

Was our victim trying to tell Ross that he was shot and killed by an FBI Agent? Why would he say, "Feeb" in response to the question regarding who killed him? Was "Feeb" a nickname for someone or something stupid like that? Do we have citizens floating around our fair city with a last name or nickname of "Feeb?" That also had to be checked out. Running down a nickname had solved a lot of cases, and I had heard a bunch of idiotic nicknames in my twenty-five years on the job. I just had never heard of anyone with a stupid nickname like, "Feeb." But, one never knows! And still, another thing to consider was that maybe Danny Martin's contact had been a Fed, and the victim was asking Ross to call the FBI.

And, finally there was the message he wanted us to pass along for him: He wanted his wife to know he loved her. That was the only thing that made sense out of the entire scene. Kathy was the only link, the only connection that Danny had between his deep cover world and the normal world.

He had been thrown into a den of lions without a lifeline. Uniformed cops, plainclothes cops, and undercover cops all have each other. For better or for worse, they have some other cop or cops to lean on, to talk to, and to vent their frustration. Danny had no one but Kathy. The mob guys saw him as a snitch. The cops, myself included, saw him as a dirt bag. His own family was ashamed of him. All he had for comfort, support, and encouragement was a tiny, pretty wife. And, during the final moment in his life, the disposable cop had sent his wife a message of love.

I shook off the romanticism and refilled my cup so I could make a better effort of getting my head on straight and focus on the job. If Kathy had truly been Danny's only confidant, then what had he told her? Cops tell other cops their secrets. So, if Kathy was this particular cop's only tie to the normal elements of the human race, what had he confided to her? What secrets did she know? When he was down and depressed or up and cocky, what had he told her about whom? That also needed to be checked out. Maybe what she knew was going to get her killed!

At quarter past nine, Winston called to say the meeting with Chief Murphy had now been put off until ten o'clock. That was it, as far as I was concerned. If these mopes expected me to sit around a few more hours waiting for them to get their shit in one sneaker and still wanted me to handle a murder investigation all by myself, they were going to have to get dished some reality.

Danny Martin had been dead for thirty-six hours and the only thing the investigation had dug up was the potential fact that he was a cop. I had been farting around long enough. It was time to kick the investigation into high gear. If the case was going to get solved, I was going to have to begin to shake some trees. I wasn't about to let the killing of a cop go unsolved. Maybe the brass had time to fiddly-dick around, but I had places to go, people to see, and things to do.

I reached out for Frank Donovan and Bobby St. John and asked them to run down the lead regarding the chick, Dee Dee. I apologized for putting them back on a case they had been pulled from, but they understood the fact that the Department was a little screwed up these days. However, I didn't mention the "Feeb" lead. That one needed to be held close to the vest for the time being.

Donovan said they would cover for me and submit the subsequent report with my name on it, but I told him, "Don't bother with that! I want these bureaucrats to know I got you doing some of the street work. In fact, put it right at the top of the report that I ordered you to do the follow-up on the lead."

I then placed a call to the Martin residence and left word with an uncle that I would be stopping by later in the day to see Kathy.

Finally, at ten minutes after ten, just as I was about to hit the bricks, a call came down from Chief Murphy's aide. The Chief wanted to see Major Winston and me over at the Federal Building, in the FBI offices, pronto. Now, there was a real news bulletin! While I had been cooling my heels at the cop shop, Matt Murphy had been chatting it up with his old cronies. At virtually the same time I hung up the phone, a second line lit up. It was Phyllis Conte.

"Mike, we have something here for you to see. I don't want to go into it over the phone, but I think it might be related to my brother-in-law's death."

"I just got something here that I have to take care of right now, Phyllis. It's important, and I have to get it done now. I'll be out as soon as I can. Okay?"

"Okay," she responded with a sigh that indicated it was not okay.

I was getting angry! I was angry about being kept sitting on my butt for almost three hours. I was angry that Major Winston and I were being summoned as if we were the tardy party. I was angry about having to go to *The Bureau's* home turf. I was angry that I had to put off the victim's family and pass up a possible lead because Matt the Chat decided it was convenient for him to meet with us now.

Most of all, I was angry because this was a clue that the Feds were going to make a move to take over our case. Why they wanted the case was a mystery to me. After all, an arrest was not imminent and the press was not hanging around. Consequently, they wouldn't be handed a cheap bust that would give them some good headlines. Why they wanted the case baffled me, but all the signs indicated they did. If they did, they were going to have to fight for it. Because of Murphy's obvious primary allegiance to his beloved FBI, it was clear I wasn't going to get much help from him. The only support I was going to have in the fight would come from Skip Winston. Once we were in the home court of *The Bureau*, the Major would be powerless, and Skip would be my only ally.

* * *

Ed Delany, the Special Agent in Charge of the Rochester Office was a guy in his early forties. Although I wouldn't call him pudgy, he wasn't the lean, jogger-type like Murphy. The man had been around Rochester for about eight, nine years. Given the length of time he had been in town and the fact that the Feds, in conjunction with my squad cover bank robberies, one would be fairly safe in assuming that we had bumped heads more than a couple of times.

Although Matthew Murphy had been the local FBI boss for about ten years before he retired, Delany now held the position; consequently, he was seated at the head of the table, with Matt Murphy on his right. Some other agent I had seen around at a couple of bank robberies, but didn't really know, was seated at Delany's left. Why a low-level agent was involved in the meeting mystified me, but I figured his role would be made clear soon enough. Chairs for Major Winston and I were arranged on opposite sides of the table, about halfway down the ten-foot polished slab of Oak. It was a well-orchestrated seating plan. The manner in which the table had been staged allowed for Winston and I to be face to face, but divided, in the hope that we wouldn't be able to collaborate.

Similar to the situation with our local Mafia organization's relationship to the Buffalo hierarchy, the Rochester FBI was actually a part of the Buffalo FBI Office. Consequently, the Special Agent in Charge, or SAC, of the Rochester office was actually an *Assistant* Special Agent in Charge, or A-SAC. Being part of our federal government, the Famous But Inept boys were very big on acronyms. A-SAC is like being called SAC, unless a real SAC was around. In that case, they always made a point of being called an A-SAC. Personally, I thought the whole thing had just a little too much pomposity.

The Rochester A-SAC made an over zealous show of welcoming us "boys" to his shop and called out to someone, "Round up some coffee for these boys."

When asked how I wanted my coffee, I declined the offer saying, "None for this boy, sir." Then, turning to Major Winston, I asked, "How about you, boy? How do you want your coffee?"

The resulting red faces of Murphy, Delany, and Agent X brought a feeling of warmth to my heart. Delany knew I was — in effect — accusing him of making a racial remark, and his stiffened posture at the rebuke brought me some satisfaction. Winston merely closed his eyes for a brief second and shook his head in the negative. I was fairly confident I could see him blushing under his brown-pigmented skin.

Deciding not to play by the Feds' rules, I slid past my assigned chair and pulled a chair up to the table, right between Delany and Special Agent X. I sat down in the un-orchestrated spot and offered an innocent but impish smile to each of the other men at the table.

Apparently, somewhat dismayed by my upsetting the seating arrangement, Delany cleared his throat a couple of times and started the meeting. The way the FBI honcho opened the ceremonies was the third clue that the Rochester Police Department was the intended victim of a hostile take over.

"It appears we have a sensitive situation here," Ed Delany said as he rubbed his right cheek with the side of an expensive ballpoint pen. "As I have been told, you already know that

Daniel Martin was on an undercover assignment working as a Rochester Police Officer on loan to the FBI."

Winston and I exchanged glances, first between us and then with the Chief. We had not known Danny Martin was "on loan" to the Feds. In fact, as of the moment, no one in any official position had told either one of us that Danny was a cop. It was a significant point, but not one that needed to be dragged out right now.

Delany stopped for a second as he noted the exchange of looks among the three Rochester cops and then continued. "There's no doubt this homicide is a state case and your agency has jurisdiction," Delany said to no one in particular. "However, The Bureau has certain interests in the case as well, and we feel we have a pressing need to be on top of the matter."

Earlier, during the three-minute ride from our shop to the Fed's shop, Winston had cautioned me five times about the importance of keeping my mouth shut, so I sat there with a I'm-just-a-dumb-yokel smile glazed on my face and listened.

"Officer Martin had been passing along some rather valuable information regarding the local Mafia's activities, and we were in the process of considering convening a grand jury to bring the investigation to a head," Delany said as he nodded to each one of us.

The use of a double qualifier, "in the *process* of *considering*," really meant that they had no intention of sending the case to the grand jury anytime in the foreseeable future, and certainly not within my lifetime.

"The work the young officer did for his community should not go without notice," Delany eulogized. "Those of us at The Bureau will make every effort to see he gets recognized as the hero he surely was."

I knew there had to be a "but" in here somewhere.

"However," Delany added with a sigh and what was supposed to be a sad face, "We here at The Bureau feel we should not go public with the matter, that is, regarding his true role, at this time."

"Why?" I asked.

"Well, Lieutenant, our feeling is that we could jeopardize a long, expensive investigation by moving too fast. We are of the belief that if we were to announce the U.C.'s true identity, some of the targets of the investigation would take off, go on the lamb, so to speak."

"I think that's a sack of crap," I said without losing my dumb yokel smile, but also without any attempt to tenderize the comment. "By the way, the 'U.C.' had a name. And, I'm here to tell you, it wasn't 'Undercover'."

Delany gave Murphy the kind of smile that one parent offers another parent whose child is acting up at the in-law's house. Murphy looked at both of us, one at a time and without any discernible emotion.

I was concerned the Feds were getting too comfortable. We were in their home court. They needed to be rattled. So, I pointed my thumb to the man on my left and asked, "By the way, who's this guy?"

"I'm Special Agent…"

"He is Special Agent William Allen," Delany interrupted in an effort to keep the upper hand. "He is the agent to whom Officer Martin reported."

"Let me interject here," Chief Murphy said directly to Winston and me. "I've chatted with Agent Delany extensively on this matter and although we have some different approaches to the matter, I think a decision needs to be forged here and now. That's why you both are here, to offer your input."

"Here comes the ol' soft-shoe," I thought to myself.

"Although there is some disagreement between myself and the FBI on the matter of disclosing Officer Martin's identity, I have decided the city will be making a public statement this afternoon that he was a Rochester Police Officer who was working under-cover."

I was more than pleasantly surprised that Murphy's decision was not in agreement with Delany's wishes. The fact is, I was in shock! My mind called a time-out and tried to decipher what was transpiring here. Evidently, by the look on the A-SAC's face, Delany and Murphy must have been going toe-to-toe all morning over the issue of releasing Danny Martin's status with law enforcement. Murphy had just declared they were going to do it his way. Maybe it wasn't really his call, and my brain reasoned that the Mayor may have become involved and told Murphy which way to go on the matter. All that aside, why did Murphy bring his Lieutenant and Major to the table to witness Delany's castration? Was he trying to show us he had severed all ties with his beloved Bureau? I would have to chew on that one for a while before I figured it out.

"That may have some impact on the pending cases," the Chief continued. "But there is no threat to anyone's life and, short of that threat, we have no reason to further strain the grief the family has experienced. If the family so desires, Officer Martin will be given an honor guard while his body is at the funeral home and he will be given a police officer's funeral."

"Way to go, Matt the Chat!" I silently cheered. The man had some balls after all! I couldn't figure why he had suddenly jumped on the RPD bandwagon. I could only surmise that one of two things took place over night and early this morning. Either Murphy had believed me when I said Kathy Martin was going to go to the press, or City Hall had gotten to him and decided to make some political hay out of the situation. My gambling intuition said it was probably a combination of both.

"Regarding the matter of the investigation, the RPD will handle the homicide investigation and will provide every assistance to the FBI in clearing up matters that are of importance to them. The Bureau's concern that we may have the beginning of an inner-mob war that has been initiated with Martin's killing is a serious matter. On the other side of the coin, I hope they will assist us in every way possible, with whatever

information they may have, so that we can successfully conclude
our case."

Skip Winston spoke up. "We look forward to sharing the
information with them, Chief. I will arrange for daily briefings by
our troops to the FBI and will coordinate their briefings with
our personnel."

I thought that offering was a kind of pie-in-the-sky thinking,
but it was probably necessary for the Major's professional
survival. There was no way the elitist FBI was going to swap
information with lowly local cops. The cocky look on my face
quickly disappeared when I heard Murphy's next comment.

"We will do better than that. Major," Murphy said as he sat
upright. "Agent Delany and I have nailed down one com-
promise. Agent Allen and Lieutenant Amato will team up and
work the investigation in concert with each other. That way,
there is no guessing about what is being shared and what is not
being shared."

"You got to be kidding me!" I said with a notable groan. The
observation was intended to be a thought, but ended up being
verbalized rather loudly.

"I kid you not, Lieutenant," Murphy said in a Chief-ly tone.
"You will work closely, *very closely*, with Agent Allen, or you will
not work the case at all! Am I clear on that matter?"

"Yes, Sir. Crystal clear," I acknowledged without any emotion
in my voice, but red-cheeked in embarrassment over having
been chided in front of the Washington suits.

"Now, I have lost a morning on this matter, but I believe it
was time well spent," Murphy said to one and all as he stood.
Then to me he said, "I suggest you and Allen take the next few
hours to catch each other up on your investigations and then
proceed with all due haste."

"May I notify the family, Chief?" I asked.

"Please do that, Lieutenant. I would appreciate that being
done as soon as you *and Agent Allen* are able to do so. I will
contact the police union so that we can make the public

announcement together. Sgt. Polson will make arrangements with the Tactical Unit to provide an honor guard, and he will also make the final arrangements with the family as well as be the Department's liaison to the family."

As we all stood and did a circle of handshakes, I found myself not trusting the fact that Matt Murphy had impressed me. Maybe it began to dawn on him that he may have been a Fed in his former life, but he now was our boss. My suspicious side thought that maybe the apparent rift between the A-SAC and the Chief was staged for a reason. It wasn't all that important right then and there, so I let go of it and turned my thoughts to more important matters, like how I was going to get rid of Special Agent William Allen.

The bosses stood and maneuvered around the table to compliment each other on their cooperation. As they went through their ceremonial, post-bureaucratic-meeting dance, Allen and I sized each other up.

Neither one of us appeared to be impressed with what he saw.

"One more thing, Lieutenant," Murphy added as he opened the door. "Ask the family when I may pay my respects to Officer Martin. Make it sometime private. I don't want it becoming a media event."

* * *

When everyone had left, Special Agent William Allen led me to a kitchen area and poured us both a cup of coffee. From there, we went into a small office furnished only with a couple of chairs and a table. Once in the room, he placed the thick file he had in the meeting room on the table and turned to face me.

"Look, Lieutenant, I probably dislike this arrangement as much as you do, maybe even more. However, the fact of the matter is those guys sign our checks; so, we do their bidding while they try to protect their political careers. I don't see us becoming bosom buddies, but I do hope we can conduct ourselves professionally and bring some credit on our respective agencies without messing with each other at every turn."

I took a second or two to absorb his intent. I reminded myself I might very well be looking into the eyes of Danny Martin's killer, and shrugged.

"Fair enough," I verbalized as I internalized the thought, "Screw you!"

With that out of the way, Allen proceeded to give me a rundown of his life. He was single and had been with The Bureau for ten years. After being born and raised in Carbondale, Illinois, he attended college there, graduated from law school and went to The Bureau the very summer he graduated from Southern Illinois University. He had drawn his fair share of low-grade assignments in Arkansas and Oklahoma before being sent to San Diego, where he worked organized-crime cases. Because he was just coming out of an engagement that didn't lead to marriage, he asked for an assignment in the New York City office, but instead he ended up in Rochester.

I offered my "mmms" and "uh-huhs" at the proper times as I sized up the six-foot farm boy. I figured that Bill Allen probably went about 175 pounds and although he looked lean, the guy was built like one of those Olympic swimmers. He probably was no slouch in a fight.

He then got the nickel tour of Mike Amato's life without the personal dribble. We then agreed that using our first names would probably make the conversation a lot smoother than trying to fake respect with titles. It was now time to get down to the case at hand.

Bill Allen started to explain the history of Officer Danny Martin's undercover assignment, but suggested that it may be better if I read some of the reports first hand. "Anything we have on the matter is open to you, Mike," he said as he made every effort to look dead serious.

With a few words of gratitude to him and The Bureau, my hands opened the folder and began to scan the relevant reports.

Danny Martin had applied to become a Rochester cop right after he got out of the Marines. At first, the Department was going to reject him because of the friends he had associated with prior to his military time. It wasn't too clear, but someone gave it some thought, saw the kid was clean, and came up with the idea that Martin might make a pretty good cop. The city was having its fair share of mob problems at the time, so someone up high in the Department got the brain fart that Danny, because of his prior associations, coupled with his Marine Corps training, might make a pretty good cop for a deep cover assignment. Arrangements were made to send him through the police academy in Syracuse in order to get him certified as a cop by the State of New York, and he still would not be known by any of the cops in Rochester. After completing the academy he was given some added one-on-one training by former Commanding Officer of the Organized Crime Bureau, and old pal of mine, Charlie Novitski.

Officer Martin turned out to have quite a flair for the job, and during his first two years as an undercover cop he turned up some fairly good intelligence on who was doing what. The kid was able to deliver the goods on a couple of large scale gambling operations as well as some crucial bits of information that led to several arrests of wanna-bes for robbery, burglary, assault and extortion.

Charlie Novitski, Officer Martin's boss and deep-cover contact, was one of the legends of the Rochester Police Department. Not only was he an outstanding cop, but he was also a gentleman. He solved some of the city's most notorious crimes during his career and he had an uncanny insight to criminal, as well as political, matters. According to the file, Novitski was pushing to get Martin brought out of his role as a mole and get him into the normalcy of the abnormal police world. Major Novitski noted in one report, "Officer Martin is showing signs of stress related to his present assignment and needs to be re-assigned to uniformed police duties, which will help insure his continued professional growth and value to the Rochester Police Department."

About the time Novitski was pushing to get the kid off the assignment, the city experienced two killings of made Mafia guys, along with a couple of bombings that were mob related. The decision was made to leave Danny undercover a little longer and have him dig deeper. We never solved the killings, but now, reading the case file, I realized where some of the information that filtered down to my squad from OCB had originated. In the meantime, Captain Novitski was promoted to Major and was reassigned as the Commanding Officer of the Detective Bureau.

After Charlie Novitski moved to his new assignment, the new OCB Commander assigned a young Vice cop to be Martin's contact. It was now a case of the blind leading the blind. A couple of years went by and Martin continued to pass along bits and pieces of information that gave the Police Department a leg up on a couple of important and not-so-important cases. However, without the guidance of Novitski, Danny failed to flourish.

About eighteen months before his death, Danny Martin's OCB contact started to get concerned about Danny's mental health. The contact cop thought Martin's usefulness was coming to an end and that it was time to bring him back to the real world. At about the same time that was developing, the FBI decided it wanted to use Danny as a means of ferreting out police corruption. They had developed some information that a couple of cops were getting cozy with some of the mob boys. They needed an expedient way of making the case. The Chief we had at the time, a guy known to us as "No Balls" Ben Westfield, had gone along with the request and "loaned" Danny to the Feds.

I thought to myself, "And all the while, I thought Lincoln freed the slaves!"

Danny Martin became the expedient way for the FBI to make the case. At the same time, without knowing it, he was also being made expendable. The Department told his OCB contact, as well as Major Novitski, that the Department was firing Martin. A story was concocted that Martin had gotten into using cocaine, and due to his drug habit and insubordination, the Department was terminating him. With that as a weak cover story, Officer Martin was traded to the Feds, and the few Rochester cops who knew his role as an undercover agent were led to believe that Danny had switched sides and gone over to the mob boys.

The little kid who used to blow the whistle dangling from my gun belt never had the chance to blow the whistle on any cops. When it came about that Danny Martin couldn't come up with the information the Feds wanted, he too became suspect. On at least a dozen occasions, Officer Martin was followed as he traveled around the city. None of the surveillances amounted to anything other than seeing the undercover officer talking to the assorted slime who hung around the city's gambling locations.

Special Agent Allen noted in a report dated about two or so months before Danny's murder, "Officer Martin is becoming increasingly more difficult to work with. He is making demands that he be re-assigned back to his Department, is demanding time off, and has been observed becoming highly agitated, to the point of crying."

Based on the word of an informant, who was not identified by name in the reports, Danny Martin was bragging about having made a "big score." According to the informant, Danny had not been around for a few days, and when the snitch asked him where he had been, Martin was reported to have said, "I was doing a thing in Buffalo with a couple of guys and we hit the jackpot!" The report indicated the undercover officer was not seen from May 23 until May 26. And, when Allen asked him where he had been, Martin said, "I went to a party." When Martin was asked about his statements regarding the big score, he told the Agent he was simply trying to keep up his role with the mob. According to the report, Special Agent Bill Allen didn't buy the claim.

The following paragraph of that same report made note of the fact that a fur storage warehouse and a large jewelry company, both in Buffalo, had been burglarized over the weekend of May 24.

There were a few more entries that made note of Danny's demeanor: the presence of alcohol on his breath, argumentative behavior, and mood swings. In typical FBI fashion, the reports added two plus two and then came up with a number the Feds wanted. They were spending a lot of money on the operation, and they were not happy with Officer Martin's failure to uncover corruption with the Rochester Police Department. In order to save their political asses with their bosses, the blame had to be placed on someone. The wind blew, the shit flew, and there stood Danny Martin!

The second last entry was made by Special Agent Allen and was dated August 11, the night before Danny's death.

It read, "Officer Martin continues to demonstrate sever paranoia and insists he has been 'used' by the mob, the FBI, the Rochester Police Department, and/or the U.S. Attorney. Martin demanded he be relieved of duty and threatened to 'go public' if his demands were not met. I advised him I would talk to my supervisors about this and would strongly support his request. Arrangements were made to meet with Martin on or about 13 August."

The last report in the folder was an interdepartmental FBI memo that was submitted by Allen to Delany on the afternoon of August 12, about ten hours before Danny's death. In the one-page memo, the contact agent made a strong case that Danny Martin was becoming unreliable in his information and should be removed from the assignment.

When I finished reading the report, Bill Allen asked me for my reaction. I stalled by telling him I was a little overwhelmed by it all. To keep from having to say too much too soon, I suggested we go tell the Martin family the truth about Danny's undercover activities.

"I came over here with Major Winston, so I'm without a car right now," I said. "Why don't you drive, and I'll give you a rundown on what we have so far."

"Good idea," the Agent agreed.

We rode the elevator in silence to the main floor of the Federal Building. Once there, I stopped at a bank of pay phones and advised Allen, "I need to make a personal call and break a date. Okay?"

With a wink, Allen said, "No sweat, Mike. I understand. I've been there myself. You go ahead, and I'll pull the car around to the State Street side of the building and meet you out front."

With my shadow out of the way, I dialed Kathy Martin's house.

"Where have you been, Mike?" Phyllis asked with a considerable note of annoyance. "We need to see you."

"I know you do, but I got buried with a couple of things."

"We got something here that you should see right away, Mike. Can you come now?"

"I'm on my way just as soon as I hang up," I advised. "Can you tell me what you have?"

"There's too many people around right now, but when you get here we'll give it to you."

"Okay," I relinquished. "Look, I got some news for the family. It's not anything great about the case, but it's good for Danny and Kathy. I'll be there in ten minutes."

"Okay, Mike. You tell us what you have, and then we'll give you what we came across. Just hurry. We got this thing here and want to see what it is."

Right then, my head didn't get the full meaning of what she was saying. However, just in case it was something I didn't want to share with the FBI, I told her, "Phyllis, I'm coming over there with a guy from the FBI and I don't want him in on everything just yet. Okay? You understand me?"

"I think so," she said with some doubt.

"If we can get alone, you can tell me what you have to say, but if he stays close, don't say anything in front of him. If I have to, I'll get together with you and Kathy later this evening when we can be alone. Got it?"

"Okay, Mike," she said with some notable annoyance. "But you need to see this. It's important!"

On the drive to the Martin home, I briefed Special Agent Allen on the official version of the RPD investigation from the finding of the body to the autopsy report. I figured they would eventually have all the reports anyway, so I might as well play the part of the cooperative local cop for the time being. Without identifying my source, I even told Bill Allen about the possible connection between the victim and Dee Dee.

"The stuff in your reports about him possibly going to Buffalo, that's a pretty serious matter, huh Bill?" I asked.

"Sure is!" he acknowledged with a nod.

"Do you believe it?" I asked bluntly. "Do you believe Martin was making scores with the mob and not reporting it?"

"I don't know what to believe, Mike. The kid was getting strange. I just reported what I came across. Nothing more, nothing less."

Needless to say, as we continued our conversations, I left out the information about Ross' verbatim conversation with the victim and the fact that I had Ross' notes locked away safely. My own Department didn't yet have that information, so I couldn't see why I should pass it along to the Feds. Nor did I mention what Phyllis Conte had just told me. If it was important information, I wanted to hear it first. Maybe, after having time to consider it, I might tell my Fed partner.

In spite of Murphy's instructions, I didn't feel I should have to give the Feebs everything. The folder that Allen had been authorized to show me back in his office had been sanitized long before I got my hands on it. Some reports I had read referred to earlier reports that were not in the file. Between the pages of the reports that I was allowed to read were tiny pieces of torn paper that were left behind when page were abruptly pulled out as Delany and his crew determined what I was not going to be allowed to see. In addition to the folder Allen had allowed me to read, there was another folder that he said he could not share, "at this time." My bet was that I would never see it, not now and not ever!

I gave Bill Allen directions to the Martin house, and then blaming a long night, I leaned back in the seat and pretended to doze. I needed the quiet time to soak in what I had just read in the FBI reports.

If everything Allen had said in his reports was true, then Martin was obviously becoming a basket case. The drinking, the mood swings, and the paranoia were all indicative of a cop going over the edge. Taken on face value, Special Agent Allen's reports painted a picture of an undercover cop going over to the other side, and if not that, at least striking out on his own in order to make his own fortune.

Being the cynic that I am, I had to consider that Allen's reports were works of fiction contrived to make Danny look like a wacko who was becoming a crook. Maybe Martin knew something about Allen that the rest of us did not know. Maybe because he knew that little secret: an FBI agent who had gone bad had marked him for death.

My tired mind told me that theories were all well and good, but I was probably going over the edge on that particular theory. Besides, in this line of business one better have proof to back up those theories. Then, for the time being, I gave up trying to mentally solve the case, and I let my mind drift to the horror that Officer Daniel Martin faced in his final months on planet earth.

I had seen it before, when Narcs, or street cops, or even homicide detectives began to close themselves off from others, they descended into a downward spiral. Without another cop to talk to, the struggling cop begins to seek his own cure. Sometimes the cure comes in the form of violence. Sometimes the violence is directed outward toward the street hoods and the scumbags. Sometimes the violence is directed inward and the cop sticks his service weapon in his mouth, pulls the trigger, and ends all the voices and the doubts.

Danny Martin didn't make the choice to close himself off from those who could support and befriend him. The Department had made that choice for him. Then, all alone in a world he could not talk about, he began to fall apart.

For some unknown reason, he had been killed. Perhaps what Kathy and Phyllis now possessed would shed some light on the who and the why.

6

Thursday Afternoon: Close to a Lead

Bill Allen eased the car into a parking spot. Due to the number of cars already there, he had to park across the street and a couple of houses away from the Martin residence. When he slipped the gearshift into park, he stopped and looked at me before he shut off the ignition.

"This is kind of foreign to me, Mike," he said with some humility. "What should I expect in there?"

"What do you mean? I don't understand what you're asking."

"I mean, I'm a WASP from the Midwest. Some of the ways up here, some of the ethnic ways are kind of, well, kind of different."

"They're Italians in there, Bill. That doesn't mean they're all mobsters or monsters. They won't attack you because you're with the FBI."

"I didn't mean that," Allen said with a hint of being offended. "What I was getting at was the fact that I don't want to offend anyone. I don't want to go in there if I'm not welcome or if I'll get in the way of what the family is doing."

I shrugged my shoulders rather than apologizing for my brash comment. If he was sincere, and I really thought he was, I owed him some consideration.

"We normally like to have the body at a funeral home within a day," I explained. "However, due to the autopsy delaying things,

121

Martin's been dead for more than a day and a half; consequently, the family is a little antsy." I paused and pointed to the car keys dangling in the ignition. Allen took the hint and shut off the car.

After we were both out of the car and moving toward the house, I continued. "The Italian people are rather big on weddings and funerals. Once a body is at the funeral home, there are usually two sets of calling hours each day for three days. Today, in an hour or so, will be the first viewing. Everyone is gong to be pretty wrung out."

"What should I expect?" he asked with some apprehension.

"Don't worry about it, Bill," I responded with a little laugh. "They aren't going to scalp you. They will treat you like a guest. Accept whatever food they offer; to turn it down is an insult. They'll be cordial to you, but keep in mind that you're an outsider. Respect that, okay?"

As we reached the side door of the house, Special Agent William Allen said he would keep that in mind.

Kathy Martin looked exhausted. The black dress seemed to hang on her small body. Her red eyes were circled partially by red-pink lids at the top and dark bags below. She was less than an hour from seeing her husband's body resting in a casket. What she did not know was that there would be a Police Officer at each end of the casket. I needed to share that with her. She already had more shocks than she needed.

In spite of everything she was being put through, she opened her arms to me and warmed me with a quivering smile. The perfume she wore hinted at the fragrance of baby powder, and as I held her tightly, I wondered who was providing comfort for whom.

I introduced her and Phyllis, along with a litany of aunts and uncles, to Special Agent Bill Allen. Along with the round of introductions, I let it be known that the Chief was going all out to find Danny's killer. I explained that he had enlisted the help and cooperation of the FBI, who were now actively assisting the Police Department with the investigation. Bill Allen's raised eyebrows made it clear that he probably didn't like my assessment that the lofty FBI was playing a support role to the local cops, but that was his problem! The collection of relatives seemed to be impressed that the FBI had entered the case. That hurt my ego, but my main interest this particular afternoon was not concerned with feeding my ego, his ego, or The Bureau's ego.

When I asked for privacy, Kathy and her sister led me off to what might be called the master bedroom. Once Phyllis had left and closed the door, I told Kathy Martin the Chief was going to publicly announce that afternoon that Danny was a cop and a hero.

Kathy's low, deep wail aroused curious looks from the relatives in the hallway. "They told you about it, Michael? They told you Danny was a hero?"

"Yes, Kathy, they told me." Okay, so they didn't quite use the word hero, but what the hell! I couldn't help myself. The woman had lost her husband and a large chunk of her life to *the job*. They didn't enjoy the fun parts of being a cop, so I thought it only right she feel some of the pride the Department *should have had i*n her husband.

"That makes me feel so proud, so happy, Mike." The tears that had never been far from the corners of her eyes since she learned of Danny's death now made an instant appearance. "I only wish Danny was here to have you tell him he was a hero."

I gave some kind of clumsy nod coupled with a hug. The motions were supposed to be comforting and a humble sign of gratitude for the compliment. I explained to Kathy that Chief Matt Murphy wanted to stop by and pay his respects, but he wanted to do it privately.

"He can come here anytime, Mike. I don't blame him for what's happened. I would be proud to have him come here." The young widow sniffed deeply and then cupped my face in her hands as she said, "He must really respect you, Mike, that he would make such a gesture."

"It's not for me, Kathy," I said with a small smile that was intended to be comforting. "He wants to do it for you and for Danny, but he doesn't want to make a big show of it."

I told her I would pass on the message that the Chief was welcome in her home anytime. At the same time I marveled at the woman's compassion. If I had been sitting in her seat, I would have told Chief Matt Murphy he could kiss my dago ass!

My personal feelings aside, I asked, "Kathy, do you wish to tell your family this information about Danny being a cop, or shall I?"

Phyllis had just re-entered the room as I uttered the last sentence and looked at both of us as if we were totally crazy. I gave Kathy a quizzed look. Evidently Phyllis was not yet convinced by Kathy that Danny was, in fact, an honorable man.

"I told her yesterday that Danny was a cop," Kathy said as she used her head to nod in the direction of her sister. "She didn't believe me then. Maybe she'll believe *you*."

Phyllis stood up and wiped her hands on a half apron that was secured around her waist. Her look was one that indicated she had heard the information, but was having a difficult time accepting it. "Why didn't you tell me before, Kathy?" she asked in a plea more than an admonishment. "Why didn't you tell me?" she repeated softer and with tears in her eyes as she sat on the bed to hold her younger sister.

Kathy Martin simply shook her head and whispered, "I couldn't. The Department wouldn't let us tell anyone. Even I wasn't supposed to know."

Again I asked Danny's widow if she wanted to give the information to the family that was gathered at the home or if I should do it.

"I could never hold myself together to do it," she said through one sniffle and then added a couple more as if to punctuate her next statement. "Besides, they would think, like my sister thinks, that I'm just imagining it or wishing it was true. You tell them,

Mike. I want it to come from you. It would be better for them to hear it from you."

"I know this is private time for the family, Kathy, but Phyllis said you had something to show me. I wanted to stop by to see what it was. Can you show me what you have before we go in and talk to the others?"

Bill Allen knocked on the door gently. Phyllis opened the door just as Kathy began to say something. The older sister said sternly in a hushed voice, "*Silenzio!*" Then, to conceal her panic that Kathy would say something in front of the Fed, Phyllis pulled her kid sister close to her as if to offer comfort. Softly, so as to conceal the true meaning of her message, she whispered Italian words that are difficult to translate literally. In essence, she told Kathy, "Say nothing in front of the government man!"

I almost smiled as Phyllis also referred to the G-man with a word that questioned the marital status of his parents at the time of his birth. I put my hands on Kathy's back and rubbed her shoulders as I whispered, "*Sta sera ritorno solo.*" My Italian wasn't first class, but she was able to understand that her news would have to wait until I returned alone, later in the evening.

Allen questioned me with a facial expression. I simply raised my eyebrows, shrugged and smiled as if I had no idea what had been said between the two sisters.

"It's an Italian thing, Bill," I said. "These little affirmations that we make at a time such as this." While saying the words, I put my arm around his shoulders in order to shuttle him out of the room. "They help the family to accept things. Give me a second or two and I'll be right with you. Okay?"

"Sure, Mike," he said graciously, accompanied by a few quick nods of his head. "Take your time. I'll be mingling." In a whisper he added, "You're right. They're very gracious people."

Closing the door with one hand, my other hand gave him the "Okay" signs with a circled thumb and forefinger but I was thinking of another gesture that I would have liked to give him.

I stepped back into the bedroom with the two sisters. I was going to say something, but by then Phyllis and Kathy were wrapped in a tight embrace with Phyllis sobbing loudly and telling her sister, "I'm so sorry, Kathy ... so sorry ... I didn't know. I really, really didn't know."

I waited for a break in the crying and then cleared my throat to let them know I had re-entered the room. For the first time in the past day and a half, Phyllis looked more drained than Kathy did.

When they looked up I asked, "What is it you have to tell me?"

Phyllis spoke. "Danny's sister got into town yesterday evening. She brought an envelope he gave her to hold for safe keeping."

"What's in it? Is it a letter or what?"

"We don't know, Mike. Danny wrote on the envelope "Hand deliver to Lt. Mike Amato only'. The word 'only' was underlined a couple of times with a couple of exclamation points after it."

"Where is it?" I asked eagerly. "Do you have it?"

"Chrisy has it with her. She's staying at her Aunt Rose's house while she's in town. She said if she didn't see you here, she'll bring it with her to the funeral home."

We discussed arrangements for me to meet them at the mortuary that evening. Although I was anxious to get my hands on the envelope, the first viewing of Danny's body was going to be traumatic enough. The family sure as hell didn't need me stumbling around in addition to everything else.

"I almost forgot to tell you one other thing. The Chief would also like to provide a police honor guard at the funeral home and, with your approval, give Danny a cop's funeral. However, before we do all that, he wanted me to check with you first."

Kathy, who was now in the process of standing on legs that did not want to do their duty, seemed to somehow will them to perform. "I think he earned it, Mike," she said before she drew a deep breath through her nose, seemed to receive strength from the new air in her lungs, and walked from the bedroom to the congregation of family.

Going back into the living room, with Kathy clutching my right arm, I asked the relatives for their attention. A cup of coffee was extended to my right hand by an aunt. A bottle of anisette appeared from the collection of bodies in the small room. The hand of another person I could not see held it and poured a long shot of the clear liquor into my glass. The same was done for Agent Allen. He smiled and mouthed words, "Thank you!" to his benefactors. His refusal was ignored with a smile and a similar pouring.

"You all know Lieutenant Mike Amato from our old neighborhood," Kathy said in a voice that had surprising strength. "Mike is a cop now, for those of you who don't know. He has something to tell you about my Danny...our Danny."

Holding up my left hand to signal for some quiet, I said, "I know this experience has been most difficult for you, but I need to tell you something before you go to the funeral home to see Daniel."

"You found the man who did this?" an aunt asked.

"No, *signora*," I said sadly. "Not yet. However, this afternoon the Chief of Police will make an announcement to the public and he instructed me to come here and tell you, *la famiglia*, the information before he told others." I took a deep breath and blurted out, "Daniel was a Police Officer and was working undercover for the Police Department."

Some of the family took the news in motionless silence. Many of the women made the Sign of the Cross. Several of them whispered exclamations to an assortment of saints as they crossed themselves.

"He was not a bad man like some of you, some of us," I corrected myself, "might have thought. Daniel was a hero who died in the line of duty. I have just asked Kathy, and she has agreed, that we have a police honor guard to stand by Daniel's casket."

"Will he be in uniform?" a cousin asked.

"No, I don't believe so," I responded. "But if Kathy wishes for him to be, it will be arranged."

Kathy nodded a very clear, "Yes."

Realizing that the Department would have to find a uniform somewhere down in the Quartermaster's Office, I responded, "It will be done, but it will have to be later today after the first viewing."

A dozen or more questions were asked and answered in the next few minutes. I answered each in turn. No, we did not know why Danny was killed. Yes, there were some leads we were pursuing. It may be weeks, perhaps months, before we made an arrest. Yes, Kathy did know Daniel was an undercover cop, but the Department had sworn her to secrecy.

After the questions were answered, I took a little more time to have a private conversation with some of the more senior uncles. This was necessary so that each of them would be able to establish his importance in the family by having facts that were given to them directly by *il padron,* as opposed to those who had garnered their information from a public announcement. With that out of the way, the family members began to break up into their sub-groups and make their way to their cars. Once they sorted out who was riding with whom, they began to leave for the funeral home and for what was assured to be a very emotional afternoon for them all.

As I helped the younger members of the family seat the older members in cars, I got close enough to Phyllis to tell her I would break away as soon as I could, perhaps after viewing hours, and meet with her and Kathy. At that time, we would be able to talk in depth without tag-along Fed.

She nodded and I was fairly confident she heard me, but the news she had just received with the rest of her family — that Danny Martin was a Police Officer and not a mob stooge — had the full attention of her senses. As I turned to walk away from the car, Kathy leaned over her sister's lap and called me back.

"That thing that Chrisy has for you," she said covertly. "Danny had her keep it in her safe deposit box."

When a question mark formed on my face, she added, "In her 'locker'."

As Danny Martin's relatives headed to the funeral parlor, Bill Allen and I headed back to the city.

"What now?" he asked.

"I vote for lunch," I responded.

"Name the spot."

Downtown Rochester is one of those typical northeastern urban cities that die at night. However, during the afternoon it was alive with the sights and sounds of people on the move. The office workers who had taken a late lunch were now hurriedly returning to their offices. Delivery trucks and cars on their way to and from places on either side of the city used their horns to make their way around vehicles that presumably had less important errands.

Bill and I grabbed a sandwich at a little place right in the center of downtown, and then we walked over to a small, narrow park on the west bank of the Genesee River. Most of the downtown lunch crowd was already back in their office cubicles, so we had our choice of tables. Selecting one close to the river and under a tree — one that would give us the privacy and shade we would need -we sat down.

"Did you know the Genesee River is one of the few rivers in the entire world that flows north?" I asked.

"You don't say?"

"Yep! It starts in Pennsylvania, comes north all the way through the entire State of New York and then dumps into Lake Ontario."

"I knew it went into the lake, and the lake is north, but I never thought about the fact that most rivers flow south," Allen said as he tried to figure what that little piece of geography had to do with Officer Daniel Martin's murder.

"Pretty messed up, wouldn't you say?" I asked.

"It sure is," he nodded in agreement, just to be friendly and to humor me.

"But," I said and then paused until I had his attention, "It's not as messed up as you guys leaving Martin out there, letting him dangle for months, when you knew good and well he was at the end of his rope." When he didn't respond, I threw him the question, "How the hell can you justify doing that?"

"He was a resource that was important to our investigation. I tried to bring him back in, but the bosses thought I was overreacting."

"A Resource? Resource? Your boss refers to Danny Martin as a 'UC'. You call him a 'resource'. He was a human being, damn it!" I barked as my right fist hit the wooden table and drew some attention from a couple of pedestrians walking toward the Main Street Bridge about twenty feet from us.

Allen didn't show any anger as he said, "Look, Mike, you're right. The kid was at the end of his rope. There's no doubt about that. But he was in there close and he was developing information for us. In spite of that, I went to bat for him twice trying to get him brought in from the cover."

"Well, I hate to sound judgmental, Billy-Boy, but you sure did a lousy job of it!"

"Come on, Mike. You've dealt with enough bosses to know they do things their way." He watched to see how that argument sat with me. "I feel bad about him getting whacked, but I don't have any guilt over it. I tried hard to do the right thing."

"So, bottom line, what did he give you?" I asked. "What the heck was he into that cost him his life? From the sanitized reports you showed to me, there wasn't one solid case in the entire thing."

"What do you mean by 'sanitized'?" Allen asked with some indignation.

"The reports you showed me this morning had been cleaned up. There were pages missing and cross-references in the folder lacked original documentation. The little pieces of paper around the metal clasps that held repots in the folders were a good indication that stuff had been pulled out. There were other things, too. For now, that's what I mean by 'sanitized'. They were cleaned up and cleaned out."

"I didn't realize that," Special Agent protested.

"Bullshit!" For good measure I added, "Now show some integrity and tell me what the hell Danny was involved in."

Bill Allen mulled over my information and the challenge in his head for a minute while he pretended to be busy chewing on his sandwich. Finally, he said, "Officer Martin was reluctant to mention any dirty cops unless he was absolutely sure they were really and truly dirty. Over the time we dealt with him, he gave us five names of local cops he felt very confident were on the take and into assorted things. We were in the process of building cases on all five."

"But now, without your star witness, your five cases are sucking canal water, right?" I proposed.

"Right," he acknowledged reluctantly. "Without some supporting documentation, at least four of the cases are, in all likelihood, down the tubes."

"What about the fifth one?"

"The fifth one is the one we were going to lead off with in the Grand Jury. We figure that once it becomes public that we took down the one cop, the other four, and maybe even some others on top of those, we will begin to look at making some deals."

"And, maybe you could even get the first cop to feel he was jammed up enough so that he would wear a wire and suck the others into making some admissions?" I asked accusingly.

The question went unanswered. It didn't need one. We both already knew the answer.

"Who's the one you were going to start with?" I asked, looking directly at Allen.

"I'm not at liberty to say," Allen said as he pretended to pick at some lettuce that had fallen into the sandwich wrapper.

"You're not at liberty to say?" I asked rhetorically. "Now ain't that just lovely? You and I are going to work together, share all our information, get down to the bottom of this, and all that other garbage that was said this morning. But, when I ask you for the name of the cop Danny had targeted with his information, a primary suspect in this murder I might add, you say to me you can't tell me that!"

"I'll have to clear it with Delany, that's all. Mike, give me a chance."

I was mad and getting madder. The wide-eyed look on Bill Allen's face told me I better calm down or I was going to be standing tall in front of Matt the Chat, explaining why I didn't play nice in the sandbox and how I ruined a beautiful working relationship with our brother law enforcement officers in the frigging FBI. I wanted to go farther and ask Special Agent Allen to clear up how the Fed creeps with their college degrees, had for years denied there was such a thing as organized crime. But, given half a chance, they sure as hell loved to hang local cops. Now, with one to hang, they didn't want to give his name to the cop who was investigating a homicide to which he might very well be connected. It made sense to Allen. It was mind-boggling to me

"Look, Amato," Allen said quietly but firmly, "You don't like us and most of us don't like you. You think were a bunch of prima donnas. Well, maybe we are because we do have a squeaky clean organization."

"With the exception of Waco," I interjected.

"Okay, maybe Waco was a fiasco," he almost allowed.

"And the cover up afterward," I added. Then, just for effect, I continued, "And Ruby Ridge. And the cover up after that. How about the Russian spy you didn't notice for fifteen years, or the four thousand pages of documents you lost in the Oklahoma City Bombing. Shall I go on?"

"All your mud-slinging doesn't change one basic fact, Lieutenant. You got a dead cop on your hands and probably one of your own cops killed him!"

"And you won't give me his name because your cooperation with local cops is just so much bullshit!"

"Look," Allen said with a louder voice. "We can fight and fuss and holler all we want. The bottom line is this, you can walk away and not work with me at all on this thing, and consequently end up being taken off the case like Murphy said a few hours ago. Or, you can bite your lip, give me a chance to navigate around my people, and together we can possibly solve this case. It's up to you, Amato. Personally, I don't give a good gosh darn either way."

I sat there in silence looking at him even after he had hit me with his very risqué, "gosh darn." I was just learning not to swear and was having a hell of a time with it. However, for Bill Allen, it looked like not swearing was a life long avocation. As much as I hated to admit it, the bastard was right. I was tied to this Feeb — and his entire organization — whether I liked it or not. Allen, by means of his argument, had taken the upper hand in the discussion, and that was not a good thing.

In an effort to take back control, my counter-argument was, "Well, based on this morning's meeting, it looks like Matt Murphy isn't willing to let you guys run the entire show. When I get back and tell him you boys in The Bureau are playing your usual one-way-street games, he's likely to tell you all to kiss his chiefly behind."

We finished the rest of our lunch in silence. It was clear that Special Agent William Allen saw the wisdom of my argument and was trying to decide what he could do about it. Rather than let him decide on a course of action, I suggested one.

"Why don't you go back to Delany and tell him we're at an impasse on this thing. Tell him he needs to contact Murphy and explain to him why he won't let you name the prime suspect on this case. I think once we let the bosses settle this, the both of us will be able to move along."

"You may be right about that, Mike," he conceded.

I then had Bill Allen take me back to my office so I could make a few calls and follow a few leads. That, of course, was a lot of baloney. What I really needed to do was look through a stack of business cards that were in the top, right drawer of my desk. We said our good-byes and made plans to meet after Murphy and Delany talked to each other.

Once I was rid of my albatross, I got into the privacy of my office and began flipping through the business cards I had accumulated over the years at conferences, training seminars, and various investigations. Finally I found the one I was looking for, the one from San Diego. Comfortable in the sanctuary of my office, the call was made to the San Diego Police Department.

Two hours later, after Major Winston advised me that he had talked to the Chief and that it was Murphy's desire to have me join up with Bill Allen *immediately*, the two of us were back in the car.

"What's the decision?" was my opening volley.

"Delany and Murphy talked, and then Delany told me I was authorized to tell you the name of the Officer who is our primary target on the corruption case."

"And?" I prompted impatiently.

"And, his name is Walter Clark."

"Wally Clark? Wally Clark who was busted almost a year ago by our guys for holding dope he grabbed off of street dealers? Wally Clark who has already pled guilty to two counts of drug possession? Is that the Walter Clark of whom you are speaking," I asked with a couple of chuckles thrown in.

"Uh, yes, yes, he's the one," Allen stammered with some embarrassment. Then he continued. "Danny Martin turned us on to Clark. We gave Danny some dope and then set it up so he would draw Clark's attention. The scam worked and Clark grabbed the dope. Working with your Vice Squad, we let them bust Clark and then we took him over as an informant."

As we traveled north on State Street, I asked Bill to make a right turn on to a side street and stop the car. Then, at my suggestions, we got out of the vehicle and walked toward the footbridge that overlooked the upper falls of the Genesee River. Half way across the bridge where we could catch a decent breeze, we stopped to talk.

My question was this: was the FBI really stupid enough to believe that I was stupid enough to fall for this line of crap? "Wally Clark is a dope head and a jerk-off. There isn't one single cop in this county, whether they're clean or dirty, who will even give him the time of day, much less bare their soul to him."

"What can I say?" the Special Agent asked lamely. "Right now, with Officer Martin gone, Walter Clark is our case."

It was obvious that the conversation — and the relationship with the FBI — was on a trip to nowhere. The Feds were handing me a bag of shit and telling me to pretend it was gold. If the case was going to get moving, I would have to run the investigation as a regular homicide investigation and not depend on Bill Allen or Ed Delany to contribute anything of value.

Later, as we walked back to the car, Bill Allen and I agreed that without other avenues to pursue, we might as well cruise the joints to see what the local hoods were up to. Chief Murphy's press conference was already in progress. Now the world, the local world at least, would know Danny Murphy was a righteous person. With that happening in the background, there were pretty good odds that we would see some activity fairly soon at the mob's clubhouses.

As for myself, I was feeling useless. The Martin homicide was more than forty hours old and the investigation was bouncing around like a fart in an eight-sided jar. All my experience had proven that if you don't solve a case or at least get a major break in a case during the first twenty-four to eight-eight hours, then there was a very good chance the case was going to end up not being solved. The killing had all the trimmings of a mob hit, but I had not moved an inch in that direction. My gut made me suspicious of Special Agent Allen, and I had not accomplished anything in that area. It was time to get this investigation rolling.

I convinced Allen that we might be able to turn up some leads if we began to lean on some of the mobsters. He agreed that some surveillance might be warranted. However, I wasn't interested in being a passive observer. I wanted to shake some trees and make some apples fall.

As we made our way over to the east side of the city, I found myself resenting the man beside me. I resented having been relegated to the passenger position in the car. That thought was driven by the fact that I was also a passenger in the investigation. I resented being told my Department was dirty and then having the messenger of the news back off and tell me he couldn't discuss who the prime suspect was. I resented being forced to work with a man who knew little, if anything, about homicides. And I especially resented having been forced to make the stupid gesture of shaking hands with a man I considered to be a good suspect in the killing of Officer Danny Martin.

We were just turning off Portland Avenue on to Bay Street when I spotted what I had been looking for. Charlie Tortero and two other mutts were heading north on Portland Avenue. I had Bill swing the car around. A couple of blocks down Portland Avenue, we pulled along Tortero's El Dorado. I hung my tin out the window and even though Tortero, always a premier jerk, flipped a finger to my badge, he pulled the car over.

"How's business, Twist?" I asked as he got out of his car to come back to meet Allen and me. His nickname was a well-earned reference to his experience as an arm twister and leg-breaking bill collector for the local Mafia organization.

"What do you want, Amato?" Charlie asked in such a manner that I immediately suspected he was not happy about our pending chat.

"I want to talk to your boss."

"So talk to him! Why you gotta bust my chops in my own neighborhood?"

"But, Charlie," I said in what I hoped would be a soothing tone. "You're the Old Man's flunky, his gopher. Therefore, I thought it only fair that I send the message through you."

"If I see him, I'll tell him. You happy now, Ace?"

I hated that nickname. I hated the press for hanging it on me. And, I hated this mope using it. The trick was that I didn't show all my hatred to Charlie the Twist.

"Charlie, Charlie, Charlie," I said slowly, shaking my head from side to side. I ran my fingertips along the barrel-chested gorilla's left shoulder, brushing off some non-existent lint. Without warning, I grabbed the man's ear lobe, squeezed it tightly and twisted it as I pulled his face up to mine. It was an old technique that nuns — masters at pain compliance — used on unruly schoolkids for a hundred years. From personal experiences in all eight years of grade school, I knew the hold was an effective one.

"Tell the Old Man I want to meet with him, I want to meet soon, and I want it private. You got that?" I hissed in my nastiest tone of voice as I snapped his head back and let his ear lobe spring free.

"I'll tell him," the man-ape said with a glare of hate as he cupped his ear.

"Tell him we can meet his way or my way. It's his choice, but I want the meeting soon. Damn soon."

"What do ya mean, his way or your way?"

"He can name the time and the location. That's his way. If I don't hear from him by tonight, a cop car will be camped outside his house until he steps out. When he steps out, he'll be busted for grand mopery with an attempt to gawk. Or maybe, if I get lucky, there will be some real crime. The cops will take him away in full view of his neighbors and he will be brought to me. Then we will sit at the curb of every goon hangout and begin to hassle the living crap out of every one of you assholes. That's my way."

The conversation ended, I walked back to the Fed car and mistakenly headed for the driver's door. Covering up my mistake and embarrassment, I bellowed to Bill Allen, "You drive, kid," and casually strolled around the back of the car and over to the passenger side of the Feeb car.

As soon as we were in motion, Special Agent Bill Allen lectured me on matters of civil rights, abuse of police powers, intimidating citizens, and other assorted nonsense that was of little interest to me.

"Cut to the chase, Bill. What's your point?"

"If I ever see you man-handle someone like that again in my presence, I'll lock you up myself!"

I turned sideways to get a good look at this hayseed, fair-haired boy and tried to figure out if he was serious or if he was just yanking my chain.

"You're serious?" I asked.

"Dead serious!" he replied without blinking.

I smiled and simply shook my head. We rode in silence for a couple of blocks as I did a slow burn. There was obviously no point in trying to educate this blue-suit Fed about the ways of the streets.

"Will he meet with us?" Allen asked after about five minutes.

"Who?"

"Vincent Ruggeri. Do you really think he'll meet with us?"

"With *us*? No. No way," I responded. "But I think he'll meet with me."

"I don't think I can permit you to meet alone with a known Mafia guy, Mike."

"I'm not seeking a permit from you, Bill," I said coolly. "If the man calls for a meet, I intend to meet with him. You're not invited, so I really don't give a squirt if you like it or not."

"Well, it's just normal in The Bureau that we ..."

"That's another reason I'm not in The Bureau," I interrupted. "Too many stupid rules!"

"What will it get you?" he asked. "Do you really think he'll tell you anything?"

"No, I really don't think he'll say anything incriminating. But, I want to see his eyes when he denies any knowledge about Martin's killing. I want to *see* him say it! I want to hear what he *doesn't* say. Then I'll know where we stand with the mob angle on this case."

"I'll have to let my people know if you go through with it," Allen cautioned.

"Bill, do whatever the heck you have to do. Make a report. So what? I'm going to make a report on the meet, so if you want to report it too, go ahead. If you want, you can make a report regarding me making out my report. The government doesn't have enough paperwork floating around. Create some more!"

"I don't mean to be a stickler about these things, Mike. It's just that we don't do these things this way in the FBI."

"I know, Bill. That's why you guys *investigate* cases, while we *close* cases."

Again, we allowed silence to be the dominant activity in the confines of the car. As the passenger on this strange voyage, I was free to look out the windows and deal with my thoughts.

Finally I said, "Take me back to the Police Department."

"To do what?"

"Look, Bill, we're not accomplishing one damn thing out here by driving around in circles," I said with a degree of resignation.

Special Agent Allen silently obeyed and turned the car around.

Sensing he was going to go running to his bosses and mine telling them that I wasn't playing nicely in the sandbox, I explained myself. "From what I saw in your reports, it looks like there's a good possibility we have some crooked cops on the Department. If that's the case, it then follows that one, several, or all of them are suspects in this murder. If that's so, I need to know their names. However, you tell me that you don't have the authority to release the names of those alleged crooked cops until you get permission from your boss. I accept that. So, my plan is this, you go talk to your boss and I'll go back and update my boss. Then, with a clear understanding of what you can tell me and what I can tell you, we get back together and start fresh tomorrow. You agree?"

Allen mulled that over for a few seconds and then nodded. "Sounds like the thing to do," he said as if he believed it. "I think we kind of got off on the wrong foot today. You're right, we need to get some clearer direction from our superiors."

As he stopped the car in front of the PD, my Fed partner extended his right hand to me. We shook hands and smiled at each other, mumbling something about seeing each other in the morning. All of that aside, each of us knew the other was going to his respective boss and try to get out of this masquerade of mutual cooperation. I walked into the Public Safety Building wiping my right hand with my hanky.

By four o'clock in the afternoon I had gotten a briefing from Detectives Donovan and St. John. They had interviewed the stripper, Dee Dee, and it looked like a bum lead.

"The woman is bedding down half the city, Lute," Bobby St. John explained. "She told us about two lawyers, a councilman, a college professor, a couple of local executives, a judge, and a priest she's hitting the sheets with, but denied any type of relationship with Martin."

"Bobby's right, Boss," Donovan agreed. "Dolores 'Dee Dee' Wilcox is very proud of her sexual escapades and makes no secret of having wanted to add Martin and half of his buddies to her trophy case of studs. I got to believe her when she says she never rolled around with the victim. To tell you the God's honest truth, I'll kiss the Chief's ass at Main and State Streets and even give him a half hour to draw a crowd if this broad had anything to do with the Martin killing."

"Dee Dee doesn't have an old man, a pimp, or even a steady boyfriend," St. John threw in. "In other words, it doesn't look like she had a motive and she doesn't have anyone close enough to even really care if she was going night-night with the victim. On top of it all, she was working the night Martin went down."

"Is it possible she could have gotten out, met the kid, shot him, and made it back to work in time for the next show, dance, or whatever the hell she does over there?" I asked.

"Hey, anything's possible, Lute," Donovan said with a shrug. "The fact is that she was working from eight in the evening until two in the morning. She says she doesn't have any wheels. But yeah, she could have gotten a car from somebody. Anything's possible, but I just don't see it with this broad."

"Regardless of what your informant told you, Boss, this chick is as ditzy as they come. Still, there's no way she makes it on my hit parade when it comes to being homicide suspect," St. John said as he sat down behind his desk.

The report was like one of those good news/bad news jokes. The good news was they had tentatively cleared a possible suspect, and the bad news was that it didn't add anything to the case. If Dee Dee was not a suspect, then Bill Allen and the crooked cops we might have on the Department were still good suspects, along with everyone in or around the Rochester mob!

Realizing, through the conversation we were having, that neither one of the detectives had yet heard about Danny Martin being a cop, I broke the news to them.

"No way!" Bobby St. John said.

"Mother of God!" Frank Donovan exclaimed.

We spent a few minutes talking about how difficult it must have been for the kid, and then a couple of more minutes putting down the Department for leaving the kid out for so long. When they moved to their computers to do the reports, I moved on to see my boss.

I checked in with Major Winston and gave him a blow-by-blow accounting of my day with Special Agent William Allen, making sure to highlight the fact that the FBI was sitting on information about a potential suspect that my new partner was

not able to share with me. Then it was time to tell him who the
secret crooked cop was, along with the related discussion that
Allen and I had about the subject. I gave the boss the
abbreviated version about me seeking a meeting with the head of
our local Mafia crew and assured him the meeting would be
documented. That wasn't a big deal for Winston. What was a big
deal was my move to get him to pull me off the detail with the
Feeb Boy Scout. To make a long story short, Winston told me I
was assigned by the Chief to work with Allen and he was not
going to change the Chief's instructions.

"Well," I began to ask as I stood up. "Can I ..."

"No, Mike, you can not talk to the Chief about it. He gave the
order. You got the order, now do the job. End of story."

Failing in that endeavor, I made a second call to Captain Felix
Santos, my contact in the San Diego Police Department. His
Sergeant assured me the Captain was working on my request but
wouldn't have any information until the next day.

At four-thirty p.m., comfortable in the driver's seat of my own
cop car, I left the Public Safety Building and headed for the
Martin home to retrieve what Danny's kid sister had retrieved
from her safe deposit box.

By now the afternoon viewing hours would be over, and the
family would be at home resting and preparing for the evening
calling hours to begin. At that point my mind went wandering
and began to question why we, an allegedly civilized culture,
were so cruel to ourselves. Why is it we put ourselves through
the terrible experience of gathering around a casket, looking
down on a lifeless body, and then repeating it again and again
over a couple of days?

Pulling off of the expressway that leads out to Kathy's
suburban home, my fickle brain shifted gears and I wondered
what Chrisy was holding for me. Although I expected it to be a
letter from Danny Martin chastising me for being so judgmental
about him, I was soon to learn it was more than that. What the
case had been lacking from the beginning was a significant lead,

a tangible piece of evidence. Danny Martin was about to take care of that situation by providing us with a clue, a clue he had sent special delivery from the grave.

7

Thursday Evening: Danny Speaks

There is something peaceful, albeit eerie, about a house that has been visited by death. The subdued voices of the inhabitants, the weak smiles offered to give the caller the impression that "it" will get better, and the very neatness of the house blend to make the home a peaceful place. The attempts at idle conversation to avoid the subject that grips the home gives an uncomfortable comfort to the guests and residences who come and go from death's home.

Such was the case within the small home of the Martin family as I entered it early Thursday evening. The first calling hours at the funeral home had just ended, and now the family was attempting to reconcile themselves to what they had just gone through and would have to go through again in a few hours.

The house was neat, dusted and vacuumed. The blinds were drawn, sheltering the home from the summer heat and light.

A young, attractive woman, who I had not yet met, responded to my knock on the door. Introducing myself to the new player, I looked over her shoulder, glancing around for signs of Kathy or Phyllis. My quest for some visual satisfaction was denied, but the aroma of freshly brewed coffee filled my nose.

"Hi, Mike," the woman said. The unexpected friendly greeting drew my attention back to her and I found myself welcomed by a warm smile. "I'm Chrisy. Do you remember me? I'm Danny's sister."

My mind made an instant trip back twenty or so years ago to a toddler with a bobbing black ponytail and baggy diapers who was clutching the hand of her big brother.

"Chrisy? Oh my God!" I said and returned a broad smile.

We hugged for a moment as I expressed my sympathy. Breaking the embrace, we moved hand-in-hand to the living room where both Phyllis and Kathy sat at opposite ends of the couch, each holding a tissue to reddened eyes. The four of us shared a few minutes of small talk about the first session at the funeral home and Kathy began to cry as Phyllis described the police honor guard. At the same moment, a cousin I had met on my earlier trip to the home in the afternoon handed me a plate heaped with lasagna.

"They made me so proud of Danny," Kathy Martin said through lips covered by the back of her left hand.

Silence erupted for a long minute. Then Danny's sister spoke.

"I need to give you something, Michael," Chrisy Polshak said as she drew an envelope out of her purse. "Danny gave me this a few months ago. He asked me to put it in my safe deposit box and told me to give it to you if anything ever happened to him. I brought it with me when I heard, you know, about ..." The words were overcome by tears and the sentence went unfinished.

The sealed envelope she handed bore the declaration that Phyllis had described earlier in the day. I held the envelope in both hands and studied it. This must have been what Danny was trying to tell the young cop about on the night he died! I was excited about the fresh piece of possible evidence Chrisy had handed me and I wanted to rip it open, but I needed to know the history of the envelope first. The envelope was slightly bulky, as if it contained a half dozen pieces of paper, and was heavy in my hands. I wanted desperately to devour the contents.

I thought about opening it and then hesitated. Deciding that patience and questions would serve the case better than my impetuous curiosity, I asked "What did Danny tell you when he gave this to you, Chrisy?"

As Chrisy Polshak began to speak, Phyllis pushed herself up off the couch and passed me on her way out of the room. The scent of her made me want to turn my head and follow her.

"He was kind of, I don't know how to describe it," Chrisy began. " I guess you could say he was kind of secretive and nervous about it. He just told me there were some things going on and if he ever got into an accident or had something bad happen to him, that I should get this to you right away." She paused for a moment to take a sip of coffee.

At the same moment Chrisy tasted her coffee, Phyllis appeared at my right side with a mug for me. I thanked the older sister and then thanked her a second time when her left hand poured a hefty shot of whiskey into the mug.

Chrisy continued, "I asked him why he didn't just mail it to you, or, if he didn't want to do that, why he didn't keep it in his safe deposit box here in Rochester. He just said that if he did that, there were ways people he was concerned about could get to it."

"What do you mean, 'Here in Rochester,' Chrisy?"

"Mike, I moved to Fredonia. I went to Fredonia State College and met my husband there. We stayed in Fredonia after we got married. Danny gave it to me when he was there visiting us with Kathy."

I nodded and asked, "How long ago was this that he gave the envelope to you, Chrisy?"

"May. The end of May."

"He went all the way to Fredonia to give you this envelope?"

"'All the way to Fredonia'?" Chrisy questioned, mocking my choice of words. "My goodness, Mike, you make it sound like the far side of the moon. It's only about a hundred and twenty miles from here, just an hour on the other side of Buffalo."

I gave an embarrassed shrug of my shoulders at the admonishment.

"We went down for Chrisy's birthday," Kathy Martin interjected from the couch. "Her birthday is May twenty-fifth. It was that weekend."

May twenty-fifth was, if I correctly recalled the information in the FBI reports, the weekend that Danny was supposed to be committing a burglary in Buffalo. The same time period when he told Bill Allen that he had gone "to a party".

Unconsciously, as I dwelled on the FBI intelligence, I slapped the palm of my left hand with the envelope.

"Open it, Mike," Kathy advised me in more of a statement than a request.

I gave her a silent nod and slipped a pen in the corner of the flap of the envelope and neatly sliced the top of it open. Inside the envelope there was a paper clip holding several sheets of typewritten paper. On top of the papers was a hundred-dollar bill. I scanned the first couple of lines of the letter and then stopped, deciding it would be better if I read it later when I was alone and able to give it my full attention. I asked Chrisy to date and initial the envelope, the money, and each sheet of paper.

The young woman looked at me with a question mark on her face.

"It could turn out to be evidence, " I explained. "If so, I'll have to prove in court how it came into my possession, and you will have to be able to testify that you gave it to me. Your initials will help establish that fact."

"What does it say, Mike?" Kathy asked, as Chrisy nodded that she understood what I had told her.

"From what I see, you know, just scanning this, Kathy, it looks like Danny just wanted me to know that he was a cop. And, he wanted you to have this hundred bucks in case you need it."

"That's all?" Phyllis asked with noted suspicion.

"I really didn't read it all, but some of it seems to deal with the case," I explained. "I need to look at it more carefully later." As I spoke, I folded the letter and slipped it and the envelope into my breast pocket. I then stood and excused myself, stammering some words about letting them get some rest before the evening session at the funeral home.

"I would really like to read it, Mike," Kathy said quietly from the couch. "If not now, then sometime later. But soon, okay, Mike?"

"It'll be a day or so, but yes, I'll get it to you real soon," I assured.

I drained the mug, finding some of that old comfort in the presence of the whiskey-laced coffee. Kathy got up from the couch and moved with me to the door. As I opened the door, Kathy said, "I don't know what's going on in that letter, but that day, the day we went to Fredonia, Danny was really nervous about being followed. By the time we got near Buffalo, he was sure we were being followed and he got off the thruway near the downtown section of Buffalo. He drove like a maniac through the city until he felt he lost whoever was behind us. It was a bad scene. I was crying and screaming at him to get out of this thing he was involved in."

She began to cry again and I held her close to me for a minute whispering lies to her that everything was going to be okay. I didn't want them to be lies, but I was sure they were. It would be a long, long time before everything would be okay for the young widow.

"You have to get some rest, Kathy," I said. I meant what I said, but my motive in saying it was so that I could leave quickly and look at Danny's letter. From what I saw in the first few lines, I was sure it contained some information I was really going to need in order to solve this murder.

"I'll be okay, Mike," Kathy Martin said with a slight, forced smile. "It's Phyllis that I'm worried about."

"Phyllis? Why?"

"She's really taking it hard, Mike. She hated Danny and everything about him. Now that she knows who he really was, well, she's feeling a lot of guilt."

I assured her that what Phyllis and she were both going through was normal, but that she really did need to lie down for a while. We kissed each other's cheeks and I left her standing alone in the driveway.

* * *

Thirty minutes later, I was back at my apartment. After I had stripped down to my underwear, turned up the air conditioner, and grabbed a beer, I opened the letter and read it.

"Dear Mike:

If you're reading this, I must be dead, dying, or disappeared. In any event, the hell I've been living for the past six months is over, and now I can tell you something that you still might not know. I'm a cop, Mike!

The reason I'm sending this letter directly to you by way of my kid sister is that there has been real shit in this game, and I trust you are the only guy that will do what needs to be done. If the FBI is involved in my demise, and they very well may be, you're the only guy I know who has the balls to go after them.

Before I get into all that, the $100 is to pay you back for the $75 bucks you slipped me when I was leaving for Marine Corps boot camp. It looked like it was the last of your money and I really appreciated it. The extra $25 should cover any interest and let you know how much I appreciate everything you did for me.

As you may now see, all the time you spent trying to straighten me out did have some impact. After the Marines, I did apply to the Department, and I made it. Right after I was accepted, I was called to a meeting with the Chief and Major Charlie Novitski (a man I know you respect) who was the C.O. of the Organized Crime Bureau. They told me they were going to put me undercover and that if I ever told anyone about it, I would lose my job and be arrested. So, instead of sending me through our academy, they put me through the Police Academy in Syracuse to get me certified with the state as a cop. After that, I went right to working undercover.

It's really giving me a great amount of relief just to tell you this, Mike, because now you'll know I didn't turn out to be a crook, and I didn't dishonor my family's name. I've seen the way you look at me and know it must have hurt you to think I went over to the other side.

The reason I'm writing this letter is that things are going to hell, Mike. When I began this assignment, the idea was for me to infiltrate the mob, work my way into some of the inner circles, and get some intelligence. I was doing just that for a couple of years, but somewhere along the line things changed. A couple of years ago, I ran across a cop that was no good. He was a guy by the name of Carl Benjamin. You probably remember the incident. Any way, he got fired because of me, and I don't regret what I did. The guy was a crook, Mike, and he was an embarrassment to the department. I'm sure you remember him and will agree with what I'm telling you. Maybe it was because of him, but all of a sudden the department shifted gears, and I was getting pressured to get information on cops.

Then, about a year ago, I was turned over to the FBI. The Chief told the OCB guys I had been fired because of something I had done, but that was just a cover to turn me over to the Feds. I guess they thought OCB was crooked, so they wanted to make it look like I wasn't undercover anymore. When I kept telling the feebs I didn't see any indication of cops on the take or doing other things with the mob, they didn't believe me. They told me to look at this cop or another cop to see if anyone was talking to the Old Man or his people. It was getting to be a witch hunt, Mike, and I didn't like it.

They turned me onto a cop named Walter Clark. The guy was a zero, but he obviously was grabbing dope off the street people and keeping it for himself. The feebs arranged it so I was carrying dope for a few days and finally got rousted by Clark. He took the dope, and that was that. A couple of days later I saw that he got busted by our guys for holding the dope. I didn't like busting cops, but Benjamin and Clark were both losers, and I don't have any guilt about getting rid of them.

The FBI kept pressuring me to get more cops, to find cops on the take, to get some dirt on some detective. They even had me checking on you. Every *time you busted balls with one of Ruggeri's clowns, the feebs were all over me asking what you did and said.*

One night I saw you and Eddy Cavaluso meeting in the parking ramp over by Frontier Stadium. You probably remember it, because you tried to catch me. (Yeah, that was me in the blue pickup truck!!!) It was back when Frankie 'Ten Times' Lanovara got hit. I kind of figured Eddy was an informant of yours, so I never told the Feds about the meeting. At that point, I figured as long as they didn't believe me on other things, there was no need to tell them stuff about you. Besides, I wasn't going to blow the whistle on a guy just because he was doing some police work, especially a cop who had been my big brother.

One thing you need to know if you don't already know it, is one of your Detectives, Al Verno, is into one of the loan sharks (Thomas Riccio) for about $1,500. Verno is always falling behind in his payments, and I suspect Riccio has been leaning on him. The long and short of it is this — don't trust Verno. He's got to pay these guys one way or another, and if he has access to information they need, he might have to get into a position where he has to trade it off in order to protect his ass. The FBI knows this, and my guess is they probably think if Verno is dirty, then you must be crooked, too.

Getting back to the FBI — Mike, everything I told them about the mob guys went in one ear and out the other. All they wanted to know about was did I see this cop, or did I see that cop, or what cops' names came up in conversations. Around January, I saw a guy talking with the Old Man, and the guy looked and acted like a cop. A week later I saw the same guy arguing with Eddy Cavaluso. I just happened to walk in on them at Teddy Carr's joint over on State Street. The whole scene was pretty heated. I told my contact, an Agent named Sam Fenser, about this guy I was seeing around and described him to Sam. To make a long story short, we never were able to identify the guy. Fenser kept showing me pictures of Rochester cops, but none of the photos were of the guy I saw. Fenser kept accusing me of covering for the guy and we had a major falling out. Then, out of the blue, when Fenser got transferred in April, I get assigned to a new agent, a guy by the name of Bill Allen. Mike, this FBI agent is the same guy I saw meeting with the Old Man and the same guy I saw arguing with Fast Eddy

Cavaluso! I tried to get that information to Fenser, but the FBI wouldn't put me in touch with him.

I don't like this Bill Allen! I don't trust him, and I don't think he likes or trusts me. So far, I don't think he knows I saw him with the Old Man or Cavaluso, but he's really concerned about how much I know, and he's pressing me to get something on local cops.

I've contacted the Chief and asked him to take me off this detail, but I think he's stalling on me. At this point, I'm useless here. Everyone thinks I'm a snitch, so they don't trust me with anything. Twist Tortero has told me to my face that he thinks I'm a rat and a couple of other goons that are close to Ruggeri have passed the word that I'm not to be trusted. The only thing I have going for me is that I am starting to get a little close with Cavaluso. He doesn't tell me a damn thing, but at least he talks to me.

Finally, I figured my time on this thing was up, so I told Chief Murphy to take me out of here and put me back in the department, or I'm going to the District Attorney or the U.S. Attorney. Evidently he told Bill Allen because Allen brought it up to me and told me that I was acting "erratic" and that he thought I was losing it.

Well, one piece of information I did latch on to was that this creep, Bill Allen, was caught banging some mob woman in California and that our mob guys know about it. They hold it over his head all the time, and I think he's cooperating with them. When Allen got on my case hot and heavy, I told him I knew about the woman in California and I knew he was leaking info to Ruggeri's people.

Well, all of sudden Bill Allen did a 180-degree turn, and he told me he was working on getting the FBI to force the U.S. Attorney to put all my information into a Grand Jury. He said that in order to do this, he would need to debrief me on everything I have seen and heard over the past five years. He then gave me some song and dance about him being a double agent and that the info he was giving to the mob was info the FBI wanted them to know about. I think it's all bullshit! Like I said, Mike, I don't trust this guy, and I get the feeling he's setting me up. I know this guy looks like the All-American FBI Agent, but he's a snake, and he's losing control. One time he tells me he thinks the mob has got a contract on me, and the next *time we talk he tells me I need to relax. Then, he tells me I should make arrangements to disappear.*

The bottom line is this, Mike: I've told Allen I'm giving him, the Chief, the FBI, the U.S. Attorney, and their whole crew until the last of July to get me into a Grand Jury or I'm going to the newspapers with everything. One way or another, that should shake things up a little.

If I come up missing or dead, Mike, you need to take a close look at this Bill Allen dude. I think he's dirty, and I think the mob has their hooks in him. I've even accused him right to his face of being dirty, and he just smirked at me. This guy is driving me crazy. Mike and I think he is doing things to discredit me with the Police Department and with the FBI.

And, one last thing: If I don't get a chance to tell you this to your face, I really appreciate everything you've done for me. I just wish I had the chance to work for you. It would have been a real honor!

The letter was signed and notarized. Danny had thought of everything! However, under the notarization Danny had added a handwritten P.S. telling me that he had been followed as he drove from Rochester to Fredonia. He said he had no idea who was following him, but he suspected it was the Feebs or Bill Allen.

I looked at the signature and then folded the letter. It was time for some Joni James. Once I slipped in a couple of her CDs, I drained the beer and grabbed a second one.

Taking the beer and the letter out on to the balcony to catch some of the cooler night air, I let the music circle around inside my head. I knew I would have to read the letter two, maybe three more times, before it all sunk into my thick skull. However, for the time being, only two things swirled around in my brain. First, my suspects in Danny Martin's killing had just grown and now included Al Verno, along with Bill Allen and the entire Rochester criminal organization. Danny had used the word "Feebs" a couple of times in his letter. Obviously, the word was in his vocabulary. Was that what he was telling Officer Ross when he was found Dying? Was he telling Ross that a Feeb had shot him? The second item to come to mind was that a good man had died, and what could have been a great police career went to the grave with him.

My heart went out to Officer Martin. He had lived in disgrace and then died alone. Alive, he was shunned by his family and the members of his profession. He had tried to live within a code that dictated he do the right thing, regardless of the personal cost. As he tried to live by that code, he was forced to forego the credo that cops help other cops. Instead of dealing with the wrongs he was witnessing, the abandoned cop was forced to look for corruption that wasn't there. With all kinds of organized crime dealings going on under his nose, Danny Martin was pushed to find something juicier for the U.S. Attorney: crooked local cops. Then, when he did find the sins of corruption that he was encouraged to seek, no one would to listen to him. It was bad enough to be abandoned, but then it was compounded by forcing him to depend on the man he feared was the most corrupt.

Someone was going to pay for this. Crooked cop, FBI Agent, or mob boss, someone was going to pay!

And in the depths where one's self-truths were entombed, I knew I too owed a debt to Danny. I, more than anyone else, had turned my back on the kid. I could tolerate the anger I had for the Department, the FBI, and Bill Allen, but the anger I reserved for myself became intolerable.

Setting my emotions aside, I began to dissect the information in Danny's letter. He had pointed me in the direction of a couple of suspects. One was Charlie Tortero. The other was Special Agent William Allen. Another was a member of my squad!

It was very possible that Tortero lost his temper one night and killed Danny. Maybe he found out Danny was working undercover, or maybe he just didn't like the kid. Tortero was a good possibility. However, I doubt he would have killed Martin if he believed — or knew — the kid was a cop. Drug dealers will kill a cop, but the mob doesn't like bringing that kind of heat on themselves.

So what about Bill Allen? It's no secret that I don't have a lot of love for the FBI. Collectively, the organization is overly impressed with itself. Individually, the members have egos that aren't supported by their balls. But, Bill Allen didn't strike me as a killer. He was a farm boy trying to make his way in the big city. By what I had seen in my time with him, he hardly could bring himself to be aggressive, much less gun down somebody in cold blood. But then again, what about this thing with him shacking up with some mob chick in California? If that was true, and, if it was true that the Old Man knew about it, then the local OC guys had Bill Allen over the proverbial barrel.

Danny had told the Chief and his FBI contact that he was going to go to the U.S. Attorney. In going to Fredonia to see his sister, he would have to take the Interstate right through Buffalo … where the U.S. Attorney had his main offices for Western New York. Was it Bill Allen who had followed Danny on the trip? Was he afraid of Danny's intentions?

Danny had also thrown a third suspect at me and it was one of my own men, Al Verno. Was Verno the reason that Matt Murphy wanted me handling this case alone? Was Matt The Chat worried about Verno working the case and covering up some leads?

That was the problem with this case. It went from having no suspects, to having too many.

Finally, with my mind going in circles, I showered and dressed, downing three stiff shots of Southern Comfort along the way. Mentally prepared for the night, I drove to the funeral home to say good-bye to a friend and to ask his forgiveness.

8

Thursday Night:
Family, History, and Ground Lions

Hospitals have an antiseptic-urine-gauze smell about them. Funeral homes reek of too many types of flowers. Both places make me want to puke. Shrinks would say I was using creative avoidance to get out of a situation I hated to face, but I liked believing it was the smell of the flowers that kept me on the steps of the mortuary, acting as an ambassador to the cops who entered the dreaded place.

Finally, I entered the building and slowly made my way to Kathy, Phyllis, and Chrisy. I offered each my sympathy and then, dragging lead feet, went to the casket to view the body of a man that I should have embraced during his life instead of kneeling next to after his death.

The two Tactical Unit uniformed officers standing at attention at either end of the casket were sharp and impressive, but not as sharp as Officer Daniel Martin, who was dressed for eternity in a uniform he had never worn in this life. I ran my fingers over the raised numbers on his badge. Tears tried to make their way out of the corners of my eyes but were forced back and kept in their place, safely in the ducts, and away from the sight of others. I had come to do what I needed to do, and now that I had completed the task I stood and made the sign of the cross.

I escaped the sickening smell of flowers and the pasty look of a man made up for death. Quickly, but trying not to make it look like that, I made for a nearby side exit where I could be alone for a minute or two. I had just lit a cigarette from my second pack of the day, when Phyllis Conte walked out of the side door of the mortuary and asked, "Hey, fella! Do you have one of those for me?"

I smiled at her Hollywood-style entrance and shook one of the last cigarettes loose from the pack. By time she brought it up to her lips, I had my lighter fired up and ready for her to use.

As she blew the smoke into the muggy, August night, I said, "Kathy tells me you're taking Danny's death pretty hard."

Her eyes avoided me when she replied, "Yeah, well, I guess I've been a real jerk, Mike. I hated him so much because of … well, because of who I thought he was, and because of the way he treated Kathy."

I wanted to acknowledge that I too had made the same mistake, but I opted for silence instead and took time to look at the woman. Phyllis wore her almost forty years very well, much the same as my ex-wife, Diane.

"Do you know I had a hell of a crush on you when we were kids?" she asked out of the blue. Maybe she wanted to throw the statement out there before she lost the courage to say it. I thought she simply wanted to change the subject.

"No, I didn't," I admitted. "But, I sure wish you would have said something way back then."

"Well, Mike," she said as she looked me directly in the eyes, "I'm saying it now. I had a crush on you back then, and I guess I still have one on you."

I'm not the type of guy that draws compliments from a lot of people. Consequently, I don't handle them well. I smiled at Phyllis' flirtatious comment, afraid she was making me blush.

There was a heavy silence between us for a few long seconds, and then I confessed boyishly, "I think I have one on you too."

"Maybe we should do something about that when this thing is over," she said as she pressed the cigarette into the pavement with her right foot.

"Maybe we will," I said like a school kid.

Then she casually walked up the steps and back into the funeral home. I stood there for a moment, trying to give some meaning to what had just transpired while watching her butt move smoothly inside her khaki-colored skirt. My mental notepad also jotted down that I needed to dig a little deeper into what she meant when she commented about how badly Danny Martin had treated his wife.

Eventually I went back inside to seek out Kathy. I had questions that she needed to answer. Taking one look at her, I knew she was in no condition to answer the questions I needed to ask. Against my better judgment, I let it go for another day.

I was standing there chatting with a couple of detectives from the Highland Section of the city when my pager went off. Due to the wonders of modern technology, I was able to keep on talking as I used the cell phone to call the dispatcher for the message.

The message for me was a short one. "Lieutenant, if you want to meet with the Old Man, you need to call 930-4237 right away."

I dialed the number the dispatcher had provided and was greeted by a bored voice asking, "Who's this?"

"Mike Amato," I said just as bored. "Who's this?"

"Mr. Ruggeri would like to invite you to join him for dinner. If you care to join him, he will be at Teddy Carr's place at eight tonight." Click!

I checked my watch. It was 7:50 p.m. After going back into the sickly sweet smelling funeral home to pay my respects the family, I drove back into the Downtown area of the city and headed south on State Street past Teddy Carr's restaurant. I continued on and made a right-hand turn onto West Main Street. If the meeting was to go right, I couldn't appear to be too eager to make the appointment. I drove down the alley that ran parallel with State Street, which was right behind Carr's joint. The alley had that typical alley stench of moist garbage. It was the right setting for a mob hangout.

The Old Man's car was there in the parking lot along with three other cars, two of which I recognized. I circled the block one more time and then parked my car directly in front of the restaurant. As I exited the obvious unmarked car, I looked across the street, combed my hair, and purposely faced the Federal Building that sat about a block to the north on the opposite side of the street. I looked up at the building and smiled, intending to give the very probable surveillance camera a clear shot of my mug.

There was a certain irony about the mob's number one meeting place being in the shadow of the Federal building that housed the DEA, FBI, INS, ATF, and the rest of the alphabet. However, the irony was nested in sharp legal thinking on the part of the mob's lawyers. What illegal conspiracy could be going on, that it had been successfully argued in court more than once and in a restaurant that was under the nose and surveillance of the entire Federal Government? Juries had bought the convoluted reasoning three times in three separate mob trials. It was a stupid argument, but one had to keep in mind that the cases were being judged by twelve citizens too dumb to get out of jury duty. Yeah, right, they were twelve brave citizens doing their civic duty, but still, they all became sucked into the American justice syndrome of focusing on procedures and how the information was gathered rather than what the information indicated.

Walking into the establishment, my nose was seduced by the smells of rich, Italian tomato sauce, basil, and garlic that had greeted me every Sunday of my life until I left for military boot camp. Trying not to be courted too easily by aromatic memories, I directed my attention to the matter at hand.

Directly ahead was my target for the evening — a half-moon-shaped booth in the back of the classy restaurant. When I got to within five feet of the booth, Charlie "Twist" Tortero faced me and put the palm of his right hand to my chest like he was some kind of traffic cop. Earlier in the day I had encountered him on my turf. Tonight I was meeting his boss on his turf. He was eager to tie the score over the humiliation I had subjected him to by tweaking his ear.

"I need to pat you down first," he said with a certain air of smugness.

"I think you love me, Charlie, and you're just using this as a cheap excuse to fondle me," I responded with obvious disdain for him and his instructions. "I'm a cop and I'm packing. Live with it and get the hell out of my way."

Charlie took a half step forward and said, "You ..."

"You drop that hand and move aside," I said in my most threatening voice, "or I'm going to rip that chubby little arm of yours out of your shoulder and it's going to end up being the largest suppository known to mankind."

The gravel voice of Vincent Ruggeri came from the booth. "Let the Lieutenant sit down, Charlie. He means us no harm."

"And have a nice day, Charlie," I said as I walked past the stubby man and walked up to the booth. In turn, Charlie suggested I do something sexual with myself that I figured was physically impossible.

Reaching across the table, I extended my hand to the Old Man and thanked him for taking time to see me. Next, I nodded to Eddy Cavaluso, who was seated to Ruggeri's left. After sliding into the booth I reached down to scratch the ear of Fast Eddy's mutt, who was under the table standing guard in the event that any loose scraps came falling in his direction. The greetings and important signs of respect out of the way, I slid into the booth and took up a position opposite the Old Man, which was at a slight angle to Cavaluso.

"I've taken the liberty of ordering linguini and white clam sauce for you, Michael. It's a specialty of our host," Vincent Ruggeri said as he pinched his right cheek and lifted his eyes to the heavens. "Of course," he continued with a slight nod, "if you prefer to order something else, please feel free to do so."

I shook my head and said, "I appreciate your thoughtfulness, Mr. Ruggeri. The linguini and white clam sauce will be fine." It would have been an insult for me to order anything other than what Ruggeri had already ordered for me. Although I didn't like Ruggeri and his chosen vocation, I was not there to insult him.

The Old Man snapped his fingers in the direction of a waiter standing ten or fifteen feet behind him and then pointed down to the plate sitting in front of me. A minute later, a platter of linguini topped with a dozen good-sized clams on the half-shell was slipped in front of my chest and my wineglass was filled with red wine. I let the drifting steam that carried the aroma of mixed herbs drift up toward my face and then drew them deep into my nasal cavities with a long, silent sniff. I smiled my satisfaction to my adversary and lifted my glass of wine to his to exchange the customary *"Salud!"* before tasting the meal.

For the next twenty minutes or so, we ate and made light conversation about nothing special. Sitting there in front of the most powerful crime figure in Rochester, it struck me how well preserved the man had remained since my youth.

Vincent Ruggeri's full head of thick hair had turned snow white. It was combed back and the thickness of it gave one the impression of a lion's mane. The years had provided the solid, neatly dressed, elderly man with a few lines and wrinkles which had eroded their way into the corners of his eyes, but otherwise Ruggeri had remained unchanged from the time I was a boy. His hands still appeared to be huge as Easter hams, although they were now spotted with the brown dots that come with over seventy years of life. His unmistakably raspy voice sounded as if the man gargled with peanut butter. My mind remembered the same voice greeting my father, *"Buon' giorno, paisano,"* as my dad and I entered the neighborhood saloon on frequent Saturday afternoons.

When my father first came over from the old country, he had worked for Vincent Ruggeri's father at his barbershop. My old man was just a kid then, and I doubt he even knew Victorio Ruggeri was a hell of a bookie back in that era. When Vincent Ruggeri hit his teens, his three brothers ran their father's book-making business, but none of them ever had anything to do with the barbershop or anything else that resembled honest work.

Vincent Ruggeri was perhaps the most industrious and the youngest of Victorio's sons. The boy was attracted to the religious leanings of his mother, more so than the nefarious businesses of his father. Upon leaving high school, young Vincent went off to Saint Bernard's Seminary on the far north side of Rochester to join the priesthood. But the life was not suited for him. When two of his brothers were killed in a short-lived mob war, the youngest Ruggeri left the seminary to comfort his mother. While on his leave from his religious studies, Vincent Ruggeri settled the matter of his brothers' killings in a manner that brought honor and respect to his father. The young man never returned to the seminary.

"Do you know, Michael, that I used to date your Aunt Maria?"

"No, I didn't know that," I admitted.

"She was a lovely woman, and most likely still is. We saw each other a few times, but it just didn't work out." After I nodded at his observation and smiled to show my appreciation for his story, he added, "Imagine that! I could have been your uncle."

"Imagine that," my voice said as my face kept the simple, stewardess-like smile.

When we had finished our meal, our napkins were set down next to our plates, signaling it was now time to conduct business.

Vincent Ruggeri spoke as the waiter appeared once more and removed the plates. "I understand you expressed a desire to speak with me, Michael."

I nodded to the man. The language learned in a Catholic High School — Aquinas Institute, the same place where Danny Martin's body had been found — and a Seminary more than a half-century earlier, had remained with him through the years. "I need to ask you a question or two," my voice said as my mind made a mental note of the coincidence of Vincent's education and Danny's killing.

Ruggeri spread his arms the width of his chest and left the palms up as he said, "Ask."

"A friend of mine was killed and I suspect one of your friends may have been responsible for his death."

The Old Man let the remark slide by him and simply nodded. "I express my sympathy to you at the loss of your brother officer, Michael. I heard it on the news today. My apologies for having failed to mention that earlier. The loss of a work associate can be as traumatic as the loss of a close friend."

"He was more than a co-worker," I corrected him as I narrowed my focus on him. "He was a friend ... a life-long friend."

"I am very sorry about the loss of your friend," he corrected himself with a slight bow of his head. Fast Eddy Cavaluso added his sympathy and I nodded my acceptance to him.

"With all due respect, *Signore,* your sympathy is welcomed, but it's meaningless if you ordered his death."

"And why would I do such a thing, Michael?" Ruggeri asked as he leaned back in the booth and furrowed his bushy, white eyebrows.

"Oh, I don't know," I said. "Maybe you would do such a thing because he was deep in your organization's shorts and some of your friends were getting worried about what he knew. Maybe you would do it because he had developed a good inside track on the rats who hang around your gambling joints. Maybe you did it simply because some of the low-life animals who frequent your joints figured he was a snitch and they convinced you that a dead snitch was better than a live snitch."

The man looked me deep in the eyes as he said the words, "Michael, I was in no way responsible for your friend's death. I say that to you in all honesty." Then he added, without looking so deeply, "I am not saying I would even know if one of my 'friends,' as you call them, did this terrible thing. However, sometimes those who think I have powers I do not really possess, come to me and ask me if I would approve of them doing certain things; or, they ask me if I will bless some of their endeavors, legal or otherwise." He looked down at the coffee cup that was devoured in his right hand and added, "Naturally, I do not condone matters of an illegal nature, and I tell them so." Looking back into my eyes, he added, "But no one came to me regarding a need to injure your co-worker, your friend."

"Mr. Ruggeri, I ask you this then, why should I believe you?"

"I have no reason to meet with you, Michael. If it was going to be necessary to lie to you, I would not even have bothered to take the time to speak with you."

I shrugged and conceded, "You may be an honorable man, Mr. Ruggeri, but those who circle around you are not men of honor." The sharp barb I threw out was intentional, and the men in the background, all of whom considered themselves to be "men of honor," shifted uneasily.

Vincent Ruggeri studied the spoon in his right hand as he asked me, "Why do you have such hatred for your own kind, Michael? Why do you regard us with such smugness, such contempt?"

As the Old Man spoke I took a quick glance in the direction of Eddy Cavaluso who had his eyes, if not his attention, focused on his coffee cup, and I wondered why he was present at the table. Was he supposed to be a witness to something or was he simply along for the ride?

"First and foremost, Mr. Ruggeri, these mopes," I said as I waved my hand across the three men seated at the table next to us, "are not 'my own kind.' They represent the worst of the Italian people. They are the reason people like my old man and all the other hard-working, honest Italians couldn't get a fair shake in this town for a lot of years."

"Think of us as you will, Michael. However, we are not evil men. We have made ourselves available to the needs of many who have come to us and asked for a favor. In our own way, we have helped ensure that many Italians, Italians like you, your own *famiglia* who would have been denied an opportunity to prosper, were given the chance to succeed."

"Oh?" I asked as I tilted my head to one side. "You're kind of like the United Way or the Red Cross, is that it?"

The Old Man gave me a sympathetic smile. "I'm going to tell you something, Michael. I tell you this not to hurt or offend you or to make you angry. I tell you this simply to make a point."

He waited for me to signal I was willing to listen to him. I did so by opening my hands to him.

"Your father, Antonio, may God rest his soul, was an honest man, a hard worker, a good father, and a good husband," he looked at me intently as he spoke the words. "You know, of course, that your father, when he first came to this country, worked for my father in a barber shop right over on Jay Street?"

I nodded and said, "I've heard the story."

"I still hold a great deal of respect for your father, for he respected many of the old ways," the Old Man continued in his hushed, raspy voice. "He had a small bakery, back around the 1950s, am I right?"

"You know you're right. If I recall correctly, you used to come in periodically. In fact, I remember taking care of you and getting the loaves of bread you wanted. I don't really remember you paying for them, but I remember you walking out with them." I smiled as I completed the recollection, and then added, "Right?"

The Old Man disregarded my insinuation that he was shaking down many of the hard working business people. Instead, he leaned forward, rested his formidable arms on the edge of the table, and began to deliver his recollections of the era.

"When the Americans in their banks would not lend your father — my friend — the money to run his business, when his American suppliers and supposed-friends would not extend him credit, who did he go to, Michael?" He didn't wait for my answer to his rhetorical question. "He came to us!" Vincent Ruggeri said in hoarse whisper as he laid his hand on the table solidly, but without animosity. "We, these 'mopes' or whatever you choose to call them, these men of which you speak about with no respect gave him the loans he needed. You're father was given the money he needed, and, by the grace of God, I am pleased to say he prospered."

"And, I'm sure you probably banged him a cool fifty, sixty, seventy percent interest for the loan," I said with a tone of faked innocence and a wide grin. "Right, Mr. Ruggeri?"

"In those days, I'm sure the rate was high," he conceded. "But it was no higher than that which our government now charges. Perhaps we were ahead of our time," the Old Man said as he shrugged his shoulders and smiled at his observation. "But the rate, whatever it may have been, was within his means, and he paid it all back and he enjoyed a comfortable life." He then returned my grin and added, "So your father, because of that favor I did for him, never begrudged me a few loaves of bread that seem to be of concern to you so many years later."

"So what are you telling me? I should trust you because you ran the Italian Small Business Administration?"

The Old Man's tanned, muscular arms came forward and he now rested the full length of his forearms on the table as he smiled sympathetically at me and leaned forward to talk to me in a low, private voice.

"The Greeks were the true origins of modern civilization. Our people would like to think it was the Romans, but it was not. The Greeks are the cradle of our system of government, democracy, and justice. If you look at the great philosophers, they were all Greeks. They were intelligent people, and they were intelligent because they observed and they reasoned."

My face must have spoken what my mind was thinking: What the hell does this have to do with anything?

Ruggeri held off my non-verbalized question with an extended beefy palm, tapping the air in front of him in a gesture that I should hold my question. "These ancient people observed a lizard who was indigenous to their land. Over time, they came to respect the little reptile. The lizard was small, but it was naturally shrewd. They called the lizard, in their own language, the 'ground lion.' In English, the two Greek words become one word: 'Chameleon.'" The Old Man leaned close enough for me to smell his cologne as he continued in his guttural voice, "All men are chameleons, Michael. The chameleons change their color in order to survive. If they are on the fence post, they are brown. When they move through the grass, they become green. Men, men like us, like your father, change their colors so that they may survive and prosper. This is not an evil thing. It is simply a fact of life. It is merely *sopravivere!* It is survival!"

Again I took a quick peek at Cavaluso, who continued to study his cup of coffee.

The Old Man hesitated long enough to sip his espresso and then leaned forward again. "I know this to be true. These men here, the men you mock, are chameleons. They will change colors and become your friend, or the friend of those bastards in the FBI, if that is what they need to do in order to survive. I know this about my friends and you should know it about your friends. All men are chameleons. You may need to look around you, Michael, and ask yourself this, 'Who do I know, and trust, and travel with, and call my friend ... and who among them is a chameleon?'"

"What are you saying, Mr. Ruggeri?" I asked with a crooked grin. "Are you telling me that Officer Martin was killed by a cop?"

"I'm simply saying that I did not order, instruct, permit, or encourage anyone to kill Danny Martin. I am telling you that so that you will ask your friends, your brother police officers, to give me and my friends some peace." There was a pause, and then with some disgust in his chafed voice, Vincent Ruggeri continued, "Ever since this afternoon, when it was announced that Martin was a cop, there have suddenly appeared several dozen cops with nothing better to do than to sit in front of every social club and confront everyone in the area with questions and accusations. I do not need that type of pressure on my friends, Lieutenant."

I disregarded the plea and wondered why I had suddenly become "Lieutenant" instead of "Michael". Not wanting to show my concern, I shrugged and commented, "You tell me you did not authorize any action toward my friend, but tell me one thing, *Signore*." Now I was the one who leaned forward and asked directly, without any kindness, "Do you *know* who killed Danny Martin?"

"I have no way of knowing who killed your associate, Lieutenant," the Old Man replied as he concentrated on squeezing the lemon rind into his small, almost empty cup of espresso. It now dawned on me that his reverting back to titles signaled that the personal conversation was finished. It was also apparent that this denial was not made eye-to-eye with me as in his earlier denials. "All I am saying is that you should take caution against looking at this matter with a jaundiced eye that sees only your perception of good and bad. Maintain your objectivity about this thing and all matters that concern you, including the value of your own people, the ground lions who are in your own backyard."

"I come to you with questions and you give me a lecture on reptiles," I said as I stuck out my chin.

"I answered your questions," he commented. "And then I talked to you as a friend, Michael. I did not mean to lecture you. I mean only to point out to you that you look to us as being killers because it is easy for you to believe. My lecture, as you called it, was simply an observation that you should look in many directions in order to solve your case. Perhaps a friend of mine did kill your friend, but I truly hate to even think that. Perhaps a friend of yours killed your friend, and with God as my judge, I truly hope that is not the case." Ruggeri pulled his upper body erect as he moved his chest and arms back from the table and added, "Many things are possible, but, Lieutenant, don't come to me and make me and my *compadre* your scapegoat. Do I make myself clear?"

The words were not angry; however, that was not the case with the man who was speaking them.

I thanked the Old Man for taking this time to share his philosophy with me and then, as I moved to stand, my toe pressed down on the Eddy Cavaluso's dog's foot, causing him to yipe loud enough to make the three men at the next table jump.

"Oops! Sorry, Max," I said without out thinking.

Eddy Cavaluso shot me a look like it was a bolt of lightening and Ruggeri flicked his eyes up at me for a split second.

"How come you know my dog's name," Fast Eddy said to me with menace in his throat and eyes.

"I get paid to know a lot of things, Eddy, like your dog's name for instance," I said with a grin that was supposed to be sardonic. "I also know that Charlie Tortero over there wears a size thirteen shoe. Fats Allocco, next to Charlie, has hemorrhoids. There's a whole bunch of things I know about this crew of yours."

Seeing that both men appeared to be satisfied with my explanation, I put a twenty-dollar bill on the table and stood up.

"Please, Michael," Vincent Ruggeri said as he gestured to the money. "Don't insult me. I invited you here. You are my guest."

"No offense intended, Mr. Ruggeri," I said as I picked up the twenty and slipped it back into my wallet. I then laid two tens on the table, pointed at it and explained, "A little something for the waiter. Please, allow me this gesture."

Ruggeri smiled, tipped his head, and said, "Of course. That is very kind of you. You are very generous. Your father, God rest his soul, taught you well."

I gave the dog, which still held an amorous affection for my pant legs, a pat on the head, shook hands with the Old Man, and then flipped off Charlie Tortero. I tried to swagger as I walked out of the joint and found myself hoping I didn't look like I was walking like a queer. It was important that I appear confident, like a winner, so Vincent Ruggeri wouldn't know he had gotten to me not once, but twice.

* * *

Rochester is a place where the names of the streets change often, but the minds of the people seldom do. State Street is one such street. On the south side of the city it starts out as Exchange Street, then, where it crosses Main Street it changes names to become State Street. A mile down the road, it changes names again and becomes Lake Avenue, and it finally sticks with that name until the road ends at Lake Ontario.

That's where I headed when I left my meeting with the Old Man, north to the lake. I turned left out the parking lot and headed to Lake Avenue, past the cemetery, past the old Saint Bernard's Seminary. My mother had prayed long and hard that I would attend the stone fortress once I received my "calling" from God. I continued on past the rows of large houses and deep lawns, past the bars and a section of the avenue that has been under construction since I was in high school, and finally to the pier that helps guide the Genesee River into the lake. The road seemed a lot longer than the last time I had made this trip to the quiet thinking spot. I swung the car into the parking lot across from the merry-go-round. Once it was in park I got out of the car like the seat was on fire. Air and space were needed so I could think and reason.

The last weeks of summer usually die with some difficulty in this part of the world. Perhaps because the season is so short, it tries to hang on as long as possible, and now, as the season was drawing to a close, the temperature climbed. As always, the humidity outpaced the temperature. Stepping out of the car and heading for the long pier that runs along the west side of the Genesee River, I blamed my damp shirt and labored breathing on the weather.

Once on the concrete pier, my steps slowed and my breathing returned to a normal ebb and flow. Now, with the cool night air coming off the lake into my face and lungs, I began to replay the meeting with Vincent Ruggeri and try to fit it in with the other pieces of the puzzle. The waves that splashed along the sides of the pier did not interfere with my thinking. In fact, they stimulated the thoughts in some magical way and allowed them to flow from my gut to my brain.

First of all, I couldn't get over that stupid move I made by calling Max by name. That was a dumb, careless, rookie mistake! It got covered okay, I think. Eddy's reaction helped me cover it, but all in all, I shouldn't have been that careless.

The second thing on my mind was what Ruggeri had said about chameleons. What did he mean? Was he telling me that he, too, suspected Bill Allen or Detective Verno? Did he even know that I was now working with — or at least was *supposed* to be working with — Allen? Or, was he telling me he *knew* it was one of them? Also, it was interesting that he looked me right in the eye when he denounced having ordered the hit, but wasn't so face-to-face when he speculated that none of his men had committed the murder. Had Tortero confessed to the Old Man that he, due to a screw being very loose, had killed Danny Martin? If so, did Ruggeri feel it was best to meet with me so as to get the cops off his back?

The possibility that Verno might in some way be involved in Danny's death gnawed at me. The guy had worked for me for probably five years or so. I liked Verno, liked him a lot. I knew he was a family man with a kid, maybe two. He adored his wife and was a solid married man. All that notwithstanding, it didn't cut any ice with me. I would slam his body into a cell fast and hard if he had anything to do with this murder.

When I got off that tangent I moved onto the next question. The burning question was why did Ruggeri even meet with me in the first place? True, I had sent a pretty strong message to him through his hack; but the Old Man was shrewd enough to know I couldn't have held up my threat without drawing a lot of heat from his scumbag lawyer. As he pointed out so clearly, he didn't have to meet with me. The fact is, I concluded, he *wanted* to meet with me. He wanted to tell me to my face that this was not an authorized hit. By convincing me he was truthful, his organization could be spared a lot of heavy-duty hassle from the cops. Still, all things considered, that was not the sole purpose of the meet. The Old Man had other reasons for meeting with me. He wanted that meet. He relished it! If I hadn't have been so quick to move, he would have eventually reached out for me to meet with him.

Was it the motive hidden in his mind that he wanted to let me know my old man had gone to the mob for operating capital? I argued with myself against that point. If he wanted to throw that in my face, he could have done it on a hundred other occasions over the past ten years. No, that wasn't an attempt to bust my chops. He had thrown in that news flash about my father only because he wanted to put me in my place. His point was well taken. How could I put him and his crew down when my own father had availed himself to the favors of *La Cosa Nostra*? That was part of the message, but it wasn't *the* message.

Reaching the end of the pier, I also reached a conclusion. Vincent Ruggeri wasn't as complex as I had originally thought. His message was sort of plain and rather simple. It had only two possible meanings. One meaning was that I had better look in my own back yard if I wanted to find Danny Martin's killer. The other possible meaning was that his own men were chameleons, and if one of them had killed Danny in order to "survive," then that maverick did the killing on his own. And, all other issues aside, I should not be blaming the entire local mob organization for one person's deed.

The only problem I had was deciding which of the possible versions to believe. On top of that, I could only believe Ruggeri when he told me he had not authorized the hit. I didn't believe him for one second when he said he didn't know who killed Danny.

I stood at the end of the pier, looking north to Canada that was a short fifty miles across the lake. Looking in the pitch-black night, my mind tried once again to solve the puzzle of Eddy being at the meeting. True, Vincent Ruggeri was always accompanied by at least one or two of his henchmen wherever he went; but still, something was screwy about Eddy sitting there without any kind of speaking role. I would have taken less note of his presence if it were he who did the talking for the Old Man. It was his *silent* presence that baffled me. Maybe I was making mysteries where none existed. I finally turned around to face the long, dark pier and put my questions about Cavaluso's presence out of my mind. There were other, more important, issues to settle.

On the walk back up the pier to my car, I glanced up to the heavens and asked my father why he had ever gone to the mob for money. The incident, as is the case with many childhood memories, was locked in my brain. This warm summer night was the first time I brought it to my adult conscious mind. My father owned a small bakery on Brown Street that turned out some very good Italian bread from the brick ovens that lined the back wall of the place. On special occasions, such as for weddings of close friends and relatives, he also produced small, frosted cookies. There had been many discussions between he and my mother about him expanding the operation and going into the pastry business, as well as venturing into bread and pizza. There was one very heated argument that had been etched into my memory. It was when my mother cried and swore at my father for selling his soul to the *disgaziati*. Her fear was that if he could not pay back the money "they" would take over the business and he would be "out on the street." At the time, I didn't understand the reasons for her fear. Now I understood them clearly.

I found myself getting angry at Pop for selling out on the values he had taught us. Had he also been a chameleon? My guess was, like it or not, he had been!

"How could you do that?" I questioned the clouds overhead. "How could you make us walk the straight and narrow, to be so honest in every damn thing we did, while you went to these Mafioso scum for money?"

Maybe the white-haired Old Man was right and it was as simple as he had made it sound. Maybe all men were chameleons who changed their colors in order to put food on the table and to make their way in life … to survive!

I watched the water of the Genesee River splash along the sides of the pier and thought about the lack of progress I had made in the forty-eight hours since Danny's body had been found. After two days of traipsing along on a treadmill, I had developed two groups of suspects: cops and mobsters.

If this case was going to get solved, I needed to put aside my emotions and my heart. I needed to step back into the role of a cold, calculating, heartless cop. It was the role in which most people perceived me, or so I had been told. Also, it was the comfortable color for this chameleon.

For the time being, I needed sleep. Tomorrow I would finally get to solve this case with one cop or another.

9

Friday Morning: Applying Pressure

I went to sleep Thursday night listening to a CD of the Three Tenors. I woke up Friday morning listening to my guts gurgle and my head pound. The night was not entirely a sleepless one; it was a night filled with short periods of deep sleep interrupted by long periods of semiconsciousness. Fortunately, it was in those twilight states unencumbered by politics, emotions, and friendship in which I was able to do my most rational thinking.

After I dragged myself out of bed and made it successfully to the shower, my body and mind came alive and the day's battle plans were drawn. It was time to get off my dead, pining, languishing rump and begin to solve this case just as if it was the same as the hundreds of other murders I had been dragged through. I knew it was well past the time to go on the offensive. Twice in the past two days I had given myself versions of this same argument. Twice I had ignored my personal ass-chewings. So far, I had been missing the guts that it takes to get the case moving.

I had spent the last two-and-a-half days trying to deal with emotions — others' and mine — when I should have been acting like a detective. Well over sixty hours had gone down the drain while I acted like a hick cop. It was time for that to stop. I had two — maybe three — real suspects to go after. Two were to be my focus of the day. The third, Charlie "Twist" Tortero, could wait until I dealt with the two most logical suspects.

I hit the office at seven fifty-five a.m., grabbed a cup of coffee, and jumped into a pile of reports. When Al Verno came in ten minutes later, I gave him three simple sets of instructions. "Get some coffee, then get in my office. Once you're in, close the door behind you."

Albert James Verno was about thirty-five years old and had one of those faces that didn't seem able to make up its mind whether to laugh or frown, so it did both and neither. When he had been assigned to me, he hadn't been my first choice to come into the squad, but in spite of that, he was a very good detective who could do an outstanding interrogation. What he lacked in skills, he more than made up for with hard work and tenacity. The best thing about him was that he wasn't one of those guys who watched the clock all day waiting for the magical strike of four o'clock p.m. The kid — he was thirteen or fourteen years my junior — had established a pretty fair reputation for breaking a string of armed robbery cases when he worked the city's west side in the Genesee Section. The press gave the arrests a lot of attention, so the person who was passing through the Chief's position at the time felt obliged to get some press for himself. In a rather glitzy press conference, it was announced that Verno was being rewarded with an assignment to the Violent Crimes Unit. Like I said, I didn't pick him, but that didn't mean I didn't like him. He did his job well and he earned his pay. That's all that mattered to me.

He was a family man who took his marriage vows seriously. I remembered hearing through the office scuttlebutt that Verno had a couple of kids. I wasn't too sure about the validity of that information because I don't really pay that much attention to the off-duty life of my guys. Some considered it a weakness of mine that I didn't work up an interest in the personal lives of my detectives, and some considered it a strength. I just considered it expedient and effective. If I didn't know their families, I wouldn't be swayed by that factor in calling them back to duty, or pushing them for the long hours that were needed in this job.

My detectives aren't usually invited to engage me behind closed doors; so, when Verno came in with his coffee and gently closed the door behind him, he was a little apprehensive. That was good. It's just where I wanted him. Now I was going to make him downright nervous.

"I understand you're into the mob for about a grand-and-a-half," I said without any preliminary greetings. "Am I right on that fact?"

His immediate reaction was to draw his upper lip into his mouth and hold it there between his teeth for a few seconds before he nodded. Finally he spoke, "It's about eleven hundred right now."

"Talk to me, Al," I ordered quietly but emphatically. "I want to know why, when, how, who."

Verno ran his finger under his nose a couple of times, sat up straight, laced his fingers together across his trim stomach, separated them, crossed and uncrossed his legs, and then readjusted his position in the chair so that he was sitting erect with his feet on the floor. Twice he opened his mouth and twice he failed to emit any sound. Having taken the allotted time for fidgeting and noting my visible lack of patience, he finally spoke up.

"I got a kid that needs a lot of medical attention. A boy. He's ten years old. He's been in and out of hospitals. I got pretty far behind in my bills about a year, fourteen months ago. I ended up going to an uncle of mine to see if he could lend me some money. He said he knew a guy that would set me up with a loan. I was going to repay it with the holiday pay we got at the end of the year, but, I don't know, what with Christmas and all, and then Kyle going back in the hospital for a few of days, well, I didn't pay it all back. Within a couple of months, the guy started hammering me for the money and threatening to go to the Chief and all that stuff."

"'The guy' you're speaking of is Tommy Riccio. Right? Am I correct?"

"Right, Lute, Riccio, Tommy Riccio." Verno, somewhat surprised by my information, confirmed the statements. He made another attempt at relaxing in the chair, but ended up sitting erect once again. "Anyway, the vig, you know, the interest, was costing me a hundred a week on top of the loan. So, even though I was paying him regular as rain, all I was doing was just covering the interest on the loan." The Detective paused to make a short, nervous sniff before adding, "I'm working two other jobs, Lute. I'm laying carpets nights and weekends, and then I'm blowing trumpet in a band once a month, on Saturday nights. Still, I just can't make it stretch far enough."

When Al Verno came up for air I remained motionless. He knew he was in the hot seat and I wanted him to feel the heat. So far, it looked like he was being up-front with me, but I still wanted him on edge when I popped the main question to him.

"Am I going to lose my job because of this, Lieutenant?" he asked.

"That depends on how deep you're into this thing, Detective." I let the thought sit with him for a few seconds before continuing with the preliminary questions. "So what have you been doing for Riccio and the Old Man?"

"What, Lute? What do you mean?" he asked with surprise and perhaps a slight hint of anger.

"Well, the way I see it, if you owe them money for over a year now, they surely want some type of compensation. If you can't come up with the bucks, then there must be other ways you've been repaying them."

"Nothing, boss. I swear to God!" he said as he raised his right hand in the air and put his left hand over his chest.

"Okay. *If* you haven't done anything, then what have they asked you to do?" It was my full intention not to let this guy off the hook. I wanted to push him and push him hard. When I put out *the* question I wanted his nerves strung out, wrung out, and hung out.

"They've been asking me to get a transfer into the Organized Crime Bureau, Vice, Narcotics, or something like that. I've been telling them there are no openings. They've been leaning pretty hard lately, so I told them I put in for the transfer and I'm waiting to hear."

"You keep saying 'they.' Who the hell is 'they'?"

A thought flicked through Verno's mind for a second as he wondered if he should give up the names. He knew better than to hold out on me at this point. The thought only lasted a second before he said, "Tommy Riccio for one. Sometimes he's with a guy called Tiny Caruso. One time Riccio was with Charlie Tortero. A couple of other times he was with the Persico brothers."

"What else?" I asked somewhat more softly than the previous questions. I had him on the defensive, so now I wanted to back off a little before I popped the key question.

"Nothing, boss. Really. This stuff just started to come up lately."

"What else?" I asked louder.

"Nothing. I swear to God. I never gave them anything, no information, no names, nothing."

"So, you say you never gave them anything," I said with a slight tone of disbelief. "You're into these assholes for over a grand. You've owed them the money for more than a year. They lean on you and ask you to get a transfer. However, you haven't transferred and you haven't paid the money." After the summary, I allowed a ten-second pause so as to give him time to let the rational points settle in. "Now, I repeat myself: what have they asked you for? What names were they asking for?" I knew Verno wouldn't like me asking the question a second time. Nobody ever does. That was tough! I wanted to hear them say he was being leaned on about what he might know about Danny Martin.

Detective Al Verno, who knew full well he was now *suspect* Al Verno, sat quiet for ten or fifteen seconds.

"I knew about the loan, Detective," I continued, not wanting his silence to last too long. "I knew who you got the money from. I knew the frigging amount of the loan. Now you better start thinking, 'What else does Amato know?' You think about that for one full second Detective, because I'm going to ask you one more time ..." I let silence fill the room before I banged my hand down on the desk and yelled, "What else?"

Al Verno's hands were hugging his shoulders and I was hoping I had pushed him to the point of tears. An interrogator loved getting a suspect to cry. It meant you had broken them and when you broke them, you owned them. However, somewhere in the back of my brain, I knew I wasn't enjoying this interrogation, and I knew why.

After a few more seconds Detective Verno dropped the grip he had on himself and said, "They wanted pictures of the guys in the Vice Squad, the undercover guys."

"And you got them, right?"

"No ... yes ... kind of," he said to the floor.

"What kind of stupid answer is that?" I bellowed.

"I gave them some pictures of my wife's cousins. They live in Arizona. They have nothing to do with being cops, but I figured if Tommy wanted pictures, well then, I would give him pictures. It got him off my back for awhile."

The Detective was breathing deep and fast. His head was down and turned to the right side of his chair. It was time to strike.

"Did you kill Danny Martin?" I asked quickly. "Did you kill that kid? Did you?" The questions came out rapidly as if spit out of the end of machine gun. The pace at which they hit Verno, the loudness of them, the very accusation they carried, left no time for the man to think.

Verno turned his head toward me in slow motion. At first all I saw was the left, rear portion of his head, then the left cheek.

Then came his nose. Next came the eyes. Deep, burning eyes. Eyes filled with agony. Eyes burning with contempt.

"Are you fucking nuts, Lieutenant? There's no way on earth I would kill Martin for any reason, for anybody, or for any price."

"Do you know who killed Danny Martin?" my voice asked slower and softer.

"On my kid's lives, Lieutenant," he protested. His right hand went up in the air and his left hand pressed to his chest. "I don't have the foggiest notion who killed Martin or why they did it. I'll take a polygraph, submit to blood tests, urine test, fingerprints, anything you want. I didn't do it and I don't know anything about it."

One can never be positive about such things, but in my mind and heart I believed that Al Verno was an innocent man whose only sin had been stupidity. We sat in silence for a full minute, maybe longer. I was not going to speak. This time he would have to be the one to break the silence.

"I borrowed the money for my kid, Lute. That's it pure and simple. It was stupid. I'm an idiot for having done it, but I'm not a killer. I'm not a turncoat."

Again there was silence in the room. Now it would be my turn to break it. Verno had been destroyed and he couldn't offer any more. He had no more to give. Now he needed to be repaired.

"Here's what we're going to do," I said. "I'll draw eleven hundred bucks out of the bank this afternoon. I'll give it to you before we leave tonight, and you will get it to this frigging idiot uncle of yours this evening. You make it clear to your uncle that he pay that loan off in the next twenty-four hours, or I personally will break his legs! You got that?"

Verno nodded with his head, but it was his face that said he understood.

"Can you trust this stupid uncle of yours? Will he pay it off?"

"He'll do it. I can trust him that he will," Al Verno said as he sniffed in the fluid that had broken loose from inside him and filled his nose.

"Then, when this case is over with, you will put in for a transfer back to Genesee Section. I will get it approved. Gene Tanny is the Captain over there now, and he owes me a few favors. I'll explain the situation to him about your kid and he'll get you all the overtime he can muster up so you can quit one of those jobs. Nothing will ever be said again, at anytime in the future, outside of this office, by you or by me, about this loan business. Am I clear on that, mister?"

Al Verno nodded his head at each of my points. Finally he stood and said, "That's fair enough, Lieutenant. More than fair. I'll pay you back every dime. I swear to God I will."

"I'll give you a year to pay it back. No vig. After the year, we'll talk about interest or whatever."

We shook hands on the agreement and I promised the broken man that his peers would never hear a word about the matter. Diane's alimony would be light and late this month, but what the heck, a good cop is more important than a wife, especially an ex-wife. Besides, it wasn't going to be the first time I missed a payment.

Verno stood by the door and then turned to open it. I don't know if he was waiting for some final words, but I offered some.

"If you ever get into a financial scrape again, you come to your friends, to cops, not those Mafia bastards. We're your family, Al. Not them. Going to them does nothing but destroy lives. You're too good of a man to turn your life over to those bastards."

He nodded to me, managed a weak smile, pulled himself up straight, opened the door, and walked into the squad room.

Alone in the office, I needed time to think through the incident that had just transpired. In order to create that time for private thought, I called over to the FBI and left a message for Special Agent Allen, advising the secretary that I would be tied up for a few hours and would call him back when I was free.

With my elbows resting on the desk, I brought my head to my hands and rubbed my eyes. Although the workday was only two hours old, it felt like the end of long, exhausting day.

There aren't any fancy words to describe it. Suffice it to say that I believed Al Verno. I was there. I saw his face, his eyes, and his body. I heard the words, but more importantly, I heard *how* the words were said, the inflections, the tones, and the little modulations. Plain and simple, the kid screwed up. He screwed up bad. I didn't know if I could keep his bacon out of the fire, but I knew I would try. He had suffered enough. The man didn't need any more pain in his life.

The next task was to seek out Major Skip Winston. Danny's letter was burning a hole in my pocket. It was evidence, evidence that would cast a shadow over Verno and Allen. The letter was explosive. It contained information that cast suspicions on a City of Rochester Detective and an FBI Special Agent. It criticized the operations of the Rochester Police Department, and it was critical of Chief Matt Murphy's handling of Danny's undercover assignment. Whoever brought the letter forward would be the messenger bearing bad news, and in police departments they do kill the messengers!

I had no problem bringing the letter forward to Murphy, Delany, or whomever. The fact of the matter was that it might be fun to watch Murphy and his sidekick Delaney read the letter and squirm. I would like to have taken the letter to them; to be there as they opened it and scanned the contents. However, a certain protocol had to be followed. I would have to share the letter with Skip Winston first. He would have to digest it and then decide the best way to bring it up the chain of command. It would be dangerous for his career, but then again, Winston had made a career of doing the right thing rather than the safe thing. Being the messenger with the letter would mean that he knew what was in the letter, and knowing that, he would be a threat. The allegations and issues Danny Martin had raised in the letter would be embarrassing to the police hierarchy. Basically, he had accused them of misfeasance and malfeasance. Suspicious eyes would look at the bearer of the letter, and in the months to come, wonder if he — the messenger — had divulged the information to anyone outside the very tight circle of police administrators. I sort of wished I could spare Skip Winston the burden, but I knew that sooner or later I would have to turn the heavy letter over to the boss and let him handle the special delivery to our leaders. What I didn't know was how my boss would react to the letter.

The good news was that Winston was meeting with the Chief and wouldn't be available for a while. Whether that was good or bad news, I didn't know. My immediate reaction to it felt like good news. Maybe Skip Winston was up in the Chief's Office right now getting me out of this unholy alliance with the FBI so that I could be turned free to do the investigation the way it needed to be done and without all the pussyfooting around.

The better news was that Wonder Boy, Special Agent William Allen, was not going to be available all morning. When his office called to let me know he was "seeing to some pressing duties until sometime this afternoon," I could have kissed the phone.

The free time allowed me to tackle the things that were piling up in my in-basket. I shuffled the stack of papers around into some order of priorities and in doing so I found what I had been seeking — the follow-up report from Donovan and St. John on Dee Dee Wilcox. After reading through the report I scribbled my initials in the "Approved" box on the lower, right-hand corner of the report, moved the report to the "To Be Filed" basket … and then pulled it back out again.

The lead on Dee Dee had come from Cavaluso. And, the lead had gone nowhere. The stripper bragged about all of her sexual encounters as if they were trophies, and yet she denied ever bedding down with Danny Martin. Either she was a liar about the alleged relationship or the lead was, very simply, no good. The woman had no obvious reason to lie, at least it appeared that way, and so the lead was most likely a bum one.

Was Cavaluso leading me down a dead end on purpose or did someone give him the bum lead and he passed it along in good faith? If he was leading me on, I had to know why he was doing it. If someone had given him the information, I needed to know who that someone was. Was Eddy Cavaluso one of the chameleons, the ground lions of which I needed to be leery, as suggested by the Old Man? Was that why Fast Eddy sat quietly at the dinner table the night before while Ruggeri talked about lizards?

I played with the question for a couple of minutes and decided it was not very likely that my informant was also my killer. Edward Cavaluso had made his reputation many years earlier. He no longer had to prove who he was and what he was capable of doing. That was the task of younger, hungrier men who still hoped to climb the corporate ladder of organized crime. If Vincent Ruggeri thought Eddy Cavaluso was a person who I called my friend, Fast Eddy would be Dead Eddy. But, even so, if Eddy was being used unwittingly to send me false leads, then he was in danger. If he was in danger, my knowing his dog's name had put him in greater danger. I lifted the phone off its cradle and placed a call to Cavaluso. I caught him at his house and we made arrangements to meet later in the night at "The Box."

By the time I had wrestled with the Eddy Cavaluso matter, Winston was called to advise he was back in his office. I grabbed a full cup of coffee and headed in that direction. When the Major saw me in his doorway, he waved me in with one hand as he signed reports with the other.

"Any good news?" I asked.

"If you consider continuing on your present assignment as outlined by the Chief yesterday morning at the FBI offices to be good news, then yes, I have good news," the Major said with a smile.

I let out a groan.

"Just ride it out, Mike. Do your investigation as you normally would and don't let the Feeb cramp your style. Lighten up a little," Winston advised lightly. "Grin and bear it. If you can't do that, well then, just learn to live with it. It's a fact. You can't change it. End of story."

I explained it was going to be difficult to pursue the investigation the way I normally would because of some evidence I had uncovered.

"Evidence such as what?" Winston asked.

I handed over the letter with a brief description of how it got to me and then sat back to let my boss read it. The man was not a slow reader, but he took a good five minutes to read and re-read the letter.

Handing the sheets of paper back to me, Skip Winston said, "I never saw that letter, Lieutenant. I do not even know of its existence."

"Yeah, right," I chuckled. "So, anyway, what do you think about what Martin says in it?"

"In what?"

Maybe it was just me, but I was beginning to feel like the village idiot! I looked at the Major with a crooked little grin and said, "In the letter."

"I don't know what letter you're talking about, Lieutenant. I never saw any letter."

"Are you jerking my chain, boss, or are you really serious?" I asked with grave concern.

Skip Winston got up and closed the door to his office. Returning to his desk, he leaned back in the chair and studied his fingertips that were pressed together in front of him in the form of a tent. Finally he spoke.

"Mike, I'm going to level with you on this. That letter is dynamite. It indicates we have a crooked cop here and in the local FBI office. It also says that the leader of this Department is inept or uncaring. Now, if either one of those two allegations is true, it's a powder keg and one I do not wish to be sitting on when it goes off. The investigation is yours. I've been taken out of the loop, and to be damn truthful, right now I am very happy that's the case." He paused long enough to get a reaction out of me. When I didn't offer one, he continued. "The Department has been through enough over the last five, six, seven years. We had the scandal with the embezzlement case, the drug squad investigation, and one thing after another. The Mayor doesn't want any more scandals and the Chief has assured him there won't be any. What you have there flies in the face of those edicts, as well as putting a smudge on the FBI. Danny Martin is dead and that is a very sad fact. However, me delivering that letter with the accusations in it would not do you, Officer Martin, or me any good. My career is just starting to move. I don't want it ground to a halt by having to deal with that thing you have there."

I couldn't believe what I was hearing, but I knew what I was seeing. Skip Winston had just leaped off the fence post and was now scurrying through the grass. I just shook my head as I got up to leave. It was the old Cop Shop Shuffle that was done when one decided it was best to cover one's posterior rather than work for one's posterity.

"You're going to have to confront Detective Verno and do something with him. It's got to be done. We just can't ignore it," the Major said as I put my hand on the doorknob.

"Ignore what?" I asked over my shoulder.

"The allegations in that … that thing you have there."

"The letter?" I queried.

Winston nodded in the affirmative.

"What letter?" I asked as I opened the door, stepped out of the stench, and slammed the cheap, city government door behind me.

Luckily, when I returned to my office I found a message that Felix Santos had been trying to reach me. I had to smile when I read the pink message slip that read, "Call Captain Santos, San

Diego PD, ASAP. He has info you asked him for." That bit of information got my mind off Winston's retreat.

I had met Santos about a year earlier at a training conference in Chicago. Although we were from two different parts of the world, we had hit it off pretty well. The two of us had tipped a few beers during the weeklong session and ended up entertaining a couple of flight attendants one memorable evening. I had no reason to put a lot of trust in the man, but then again, I had no reason not to trust him. I decided I would make the call and evaluate the trust thing after we spoke.

It took a few minutes to get through to Santos, but when I got him on the line I couldn't help but jump right into the subject.

"So, what have you got for me *jefe*?" I asked.

"Very good, *gringo*," he laughed. "I see that you remember some of the Spanish I taught you."

We joked for a few minutes about my poor Spanish, his poor Italian, and two benevolent flight attendants before we finally got down to the matter at hand.

"What I'm telling you, Mike, is very sensitive. It's all off the record, and it can't come back to me. In fact, it can't come back at the San Diego PD in any way, shape, or form. Understand?"

"Understood," I acknowledged. "You got my word."

"If it wasn't for the fact that it was a cop who got killed up there, I wouldn't even be passing the information along. It's that sensitive."

I offered a blood oath and swore by all that was holy that I would not go official with the information, but would only use it off the record and only if I really had too. When he questioned the possibility of the Police Department monitoring the office phones, I had to acknowledge the possibility of such an act. To sanitize the private conversation, we switched over to cell phones and re-initiated the call through the microwave route that would be more difficult to be monitored. With that out of the way, Santos gave me the low down on Special Agent Bill Allen.

"My source tells me that Allen was a pretty good Agent. In fact, he was better than most. The guy made some good cases for the Bureau while he was here, but it seems he got too engrossed in his work and started to take it home with him."

"How so?" I asked.

"One of his snitches was a part-time girlfriend of one of our local Mafia dudes. Bill Allen got close to her ... real close, in fact. They started doing some horizontal bed dancing, and pretty soon they were shacking up on a regular basis. The mob got wind of it and they got the broad back in their corner. It seems that she was able to get Billy captured on some pretty good skin flicks and once that was done, well, you know how it goes. The mob started to lean on him for information with the threat they would send the pictures to Washington."

"So, he's not the red, white, and blue Fed that he likes to strut around and pretend to be," I commented.

"Exactly," Felix Santos said. "However, our boy had the good sense to go to his bosses with the unpleasant news. In the end, the entire thing was handled unofficially within the FBI ranks."

"How so?"

"Well, I hate to slam your home town, Mike, but his punishment was that he was sent to Rochester. That's exactly the way my source put it," Santos added with a laugh. "My guy says, 'The Bureau punished Allen by sending him to Rochester, New York!' I hate to be the one to tell you that, Mike. But, the way they look at it here, being sent to Buffalo or Rochester is worse than going to hell."

I took a pass on the cheap shot about Rochester and asked, "Do you know if the Rochester FBI office was told about Allen's sins?"

Santos hesitated slightly and then said, "The way it was given to me was that these matters are handled very quietly and they pretty much stay in-house. So, based on that, my guess would be that his new boss up there doesn't have any idea about the boy's past here in the land of milk and honey. However, you know how tight the boys in The Bureau are, so he may have gotten an unofficial word about it."

Felix Santos gave me the name of Bill Allen's bed partner. We then said our good-byes after quibbling about whether I owed him a favor or if this made us even for the blonde stewardess I had fixed him up with while we were at the conference where we had originally met. The argument wasn't settled and was left for a later time.

* * *

I got out of the office and headed for Kathy Martin's house to tell her that our case had developed three suspects. One suspect had already been cleared, I told her, and the second one would be interviewed later in the day. I didn't feel it was necessary to tell her that the third suspect was the entire organized crime family in upstate New York.

Also, in great detail, she shared her news with me. Chief of Police Matthew Murphy had come to the funeral home the night before.

"He came in very quiet, Mike. It was right at the end and almost everyone was gone. He just walked in like he was no one and came right up to Chrisy and Phyllis and me, and he very quietly expressed his sympathy. He was so kind, Mike and so gentle."

I told her I was glad he had made the effort to show his respects to Danny, but in my head I was cursing the man for showing his kindness too late.

Kathy was pouring us our second cup of coffee when I said, "I have to ask you something. It's something I've been holding off asking you about because it concerns the night Danny was … got hurt, and well, I just didn't want to make you drag all that up while you're in so much pain."

She gave me a sympathetic smile and said, "If it will help you find who did this, Mike, then you ask me anything."

"On that Tuesday night before Danny left, did he say where he was going?"

"He said he had to see a guy. That was it, just that he had to see a guy."

"Did he say it was a guy, one guy, or maybe some guys, a couple of guys?"

Kathy took a sip of coffee and I could see her thinking. Finally she responded, "Danny had been on the phone most of the evening. A couple of times he called out, and a couple of times he received calls. Then, I don't really know the exact time, maybe about nine o'clock, he said he had to go out and meet a guy. That's how he put it. 'A guy.' He said that he would only be an hour or so and that he would be back before midnight."

The small woman began to cry and I hesitated before I pushed her farther. After we both took another swallow of coffee, I asked, "What was his demeanor? How was he acting?"

"He was sort of relaxed, Mike. Sometimes I could see he was nervous and jittery when he went out. But that night, Tuesday night, he was kind of mellow. Like I said, he was relaxed."

Phyllis came in carrying a clothesbasket piled high with freshly washed laundry. We exchanged greetings, and after setting the basket down she filled the coffee cups in front of Kathy and me. Taking the cue that Kathy and I were into something private, the older sister went into the living room and began folding the wash.

"Is there anything else, Kathy?" I asked. "No matter how small it was, no matter how unimportant it seems, was there anything else he did or said that night?"

Again she stopped to think and I allowed her the time she needed. Her head was turned slightly to the right and it appeared she was staring at a tiny, spot on the wall on the other side of the kitchen.

"Before he left," Kathy said, as she continued her distant gaze, "Danny kissed me on the cheek. He said he had to 'make contact with a guy' and that he wouldn't be more than an hour or so." She returned her eyes to mine and said, "That's it, Mike. That's all I remember."

"That's fine, Kathy. You did fine. Really you did. That helps a lot," I said in an attempt to make her feel better.

* * *

It was almost noon when I headed out to the diner I frequented over on Thurston Road. Margaret *"Sitto"* Tannous greeted me at the door and advised me that I would have a nice bowl of her green pea soup and a large salad.

In her usual candid manner she told me, "You look like death warmed over, Mister Big Shot Detective. Eat a nice salad," she pleaded. "It's good for your bowels."

I thanked her for her concern and warm words about my potential to defecate freely, but ordered a liverwurst sandwich as I grabbed the sports page off the countertop. Later, when the sandwich I had ordered — along with a very large salad I had not ordered — was slipped in front of me with an admonishment, "Shut up and eat it!" I just smiled and dug in to it.

After the meal I lit my fifteenth cigarette of the day and blew the smoke into the air. Taking a momentary time out, I silently thanked my father for answering my prayers and coming through for me. Maybe I'm not the most religious guy in the world, but I figured my old man helped, in some way or another, in getting the San Diego information to me.

Another lead had fallen into place along with Felix Santos' news, and that was Kathy's recollection of the last time she saw her husband alive. Danny's final words to Kathy, at least as she recalled them, had indicated he was going to make contact with a guy. Maybe what he really said was that he was going to meet his contact! If that was so, then Bill Allen just went to the top of my personal hit parade.

I hoped the local phone company would be able to pull up the records of those last few calls to and from Danny Martin's house. But, getting those records would take a few days and maybe as long as a week. If I knew who he was calling, as well as who was calling him, I would be a leg up on the entire case.

Then, I made mental plans to ruin Bill Allen's afternoon and possibly his life. I was going to have to find out what he had been up to all morning; and, once we got past that I was going to have to weigh up the situation before I lowered the boom on him. If all went well, by this evening I would be wrapping up this case and would have good news for the Martin family before they lowered one of their own into the ground tomorrow morning.

That turned out to be wishful thinking on my part. Things are never as simple as they appear. If something can go wrong, it will. In this job, Murphy's Law is a way of life. In fact, there's a rumor, and I do believe it: Murphy was a cop!

10

Friday Afternoon: Caging the Suspect

According to local cops, there is a strange ritual to be experienced whenever one of us enters an FBI Office. The ritual is referred to as "having your brain sucked." Having experienced the ritual several times, I no longer consider it a myth or an old cop's tale.

The manner in which brain sucking is performed is rather interesting to observe. It begins when a local cop is admitted to any FBI office by a smiling, although distant, receptionist who immediately offers coffee, soft drink, hot chocolate, or a glass of water. Next, a smiling Agent emerges from the inner-office and apologizes for having kept the local copper waiting. To prove the extent of his caring, he may even admonish the receptionist for having been so rude to a brother officer as to keep him sitting in an anteroom.

The FBI Special Agent makes quite a ceremony of introducing the neophyte and assumed dumb, local cop to The Bureau's Senior Agent in Charge. The SAC welcomes the visitor and tells him how much The Bureau respects the local "boys in blue" and assures him that the entire FBI organization stands ready to assist in any way. The boss makes a point of instructing the host agent to share all of his information with the local police, often reminding him, "We're in this thing together, you know!"

Theoretically, according to the Feds, at least, the street cop has now been lulled into thinking he's just one of the boys. To bolster his ego while weakening his defenses, he will now be told how much better the local cops fight crime than the suits from Washington.

The stage is set. Now, the brain sucking starts.

As the host agent retrieves a file of information he allegedly is just dying to share with the cop, another agent will stop by the desk and pop an, "Oh, by the way ..." question. That agent is then joined by a second one, then a third, and possibly a fourth. The local copper is stroked about what a great Department he comes from, and thrown in with the lavish compliments and questions about who is doing what, how bad is the narcotics situation, possible corruption, identities of informants, leads on old cases, his shoe size, and his chief's favorite color.

By the time the cop makes it out of the office he realizes he has not received one solitary piece of information, and he has a splitting headache, which is the result of having his brain sucked.

In other words, the Feds take, but they don't give.

After lunch, I called the local Feeb office. Due to my respectful fear of having my brain sucked, I declined Special Agent Allen's invitation to meet him in his office, even when he told me that he had a lot of information to share with me. I suggested he bring the information with him, and we would go somewhere we could talk. He wasn't too crazy about the idea of losing an opportunity to bring in a fish for brain suction, but finally conceded the point. His failure to lure me in for brain drainage probably cost him several brownie points with Ed Delany, and I considered that a further win.

The next issue to be settled was who would drive whose car. I let my tone of voice tell him I was not in the mood for these chicken-shit issues when we had some serious police work to get done. We finally, after negotiating all the possible options, settled on the fact that I would pick him up in my car in front of the Federal Building about two-thirty p.m. I considered the negotiated settlement another win because I wanted total control over the entire afternoon, including where we went, when we stopped, and how long we were out. I had questions for Mister Allen and I didn't want him having dominion over the vehicle and the day's activities.

The clock told me I had a little over an hour until our meeting. I planned to use the time to catch up on some of the administrative things that had been taking a back seat to everything else since Tuesday. However, after less than five minutes into the planned tasks, the phone rang, and I was on my way in another direction.

I was not displeased to hear Phyllis' voice on the line. Truth be known, I was quite pleased. She needed to talk to me, and she needed to do it right then. We agreed to meet at a little restaurant out by the airport, which was a point that was about halfway between my office and her sister's house. The meeting fostered the possibility of being late in my arranged chauffeuring of Bill Allen, but Phyllis sounded like she truly needed to talk.

When I arrived at the hamburger joint, Phyllis was already there, seated near the back of the place. My beaming smile to her unsmiling face was welcomed with a slight, forced grin. I slid into the squeaky vinyl booth across the table from her. We spent the next minute discussing the virtues of malts over sodas and sundaes over frappes. When the waitress came by, we discussed whether or not to order lunch and finally settled on having coffee.

After the two cups of coffee arrived and the waitress disappeared, I asked, "So what's going on?"

"Kathy's really having a bad time with this thing, Mike. She's totally withdrawn and won't talk to anyone. She just sits there doing nothing, only looking into space."

"It's to be expected, Phyllis. She's been through a lot. Sometime a person's system just shuts down rather than have to deal with the pain." When she didn't reply, I took a sip of coffee and added, "The Department's psychologist will be in touch with her soon, and she'll learn to open up again." Still my coffee companion remained silent, looking into her cup for words she wanted to say. I continued to hold up my end of the conversation until she was ready to jump in. "In fact, I'll get in touch with Sergeant Polson, Chief Murphy's aide, and I'll have him get the shrink out there today, if at all possible."

Phyllis continued her silence even though her lips initiated some movement a couple of times. I took a swig of coffee, and sat back.

"She's feeling so guilty, Mike," Phyllis said to the table and then looked up to me.

"Guilty? Guilty about what?" I asked, remembering a very similar conversation with Kathy the previous day, in which she voiced concern about Phyllis' feelings of guilt.

Phyllis closed her eyes, took a deep breath, and let it out slowly. "Danny was no angel, Mike. He's dead and gone, God rest his soul, and I don't mean to speak ill of the dead, but he was not the hero he's being made out to be." With the main course of the conversation out on the table, my lunch date looked back to her coffee cup.

"It sounds like you know something I don't know," I said flatly, and then went silent. It was her ballgame now, and she had to take the lead. To force the issue, I encouraged, "So, tell me about it."

"Danny was running around. He was screwing around behind her back. She's almost positive. Kathy told me today that you asked her about Danny's last night at home. What she told you was the truth, it just …"

"It just wasn't *all* of the truth," I volunteered in order to help her finish the sentence. Then I asked, "What did she leave out?"

Phyllis took another deep breath, but it was quicker than the last one. She was now ready to dump everything. "Tuesday night, before Danny left the house, he was on the phone a couple of times, like Kathy said. In one of those conversations, he was talking to someone and saying things like, 'Don't believe the bitch ... she's full of crap'. It went on for a minute or so. Danny didn't know Kathy was in the hallway and could hear him. From what my sister made out of the entire conversation, Danny was screwing around. The woman must have told someone, and he was denying it to whoever he was talking to."

My mind wandered and wondered if Phyllis Conte could put up with the life as the wife of a homicide cop. I thought for a moment that the sex would probably be great, but she would also tire of my long work hours and frequent absences.

I didn't know what to say, so I told her exactly that. "I don't know what to tell you Phyllis. I swear to God, there's no sign in the investigation that he had a woman on the side. If he did, well, I'm not going to defend him. But still, even if he had fifty women out there, that's no reason for Kathy to feel guilty." When she didn't take the lead I had thrown her, I pushed it with the question, "So what is it that's making her feel guilty?"

"Danny beat her, Mike. At least once that I know of, but there were probably other times. I saw her with the busted lip and the swollen cheek. I know he did it to her. I asked her about it and she told me it was him that did it. She made all kinds of excuses for him. She said he was under a lot of pressure and she had been nagging him. Still, Mike, there's now reason for that. No reason!"

Now it was my turn to stare at my coffee cup. As far as I was concerned, the second lowest form of the human species is a wife beater. It turned my gut to think that Danny would hit his small, delicate wife. However, for the time being I had to set that aside and get to some facts.

"When was this?" I asked, "And why? What was it all about?"

"It was right after they came back from seeing Chrisy in Fredonia. Kathy says Danny was becoming a basket case. He was paranoid and suspicious of her and everyone else. Kathy says the least little thing would set him off. One night she tried to convince him to get out of what he was doing. She threatened to call the Chief of Police and tell him that Danny needed a break. He went into orbit and slapped her a couple of times." Phyllis paused long enough to swallow the emotion that was pushing up inside her throat. Having controlled it, she continued. "Of course, at the time I didn't know the entire thing was about the cop stuff he was doing. Back when it happened, she just said that Danny was under pressure. Now, since all this came out about him being undercover, she told me about her wanting him to get out of what he was doing. Back then, back in May, Kathy just told me he was under a lot of pressure. I told her then to leave the bastard." She caught herself and made the sign of the cross. "Not to speak evil of the dead, but at the time, I didn't know about all this undercover stuff."

"Is that what her guilt's all about?" I asked. "Was she going to leave him?"

Phyllis Conte nodded. After a few seconds she said, "He hit her again a few weeks ago. Not as bad as the other time, but he hit her. I finally convinced her that it was going to get worse, not better. She had just about made up her mind to do it when this thing, him getting killed, happened."

We talked a few more minutes and each of us downed another cup of coffee. When I asked the million-dollar question, that is, did Phyllis believe that Kathy was mad enough to kill Danny, she laughed out loud.

"That's just not possible, Mike," she answered. "She loved him too much, and more to the point, my sister just doesn't have the guts for that. If you think she killed Danny, you're a hundred miles wrong, Mike. A thousand percent wrong!"

"When was she planning on leaving?"

"This weekend," Phyllis said so lowly I hardly heard her. "She knew he would go out late Friday night and not be back until early Sunday morning. It was getting to be a ritual with him. She could bank on him being gone at least twenty-four hours over the weekend. She was going to wait for him to leave, and then she was going to pack her bags and move in with our cousin Connie, you know, until she got on her feet."

I let it go at that. There was nothing more to say. Danny had been losing all control over his life, his emotions, and perhaps even his mind. In his mental state, he had sunk to the depth of being a wife beater. Kathy, strung out as far as she could go and without anywhere to turn to get help for herself — and her husband — was going to bail out on the man she loved. And now, instead of leaving him this weekend, she would be burying him. I hoped, but doubted, the Department's shrink could help her work through that.

After Phyllis and I parted ways in the parking lot of the restaurant, I drove around the city streets and tried to clear my head before I met the person I believed was the most likely suspect in Danny Martin's killing. I was going to be late in picking up Allen, but I figured the wait would do him good. As I drove, I realigned the batting order of murder suspects. Bill Allen, as far as I was concerned, was still the leadoff man. Assorted mob members, such as Charlie "Twist" Tortero and fifty other mob guys who wanted to make an impression on Vincent Ruggeri, were all in second place. And now Kathy Martin had moved into position number three, pushing Al Verno to the clean-up spot.

I pointed the car in the direction of the Federal Building and assessed my list of suspects. Two cops, half of the Rochester Mafiosi, and the victim's wife. It was a goofy list; but then again, this was a goofy case. I had a hard time featuring the diminutive Kathy Martin as a killer. However, on the other hand, hell hath no fury …

* * *

"How you doing, Mike, old boy?" the Illinois farm boy asked as he hopped into the passenger side of the city car.

"Pretty good, Bill. How's everything with you?"

"Things are great, Mike. I just got it settled with the SAC that I could open the entire file to you. No more secrets," Allen said with a broad smile. "That's what kept me tied up all morning. I told Delany, 'We either play on an open, level playing field with Lieutenant Amato, or we shouldn't be playing at all.' He finally bought it and caved in. I'm sure it might cost me some little favor in the future, but Mike, I feel very strong on this issue."

Allen was sucking my brain so hard I thought I felt my ears pop. However, instead of being my usual sardonic self, I just smiled and said, "Way to go, Bill. I appreciate the support. I've got some stuff to share with you also." Oh boy, do I have stuff to share with you!

I turned right on Church Street and then left on Plymouth Avenue. As I approached the Public Safety Building, Allen cautioned, "I really don't think we should go here, Mike. We should really go some place private for what I have to say."

"I agree, Bill. Good point!" I said as we passed the PSB. It was never my destination in the first place. I made my way through a maze of streets in the Cornhill neighborhood and smiled to myself as I realized that the Feds must have their own myths about local cops being brain suckers.

"Where are we going, then?" my passenger asked with a hint of apprehension.

"Genesee Valley Park," I responded. "It's too nice of a day to be cooped up somewhere indoors. Besides, it's private enough and there will still be enough witnesses around to settle who hit who first."

"What ... what do you mean by that?" Allen stammered.

"Just kidding, Billy," I said with a hearty laugh as I patted his left leg a couple of times and then squeezed his knee ever so slightly so as to make him more nervous. "Relax."

Relaxing was the last thing I wanted this guy to do. This was going to be a day of reckoning, so I wanted this S.O.B. stressed out. I had picked the park because it was open and public, so Allen wouldn't get any strange ideas if I made him panic just a little too much. If he killed Danny Martin and then realized that I knew it, it was an even bet he would try to whack me. I wanted our meeting out in the open where he would have to have second thoughts about killing me. Besides that, the park would have plenty of black people around, and that would help force the white-as-rice Special Agent out of his comfort zone. Like I said, I didn't want this guy to relax for one single second.

Genesee Valley Park, also called South Park by some of the older locals, is a spacious area of green trees and rolling, grassy hills situated in the southwest corner of the city. My best guess was that it encompassed over a hundred, maybe even a couple of hundred acres. It began at the edge of the 19th Ward neighborhood, a nice section of the city with large, two-story homes, and then spread out south and east to the border of the suburban towns that touched Rochester. The park was the setting of some great childhood memories, and some even better, off-duty police party memories. As a kid, I swam in the park's huge pool, and as an adult I hacked at small, white balls on the park's golf course. It was also the scene of some wild cop parties on hot summer nights after some long swing shifts. The place held a lot of memories for me, and my hopes included that it would — from this day forward — be the source of a new happy memory of Bill Allen confessing he killed Danny Martin.

I pulled into a small parking area off of a narrow residential street that bordered the extreme northern edge of the quiet place. Once the car was parked, I grabbed my notebook and case file, exited the car and said, "Come on, Bill. Let's get this show on the road."

Allen got out of the car and looked at me, not too sure about what we were doing. That made me feel good.

"Aren't you going to wear your sport coat?" he asked.

"Why? It's too warm and muggy for a frigging coat."

"Your gun," he said as he pointed to the right side of my waist.

"It goes with this," I answered, pointing to the badge on my belt next to the gun.

The Feds have a thing about exposing their guns. Maybe the shrinks were right when they speculated that to many cops the gun is a phallic symbol. At the very least, it seemed to apply to the Feds. Maybe that's why they don't like having their guns exposed to the general public. I never understood the reluctance, but it was one of the many hang-ups carried in the federal baggage.

"People might get concerned when they see men carrying a gun in a public park," Allen offered.

"Bill," I said with some tone of exhaustion, "every person in this park knows we're cops. They can tell by the way we dress, the ugly car we drove up in, the way we walk, and our haircuts. Give it a rest and relax a little, man."

As I waved the G-man over to follow me, I realized I was pleased Bill Allen chose to wear his coat. If we went for a quick draw, I was going to have the advantage.

We walked in silence to a picnic bench about fifty yards from the car and about twenty yards from a group of kids who were obviously enjoying a near-the-end-of-summer outing with their church group. The scent of fresh-cut grass was a welcome summer scent and it mixed nicely with the cheers and laughter of kids at play. I found myself somewhat perplexed by the nicety of the setting and the nastiness of the situation.

"So," I said as we sat down across from each other at the picnic table. "What have you got for me?"

"Like I told you, Mike. I'm going to give you the whole enchilada here," he said as he spread his hands across the table's surface. "You may not like some things I'm going to tell you, but I feel you should know about them. Okay?"

I liked the fact that he was trying to play his role very seriously, but he was betrayed by the movement of his eyes in the direction of the laughing children who were involved in an aggressive game of dodge ball.

"I'm a big boy, Bill. Shoot." As soon as the word left my mouth, I realized it was a bad verb to use.

"The Bureau," he intoned as if he was speaking of some sacred monastery, "is leaning toward the possibility that Officer Martin was killed by a Rochester cop, a detective."

"Really," I said with a tilt of my head and raised eyebrows. I left my mouth open, hoping it would look like genuine shock and not appear to be as phony as it felt.

"The guy works for you, Mike, so this might rile you a little, but please hear me out. The Detective is into one of Vinnie Ruggeri's loan sharks for quite a bit of money. Danny Martin was well aware of the situation and it might be that the Detective got wind that Martin was a cop and he killed Martin to cover his tracks."

I nodded thoughtfully as the information was given to me before asking, "Who's the loan shark? Tommy the Tape?"

"No, I don't think so. The guy's name is," he started to reply and then trailed off as he began to flip through his file. "The man's name is ... ah, here it is, Thomas Dominic Riccio."

"Yeah, that's what I just said. They call him, 'Tommy the Tape' because he thinks he's a frigging accountant. He's always carrying around bits of adding machine tape."

"Oh," Allen said with a nod and a smile, obviously feeling somewhat foolish. I was glad he did!

"And, who's the cop, Al Verno?"

Silence and a wide-open mouth were his first responses. It was followed by "You know?"

"Of course I know, Bill. It's old news. The guy works for me, for crying out loud! I know everything that has to do with my people. In fact, if you want the full story, it goes like this. Verno's uncle interceded for him when Al's kid was in the hospital about a year ago. Verno needed the cash and went to his uncle, and then the uncle went to Tommy the Tape. But that's ancient history. The money's been paid back for quite some time now." It was strange, but I almost enjoyed lying to the hayseed.

"How long ago was it paid back?"

"I don't have the date, Bill. They usually don't give receipts and loan account summaries. Suffice it to say it was some time ago."

"Still in all, Mike," Allen countered. "If he knew Martin was a cop and that Martin knew he was doing business with this Tommy the Tape fellow, Verno could have panicked and decided it was necessary to take Martin out of the picture."

"I can't buy that, Bill," I said with a groan. "Number one, there's no way that Verno knew Martin was a cop. I didn't know it. The mob didn't know it. And, I'll bet my year's wages on this, Verno didn't know it. Besides, even if the news leaked out, what was Verno going to get? I already knew about it. My boss probably knew about it. What was the worst thing that could have happened to Detective Verno? He could maybe get a ten-day suspension or thirty days at the most. That's hardly a motive to kill someone."

Special Agent William Allen was going to say something, but he changed his mind. Then he changed it back again and proposed, "But it would have ruined the man's reputation! That's motive enough."

"Bill, let me tell you something," I said with a little edge of annoyance. "There wouldn't have been any public disclosure. The case would have to have been handled strictly in house as a personnel matter. The reason for that is the Rochester Police Department has a damn strong union. That union protects cops from double jeopardy."

"So?" he asked in a schoolyard retort. "Where does the double jeopardy come from?"

"So?" I responded with a hefty edge of annoyance. "When I found out about this loan, I gave Verno an official RPD typed on blue paper, per regulations, letter of reprimand. Once I did that, the Department couldn't hit him with anything else. The case was closed. Consequently, Verno had nothing to fear even if he knew Martin was a cop, and even if he knew Martin knew he had a loan from Tommy the Tape, et cetera, et cetera."

"You, in effect, you protected him," Allen said as if the fact was incredible.

"So what else do you have, Bill?" I asked with apparent eagerness, ignoring his astute observation.

"Delany thinks we should look hard at Verno."

"It would be a waste of time," I said. After a pause of about two or three seconds I asked, "So what else do you have for me?"

"I was thinking I could start running his financial background. You know, pull his bank records, stuff like that."

"You would be wasting your time, but what the heck, go for it. But I'll save you the trouble and give you his up to date financial picture by tomorrow morning." Pause. "Now then, what else do you have?"

"How would you do that so quickly? I mean, even for *The Bureau* it takes a few days to get that kind of information."

My smile was probably too cocky, but it felt good to wear it. "I would try something radical, something strange and totally off the wall." There was a pause for effect. "I would ask him for it! That's something The Bureau never thinks of — going in the front door and using the direct approach."

"We should at least put a tail on him, Mike. We need to see where he goes, who he sees," Allen insisted, although not too strongly.

"No need for that, Bill. He goes home, lays carpets in the evenings and on Saturdays, plays in a band on weekend nights once a month, and comes back to work." Pause. "What else do you have to share?"

"Nothing," he said after he cleared his throat and then looked nervously at a soccer ball that bounced up against the picnic table at which we were seated. For a second I thought he was going to reach for his gun, but instead he just looked from the ball to me as if to ask, "What now?"

"That's it for the 'open, level playing field?' " I asked as I got up to retrieve the ball for the kids. "That's the whole enchilada? That's it for all the information you've been cleared to tell me?"

I threw the ball back to the kids and one of them yelled, "Thanks, Five-O!"

"Not bad for an old white dude, huh?" I yelled back. The kid laughed.

I sat back down at the picnic table, rested my forearms on the top of it, and folded my hands together. "See?" I asked Allen. "I told you!"

"Told me what?" he asked as if insulted.

"The kids already knew we were cops."

"What makes you say that?" he questioned.

"The kid called me 'Five-O.' It's their name for us. It comes from an old cop show on TV." I smiled a friendly smile, then added, "But that was probably before your time."

Again I could see that the man felt foolish. He knew he was on my turf. He understood we were playing on my kind of "level playing field," on the streets, in the ghetto, in my world.

"Now, let's cut through all the garbage and start being honest with each other."

"I have been honest with you, Mike," he protested with some indignation.

"Yeah, right!" I snickered. It was time to let the chips start falling. I stood up, put my right foot on the seat of the park bench and leaned into my suspect across the park picnic table.

"That file you showed me the other day was big enough to hold about four inches of reports." I let him absorb that observation for a few seconds before continuing. "In fact, going by the bend marks in the little metal thing at the top of the folder that holds all the reports in place, I would say it did, at one time, have at least four inches of paperwork in it. When you showed it to me it had about an inch, maybe and inch and a half, of reports and forms." Again I let a short pause do its work. "Don't I get to see those reports, the ones that were there once upon a time, but are gone today? I mean, what the hell, we do have this open, honest, level-field relationship that you hammered out with Delany this morning, don't we?"

Allen shifted in his seat, then stood, removed his suit coat, folded it neatly, laid it across the table next to him, and sat back down. I could see he needed time to think, and I was willing to give it to him.

"There are some aspects of this case we can't divulge right now, Mike," he said with some noticeable embarrassment. "I'm on the spot here. I know that, and I hope you can appreciate it." Now it was his turn to pause. After five seconds of lip licking and another five seconds or so dedicated to biting his lower lip, he continued, "I did argue with Delany this morning about turning over a lot more to you, but he was dead-set against it. All I can tell you is that there are some things in the works that blend in with the stuff that Danny Martin was working on, and The Bureau doesn't think it's appropriate to release those things at this point in time."

I studied the man's face and hands for a moment and then began to speak slowly and deliberately so my words would sink in to his mind and his nerves.

"Okay," I said after lighting a fresh cigarette. "If you won't open up your information to me, I will at least keep my end of the bargain and open up my information to you. I'll caution you just as you cautioned me a few minutes ago, Bill."

"What do you mean by that?" he asked defensively.

"Just as you told me, I'm going to say some things you might not like, but I want you to hear me out. Okay? You may get riled. Isn't that word I think you used? But if you do get riled, don't get mad and don't interrupt me. I just want you to listen. Okay?"

"Okay," he agreed and cleared his throat once again and crossed his arms across his chest.

"I'm pretty set on the possibility that you killed Danny Martin, Bill," I said evenly and without emotion, as if I was stating a known fact. "Not Verno, not some hit man, but you!" Now I let the emotion begin to build.

My picnic table companion looked up at me and started to utter a sound, but I stopped him by putting my finger to my lips.

"I have reason, good reason I might add, to believe the mob was leaning on you for information and cooperation. They had you by the short hairs and they were hitting on you to give a heads up to them on what the FBI was up to. In fact, you and Eddy Cavaluso had a big, nasty argument about it one day inside Teddy Carr's joint." I let that sink in for a second or two and then cautioned him, "Don't even think about asking me how I know that. I just know it, and the important thing is that you know it too!"

Allen didn't interrupt and I could see in his eyes that his mind was racing in high gear. It was time to go for the throat.

I continued, "When you got handed the job of being Officer Martin's contact, you realized he had some very interesting information *on* you, not *for* you. Martin had already told your cohort, Agent Fenser, that he had seen some cop-looking dude arguing with Eddy Cavaluso. He described you to Fenser. When Fenser debriefed you, just before he got his ticket out of here to someplace decent, you knew that your undercover guy had some shit to lay on you! Danny knew you and the mob were playing footsie, and he was clamoring to get pulled off the assignment so he could get himself into the grand jury. Ah, but you put two and two together, and you damn well knew once he got behind those closed doors and began to testify that he was going to throw your name in the hopper. That made you nervous. You panicked. You killed him."

Bill Allen looked at me with hatred in his eyes and waited in silence to see if I was done. When he sensed that I was, he spoke.

"You're a sick, twisted man, Amato. What you just said is the dumbest, most full of crap, convoluted piece of thinking I ever heard." He continued to stare at me for a half a minute and then made his case. "Why on God's green earth would the mob be leaning on me? *I* don't borrow money from them! *I* don't sit down and have dinner with them! You and your rag-tag collection of Detectives do, but I sure as hell don't!"

"You're right. I do eat with them." I conceded. "But, you hit the sheets with their women. We don't, but you sure as hell do!"

"What? What is that suppose to mean?" Allen asked with a little snicker of his own. He was testing the waters and wanted to see if I was bluffing. I had made the bet and he had raised it. Now he wanted to see if I had the chips to stay in the game. I did, and he was going to be sorry he upped the ante.

"Does the name Gail Sampson ring any bells with you, Billy?" I asked with wide eyes.

Allen paused before he answered. It was a short, half-second pause, just long enough for him to flick his eyes off to the side, toward the kids, and back to me. "She was a snitch of mine. Why? How do you know her? What do you mean?"

"Why?" I repeated. "Because you were banging her. You asked me how I know her, well I don't know her, but I sure do know her friends. And, to answer your last question, what I mean is that you were up close and personal with the woman, Miss Sampson. She started out as your informant, but you started thinking with your other head, and pretty soon you were tapping her bones. Then, your buddies in The Bureau, back in sunny San Diego, found out about it. They didn't like the fact that one of their Agents was making the motel circuit with a mobster's broad. They also didn't want to ruin their careers by exposing it to the rest of The Bureau. That would have been admitting they had a problem in their office, and The Bureau doesn't like to have SACs who have problem employees. So, the best thing your boss could do to solve his problem and protect his ass was to ship your young butt to Rochester."

"Even if that's true, and I'm not saying that one word of it is true, what would lead you to believe that I would cooperate with the local Mafia here?"

"Oh," I said casually. "I don't know. Maybe good old Gail's boyfriend back in California thought he would do the mob here, and himself, a favor and tell them about you. Maybe the Rochester mob was very happy to get the news and they confronted you with it. Maybe, just maybe, they threatened to tell Washington about your sexual exploits. Maybe, and you need to follow me closely here, Billy, maybe they told you that you would either do them a good deed or they would do you a bad deed. Maybe they even talked about you in front of Danny and he knew what they knew. And, maybe when you realized your entire career was going down the tubes you figured you would do them, as well as yourself, a favor and take Danny out of the picture." Then, for frosting on the cake, I asked rhetorically, "What was it you said about a ruined reputation being motive enough to kill someone?"

"You're shooting in the dark, Amato. This conversation is over. Take me back to the office." Allen began to get up from the table.

"Sit down, you piece of shit," I said with a great deal of menace in my voice.

"Go to hell," he said. "You can talk all you want, but you don't have the tiniest piece of evidence to prove any of what you're alleging."

"I have the video the mob shot of you bed bouncing with the vivacious Miss Gail. And, much more important, I have a couple of notarized letters from Danny." I casually told the assortment of truth and lies as I folded my arms across my chest.

That stopped him.

"Do you want to see the letter now before I show you the video later?" I asked as I pulled a copy of the letter out of my notebook and threw it on the table. He didn't say no because he couldn't say no.

My eyes never left Agent Allen's face and body as he picked up the letter. His long fingers held it gingerly, as if it had come off of a hot stove. I watched with intense hatred as he opened the letter and began to scan it. Although he read the letter in silence and without moving, it was obvious he was weakening.

When he finished the letter and began to fold it, I asked, "So, why did you follow him to Buffalo, Bill?"

"I thought he was going to meet with the U.S. Attorney there," he said with noticeable resignation. "He had been threatening to do so. He was convinced all of the Federal agencies here in town were together in some big conspiracy, so he was talking about going to the main office in Buffalo or even New York City. I just wanted to see if he was going to do it."

"So, fearing that he had done just that, you made out the report about him supposedly saying that he had scored a big job in Buffalo. And, that not being good enough, you resorted to the old FBI stock in trade and made the innuendo about the warehouse and jewelry store heists in Buffalo that same weekend."

Allen didn't nod. He didn't speak.

"In one of the other two letters he gave to me, Danny gave his version of what he heard when you had your argument with Eddy Cavaluso." I paused long enough to see if he bought my bluff. He did, so I said, "Give me your version."

"Cavaluso was getting pressure from Ruggeri to turn me into an informant for them. You're right, the mob in San Diego told Ruggeri's people here about Gail and me. Consequently, Eddy was pressuring me. I told him to go to hell. When he threatened to turn me in to the Attorney General's Office in Washington I got scared, so I went to Delany and told him everything."

"And?"

"And Delany said not to worry about it. Hell, he was more upset with the San Diego office for not telling him about Gail and me than he was about the organized crime guys pressuring me. He said I should play along with them and make it look like I was helping them. From time to time I would give them some phony information like, tell them about wire taps and bugs where we didn't have any so that they would talk more openly at the places where we really did have the taps and bugs."

I couldn't figure out why Allen was giving up his information so easily. I decided to ask him. "So then, if Delany knows everything about you and the mob lady, and you don't have anything to worry about from him, why are you supposedly being so up front with me? Why is it that we're finally getting to the down and dirty honest to God truth?"

William Allen turned his head up from the table top he had been studying for the past few minutes, looked at me directly, and said, "Partially because I'm sick of it, Mike. I'm sick of all the running and lying and hoping nobody else finds out about Gail. But mostly, and I mean this one hundred percent, I don't want you thinking I killed your friend Danny. I mean, the man was taken out, shot in the back like a dog, had his chain and medal ripped off his neck, and it ... what's the word that can describe it? It hurts, and that's the only word I can think of. It hurts to hear you say that you think I did that. I know that sounds like just so much drivel, but it's true, Mike. It tears me apart to know you think I would do that."

I looked into the eyes of a broken man for the second time in this short day. I halfway believed him. I mean, I didn't want to believe him, but I did almost believe him. Maybe he had been living so many lies that he just lied a lot better than most people did. Maybe he was telling the truth. I had to push the issue.

"You're right, Bill. It does sound like a lot of baloney." I waited for that insult to hit home and then asked directly, right between the eyes, "Did you kill Danny?".

"No way, Mike. Absolutely not," he said emphatically but without emotion.

"Do you know who did?"

"The mob killed him," he said matter-of-factly as his head gave short, almost unnoticeable nods.

"Who in the mob?" I asked.

"I can't say, Mike. I gave my word I wouldn't say. It would mean my job if I told you. Please, don't push it. I can't tell you."

"But you do know who killed him?"

Allen nodded and almost whispered, "Yes, I do."

"If you can't, or *won't* tell me who did it, then tell me how you know for sure it was the mob that hit him."

"Just leave it alone for now, Mike. I can't go into it. I shouldn't even have told you what I just told you."

"You better tell me," I said through clenched teeth as I banged my fist on the table. "You feed me this company line about being open with me, then you throw me off on some wild goose chase about Al Verno, knowing full well it's just that, a diversion, a detour for me to take. You seem to know it's a mob guy that did Danny, but you want me to chase one of my own guys. Just tell me one thing, Bill. Where do you guys get your ethics? Do you bastards even have any ethics?"

Bill Allen got up from the table and started to walk over to where I had parked the car. I got up, took a giant step and grabbed him by the left elbow, spinning him around.

"How long is this deceit going to last, Bill?" I asked as I peered directly into his watery eyes.

"I don't know," he said down to his chest. Then, raising his head slightly but not his eyes, he added, "It might be another six months, maybe a year."

"Why did you mislead me with that cock and bull story about Al Verno?"

"I was told to," he answered. "I was supposed to buy the time The Bureau needs." This time, when Allen referred to his place of employment, there was no reverence in the words, "The Bureau".

I just smiled and shook my head. "Just like Hitler's guys, huh, Bill? You were just following orders, huh?"

We both sat down again at the picnic table as Bill Allen said, "The Bureau is afraid of you. They're afraid that you'll break this case. Even if you don't, they are very concerned that if we tell you what we know and how we know it, that it will blow an investigation we're doing. I was told to feed you Verno. It was wrong. I know it was wrong, but I did it."

"So that's it?"

"That's it," he said with a nod.

"You guys got the morals and integrity of a low-life snake," I said and then spat. "We got a dead cop that's going into the ground tomorrow and you people are worried about next month's publicity. You and your holy Bureau make me sick. You guys are worse than the mob ever thought about being."

My pretend partner did not bother to reply.

Special Agent William Allen got up and walked slowly toward the car, but I sat at the picnic table and lit another cigarette. Smoking, I tried to decide if I should or should not believe my number one suspect. The answer was, he came across as if he was telling the truth. The right moves, the correct amount of eye contact, and the appropriate inflections were all in the right places.

I just wasn't convinced that he was truthful. All the interrogation stuff aside, one thing, one new and really big thing, bugged me.

Where did Bill Allen get this little tidbit about Danny having his chain ripped off his neck? That would account for the scratch on the Martin's neck, but how did Allen know about it? I hadn't told him about the scratch on Danny's neck, and I sure as hell didn't show him the Medical Examiner's report. Was that part of the proceeds from the big fed investigation, or was it first-hand information that Allen had because he was the guy who killed Danny?

The trip back to the Federal Building was made in total silence. I wanted to ask him about the chain being ripped off Danny Martin's neck, but opted to put it off. I had to think about it first and get all my facts together before I popped that question. As Allen opened the car door to leave my world and get back to the safety of his, he said something about seeing me the next morning.

"Tomorrow's the funeral. I won't be in much of a mood for you or work."

"Okay," Bill Allen said, sounding somewhat resigned to the fact I didn't really care to be in his presence ever again.

"But do me a favor when you get in your hallowed halls. Tell Delany I knew about Verno, that I know about the smoke screen you guys tried to pull, and then tell him he can expect me to punch his fucking lights out the next time he tries to talk to me."

Not waiting for the door to close, I pulled away from the curb. My day to break this case was ending just the way it started. I was sitting there holding an empty bag! I had gone to bat twice and popped out both times. All I had done was possibly clear Verno as a suspect. Other than that, the day was amounting to a big, fat nothing, and I really wasn't looking forward to tonight when I would ask Kathy Martin if she killed her husband.

11

Friday Night: The Third Suspect

The Department's psychologist probably had a fancy medical name for how I felt about the funeral home where Danny was laid out. I hated the thought of going anywhere near the place, but I couldn't stay away. When I was there, I felt useless. When I was away from the dreary place, I felt it was important for me to be there ... as if my presence would make any difference to the living, or for that matter, the dead. My father would have said that it was my duty to be there. He would have labeled it "a matter of respect," and perhaps that was true. Maybe it was respect for Danny, a respect I had never given him in life that drew me to the sickening smell of flowers and the drone of voices.

On Friday night, as I drove in the parking lot of the mortuary, I told myself I had to go there. I had work to do. I had a question to ask Kathy ... in fact, several very important questions. The answers to the question were going to have far-reaching implications for me, for her, my career, the Police Department, the FBI, and especially for Special Agent William Allen. Her answers may clear him, only to implicate her.

A few hours earlier, before leaving the office, I had made a call to Dr. Carl Chandler, the forensic pathologist who had done the post-mortem on Danny Martin's body. Although I had seen the guy face-to-face, my mind enjoyed drawing a ghoulish, exaggerated caricature of his rather mundane features, which were accented by deep-set eyes. His deep, bored, dragging voice contributed greatly to my mental vision of a hunched-back, bulky guy in a white lab coat and a Bela Lugosi voice welcoming frightened visitors to his "la-BOR-a-tory".

It was late in the day when I made the call. The good doctor wanted to be home, sipping a Manhattan and playing with his wife, so he wasn't too happy with my call as he was about to beat feet out of the office shortly before five o'clock. Nor was he too happy about my many seemingly petty questions, as was evidenced by his often repeated, "Read my report, Lieutenant."

"I read your report, Doc," I said in a voice that hinted at my own frustration. "I read the report three times. What I need to know from you I need to know in plain, garden-variety English. So just cool your nine-to-five heels and talk to me as if you really don't want the County Exec knowing about the last two times you were stopped for playing Bounce-the-Curbs while a heavy odor of gin hung on your breath."

Now and then it came in handy to know many of the little secrets about the citizen dredges we cops deal with on a day-to-day basis. In this particular case, it came in very handy. Chandler — known to one and all as "Chiller Chandler" — being one who wanted to avoid any ill dealings with the County Manager, spent several minutes giving me the details I needed to know in the terms that I needed to know them.

"The narrow abrasion that I referred to in my report, was just above what lay people call the 'Adam's apple,'" he finally said in words I could understand.

"Could it have been caused from a wire, something that may have been used to try to choke him?" I asked.

"Not really, Lieutenant," he admonished my layman's question with a definite tone of exasperation. "This mark was caused by something being pulled up and away from his neck. Totally different from a ligature mark."

"How about if a jewelry chain was grabbed and, how do I put this correctly, if the chain was ripped off him?"

"That would do it," Chiller said. "I can't swear to it in court, but that would be consistent with the type of mark that was on the body."

Sensing that our business was out of the way, Chiller said, "I don't like being threatened, Lieutenant."

"And, I don't like being ignored, Doctor."

"Don't do it again," he said in a monotone that was supposed to be an angry warning.

"Drive sober," I responded. The two words hung on the telephone line for a few seconds before I added, "Thanks for helping me out, Doc." After all, there wasn't any reason to burn the entire bridge.

* * *

Armed with that information, I was able to go into the funeral home, seek out Kathy Martin, and escort her to a private room where we could talk with some measure of privacy.

"Did you get all of Danny's personal property back, Kathy?" I asked after we gave words and hugs of support to one another.

"Yes, Michael. The same day I went to see, to identify Danny's body. The coroner, medical examiner, whatever he's called, gave me everything in an envelope."

"Was everything there?"

"Mike, all that was there was his wallet, some money, about thirty or forty dollars, his watch, comb, hanky, and wedding ring," she then paused to search her memory. "That damn pinkie ring," she continued after a short pause, "and his little pocket-knife. Why?"

"Was anything missing, anything at all?"

"Like what?" Kathy asked as she pulled her head back slightly as if to study to me, to see if she could look into my eyes and find what it was I was asking of her.

I had to be careful with the next question. I didn't want it to come back to haunt me in some future months when I went to court to prosecute the killer. The question could not be leading in any way. It had to be asked as a multiple-choice question, without offering any hint of the word I was seeking. More important than court testimony, *I* had to know the information was good and was not the result of any hints I may unconsciously have offered.

"Anything like, oh, I don't know," I hesitated so Kathy would believe I was searching for information I didn't already suspect to be a fact. "Things like a bracelet, ring, necklace, a lucky charm, or something like that," I rattled off the list and prayed to hear her say the right word.

"No, nothing valuable," she said as she continued to look at me inquisitively, wondering why I was pursuing the line of questioning, and where I was going with the discussion.

I remained silent and allowed her to do a mental inventory of her husband's body, of his hands, his arms, wrists, face and neck, as she clicked off, "His wedding ring, watch, silly looking pinkie ring …" Then the light went on, and I could see it in her eyes and in her open mouth.

"Oh my God, Mike! Danny's Saint Christopher medal. His mother gave it to him when he went into the Marines. It wasn't with his things."

"Do you know if he was wearing it that night, the night he got, uh, got hurt?"

"Danny always wore it. His mother gave it to him. He never took it off. He used to say it got him through the Marines and it would get him through this, 'this journey,' as he put it."

"The medal would get him through what journey?" I asked for clarification.

"Saint Christopher is the Patron Saint of travelers, Mike. You know that! What he meant was that the medal would help protect him as he got through the assignment he was on. It was supposed to protect him, Michael. Saint Christopher was supposed to protect him," she said as if some promise, some contract, had been broken by the Saint.

I had my own suspicions about certain patron saints being derelict in their duties from time to time, such as whenever I called upon them for some little favor, a little nudge in the right direction on one investigation or another. Having been personally upset with Saint Michael, the Patron Saint of Police — not to mention *my* patrol saint — on more than one occasion, I just chalked up this instance as sustaining my suspicions that some of those saints were taking long lunch breaks when I went knocking on their doors. But that was not my concern on this particular night. My thoughts were on evidence and using that evidence to nail a killer, regardless of who that killer was or for whom he worked.

"How did he wear it, Kathy? Was it pinned on him? Did he carry it in his wallet? What?"

"On a chain, Mike," she said as if I was the dumbest person alive. "He wore it around his neck on a regular, simple, silver chain." While the next question was formulated in my mind, she asked one more, very salient question. "What happened to it, Mike?"

"We don't know, Kathy. We really don't know. My guess is that whoever hurt Danny also took the necklace and medal."

"Why would they do that? It wasn't valuable. It was just a medal with an ordinary chain."

There was no answer for her question, so I offered none. There was a moment's delay before the next question, the one that was burning a hole in my head, was asked. "Kathy, I need to ask you something else," I prepared her for the invasion I was to make.

"If it helps what you're doing, ask anything, Mike."

Based on her response and surprise at remembering the missing necklace and religious medal, I really didn't consider her to be high on the suspect list. However, it was a stone I had to turn. The question could not go unasked; nor would I allow it to go unanswered.

"This may be embarrassing for you to answer, but I really need to know." With that out of the way, I blurted, "Did Danny slap you around a couple of times? Did he bruise you a few times?"

Kathy Martin stood up and moved to the center of the small, private room in which we were meeting. She had her back to me as she said, "Once, Mike. Only once." I was going to ask why and when, but it seemed she needed to go it on her own, to deliver the information at her own pace.

"Danny was becoming a mental wreck over the past few months, Mike. He was nervous, edgy, and paranoid. He was concerned about where I was going, whom I was seeing, and what I was saying to people. He didn't want me seeing Phyllis, my own sister! Danny was so nervous, so edgy. It was scary, Mike. He kept the house locked whenever he was home. Whether it was day or night, the doors were locked and the blinds were drawn." She paused long enough to blow her nose into a crumpled tissue.

Turning to face me, Kathy took two small steps and sat down to my right. Once seated, she turned in the chair to ask me, "Who told you about this, Mike? Has Phyllis been talking to you?"

"We talk to everyone when we get a case like this, Kathy. We hit the neighbors, friends, relatives, and the clerk over at Wegman's Supermarket ... everyone. It isn't important who said it. What's important is whether or not it's true."

Her voice, her eyes, and her hand's grip implored me. "Don't think badly of him. Danny was a good man, a very devoted man. He was so wrung out over everything that was going on. I'm sure I don't know the half of it, but he was going through a lot." Again she stopped long enough to blow her nose into the abused tissue. "The weekend we went to Fredonia to see Chrisy, Danny was a basket case. I thought he was going to have a nervous breakdown. Once he got around Chrisy and her family, he finally calmed down, but on the way back to Rochester he tightened right up again. By the time we got to our house, I was begging him, even ordering him to quit the job. Finally I told him I was going to the Chief to demand that he take Danny off the case."

Kathy stood up again and turned her back to me. "That's when it happened. He just blew up. He slapped me across the face and told me to never, never interfere in his business. He told me that everyone was against him and he didn't need to have me turn against him along with everyone else. He slapped me, Mike. Once, just once. The instant he did it he was sorry. I could see it in his face." The young widow rubbed her nose with the shred of tissue, and then added, "He cried over it," she said finally and then sat down again.

"Were you going to leave him?" I asked brutally.

"Not really. I wanted to get away from him, to give him some space. I felt I was maybe part of the problem, that I was nagging him too much. I thought that if I gave him a time limit, like two or three months, and then left him alone, that he would finally be past this thing." Kathy Martin again turned to look me in the eyes. "I loved him, Mike. He was the center of my life. I loved him too much to ever leave him."

"Kathy," I said softly. "Look at me, honey. Look at me."

Her face turned to mine and I swallowed hard. Her eyes asked me why I needed, demanded, her attention. I answered the question on her face with a blunt question of my own.

"Did you love him so much that when he hit you he hit your heart? Did you love him so much that you had him done away with?"

It was the hardest question I had ever asked anyone. The look that it brought was the harshest look that I could ever imagine. Her eyes burned into my eyes, her breath drew deep and quick. Her words cut into my heart.

"You bastard, Mike Amato! You dirty bastard!"

I knew the answer to my question, but I had to hear her say it. I needed to hear the sounds, the way she said the sounds. She had the offensive and I could not permit her the upper hand.

"Did you, Kathy? Did you kill Danny ... or have him killed?"

Her answer came in the form of questions. "Do you have ice water in your veins, Mike Amato? Do you not trust anyone? Is everyone a killer to you? You dirty, rotten bastard! How could you even ask me that? How could you?"

"Did you kill him?" I repeated.

"NO! No I did not! I loved him. I loved that man! How could you? I loved ..."

I went to the woman I had just emotionally destroyed and hugged her close and tight as she squirmed to break my grip.

"I had to ask, Kathy. I'm so sorry, but I had to ask. I had to. I had to."

* * *

I left the funeral home feeling as exhausted and drained as Kathy had appeared. In my movements I was walking away from the place, going calmly to my car. In my mind, I was fleeing from it and all that it held. The distance between that horrible place and my car grew rapidly as I drove towards the expressway and accelerated down the on-ramp. I had plenty of time to make the meeting with Cavaluso, so time was not the problem. Distance was the problem. The only thing wrong was that there just wasn't enough distance to put between that horrible place and me.

The Friday night crowd remaining at the Robe and Gavel gave me some comfort as I downed a couple of Genesee Cream Ales, a local brew called "Jenny" by Upstate New Yorkers. Looking at the faces and listening for bits and pieces of inane conversation did a fairly adequate job of occupying my brain cells and kept me from dealing with the information I would have to deal with sooner or later.

I guess I was in one of the foul moods that Diane often complained about while we were still married. I knew I was furious inside and could feel the heat of anger welling in the pit of my stomach. I looked in the mirror behind the bar, and scanned it, searching for a friendly face, someone from whom I could draw comfort. The truth is, I was looking for Diane's face in the crowd.

Instead of finding solace in the faces, I found hatred for the people sitting in the bar, celebrating the last workday of the week. I resented them not mourning the loss of my friend. Also, I was angry with myself.

Carl Herzog, an Assistant District Attorney, said hello as he stood beside me and tried to grab the bartender's attention.

"I hear you're working with the Feds," he said in a thick tongue.

"It's a dirty and thankless job, Carl, but somebody's got to do it, and well, I took the oath," I said sardonically.

"Personally, I don't see what the big mystery is all about," the ADA commented. I instantly knew I was going to get an opinion I didn't solicit, didn't want, and didn't value. "It's a mob thing, pure and simple. You wops always had a thing for killing each other. Write it up as 'unsolvable' and forget about it, Mike. That's what you do with it. File it and forget it!"

"Thanks, Carl," I said, as I looked down at the chubby, bald little German. "And, by the way, remember us wops do it face to face with people who can defend themselves. We don't throw them in ovens like you krauts."

"Whoa! Well, excuse me," the roly-poly lawyer said as he threw up his hands. "It sounds to me like you would just love to pick a fight with someone."

"You're right, Carl. Dead right! I would love to have a fight right now, Carl. I would enjoy every minute, every second of pounding the living stuffing out of some human garbage. Now then, you fit the latter part of that description but not the first part, so why don't you just get away from me and crawl back under the rock you came from."

I knew the beautiful moment Herzog and I were sharing would have to be apologized for at some future time, but I really didn't care. With everything else going on, I really didn't need his line of crap. Deciding it was better that I left the company of humans, I picked up my beer and walked out to the parking lot.

In the cool, late summer night air, my thoughts went to the job that was ahead of me, the job that had to be done. In a half-hour I would be meeting with Eddy Cavaluso to clear up some odds and ends on the case. Then, tomorrow morning, I would attend Danny Martin's funeral and watch his body and his future lowered into the ground.

After the funeral I would deal with Bill Allen and all his lies. With the exception of Kathy Martin, Special Agent Allen was the only person who knew that Danny's chain and religious medal had been ripped away from his throat. Depending on what he told me I just might end up with enough to legally arrest Allen. If he didn't cough up enough information to give me a legal bust, I would still arrest him and let the news media deal with him. Either way, the fair-haired, farm boy Fed would pay for what he did to Danny. Maybe I would even get lucky and the suit-and-tie pseudo cop would resist me and then I could bust his face! My anger was directed at myself as well as at the Fed. I couldn't believe I was gullible enough to have halfway believed him.

* * *

Our local baseball team, the Red Wings, was on a road trip, so the parking ramp across from Frontier Field was virtually empty when I pulled into it, checked out the seven floors, and pulled into a stall on the fifth level. The sun had already set behind the suburban bedroom communities of Gates, Chili, and Churchville. People there would be sitting in their back yards and sipping iced tea as I smoked a cigarette in the dark high-rise parking garage in the center of Rochester and awaited the arrival of Fast Eddy Cavaluso. While waiting, a smile crept across my lips. This had been the very spot in which I stood many months ago as I met with Eddy Cavaluso and watched the suspicious pickup truck across the street in Kodak's parking lot. At the time, the mysterious truck had caused me a great deal of concern. Now that I knew who was in the truck and why it had been there, the memory of the truck only made me smile. It was surprising how comforting a little knowledge could be.

When I unconsciously looked down to the street, the sensation of falling hit me instantly. Damning my vertigo, I quickly shifted my eyes up and out to the west, at the dark form of the baseball stadium. The ballpark fitted nicely into the city's framework. Although it was less than a decade old, it was made to look like one of those old-time ball fields, like Wrigley Stadium or Ebbets Field. The place had a brick front and a cobblestone walkway leading up to the main gate. My thoughts were on the baseball field and the games I had seen there, when I suddenly heard a car coming up the ramp. I stepped back into the shadows to wait.

Eddy's Lincoln rolled by me and I had to smile when I saw Max standing on the mobster's lap, leaning out of the driver's window, the white fur along his face blowing in the breeze and his tongue lapping the air. Cavaluso parked the car and got out slowly, followed by his best friend. I was impressed with the way in which Max had patiently waited for the old man to rotate his legs out of the car, get a firm grip on the doorframe, and finally pull himself out of the car. Only then, after his master was safely out of the way, did the dog make the leap from the car seat to the pavement.

I shook hands with the man, and commented on the strength in his old large hands. He passed the compliment off with a wave of his hand, and his hallmark comment, "Forget about it!"

"Sorry about that slip at the restaurant, Eddy," I said right away, as we finished our greetings and I gestured to the dog with my left hand.

Characteristically, he said with a shrug, "You covered it okay, I guess. It rattled me for a second, but I don't think none of them caught on to us."

I saw something different in Eddy that I had not seen before. He looked drained, haggard, like someone had let the air out of him.

"You okay?" I asked.

"I'm old and worn out, filled with arthritis, and all alone, Mike." His eyes were on the dog as he spoke. They shifted to me for a fleeing instant and then went back to rest on the dog. "Forget about it."

I decided to let the matter drop, and moved to the reason I had asked for the meeting.

"There are some things I need to clear up with you, Eddy."

"Like what?" he asked as he turned his back to me and looked out of the ramp garage, over the street below us.

"Well, for one thing, when I talked to you the last time up on Cobbs Hill, I had no idea that the kid was a cop. I want you to know that. I wasn't feeding you a line. I really didn't know."

"I believe you, Mike. The papers said he was working undercover for the past five, six years." He turned to face the street and rested his elbows on the ledge.

With that out of the way, I moved on to the next item on the agenda. "Where did you get the information about Martin screwing around with the stripper, Dee Dee Wilcox?"

"What do ya mean?" he asked as he turned around part way and looked at me over his right shoulder.

"I mean it was bogus information, Eddy. Whoever gave you that information was lying."

"It was common knowledge, Mike. I don't know who I got it from. Around, that's all. The information was just around."

There was a word our polygraph examiner used to describe a guy who gave up, a person who just didn't care about what happened. The word bounced into my mind as I stood there looking at my long-time acquaintance, trying to figure out what was going on in his head. Parasympathetic was the word. Now, looking at Eddy, I finally understood the condition the word was intended to describe. Eddy was parasympathetic. This was a guy who just didn't care anymore.

"I got one more thing I need to ask you about, Eddy," I mentioned, hoping I sounded casual.

"And, that is?" he asked as he turned to face me again.

I crouched down like a catcher behind home plate and scratched the Westie's ears. It was important to me that Eddy was not intimidated by my next question, so I tried to convey a casual manner to him by showing attention and affection to the one thing about which he still cared.

"Back about six months ago, you had an argument with a Fed, an agent by the name of Bill Allen."

"I mess with all of them," Eddy said with a hint of a grin. "Refresh me on the circumstances."

"You were in Teddy Carr's joint and you were seen getting nose-to-nose with this Allen guy. The way I hear it, you were pretty hot." I stroked the dogs head and ran my fingers under his chin as I asked, "What was all that about?"

"The guy's a jerk, Mike. It could have been about anything."

Eddy needed a little prodding on this point, so I decided to pull out all the stops. "Did it have anything to do with Gail Sampson?"

Cavaluso smiled at me and asked, "Yous guys know about her?"

"*I* know about her," was my response, so as to let him understand it was my piece of information and not the Department's. "There ain't much that goes on around here that I don't hear about in one way or another."

"I'll say this about you, kid, you sure do your job. Forget about it! You do your homework, Mike." He shook his head and added, "You would've made a good living if you was a crook." The old man nodded to himself as he smiled.

"So tell me about it, if you can."

"We asked the guy for a little favor. Nothing special, just a little something and he tried to get in my face about it. He was telling me that I was running a scam on him by accusing him of fooling around, so I dropped the broad's name on him, you know, just to let him know I wasn't giving him no con."

"That was it?" I asked as if the information was of no consequence.

"If that's the instance you're talking about, that was it," he confirmed as he turned to look out over the street once again.

"Did he buckle under?" I asked, knowing I was getting to the outer edge of our agreed upon relationship.

"That's not up for discussion, Mike," Eddy said in a gentle way.

I joined him at the railing of the garage, careful not to look down, so that my vertigo wouldn't kick in. Lighting a cigarette, I looked out at the street, the parking lot across the street, the Kodak office building, and the stadium, to see if I could determine what he was looking at. I saw nothing.

Eddy drew in a deep breath, exhaled it, and said, "The last time we was up here, we got spotted by someone. Remember?"

"Yeah," I admitted. "Did you ever find out who it was?" I asked of him before he could ask me.

"How would I find out?" he asked with some tone of hostility. Then he turned to face me once again and asked, "You interrogating me all of sudden, Mike?"

The inquiry sounded like a simple enough question, but there was an accusation hidden in it somewhere, somehow.

I made a quick decision to stay on the offensive and fired back, "What do you mean by that?" As I asked the question, my eyes caught sight of Max doing a fine job of vacuuming the garage floor with his hyperactive nose.

Eddy's face softened and again the word "parasympathetic" popped into my head. For a second or two there had been life in those eyes as we exchanged challenges. But the life had gone out again, and there was nothing.

"Max has gotta go," he said casually. "Let's walk a bit."

We walked to the south side of the ramp garage, and I'll be darned if the dog didn't walk but ten, maybe fifteen feet, before he squatted his butt down and began to push out a couple of logs. It was difficult to believe stools that big come from a dog that small. Eddy had evidently become well acquainted with the toilet habits of his little companion.

"Don't watch him," Eddy said with a deadpan face. "He gets embarrassed if you watch him do his duty."

I had to laugh at this big, rough and tumble Mafioso using the term "do his duty." It was said that Eddy had whacked a half-dozen or so guys in his lifetime. One word from him could cost a man his health. A nod of his head could result in a gambler being shut off from ever again gambling in or around Rochester. Another nod could get an advance of five or six grand for another gambler. He was a powerful man, so his concern over the potential embarrassment of his pet seemed all the more incongruent.

"I'm serious!" Eddy said to my laughter. "He can't finish going if you watch him!"

I looked out at the city and stifled my laughter as the mobster and the cop waited for the mutt to relieve himself. I knew this would make a great war story at the next cop party, but I could never tell anyone about the meeting. Besides, who would believe it?

There was another question I had to ask, but I couldn't just blurt it out. It had to flow naturally, as if it was part of our conversation. As Eddy and Max turned toward me, I let a little

smile show on my mug as I tossed the subject into our clandestine meeting.

"By the way, Eddy, what was the deal with you and Ruggeri
last night?"

"What do ya mean?" he asked as he watched Max's busy nose
investigate the lower edges of my pant legs.

"I kind of thought he and I would meet alone, you know, in
private. I was surprised to see you stay."

"We was talking business," Eddy responded with a shrug.
"When you got there I got up to leave, but he told me to stay
put. Why you asking?"

"I don't know. It's no big thing. It just kind of looked strange,
like maybe you and him were at odds about something."

Eddy blew out a long, slow breath before he answered. "Truth
is, Mike, I told him not to meet with you. Forget about it. I was
telling him that if you and him met and he asked you to have the
cops back off, that you would just put on more heat."

I shrugged back and muttered a noncommittal, "Oh."

"He told me you would listen to reason, and I told him all
yous cops was alike and you liked throwing heat our way."

The explanation put my mind at ease. I was glad I had asked
the question. I didn't know if Eddy was being totally honest with
me, but the explanation made sense.

Eddy closed the matter with his usual, "Forget about it!"

We were walking back toward our cars when the mood shifted
with Eddy saying softly, "Mike, let this one go. Don't push it."

I knew what I heard, I just didn't know if I understood it.
"What do you mean, 'Let it go'?"

"This Martin caper. I would appreciate it, you know, consider
it a favor, if you let it go."

I wanted to ask fifty, a hundred new questions about the
remark, but instead I said, "I can't, Eddy. I owe it to the kid.
Besides, it's my job. I can't turn my back on it."

"I understand." The old man exhaled the words more so than
speaking them.

"Why are you asking me to step away from it, Eddy?" I asked as I put my right hand on his left forearm and stopped him in his footsteps. "Was Ruggeri playing with me when he told me it wasn't a mob hit?"

"No, I don't think so," he answered. "Forget I mentioned it." The man they called Fast Eddy turned to face me and said gently, as a father would say to his son, "Do your job, Mike. Do what's right. Do what you have to do."

I watched the man and his dog get in the car and waved to both of them as they pulled away. Alone in the garage I wondered why the mob, at least the mob in the form of Edward Cavaluso, wanted me to drop this case.

The prudent thing I should have done was go home, get a full night's sleep, and rest up for the next day. But the cop car refused to wander north to my place, and instead it roamed west toward the home of Kathy Martin. My conscious thought was that I would drive by and see if the house was dark, and in doing so, would be assured that Kathy and Phyllis were getting a good night's sleep. My covert subconscious was hoping the lights would be on and in the house I would find the company I needed.

The car slowed as it neared the home and was about to accelerate when it noted the absence of light from the windows of the residence. However, when I saw the figure seated on the front steps of the house, the car slowed to a stop.

"Michael?" Phyllis asked from her perch on the front steps.

The car stopped and I got out. Nearing the front of the house, I asked, "What are you doing up? I was checking to make sure everything was okay … to see if everyone was sleeping."

"I couldn't sleep," she almost apologized. Then standing, she asked, "Do you feel like walking?"

Without an answer of any sort on my part, she moved toward me, took my hand, and began to walk away from the house. We passed a few homes in silence before Phyllis commented on how much she missed the simple pleasure of a walk around the neighborhood on a warm summer night.

"Kathy told me about what you asked her tonight," Phyllis commented as she watched her feet take steps.

"It was a bad scene, but I had to do it. It had to be asked," I offered in a manner of apologizing.

"I understand you have to be hard and cold to do what you do, Mike. But damn, that was cold!"

I hoped that silence would settle the matter for her, and feared that anything I did say would ruin the walk.

Finally, I broke the silence, and changed the subject. "I was thinking, it's kind of strange that none of us ever had any kids," my voice said almost in a whisper. "It's as if we all decided, for whatever reason, not to have any children."

"Oh, I don't know," Phyllis responded. "Chrisy has two kids. And I know Kathy would have loved to have at least two, maybe three of her own."

"Why didn't she and Danny have any kids?"

"Danny always wanted to wait until things were, as he put it, 'more stable'." There was a four- or five-step period of silence before she added, "I was always glad they didn't have any kids, but that was before I knew the situation."

I slipped my hand from hers, pulled the pack of cigarettes from my shirt pocket, and withdrew one. When the pack was extended to Phyllis she waved it off. After lighting the smoke, I exhaled into the night air, and casually slipped my left arm around her waist.

"Tell me about you," I prompted.

"Tell you what?"

"What do you do for a living? Why don't you have any kids of your own? What do you do for fun and relaxation? What music do you like?"

"Why do you want to know? Am I auditioning for something?" she asked in a teasing manner.

There was another moment of silence, but it wasn't long enough for my head to edit my mouth. "I think I'm falling ..."

"Don't say it, Mike," Phyllis said as an advisement more than an admonishment. It was said the way one would say, "Be careful." It wasn't an order. It was more of a caution. After a few more steps in silence, she added, "I know how you feel ... I feel it too. But let's wait until this is all over with, and then we'll see where our emotions lie."

As we continued our walk in silence, my head was doing a good job of chewing out my mouth for its lapse in judgment. My sentiments may have been well placed, but the timing sucked!

I dropped my arm from Phyllis' waist, but she reached down and put it back where it had been. After offering me a brief smile, she spoke.

"I got married when I was 20. He was a nice Italian boy, a good Catholic and all that crap. The problem was he drank too much and his hands struck too hard. After a couple of beatings I began to devalue myself, and actually believed I deserved being slapped around. That went on for a while, but for some reason or another, I got past it. I finally figured out he was the asshole, and I wasn't. One cold night, after he had beaten me pretty good and then passed out on the couch, I left him. I got myself some help, got my head screwed on straight, and took advantage of some educational programs that were around for battered and unemployed women."

Phyllis stopped long enough to say she would take the cigarette I had offered. I took two of them from the pack, lit them both, and handed one to her. After we both took a long drag on the instruments of death, she continued.

"After I left the jerk, I waited tables. It didn't take me long to learn that a woman could make a whole lot more money and lift a lot less weight if she was serving drinks. I put myself through

Monroe Community College by tending bar. After I got my degree, I went …"

"Got your degree in what?" I interrupted.

"In computer science," she answered. "After I got the degree I went to work at a place doing computer programming for telecommunications. It's a nice job, and I don't kill myself." There was a pause as she took a drag on the cigarette. "But on most weekends I still tend bar."

"Why?" I asked. Then added, "Where?"

"Where? At a place in the Town of Webster called Skelly's. It's a nice joint that attracts a mixed crowd of middle aged people, some Xerox workers, some professional people, and a few, shall we say, interesting people. The music is great. It's jazz, mostly, with a little blues tossed in."

"Why?" I repeated, more out of wanting to hear her talk more and wanting the walk to last, than out of true curiosity.

"The money's good, and, bottom line, it's fun. I enjoy it."

We had made it all the way around the block and were nearing our point of origin. Phyllis stopped and turned toward me. She didn't say anything, and neither did I. Our voices were silent, but our eyes spoke. Slowly, with plenty of time for either one of us to change their mind, our faces moved toward each other and we kissed.

When our lips parted, she said, "We shouldn't have done that."

I said, "Bullshit!"

* * *

Back in the car and heading toward the apartment, my thoughts skipped back and forth between the sweet sensations of the night, and the frustration of the day. It wasn't until I was standing on the balcony of my apartment, with a Southern Comfort in one hand and a cigarette in the other, that I finally was able to focus on the events of the day.

That morning, Skip Winston had made it clear to me that he wanted nothing to do with the case. Bill Allen had told me in the afternoon to, 'Just leave it alone.' And, Eddy Cavaluso had just asked me to, 'Let it go.' What the heck was going on with this case? Why were the mob and the FBI wanting me to drop the case? It wasn't making any sense to me. Nothing in this case made any sense to me, and that was beginning to piss me off big-time!

Was the FBI in cahoots with the mob on this killing? Was Winston in on the deal also? Besides not having the balls to deal with it, why did my Major want me to bury a piece of evidence?

The case had handed me an assortment of suspects. I felt that two of them — Kathy Martin and Al Verno — had been cleared. I felt sure that Kathy lacked the motive, opportunity, and ability to kill her husband. Al Verno also lacked the motive. He never even knew Danny Martin existed, so why kill him? That left me with two suspects: the mob and Bill Allen. After my meeting with Eddy Cavaluso, I felt better about Vincent Ruggeri's assurance that Danny Martin's killing had not been an authorized hit. That left Bill Allen as number one on my hit parade, and in the second slot, any one of a hundred different renegade Mafia goons who may very well have acted on their own, without the permission, knowledge, and blessing of the Old Man, Vincent Ruggeri.

It would take a few days for me to determine that maybe I should have listened to the Feds and the mobsters. Maybe some things are better left unsolved. Maybe it was good to just let go every now and then. I would come to know that in a few days. However, right then, at that moment, as I stood there, flicking my last cigarette of the day into the night, I had no way of knowing that ignorance is sometimes truly bliss.

Chameleons, being as they are, were getting more and more difficult to see. As for the ones I could still see, well, they would soon begin to change their colors.

12

Saturday Morning: Saying Goodbye

Officer Daniel Albert Martin, while alive, never knew the comfort of his brother and sister officers. However, on a very warm Saturday in August, three hundred and fifty police cars, filled with over seven hundred cops, followed him to his grave. They came from Rochester and all of its suburbs, from all of the state's bigger cities like Albany, Syracuse, Buffalo and, of course, New York City. Most of the state's smaller towns, such as Brockport, Lockport, Middletown, Jamestown, and Lavonia where represented, and because of Chrisy's connection, even tiny Fredonia and it's neighboring city of Dunkirk were represented. Toronto, Canada, just fifty miles across Lake Ontario from our city, sent an honor guard of six officers. The New York State Police sent an impressive twenty-man and woman group standing tall in their gray uniforms and Stetson hats. The Secret Service, Immigration and Naturalization, Drug Enforcement Administration, Alcohol Tobacco and Firearms, Customs, and my friends at the FBI all sent their top brass to see Danny off.

But Danny knew none of them, and almost none of them had known him.

The long procession wound its way from the funeral home, through the city, and past the flags at half-staff in front of the Public Safety Building, to show Officer Martin the outside of a building in which he had never set foot. We headed north on Plymouth Avenue and then west on the expressway toward the suburban town of Gates, New York. The parade of police cars that silently transported the revolving and flashing red lights above them, stretched out well over a mile. When the hearse and family cars turned into the parking of Saint Theodore's Church, the tail end of the long procession was still on the expressway.

People stopped what they were doing. Some shoppers leaving Wegman's Supermarket waved handkerchiefs at the seemingly endless line of cop cars. As each squad car turned into the driveway leading to the church, the driver turned off the flashing lights and guided the car into a parking spot. When the parking lot was filled, cop cars lined both sides of the streets, and when both sides of the street became filled, the drivers of the last twenty or so cars parked their vehicles right down the middle of Lyell-Spencerport Road.

The elderly residents of Dunn Towers, which was situated behind the church, waved timidly at the cops who were walking quickly to the emerging formation. Some of the senior citizens made the sign of the cross; others blew kisses from their finger-tips to the uniformed men and women below them.

It took a good five minutes to arrange all the cops in columns on both sides of the entrance to the church. Once they were in place, Sergeant Donald Banion's husky voice filled the parking lot from the black tar pavement up to the breaking morning clouds with the order, "Ahhhh-tennnn-hutt!" In response to his command, well over fourteen hundred heels clicked. With the bark of, "Pre-zennnt... harms!" more than seven hundred right arms raised and bent at the elbows, allowing the tips of their fingers to touch the brims of their hats.

The cops held their statue-like poses as more than a few civilian men and women pressed handkerchiefs to the corners of their eyes, or wiped them under their noses. A dozen or so civilian cars occupied by the inquisitive stopped and double-parked next to the cop cars along the roadway in front of the church.

Finally, Danny was getting a sign of respect, official, military-type respect, from a bunch of quasi-military men and women who feared that someday his fate would be theirs. Because the family was entitled to the same respect as the officer, we held the salute until the family and the casket entered the church. They, too, had earned and deserved our respect, for they also had served and suffered.

The Catholic Mass was a blur to me and I remember little of it. Frank Donovan genuflected in the aisle and then stepped aside and ushered Al Verno, Bobby St. John, and Jimmy Paskell into the pew. Only then did he slip in beside them. The seat along the aisle was left for me.

On the other side of the aisle, just two rows in front of me, were a half-dozen Special agents from the Rochester FBI office. Ed Delaney nodded in my direction, and shortly after, Bill Allen turned, offered a thin smile coupled with a nod, and then turned back. I couldn't control the feeling that the son-of-a-bitch was laughing at me. A deep breath calmed my queasy stomach, and my eyes focused on the front of the church.

Danny's brother, Anthony Martin, gave the eulogy and did a fine job of tracing the young cop's life from Troop Street to this suburban church where he and his family worshipped. The priest called on the saints in heaven to welcome the soul of the fallen parishioner into eternal happiness. I asked — maybe told — Saint Christopher to get off his dead butt and be there for the welcoming. If he wasn't doing his job when Danny was alive, then I thought he better start doing it now that the kid was there with him.

It was almost an hour later when we left the church and headed north to Holy Sepulcher Cemetery on the city's far north side. The motorcycle cops — there were over forty of them from twelve different departments — roared past the motor-cade, blocked off the next four or five cross-streets, waited for most of the cars to pass, and then roared passed us again. The leapfrogging continued all the way to the cemetery, leaving one heck of a traffic jam of Saturday morning shoppers behind us.

The citizens seemed more awed by the spectacle we created than angered over being delayed. A few of them wiped tiny tissues and handkerchiefs under their eyes as the eternity of flashing and revolving red lights passed by. We all suspected that one or two members of the crowd would write a letter — and the assholes did — to the newspaper in the morning complaining about the traffic tie up and wondering why the crime rate was so high if there were that many officers available for a funeral. The letters would just confirm our suspicion that eighty percent of the population consisted of fairly decent people, ten percent really didn't care one way or the other about anything, and the remaining ten percent were too classically stupid to matter to the rest of us.

Once at the cemetery, the cops were again assembled into neat, straight columns and rows. Then we waited for the family members to leave their cars and make their way over the lawn and assume their seats in front of the open grave.

Again Banion's voiced boomed out to fill every corner of the sad place, and once again heels clicked and hands saluted.

Then began the strange ritual those of us in the "civilized" world put ourselves through at our saddest of times. We gathered to witness a loved one lowered into the ground and be covered with cool, dark earth. I had sometimes wondered why we did this to ourselves, why we put ourselves through the agony of watching such a dreadful event.

The priest said his words of good-bye to the poor soul and provided a second reminder for the saints to be assembled at the gates of heaven and salute Danny's arrival. And, once again, I reminded Chris the Saint that he had better be there when it happened or I would personally kick his saintly ass if I ever got to the place, an accomplishment I did not really anticipate happening. My peripheral vision caught a glimpse of a detach-

ment of Marine Corps Reserves beginning to move, and my
stomach began to churn. My heart knew the worse was still to
come.

Silence — for a lonely minute — fell over the area like a
comfortable blanket.

Then it began.

The commands rolled out of Don Banion slightly lower this
time than before.

"Ready! Aim! Fire!"

The volley rang through the quiet, peaceful place. Kids
jumped. Women cried.

"Ready! Aim! Fire!"

A second thunder of gunfire cracked and echoed and the kids
held their ears.

"Ready! Aim! Fire!"

The third volley of shots sent shivers through most of us
because we knew what followed the 21-gun salute.

Taps.

A lone bugler somewhere behind us, hidden over a small
knoll, pushed a trumpet to his lips and blew the sad, long notes
that wailed mercilessly through the curved tubes of the
instrument, out into the summer air, and into our souls and
hearts.

The children looked around to see where the music originated.

Women sobbed openly.

Men sniffed their noses and blinked their eyes to halt the tears,
but their blinking and sniffing only slightly delayed the
inevitable.

Embarrassed by my emotions, I led the chorus of sniffles as a
very impressive squad of young coppers from the Tactical Unit
gathered at the four corners of the casket, gripped the flag that
draped it, and snapped it taunt. Methodically, the flag was folded
until it formed a neat triangle with only thirteen crisp white stars
showing on a field of blue. The flag was marched slowly to
Matthew Murphy, who in turn presented it to the widow.

The crowd now made their way back to the cars that lined several roads of the cemetery. I stayed behind long enough to watch Danny Martin the little kid, Dan Martin the Mob Wanna-be, Officer Dan Martin, my brother police officer, be lowered into his grave. I then turned and walked across the green grass to return to my car and await the arrival of my driver of the day, Detective Frank Donovan.

In the car I wept openly, without control, hoping that somehow Danny would find comfort in the old, faded and chewed plastic whistle that rested in the coffin where I had tucked it, next to his right hand.

The street in front of Kathy Martin's home, along with all the streets within two blocks, were filled with a wild assortment of blue, white, black, and green police cars. Inside, the solemn after-funeral wake was in progress. The cops mixed with the civilian members of Danny's family and friends, as platters piled high with food of all tastes and descriptions were devoured, and beverages of many tastes were poured from bottles of all shape, sizes, and colors.

A conservative guess was that the spread had set the union back fifteen hundred, maybe two grand. However, unlike the politicians who were only too glad to take advantage of the photo opportunity the funeral had presented, the president of the union stood in the background commenting about the wonderful feast the family had prepared.

Small groups of cops gathered on the lawn in front, alongside, and behind the house. Each one of the groups became engaged in its particular war story from the streets. Occasionally a small round of laughter emerged from one of the groups as a joke was shared. I found myself tightening up before reminding myself that people there needed laughter to take their minds off the sad day when the same groups would possibly be gathered in and around their own back yard.

Dick Grassler, the president of our union, made eye contact with me and in that second he signaled me to follow him to a quiet corner of the backyard. I excused myself from the group of Buffalo, New York cops with whom I had been conversing, grabbed a beer, and walked casually to the meeting spot.

Grassler's official position within the Rochester Police Department was that of an Investigator. In spite of that somewhat minor rank, as president of the union, he commanded a great deal of fear and apprehension among the city's officials. A man in his mid-30s, of average height and build, Dick had a manner about him that dictated a feeling of calm blended with awesome power. His words could spark a lengthy and expensive legal battle for the city, and his handshake could end one. The man wielded his power carefully and humbly, and consequently he was granted a great deal of respect.

Not being one to waste words or time, Grassler got to the meat of the subject as soon as we shook hands and I thanked him for the fine spread the union had provided.

He shrugged off my words of thanks and said, "I don't know where you are with your investigation, Ace, but the city is trying to screw over the family."

"How so?" I asked with more than average concern.

"I was checking on his benefits for the family, and the city is taking the position that he was killed off-duty and is therefore not entitled to any line-of-duty benefits."

"How the hell did they reach that conclusion?" was my question.

"Quite easily," he answered as he accepted the cigarette I held out for him. "Brother Martin," he said, referring to Danny in the traditional union manner, "was carried on the books under a cover name and position, and because everyone has to be somewhere, for convenience sake, he was carried as working on the day shift. Therefore, as the assholes in City Hall figure it, he was off-duty at the time of his death."

"Don't they realize …?" I began to ask before he held up a hand to silence me.

"I made the arguments, told them he was undercover, that he didn't have normal duty hours, that he worked all kinds of split shifts and hours, and so forth. As you know, our leaders don't use a lot of common sense, so they're going to fight it." He took a drag on the cigarette and added, "Of course, with one call to the right reporter, I'll have them seeing it our way. However, I don't really want to drag the press into this one at this time."

I didn't ask why the media was not a viable option but Grassler knew it was going to be my next question. "There's reasons," he said. "I can't go into them, but take my word for it. So what I'm saying is this, I hope the investigation turns up something to establish that Brother Martin was carrying out his police duties at the time of his death." He then closed the conversation with, "Enough said?" and walked away.

Yes, enough had been said. Several people wanted me out of the investigation, others wanted me to drop the investigation, and now the union wanted me to insure it came out a certain way. I drifted through the crowd of people in an effort to look for Phyllis, and in doing so, also noted that none of the Feds had bothered to show up at Danny's house. Maybe they didn't feel welcome. Maybe they took the hint!

One of Danny's uncles engaged me in conversation and saw to it I was introduced to an assortment of cousins, aunts, and other uncles. As I shook hands or embraced each of the relatives, I had the opportunity to make eye contact with Phyllis a couple of times. Each time we exchanged smiles, I could swear she winked at me.

It took a few minutes before the two of us managed to get off to a quiet spot.

"You're a handsome man, Mike Amato," she said in an obvious attempt to flirt. She then ruined it by saying, "But you really piss me off!"

Trying to be cool about her statement, I commented, "Not many women would say the first thing you mentioned, but almost all of them have said the latter. However, why is it that I piss you off?"

"Last night, at the funeral home, did you ask Kathy about Danny beating her?"

"Yes. I had to, Phyllis. It had to be done."

She took a few seconds to think about what I had said, and then, with an expression that told of some of her personal shame, she said quietly, "She knows I told you. She ... she's very angry at me for telling you."

"And highly pissed at me for asking her if she hurt Danny."

"She'll get over being pissed at you. She knows you were only doing her job. As for me ... I don't know."

"She'll get past it. She'll realize you were only trying to protect her."

"Did you really consider her to be a suspect, Mike?"

"No, not really," I lied. Then I truthfully added, "This isn't a family thing. Families don't kill this way."

Phyllis went up on tiptoe, leaned forward, wrapped her right arm behind my neck, and kissed me full on the lips and then disappeared into the crowd.

The brief conversation left me a little confused. On the surface it appeared that she was greatly relieved her sister was not a suspect. Below the surface, if I hadn't have known better, it appeared that in some way she was relieved that *she* wasn't a suspect.

It was almost two o'clock in the afternoon before I was finally able to find Kathy. There were things that needed to be said to her; apologies to be made. The crowd was beginning to thin out, and the small woman appeared to be exhausted. Taking her hand in mine, I whispered an apology to her and asked for forgiveness. She nodded and told me how I had hurt her, but in the same breath acknowledged she knew I had to ask her the question.

"It hurt me to have that question asked of me, Mike," she said in a quiet, simple admonishment.

"It hurt to have to ask it," I offered back as a lame excuse.

Our conversation drifted to other times, better times. As we talked about the old neighbors, Chrisy came over and introduced me to Danny's brother, Anthony. I shook the man's hand and passed along my sympathy over his loss, along with compliments on his eulogy. Then, turning to Kathy, I told her I would try to get the remaining cops to begin to move out and leave her in peace.

"No, Mike! Let them stay," she scolded in a friendly way. "Don't do that. They can stay as long as they want. Danny would have loved it. He lived for the day he could have a big, backyard cookout with all the guys. He had to die in order to get it, but he has it now." She looked up to me, offered a warm smile through two streams of tears, and repeated, "Let them stay, Mike. Danny's getting a real kick out of it."

"I need to ask you something, Kathy," I said as she walked me in the direction of my car. "It's got nothing to do with the case. It's something that has been bothering me ever since I found out Danny was on the job."

"What is it, Mike?"

"Did Danny's mother know he was a cop?"

"I promised Danny I would never tell anyone this, but, under the circumstances and because it's you, Mike, I guess I can tell you." The tiny woman stopped walking and turned to face me. "The night before she passed away, she was getting very bad and the doctor said she wasn't going to last the night. Danny spent a lot of time with her and told her he was working undercover." Kathy began to cry again. "He said he didn't know if she really understood him, but she smiled and she squeezed his hand. That made him feel good."

"And now," I added in some clumsy effort at comfort, "she knows for sure."

We hugged tightly for a long time and cried.

The funeral was over. Now it was time for the investigation to move along. On the way to my apartment, I mulled over my conversation with Grassler. His suggestion that the case end a certain way was well taken. If the city was trying to screw Danny's family out of the little bit of money they had earned by their years in hell, then I would do my part to insure that it was City Hall that got the screwing.

Some people wanted me off the case and others wanted me on it. Some wanted it to stop and some wanted it to continue. My reaction was, "Screw all of them!" I was going to work the case my way and it would come out the way it came out. The chips would fall where they may. But, if I could somehow stack the deck in Danny Martin's favor, so be it!

And now that I was finally making some progress in the case, the powers that be were planning to take me off the case.

13

Saturday Afternoon: Finding an Ally in an Enemy

It was almost three o'clock in the afternoon when I returned to the apartment that I call my home. It's a bare-threads place without a lot of furniture to clutter it. The living room contains a couch, chair, and a good stereo system, all of which were salvaged from — or added after — the divorce. There's a small table, a couple of chairs, and the usual appliances in the kitchen. Other than a bed and a nightstand in the single bedroom, that's about it for my palace.

I poured a Southern Comfort and ran it down my throat. I felt good, so I poured another one and added a water chaser in a mismatched glass. Next, I got out of my funeral duds and slipped into a pair of running shorts. I was hot and sticky from the muggy, oppressive humidity of the season we Rochesterians call summer. Looking for music that felt right for my moodiness, I started flipping through some CDs. When I came to a Joni James disc, I slipped it into the stereo, turned down the volume, and went out onto the balcony. Shirtless and barefoot, I dropped my butt down low into the cushion of an old patio chair, threw my feet up on the railing, and allowed my brain to slowly engage. The Southern Comfort went down smoothly, so smooth that I

dumped the chaser into a potted plant that appeared to need the
water more than I did.

Like fine paintings, investigations look better when you step
back a pace or two. Similarly, there's a time in an investigation
when the investigator needs to cleanse his mind and step back
from it. Now was the time for stepping back. There was work to
be done, but it was work better saved for the darkness and
coolness of night. For the instant hour — maybe two — there
was the need to think, to analyze, and to plan the next move.

Danny Martin was dead. God rest his soul. I had to let go of
that baggage. Nothing would change the weeks, months, and
years already passed. The only thing I had control of was the
future of the case. The things to be done and said in the coming
hours and days would impact the outcome of the case.
Consequently, I had to use this time-out to assess where I was
and plan what was going to happen next.

William Allen is alive. That's a fact. He's the main suspect.
And, that's another fact. Something needs to be done about
those obvious facts, I reasoned as I sipped the liquor. I'm the
person who needs to do something to change his status from
suspect to defendant. Things concerning him could change in
the days and weeks to come. The boys in The Bureau had
moved him once when he became an embarrassment, and, if the
need arose, they would do it again. I didn't have time to wait.
This guy had to be broken. If his bosses got together and
shipped him off to Butte, Montana, I would never get a chance
at him.

The case. The investigation into the murder of Daniel Albert
Martin was mine. No matter who they paired me up with, the
case was mine. It would always be mine. That had to be my
focus, the center of my attention, my object of concern. There
wasn't time for politics, nor was there room for emotions.

Phyllis filtered into my mind and I pushed her out. This was
not the time for love affairs or even thoughts about them.

Just do the investigation. Get it done. Proceed. Move forward. Forget about the chips in this game. Let them fall where they may. Either my career or Bill Allen's career was going to suffer and die. That was unfortunate. But so was the murder of Danny Martin.

I pressed the cold, sweating glass of booze to my forehead and listened to Joni float from one note to another effortlessly, like a breeze. Without catching it, my mind drifted to a barefoot Phyllis Conte gliding across her sister's kitchen floor. The thought emerged that I should sit down and talk to her in some quiet place. She may have information she's reluctant to discuss in front of the family, I supposed on the cop side of my brain. Besides, my last encounter with her had been a strange one, one that I couldn't read well. While I made those honorable arguments, the phallic side of my brain also kicked in and told me I may simply be searching for a reason to be with the woman and to hold her close to me one more time.

My mind got back to business and I began to think about the best way to get inside of Bill Allen. I let Joni James work her magic, and as the music filled my ears, my mind began to develop a plan to work on Bill Allen. With my mind totally engaged in thought and sound, I jumped a foot when the phone rang and slam-dunked me into reality. My heels came off the railing and slapped the concrete floor of the patio.

"Lieutenant?" Skip Winston asked only as a formality as I picked up the cordless phone next to me. He didn't wait for an answer. "I need you to come in right now."

"We got a homicide, boss?" I asked more to give me a chance to think rather than get an answer. There was something in his voice that made me cautious.

"Something came up. No homicide, just something we need to discuss."

"Gee, Major," I stalled. "I was just on the way out the door to meet my aunt and uncle. I promised them I would stop over and take care of some things for them."

"I'd like for you to put it off for now and come right in."

"They're kind of old and need a lot of help."

"Call them. Put it off. Come in." He knew I was trying to figure out what was going on, so he wasn't wasting a bunch of words.

"How long should I tell Aunt Sofia it will be before she can expect me?"

"It won't take long. It just needs to be done face-to-face and it needs to be done now!"

I took my time slipping into a pair of slacks and some loafers. There was no sense in hurrying to an inevitable ass chewing. That's what it was, a chewing out for something gone wrong, perhaps something one of my guys had done. Or, more than likely, something I had done to offend the FBI's sensitive ego. Had to be. Winston always used my first name whenever I was off-duty. Even when he had to call me at the apartment to get some information related to an investigation or some other pending police matter, he always referred to me as, "Mike". It was just a habit with him. The title was only thrown in at official happenings, such as homicides, or when the public or another boss was around. He had to have a boss in his office right then, when he called me. His voice was neither happy nor angry, just kind of official and slightly unsettled. So, if Skip was upset and there was a boss there with him, he must have already been called on the carpet. Being a fact of nature that ass chewings, along with other things, roll down hill, I was now in line to be hauled over the coals.

I was going to take the Corvette, the real love of my life, to Headquarters but I figured as long as I was being ordered in, I would use the city's gas. I got into the plain-wrapper cop car and took my time heading south to the center of the city. As I drove, I wondered what I had done to earn a Saturday ass-reaming. Another burning question was who was in Skip's office. His immediate boss was our sawed-off Deputy Chief Ernie Cooper, who thought of himself as a great cop. However, the truth is the only person who held that opinion was Deputy Chief Ernie Cooper, himself. Besides, Cooper had been out the picture ever since Matt Murphy jumped the chain of command and began dealing directly with Skip. Consequently, the boss sitting in with the Major must be our one and only Chief of Police, the chatty Matt Murphy. On the other hand, Cooper had been at Kathy Martin's home after the funeral. He may have seen me chugging down a couple of beers in the back yard, and then later, he may have seen me driving the city car. According to "the book", drinking and driving a city car was a real no-no. Cooper might be a piss-poor cop, but he was a stickler for the "Good Book" of the Rochester Police Department, the blue, four-inch thick, three-ring binder of Departmental General Orders.

A weekday bawling out could be for anything. On a Monday through Friday one could easily earn an ass-chewing for being late, taking too long for lunch, being seen changing lanes unsafely, or for a tie that didn't match your suit. But, getting ripped out on a Saturday, that had to be prompted by some major infraction of the many rules, and it would have to be driven by some high-ranking, low self-esteem boss who had nothing better to do on a weekend than hassle the working troops.

By the time I pulled off the Inner Loop, an archaic expressway that circled the central portion of the city and headed south on Plymouth Avenue, my temper was beginning to stir. I had a big enough mystery centered on the Martin killing. I surely didn't need this kind of cat-and-mouse game.

As I parked the car at the front of the Public Safety Building, there were two things I knew. One, Skip Winston was going to pitch a major beef at me. The other bit of knowledge I had surmised was that Deputy Chief Ernie Cooper was behind it. What I didn't know was the subject of the chewing-out. What had I done? Or, more to the point, which one of the many things that I had done had now come to someone's attention?

I pushed through the heavy glass doors at the street level of the building and made my way for the escalator that would bring me to the main floor. Once there, I gave a wave to the cop sitting behind Headquarters Desk. Not stopping to talk, my legs quickly crossed over to the far wall where I pushed the button to summon one of the three elevators.

The fourth floor was totally vacant, so my heels clicked loudly on the worn tile as I moved down the corridor to my boss' office. Winston's door was wide open, so I walked in without knocking. Like me, he was in casual clothes. It was easy to see he also must have been called in to work from home. He was leaning back in his chair, chewing on the eraser end of pencil. His eyes were fixed on the wall to the right of his chair. Hearing or sensing my approach through the short hall leading from his aide's office to his domain, Skip rotated the chair in my direction.

"You're off the Martin killing," Winston said as soon as I crossed the threshold into his office. It wasn't said harshly. It was just said.

"What?" was all I could manage to respond.

"You're off the case," he repeated flatly.

"You've got to be kidding."

"I'm dead serious. After the funeral the Chief had my butt for lunch, Mike. He says you're off the case, so you are off the case."

"Why? For what reason?"

"Did you accuse that FBI guy, Allen, of killing Officer Martin?"

"Sure I did," I admitted. "So what?"

" 'So what?' " Winston asked incredulously.

"Come on, Skip! Remember that letter I showed you ... the one you didn't see?" I just had to get that shot in! "Martin just about named Bill Allen as his killer. What was I supposed to do? I had to pop the question to him."

"Well, Delany got a hold of the mayor and pitched a giant-sized complaint. The mayor then jumped all over Murphy.

Consequently the Chief is up in arms about you ruining the relationship he's been trying to build between the other agencies and us. The way he sees it, you're intentionally trying to offend the FBI."

"Relationships? He's mad because someone is putting his outfit under a microscope the way they like to do to everyone else."

"His ex-outfit," Ken Winston corrected.

"Baloney, Skip. Remember what it is that they like to tell everyone, 'There's no such thing as an *ex*-FBI Agent'."

"Regardless, Mike. We're off this one. Murphy's going to turn the entire case over to the Monroe County Sheriff's Department on Monday morning."

"The Sheriff's Department?" I asked rather loudly. Now it was my turn to be incredulous. "The county mounties? Is he nuts? What's the reason for that?"

"He says he realized, while at the funeral this morning, that we're going to get criticized from all directions, no matter how we solve this case. The defense, the man in the street, is going to say we just picked on someone because Martin was one of ours. So, Murphy feels it would be better if we let an objective party investigate the matter."

This was madness. I got to my feet and began to pace the floor as I ran my hand through my thinning hair. Politics had evidently reared its ugly head once again in the halls of the Rochester Police Department. Martin's killing was grabbing a lot of publicity with the local media. Obviously the mayor was afraid that if we got the killer, there would bad press if it was indeed another cop. If we didn't make the arrest, there would be more bad press. If we arrested someone controversial — such as an FBI agent — there would still be bad press. And, the bottom line of it all was, no mayor wants any bad press in an election year. Therefore, the politicos must have figured it was better to let the County Sheriff's Department get stuck with the limited good press of the arrest ... and get hurt with the potentially negative press.

"I've got to talk to the Chief," I finally said.

"No way, Mike."

"Way, Major," I answered as my teen-age neighbor would have responded. "I want permission to see him. He's always saying he's got an open door policy, well, I want through that door."

"I'm not going to allow it, Mike. Permission denied."

"Why?" I asked as I turned to face him with my right hand halfway through my hair and resting on the top of my head.

"You're hot. You're steaming hot. You would say, probably do something stupid that would mess up your career, my career, or, more likely, both of our careers."

"Chuck my career. My career doesn't matter if I'm not allowed to work a case, a city case, without this kind of lunacy. I'm not worried about my career."

"Well, pardon me, but I *am* worried about mine."

My face worked into a stupid little grin as I asked, "That's it, *Major*? You're folding your tent because finding a cop's killer, a Rochester cop's killer, might dampen your career?"

"I worked too hard to get where I am, Mike. Murphy's going to be here another couple of years before he heads out to a bigger department and a bigger paycheck. When he does, I want to be in line."

I shook my head in disbelief. "Don't go Uncle Tom on yourself at this point of your life, Major. It doesn't look good on you."

I regretted the insult as soon as it was out of my big mouth. I regretted it more when I saw the hurt on my boss' face.

"I'm going to talk to him, Skip," I said firmly. "With or without your permission."

"He's gone, Lieutenant. He's left for the day."

"I'll go to his house," I said matter-of-factly.

"You do and you'll be up on charges Monday morning."

"Prepare the charges. I think there's room in my personnel folder for another charge or two," I answered as I moved toward the door.

"Lieutenant!" Winston barked as I reached the door.

Holding my position and without turning around, I asked coldly, "What?"

"I'll let you talk to him on the phone, *my phone*, from here, with me present. That's it!" Winston's voice was one of resignation.

"Good enough," I said, and moved back toward his desk. I was confused about my feelings toward the man. There was a certain amount of anger in my range of emotions for the Major, but I also felt sorry for him. Although I respected his caution and his plans to perhaps become our next chief, I found myself lacking any respect for this commander I had once admired. The thought struck me that Skip Winston was yet another demonstration of Vincent Ruggeri's philosophy regarding the nature of men and chameleons.

As the Major dialed the Chief's home phone number, I said, "Thanks, boss." The words went unacknowledged.

I waited patiently as I scanned every inch of Skip Winston I could see. His entire being offered no clues as to what he was thinking or feeling. His eyes went up to the ceiling as he waited for an answer and they remained there as he asked the person answering the phone to get the Chief.

"Chief," he finally said into the phone. "I have Lieutenant Amato here in the office. I gave him your instructions and he understands them clearly, sir. However, he's asked to speak to you directly." He took a breath of air and continued, "So, knowing the importance you put on having an open door to the men and women of the Department, I've called you to see if you wish to speak to him, sir."

I waited patiently as Winston said, "Yes, sir…no, sir," a couple of times. Then he held the phone out to me with his right hand as his left hand cupped the mouthpiece.

"He asked me if you were pissed off, and I told him you were. He said, 'Good'. Don't blow it, Mike. He's expecting you to go off on him. Keep it cool. Use your head."

I promised I would behave and would not swear or do anything to bring discredit on Winston. Then I took the phone.

"Chief?" I asked into the plastic phone.

"Yes, Lieutenant. I understand, from Major Winston, you need to chat with me about my instructions."

"That's right, sir," I answered. "I'll be at your house in about fifteen minutes to speak with you." Winston glared at my forwardness. "I believe there are some things in regards to this case of which you are not aware."

"Now's not a good time, Lieutenant."

"Chief, if you need time to clean up a little and put some coffee on, I'll delay a little and be there in twenty, twenty-five minutes." Skip Winston's eyes rolled up to the ceiling. "Or thirty minutes, but, I will be there," I stated flatly. "The point is this, Chief; one of your officers is dead and I would like to have the opportunity to discuss that matter with you, to chat about it. If you're planning on taking me off the case for whatever reasons you may have, I want to use that open door to present my side of the coin. Someone is blowing smoke in your direction and I want the opportunity to clear away some of that smoke. I think that's fair enough ... don't you?"

There was a pause that lasted no more than five seconds. Finally I hard Murphy say, "Fair enough." The concession sounded sincere, but was accompanied by a faint hint of a chuckle. "I'll have the coffee on."

As soon as the phone was down in its place, Winston said with a tone of resignation, "You've got more guts than brains, Mike."

"Hey, I had no choice." I said with my hands raised in innocence. "The man invited me over to his house. What could I do? Refuse an invitation from the Chief of Police?"

"You're so full of it, Amato," Winston said in resignation.

"Don't worry. Boss," I said, and left his office. "I won't tarnish your oak leaves."

"Mike, I just want, you know …" Skip Winston let the sentence drift off.

I don't know if he was going to offer an explanation or apology for wanting to save his career. Whatever it was, the man could not manage to get the words out, so I told him, "Forget about it, Skip. It ain't no big thing."

* * *

Chief Matthew Murphy's house was on the south side of the city in an area where chiefs had bought houses for as long as I can remember. It was the same area in which George Eastman had built his home as Kodak became a major industry. I guess it kept the chiefs far enough from the stench of the city while they preached the importance of city residency to the rest of us who could not afford to live in the Tudor mansions of the city's southeast quadrant.

I thought about that and some other things as I made my way from Major Skip Winston's office in the PSB to the stylish home of Chief Matthew Murphy. One of the items that crossed my mind was that I had a score to settle with Murphy. He had, in effect, lied to me a few days ago when he fed me the line about Danny Martin going into the grand jury as a witness against his friends in the mob. Sure it might have been true that Danny would have to appear at the grand jury, but Murphy never told me the kid was a cop. It was a bone I had to pick some day with Matt the Chat, but this day, at his home, was neither the time nor the place. Today I needed a favor, so it would not be prudent to draw lines in the sand and try to settle old scores.

The man was a died-in-the-wool member of The Bureau. It was to be expected that he would take their side over mine. I had to win him over to my side, and I doubted that could be done. However, I was prepared to take a decent shot at it. Besides, regardless of what he was about to say, I was still going to investigate the case, even if I had to hand in my badge to do so.

After two wrong turns, I finally made it to the Chief's place. It was a nice, rustic home framed in red, weathered brick. The home was not too large, but appeared regal in some way or another. After parking the car on the street in front of the Murphy home, I cut across the front lawn that was dissected by a red brick walkway, which curved slightly right, and then back to the left. I rang the doorbell mounted on the right side of the large, heavy wooden door, and waited until the Chief opened the door and welcomed me into his home. As we moved through the house I did a survey of the visible contents and determined the guy and his wife must be rather conservative in their tastes. There was the notable absence of a television set. The walls held a few paintings that were not to my liking, but were in keeping with the English Countryside style of the home. We walked in silence through the living room, dining room, kitchen, and finally out the back door of the house, to a small, brick patio that provided the setting for a black, metal table and matching chairs. Brightly colored chair cushions mitigated the bleakness of the patio furniture. An open umbrella, in the same flowered pattern as the chair cushions, shaded the table from the hot, afternoon sun. The table was already set up with coffee mugs, sugar, cream, spoons, and napkins.

Gesturing for me to have a seat in a chair opposite of where he stood, Matt the Chat said, "I don't think you're going to change my mind on the matter, Lieutenant, but let's chat. I'll give you the opportunity to be heard."

"Fair enough," I responded just as he had said less than a half-hour earlier.

I took the next ten minutes to tell Murphy about Danny's letter, the references it made to Special Agent Allen, the Agent's argument with Eddy Cavaluso, and my suspicions about Special Agent William Allen. Next was a rather accurate and objective accounting of my conversation with Allen at Genesee Valley

Park, but I left out my reasons for selecting the park as our meeting place. When I got to the part where Allen made reference to the fact that the killer had ripped off Danny Martin's religious medal, Matt Murphy never batted an eye. However, when I continued with the information about Kathy Martin confirming the fact that Danny wore such a chain and medal, along with the Medical Examiner's assessment of the small, horizontal scratch on the victim's neck, I got Matt Murphy's attention. The Chief raised both eyebrows as he looked at me over the rim of the coffee cup that was positioned at his lips.

I concluded by saying, "Chief, I respect your relationship with the FBI, but I'm telling you all this in strictest confidence. I hope you will respect that confidence."

"You have my word on it, Lieutenant," he said in a manner that made me believe him.

He then asked a couple of questions about the letter and how I had gotten it. I told him about Danny giving the letter to his sister for safekeeping. I also told him the victim's wife had let me read it, although she would not, for personal reasons unknown to me, surrender it to the Department. That may have been a stupid move, but I felt it was necessary, at least for the time being, to keep the letter away from Murphy.

"Then how was it that you were able to let Agent Allen read that letter, Lieutenant?" he asked with a hint of accusation.

"The wife trusts me. She gave me a copy as long as I promised to use it only if I had to, only when I really had to, you know, in order to further the investigation." The answer seemed to satisfy him, but then for good measure I added some embellishment, self-serving as it was. "And, I thought in all fairness I owed it to Bill Allen to let him read it, rather than just tell him what it said."

"And besides, you wanted to see his reaction to the letter, didn't you Lieutenant?" he asked with a confident grin that told me he saw through my bullshit.

I shrugged and smiled, but didn't answer.

Murphy pointed to my cup and raised his eyebrows. I accepted the offer, believing that as long as we had coffee, we were going to be chatting.

"What makes you believe Agent Allen is a target for the Mafia's interest?"

"Sir?" I asked as I tried to decide if I should tell him about the woman in San Diego.

"You said the mob here was trying to lean on Bill Allen, and that you confirmed that information with a source of yours. Then you said that even Allen eventually confirmed the information." Murphy said his words casually but as he spoke, he studied me closely, looking for ... what? "What was it that made them think they could lean on Allen? Do they have something on him?"

Asking for a promise of confidentiality, and receiving it, I told him about Gail Sampson and her relationship with Allen. I added, "That's why he got sent here. It was punishment for having screwed up in San Diego."

"The Bureau does like to sweep those things under the rug," he admitted with a sigh. "Ed Delany probably doesn't even know about the San Diego affair."

"He didn't know it at first, but he does now. Bill Allen told him."

"Oh?" Murphy commented. Retired agents may think there is no such thing as an ex-FBI Agent, but those Feebs who are still on the job sure do consider the retired guys ex-Agents! Consequently, the Feds who are still active in the organization don't tell the retired agents everything.

"Well then, if Allen already let the SAC know about the attempted shake-down," Murphy mused, "why would Allen still feel it was necessary to kill Officer Martin?"

"I think Allen was in deeper than we know, and I think Danny Martin knew just how deep." I let the boss think about that for a few seconds and then added, "Why else would Allen be trying so hard to discredit Martin with the Buffalo innuendoes, if he had nothing to hide?"

There was a one-minute pause in the conversation as Murphy studied a tree farther back in the yard and thought about the situation. His eyes narrowed ever so slightly, then they seemed to slowly return to normal before they widened. It was obvious he was having some internal discussion and I knew the result of that self-conversation was going to impact my involvement with the case.

"Lieutenant," he finally said. "I stand by my decision."

My heart sank. I leaned forward to speak, but was silenced by the Chief's extended right hand and raised forefinger.

"I know you hold the FBI in low esteem and don't trust them and some of their investigations." I was going to protest my innocence, but knew my mouth had done a fine job of letting everyone know how I felt about the FBI ... as well as many other matters. The effort was going to be useless. I decided to shut up for once and listen.

"Ed Delany and I do not always see eye-to-eye," Murphy admitted. "All things considered, some of your mistrust and apprehension about my former co-workers may not be misplaced." Murphy stirred his coffee and tasted it before he continued. "However, just as I am your boss, I have my bosses. And, the truth is, between you and me, Ed Delany has seen fit to seek out my bosses and make his concerns known to them. Therefore, I have my set of orders and I will follow them."

"But the Monroe County Sheriff's Office is going to ..." I started to say before I was again silenced by the Chief's extended hand.

"As of Monday you and the Rochester Police Department will turn over the Officer Martin homicide to investigators from the Sheriff's Department. We are doing that to protect the integrity of the case. We're too close to it and we're going to get nailed by the press, by everyone, if any small error is made."

"But ..." I started to say before I was silenced by the same gesture from Murphy.

"However, this being the weekend and all, it's very difficult to contact everyone and issue such an order. Therefore, this conversation is not taking place. It being the weekend and all, I have to assume you have taken the opportunity of your days off to get out of town and recharge your batteries, so to speak. Do I make myself clear?"

I couldn't believe it! The guy was giving me a free ride for the next day and a half! It was not a big deal as far as the amount of time was concerned, but it did give me time to move. "Very clear, Chief" I confirmed.

"However, on Monday, I will call you in and give that order. I will then, as of Monday morning, expect the order to be followed to the letter and in the spirit of my instructions."

I mumbled a word of thanks and drained my coffee. As we stood to shake hands, my boss said, "If this works out well, we'll both come out of it looking good. If it works out badly, your butt, and your butt alone, is going to be hanging way out there." Chief Murphy paused long enough to let it sink in that I was going to be swinging all alone if anything went wrong with the case. Then he added, "Lieutenant, I want you to know that this is not a license to run wild. It is only some slack to allow you to do your job. If you step out of line I'll have your ass mounted on my office wall!"

"I understand, Chief. I won't embarrass you."

"Don't worry about me," Murphy said as he escorted back through the house to the front door. "Just don't embarrass The Department."

I had no time now to linger on his patio. There were less than forty hours until Monday morning, less than forty hours to catch a killer.

14

Saturday Evening:
A Friend Found, A Friend Lost

One valuable lesson I had learned over the years was that an important difference separated an average cop from a good cop. The average cop waits for luck to happen. A good cop makes his luck happen. The good cop goes out and shakes the trees, knocks on doors, has some good informants lined up, and asks a hell of a lot of questions.

It was time for me to make some luck happen. I had been waiting for luck to find me. It was time to go out and make some luck! Maybe it was the pressure of the time limit that had been placed on me, or maybe I was just fed up with pussyfooting around. Whatever the case, when I left Murphy's house I was bent on getting this case into overdrive and bringing it to a close.

After arriving back at my apartment from my sojourn downtown and to the Chief's place, I slipped a big-band disc in the stereo. This was not a time for mellow sounds. This was the time to pick up the pace and make things happen. The sounds of Benny Goodman, Artie Shaw, and a jamming drum solo by Gene Krupa filled the place as I took down the espresso machine and whipped up a full cup of the strong, black-brown liquid. A stiff shot of sambuca added the sweet, anise flavor I

loved. Taking the early evening refreshment with me out onto
the balcony, I went through my plans for the night.

Bill Allen had to be handled exactly like any other suspect. He
needed to be confronted directly, head on, with the evidence.
Just like any other homicide suspect, he would have to be
slapped in the head — so to speak — with the facts of the case.
Sure, he would want to toss out some excuses, and would
probably even offer up some type of denial, the irrefutable facts
of the investigation that would eventually shake him. Then he
would have to decide whether to be smart or dumb. If he elected
to be smart, he would admit to killing Danny Martin and be
done with it. Later, in court, he could lay out a temporary
insanity plea, or try to make some bullshit type of self-defense
case. That was his choice. On the other hand, if he wanted to be
dumb, he could try to kill me. The choice was going to be up to
him. I didn't really care. I was ready to play it either way.

The swing music was still doing a nice job of keeping me
rolling straight ahead, on steady course toward wrapping up this
case. After draining a second cup of sambuca espresso, I showered and shaved. Afterward, I moved methodically, slipping into
a pair of slacks and an opened-collared shirt. Next, a casual sport
coat was drawn out of the closet and laid over the back of a
kitchen chair. Only then was it time to assemble the tools I
would need in order to do the job.

I checked the action on my 9mm, loaded it, chambered a
round, slipped the pistol into the holster, and laced my belt
through the holster. Next, I pushed the rotating portion of my
handcuffs around a couple of times. Satisfied they were moving
smoothly, I shoved one of the cuffs behind the waist of my
slacks and allowed the other one to swing freely between my
pants and the sport coat. Next came the small .25-caliber backup gun. I loaded the hide-away automatic and shoved it into the
back of my pants, next to the handcuffs, right at the hollow
created by the spine going to the tailbone. I gave some thought
about putting on body armor, but finally rejected the idea. If the

arrest didn't go down easily, it was likely there would be a pretty good fistfight. In that case, a bulletproof vest wasn't going to help me. It would only get in the way.

Before leaving the apartment, I gave a quick call to the Martin home. Phyllis Conte answered the phone.

"How's Kathy doing?" I asked.

"It's beginning to hit her now. It's hitting her hard," the older sister said softly. There was a few seconds of silence before she asked, "Are you going to stop by, Mike?"

"I can't, Phyllis," I answered, but my mind toyed with the idea. "It's a bad time for me. Besides, Kathy needs some rest."

"I would really like to see you, Mike," Phyllis said in a whisper. I was flattered that she was thinking of me, but my ego dropped back in place when she added, "Something came up today about Danny's insurance and I wanted to ask you about it."

Thinking that she was talking about a life insurance policy someone may have taken out on Danny Martin's life, I asked "Like what?" The thought of a fresh lead in the case intrigued me.

"I was talking to one of the officials from the police union and he said they have some inkling the city is going to balk at covering Danny."

"Don't worry about it, Phyllis," I said with a little laugh. "They can't do that. Besides, I already took care of the issue." I wasn't too sure about that last sentence, but she needed to hear it.

"And," she hesitated, " I would really like to see you ... to take a walk or ... I don't know."

"It'll have to wait. Something just came up and I have to jump on it."

We said our good-byes with some assurance that I would see her and her sister the next day. I hoped that prophecy was going to be fulfilled.

* * *

The sun was setting into a haze at the western horizon when I made it to Kenny's Joint, a little neighborhood bar on the edge of the city's downtown district. Along the way I had given some thought as to whether or not I could take Special Agent William Allen in a toe-to-toe, bare-fisted brawl. I was giving up a twelve, maybe thirteen year age advantage to the Feeb, along with two or three inches of height. If it got down to throwing punches, I would rely on street fighting and let him use the stuff he had learned in the FBI Academy at Quantico.

Once in the saloon, I ordered a bourbon and ginger ale, and asked Steve, the bartender, for the bar phone. When he placed the instrument on the bar, I dug out Allen's pager number. Bill Allen had my home, office, and pager number; so, I didn't want him recognizing the number he was going to be asked to call. If I had been told that I was supposed to be off the case, he had probably been given the same information. Consequently, being the type who obeys all orders and regulations, he would probably avoid calling me if he recognized one of my phone numbers.

I placed a call to Allen's pager. On the electronic cue, I entered the number of the bar phone. It took about five minutes for the phone in front of me to ring. After the third ring I picked up the receiver.

"Kenny's," I said briskly.

"This is Bill Allen," the Midwest accent said. "I was paged to call this number."

"Right, Bill. This is Mike. Look, I was wondering if maybe we could get together and talk some things out."

"Sure. Why not?" he responded casually.

The mirror behind the bar caught the surprise on my face as Allen readily conceded to meet. Hoping to sound more casual than my face looked, I managed to say, "I know it's the weekend and all, but I was hoping we could meet tonight."

"I don't see any reason why not." He sounded too chipper, too pleased. Hadn't he been told I was off the case? Wasn't he still pissed that I had called him a murderer?

"How about if you meet me over around Upper Falls Park? It's a decent night," I offered casually. "We can walk and talk. Okay?"

"Can't do it, Mike. Wish I could get out, but I'm tied up here all night."

Here? Where was, "here"? Was I being sucked into meeting him on his terms, at his apartment? I had imagined having the meeting on my turf, my streets.

"So, where are you?" I asked.

"I'm at the office. I've got desk duty tonight, all night." He waited a second, and then added, "We pull it on rotation. I was up for it this weekend. If you want to meet, we'll have to do it here."

My instincts suggested putting off the meeting until I could get it set in a better playground, but my impetuous gut cast off the thought. The clock was running. A couple of more hours could find me on the outside looking in. It was a thought I did not relish.

"Okay," I said happily. "That works for me. Are you sure you don't mind if I come there?"

"Not at all, buddy," he answered just as happily. "I could use some company. I'll call downstairs to let the guard know you're coming."

We gave each other friendly salutations and I hung up the phone. It took another cigarette and a fresh drink for me to work out the details of my thoughts. If I was going to Allen's home court, it was going to be necessary to be on my toes. He would have a mental edge that would give him a certain confidence. Maybe that wasn't a bad thing! He could also be lulled into being too confident, and his confidence would breed carelessness.

I thought about ordering a third drink, but quickly cast the idea aside. Instead, I left the bar and took a leisurely walk around the block.

The average, smoking gun, homicide case always has a couple of surprises that pop up in the investigation. However, as weird as this case had turned out, it had more than its fair share of surprises. In fact, by all counts, it had far exceeded the surprises one could expect. It was a surprise that Danny was a cop. Another surprise crept in when it was learned that the farm boy, Special Agent Bill Allen, has been parting the sheets with a mob broad. Another significant surprise had surfaced when Bill Allen let the cat out of the bag in regards to knowing about Danny wearing a religious medal on a chain around his neck — something even Kathy didn't remember until her memory was severely jogged. There was the sad surprise that Skip Winston had been lulled away from the ranks of street cops and had gone over to the suits. Then came the two-pronged surprise of being taken off of the case, but Murphy allowing me the weekend grace period. And now, now came Bill Allen's willingness to meet with me tonight. This case didn't need any more surprises. However, as I walked in the warm end-of-summer evening, I was too dumb to know there were still two more surprises to come ... and Bill Allen would deliver both of them.

At the time of the stroll, what bugged me the most was the Feeb's light-hearted response to my call. If he had been told I was off of the case, he should have been reluctant to talk to me, especially on an office phone. But he had not been reluctant. Much to the contrary, he sounded pleased to hear from me. That meant one of three things. One, because the decision to remove me from the investigation had been made on Saturday, he had not yet been told I was off the case. Two, he knew I was off the case but didn't care. Or, three, he had his own plans for the night and me. The first option seemed likely. The second one was possible, although not highly probable. The third one simply didn't sound appealing. Allen sounded *too* eager, *too* pleased to have me come to his brain-sucking den. Maybe he liked the idea of confronting me while he was in his own sandbox. Was that it?

Was the country boy federal agent going to confront me? Was this going to be the showdown?

Good! I thought to myself. Let's get it on! This guy's a killer and I was tired of treating him as if he were a partner.

Ten minutes later, I parked the car on State Street, directly in front of the Federal Building. Walking toward the building, I looked up and saw the lights on in a couple of the FBI offices. That was bad! If there were a couple of other agents hanging around Allen, he would have too much support, and I wouldn't be able to lean on him like I wanted to lean on him.

A young, square-jawed, blond guard sitting behind a small desk in the lobby of the Federal Building nodded and said he had been told to expect me. I signed my name into the register and was handed a visitor's badge. The two of us rode the elevator in silence. The Nordic security officer walked to my right after we exited the elevator, and remained there on our short journey to the main entrance of the FBI offices. Only after Bill Allen opened the door did the guard back away from my right side. When it was established that I was the person the agent was expecting, the escort gave a smile accompanied with a nod, and left.

Bill Allen welcomed me into the offices, offered coffee, complained about the weekend duty, and commented on the weather, all in the time it took to walk from the main door to his desk, a distance of about thirty feet. His verbosity was a warning he was nervous about the meeting. That was good. Finding out he was alone was even better! All the good signs set aside, I was still cautious about being alone with the man. Something wasn't right here. This boy had his own agenda, just as I had mine. I didn't like being left to guess why he was so happy — yet nervous — about seeing me.

"They shut down the air conditioning on the weekends," he explained as he indicated his loosened tie and short sleeves. "The government tries to save every nickel it can." He looked to me for the nod of agreement I offered, "I'll grab the portable phone and we'll go up on the roof. There's a breeze up there, so it's a heck of a lot more comfortable."

The roof? A rooftop is a place far out of my comfort zone. I don't like heights and I don't like looking down. The fact is, I would rather jump into a bar fight at some Polish pub than stand on a tall building. However, refusing the offer would be a sign of weakness on my part, and showing weakness was not an option at this time.

"Sure," my lips said casually as my stomach questioned why my mouth was acting stupid.

Allen led me through a maze of cubicles to a back stairway. We climbed the two flights of stairs to the roof. As we did so, I made a conscious effort to save my wind. The agent used a key to unlock the door at the top of the stairway, and stepped out onto the roof. Politely, he held the door open for me, and smiled as I stepped onto the gravel-covered floor.

By the time I saw the fist, it was less than a couple of inches from the left side of my jaw. The punch drove me backwards and slammed my back against the door that had just closed behind me. Instinctively, my fists came up and my elbows pulled in close to my gut. With my face and belly protected, I tried to shake off the blow that had wobbled me. I prepared for his second punch.

In that short second, I tried to sort out what had just happened. The son-of-a-bitch had sucker-punched me! That was my first thought, and then it was followed instantly by a second revelation. The fair-haired, farm boy had some street sense!

"Put them down," Allen's voice came through to my stunned head. "I'm not going to hit you again. I owed you that one, but it's all over now."

My mind was not doing a good job of sorting out what was going on, so, I threw two quick punches. One caught him over the right eye and the other landed solid under his chin.

With him flat on his back, and blood dripping from the corner of his eye, I conceded, "*Now* it's over!" And followed it with, "What the fuck's going on with you?" Although I fired the question, the answer was obvious. We both had decided to settle scores this warm summer night.

"You've ridiculed me for two days now, accused me of being a murderer, insulted The Bureau, and humiliated me with my bosses, Mike. You had that coming." He stopped long enough to wipe the blood away and then looked at me to see if I understood him. Getting up from the gravel that covered the rooftop he commented, "Back home you get what's coming to you, and you had that coming."

The temptation to add a kick to the groin — in addition to the two punches I had given him — was gaining a lot of acceptance in my psyche, but I opted to take advantage of his moment of weakness, which was being demonstrated in his somewhat limited apology.

"Oh, yeah? Well, I got another news bulletin for you, Billy!" I said evenly. "You messed up yesterday when you made your little 'I'm-so-hurt' speech denying you had anything to do with Danny Martin's death."

"When?" he asked as he edged toward the west side of the roof, overlooking the State Street traffic six floors below us. "Was it when I mentioned that the killer had ripped off Officer Martin's chain and religious medal?"

"Yes, as a matter of fact!" As I spoke the words, I wondered why my revelation hadn't surprised him. My mind was wrestling with a few other questions at the same time. Here I thought I had caught him in a screw-up about the information he gave up the previous day at the park, but he obviously had purposely planted the information with me. I shook off the questions floating around in my still shaken brain and went for a direct question. "If you didn't kill Martin, then how did you know what no one but his wife knew?"

I was about five feet from the edge of the roof when I made the mistake of looking down to the street. I felt that strange sensation, almost like a tingle, in the palms of my hands and the soles of my feet as the vertigo kicked in. The spasm in my stomach blocked out what he replied, so I had to ask him to say it again.

"I got it from them," he repeated as I backed away from the edge of the roof.

"Who," I asked, wondering if he was seeing other people on this rooftop.

"Them," Bill Allen said as he pointed with his chin out toward State Street, in the direction of Teddy Carr's restaurant. "Yes, I slipped when I mentioned the chain. But afterward, well, I thought it might work out all right because you would put two and two together and realize I got the information from the Mafia guys. Evidently, you didn't."

What was he saying? Was he trying to make me believe the Old Man had told him that the mob killed Martin? That didn't compute.

I moved closer to the edge, concerned that if I stayed back as far as I was, Allen would sense my fear and exploit it. Moving to the suspect's weak side, his left side, but staying slightly behind him, I assessed the moves I had available to me if he made a move to shove my soul off the roof. I hated being afraid, but Bill Allen would be wise to shove me to my death. I was the only person who could testify about his involvement in Danny's death. Once I was being sponged off of the sidewalk, he could easily allege he had invited me to the roof to talk, and then, when I attacked him out of rage, he had to defend himself. That scenario was a viable act for a man I considered to be very vulnerable. He could easily explain how I had attacked him. The cut over his eye was proof enough. It was then a matter of him explaining how he was forced to counter my attack, and how he had tried to ward me off. He would shake his head in his farm boy way and describe how I stumbled back from his punch, and had gone over the edge of the building falling the seventy or so feet to the concrete below. He would probably add a little scenario about how he gallantly had reached for me, but how my weight and momentum had pulled me from his grasp. The boy would probably end up getting an award out of the deal.

"I don't get you," I said, and realized my voice was giving away my uneasiness about the height. Still, if he had some plausible explanation for the garbage he was feeding me, I wanted to hear it. He had some explaining to do.

"We've got a wire over there," he said as he pointed to the mob meeting place where I had had dinner with the Old Man a few nights earlier. "Here," he said as he beckoned me closer to the edge with his right index finger, and then pointed to a rectangular, gray box mounted on the southwest corner of the Federal Building. "This surveillance camera picks up who goes in and out. The recorders downstairs pick up the conversations. Between the two devices, we can verify for the courts who was there when a certain conversation took place."

I was about two feet from the edge of the building now and my hands were sweating as the vertigo attacked my system and warned me to step back to the relative safety of the center of the roof. My mind created the feeling of the rooftop beginning to slant downward, toward the street. To cover my phobia, I pulled a pack of cigarettes out of the inner breast pocket of my sport coat. I dropped the first cigarette and rather than bend over to retrieve it, pulled out a second one. Cupping my hands around the lighter I rotated the wheel against the flint a couple of times before muttering something about the wind. With that excuse, I stepped back from the edge of the roof, closer to the door that had brought us to this frightening place from the hell of past nightmares. I used the wall and door to shelter my lighter from a non-existent wind and to support my weight as I leaned against the solid concrete blocks.

The explanation Allen offered was believable, but he had not quite sold me. "Quit giving me the one-liners, Bill. If you have an explanation for knowing about Danny's medal, lay it on the line. Cut the bull and give me the details."

He began to move close enough to me so that when I wanted to, I could put my gun to his head, have him turn around, and then cuff him.

"Thursday night, just before you met with the Old Man," he began. "They were in there talking about Martin being a cop. It had just been all over the news about Danny Martin being undercover. Ruggeri was whining and moaning about all the heat it was bringing on the mob's operations. Then, out of nowhere, the Old Man asked Cavaluso if he had whacked Martin. Cavaluso kind of hemmed and hawed, but he admitted he had killed the cop."

"What?" I asked in disbelief. "Are you telling me that Eddy Cavaluso killed Martin?" I couldn't picture Fast Eddy with the inclination to kill Danny Martin. If he had done it, *everyone* in this case had been lying to me. Worse than that, I had been suckered into believing all the liars. Was it possible I had believed Murphy when he said Danny Martin was simply an informant? Was it also possible that I believed Eddy Cavaluso when he denied having knowledge about Danny's killing? And now, was I being sucked in by halfway believing the song-and-dance Allen was putting on for me?

"You can listen to the tapes, Mike," Allen offered. "He admitted it, even bragged about it to Ruggeri."

"Why?" I asked loudly, still in denial. "Eddy Cavaluso hasn't whacked anybody in twenty years. He doesn't have to. He's got a crew that will do it for him."

"Cavaluso told Ruggeri he found out, from cops as a matter of fact, that Martin was a snitch, so he killed him. He said he took the kid for a ride and told him he knew he was an informant. He said the kid went ballistic on him, so he had to kill him."

"Ruggeri would have whacked Cavaluso if he thought he killed Martin," I said with an arrogant snort. "This sounds like more bogus FBI information to me."

"Hear me out, Amato!" Allen said sternly. "Then, when the Old Man complained about that being a dumb move to make without his approval, Cavaluso said he had to do it because of the way the kid was going off. That's when he told Ruggeri that he made the killing look like a robbery, and that he had taken the kid's religious chain. He said he was going to lift Martin's wallet, but he saw headlights coming, so he split."

"If you have all this on tape, then why are we handling the case like it's some kind of big mystery?" I challenged with my face up close to Allen's.

"If we go after Cavaluso, we'll have to produce the tape. If we produce the tape, then we will lose the advantage of having the bug right where they do most of their talking." The Feeb looked at me with some hint of sympathy in his eyes. Then he explained. "Remember? I told you the mob was leaning on me about the matter with Gail Sampson. I also told you that part of my role was to supply them with bad information. Some of that bogus information was getting them to believe other places were bugged so they would talk more freely in the places where we actually have an operating bug. Well, that restaurant is one of the places in which we want them speaking freely."

"So, you blow the cover on Carr's place and you close out the homicide. Then, you still get to pick them up on other bugs in the other places," I reasoned.

"It wouldn't be economical for The Bureau to let the Cavaluso cat out of the bag, so to speak, because then they would have to start all over again with another bug at another location. Right now the Mafia crowd feels comfortable in Carr's place."

"You scum bags! You cold, rotten, low-life fed scumbags! You would let a homicide go unsolved just because closing it wouldn't add up in your cost-benefit ratio books?" The words were spit at the man as I grabbed the front of his shirt.

"The Bureau considers the murder case solved now, and sooner or later, when the investigation into Ruggeri is over, all the tapes will be presented in court and the murder will be closed officially." He looked down at my hands holding the front of his shirt. I responded by letting go of him.

"What about the family?" I asked with a degree of sarcasm. "Does the frigging Bureau think the wife, the sister, and the brother have a right to know who killed Danny?" The question was rhetorical, and Allen knew there was no answer necessary. I continued the tirade. "You sit in your smug little offices with your smug little federal government smiles, and you make all the decisions for all the people because you are the almighty FBI. With all your crap about integrity, ethics, and all the rest of the crap you deal out, you look down your noses at the street cops. But when it's all said and done, it's the cops that have the integrity, and you three-piece suited, briefcase carrying, cappuccino sipping, Washington-based Feds are left with your economically beneficial decisions."

"I'm not defending it, Mike," Allen said with little emotion.

"Of course you're not defending it! How the hell could you defend it?" I bellowed, not really caring if the people on the street could hear me. Then, in a more quiet tone, I told him through my teeth, "The way I was taught was that the victim comes first. We do it all for the victim. We might have our butts dragging and our wives hating us, but we take it a step farther, we go another few hours, we stick our necks way out there on the chopping block, and we do it for the victim. Not economics! The *victim!*"

Bill Allen said nothing. He simply stood there and nodded while he stared at his shoes. Finally, with his eyes looking out over the western portion of the city he conceded, "You're right, Mike. What can I say? You're right. Sometimes we lose sight of that. We get caught up in the sensationalism of the case rather than the guts of it. We lose the perspective."

I stayed silent for a few seconds and tried to determine if Allen was being straight with me. I guessed he might be, but I wasn't sure about anything anymore. I had already heard — and accepted — too many lies

I was ready for an argument to accompany my request, so I said it as an order, "I want to hear those tapes you got." I was ready to back that up by telling Bill Allen I was prepared to go to the Monroe County District Attorney, the local media, and, if need be, to the Pope, with the information he had supplied this night on the rooftop of the Federal Building. To my surprise, there was no need for threats.

Bill Allen looked past me, and his eyes narrowed in thought as he processed some information internally. It looked as if he was trying to make a decision, and then, after apparently arriving at a conclusion, he looked down to the stone-covered roof. "Normally, I would have to deny that request, Mike," he said with his head down. Then he took a breath and brought his head up to look me in the eye. "However, with the way things are going around here right now, I really don't give a darn about what The Bureau likes or doesn't like." Holding the stairway door open for me, he said, "If you want, you can listen to them now."

I didn't fully understand why Bill Allen was giving in so easily. By allowing me access to the tapes, he was jeopardizing his job. The FBI didn't approve of this kind of assistance being provided to local cops. I knew that, and more importantly, he knew it. If he was rolling over this easily, there had to more to this game than was evident. Was I about to be exposed to more FBI mis-information?

Back in the hallowed halls of the FBI, Bill Allen fixed me up with a set of headphones attached to a fancy digital recorder, the likes of which I had never seen before. As he listened to the tape with his set of headphones and searched back and forth for a minute or so, I looked at the back of the man and wondered what made him tick. He had been covering for the FBI for days.

The information he shared with me since he became my alleged partner had ranged from total bullshit to somewhat weak. He looked like the fair-haired mid-west farm boy, but he had also bedded down with a mob princess. I thought of him as spineless, but now he was making some major decisions that were going to impact his life, if not out-and-out ruin it. All of his actions, his words, his demeanor, had led me to believe he would fight by the Marquis of Queensbury Rules; yet, he had knocked me square on my ass with a beautiful, street-wise sucker punch. Bill Allen was becoming a mystery to me, and as I said before, I don't like mysteries. The man was turning out to be rather complex, and as is the case with mysteries, I don't care much for complexities either.

After Allen found the relevant conversation, he slipped me a pad and pen, unplugged his set of headphones, and plugged mine into the recorder. He then excused himself, and as he left the room he said over his shoulder, "I guess this will cost me my job."

His parting comment caused me more concern. Was it an observation said out loud to him or was it said for my benefit? I smelled a set up and began to believe the entire thing was being staged for my benefit. However, my presence in his office on this night was totally unplanned, and he had no way of knowing I was going to call and ask to meet with him.

I listened to the voices of several men on the tape as they talked about baseball, food, and women. When things quieted down a bit, Ruggeri dispatched Charlie Tortero to call me with the invitation to join him for dinner.

"This kid getting killed usually wouldn't mean a thing to me one way or another, Eddy," Vincent Ruggeri said in his customary low, gravely tone. "But he was a cop. That means trouble we don't need right now. This has brought a lot of heat on our businesses."

"I know what you're saying, Vincent," Eddy Cavaluso's voice said.

"We got union things going on, that trouble with the Buffalo people, you know what I mean? We're coming into prime betting season for baseball. The football action will be starting. We don't need the kind of trouble this thing will bring us."

"Uh, huh," Eddy said without any emotion or commitment.

There was a silence that lasted an uncomfortable amount of time.

"So, from what I hear, you were going to take the kid with you for a drink or something," Ruggeri commented. "That was the night he got killed, Eddy." The statement was dropped into the conversation as a simple observation, but it carried a tone of accusation. I wondered if I was reading too much into the Old Man's statement, but two second later I learned my observation was a correct one. "You killed him," Vincent Ruggeri said flatly as if he was stating a simple, known fact. "Why?"

"Vincent, the kid was too nosy. He was always asking about who was who and about this thing and another thing. He was getting into my business. Forget about it. I knew he was a snitch. I didn't know he was a cop, believe me! But I knew he was a snitch."

"How do you know that?"

"There was a couple different things I seen him do that I didn't like. I seen the kid talking to one of the Organized Crime cops once. I asked some cops about it. They told me, in so many words, they thought the kid had a screw loose. Now don't get me wrong, Vincent. I didn't know the guy was a real cop, but I had to dump him. Besides, what was I supposed to do? I tried talking to him, you know, telling him it ain't so good to be asking all them questions all the time. He laughed at me and told me not to worry about it. Hey, forget about it! What am I supposed to do? I finally tell him if he comes around I'll cut his ears off and he tells me to back off. He got out of hand. He had to go. Forget about it!"

I played back the segment a second time. My heart was having a difficult time accepting what my ears were hearing. I didn't want the information to be true. Somehow it was easier for me to believe a Federal Agent was the killer of Danny Martin than it was for me to believe Eddy Cavaluso, a Mafia killer, was the murderer.

"That was a bad move, Edward. Bad move," Ruggeri intoned.

"The guy was no good," Eddy stated as he tried to make his case. "He's beating up on his old lady. I got the family coming to me saying they wouldn't mind if he got hurt a little, or if he even ended up dead. He was a punk."

The family? I looked at the recorder, hoping it would explain. Who in Martin's family wanted him dead? Did his wife go to Eddy and ask him to whack Danny?

"The family paid you to kill him?" Ruggeri asked in noted disbelief. "Is that what you're telling me?"

"No, they didn't pay for it," Cavaluso protested. "But, a member of the family asked me to do the favor for her. Forget about it! With him being a snitch and showing me no respect, and one thing or another, I figured we was better off without him."

"Since when do you make those decisions on your own?" Ruggeri asked without any hint of anger.

"Vincent, you tell me to run things, to handle things. Am I right? You tell me to take care of things. Right? I took care of it. Don't worry about it." There was a pause before Cavaluso, continued, "The fact is, I wasn't even gonna kill him, but it turned out I had to. Besides, it ain't gonna come back on us."

"I feel it will come back on us, Eddy," the Old Man countered with a hint of indignation.

"Forget about it," Eddy countered. "The cops are gonna figure the whole thing as a robbery."

There was a short silence and all I could do was imagine Ruggeri questioning Cavaluso with a look.

"I ripped the kid's necklace off his neck," Eddy said. "In fact, I was gonna grab his wallet too, but then I saw headlights pulling in the driveway, so I had to get out of there."

Again there was silence except for some silverware being moved around.

"Did the Martin kid know about this fed, Allen, being in our pocket?" Ruggeri asked.

"I don't know if he knew it for a fact," Eddy responded. "But, he sure wondered about it. He was asking me some time ago about me and the fed hollerin' at one another, you know, when I asked the Fed about his old girlfriend in California."

"So why kill him without coming to me first?" Ruggeri asked as if he was some CEO inquiring about an unauthorized expenditure.

"I was gonna talk to the kid. But, forget about it. He wouldn't listen. He threatened he was gonna blow the lid off everything. I pulled the gun, you know, to make my point. Martin grabbed for it, and one thing and another, he ended up getting shot."

"Amato's here," a voice, evidently Twist Tortero's, advised in a hushed whisper.

"Let me handle this," Ruggeri said. "Just keep quiet and let me try to redirect Amato's attention someplace other than us."

"I already done that," Eddy said in a similar whisper. "He leaned on me the other night when I was coming out of the State Street Club. I told him the kid was banging a stripper and that her old man was on to it."

"*Silenzio!*" the Old Man ordered just as my voice was heard discussing Charlie Tortero's attempt to pat me down for a weapon.

I slipped the machine's lever to fast forward through my conversation with the Mafiosi, checking every so often to see if it had gotten to the dialogue that took place after I left. Finally, I found it, just as Bill Allen returned to the room where I was hunched over the recorder. Following his suggestion, I unplugged my headset, and we listened to the remainder of the conversation directly from the speaker of the recorder.

"I don't know if he caught your drift," Eddy said.

"He caught it," Ruggeri confirmed. "He knows your dog's name, and who's got hemorrhoids, and everything else," Ruggeri said with a laugh. "A man like that needs to be lightly tapped, not struck with a hammer," the Old Man commented. "If the need comes up, we can send someone to him with the message that the fed has some past friendships in San Diego that needs his attention. It will be implied that Martin knew it also."

"Did they?" Bill Allen asked over my shoulder.

"What?" I questioned.

"Did they send you someone with the information about me and Gail?"

"No, Bill. I got that on my own."

"Can you tell me how you got it?"

"Sorry," I said, and the man knew I was not going to reveal my source. Then I threw in a question of my own. "What was that about you being 'in their pocket'?" I asked.

"I already told you about that, Mike. After they made a move on me with the information about Gail, we played along. From time to time, following Delany's instructions, I fed them bits and pieces of bogus information." He paused and smiled. "That's why they felt so comfortable talking at the restaurant. I had them convinced most of their other places were bugged."

I picked up my notes as Bill put the recorder, tape, and headphones away. When he was finished, we walked back to his desk.

"You said you wouldn't normally have let me listen to that tape," I reminded him. "So why did you?"

"I'm all done here, Mike. My career with the FBI is gone," he said with just a slight tinge of remorse. "No matter where I go, that thing in San Diego is going to keep coming up. My reputation is shot. Letting you listen to the tape is just frosting on the cake. My resignation is in the computer. Delany will get it Monday morning."

"Reputations change," I commented. "What finally made you make the decision to bail out?"

"It's like you said, our perspectives and priorities are all screwed up. The Bureau isn't like it used to be. We get bogged down in protocol, running to Washington for permission on everything. We spend more time and resources fighting cops than we do fighting the likes of Ruggeri and his people." Allen gave me a shrug and added, "It's not only me. A number of guys are feeling it. In fact, why do you think Matt Murphy retired? He got fed up too. He hates Delany." The fed leaned back against the wall and crossed his arms over his chest. He continued to act as if he was talking to me, but he was really vocalizing what was going on in his head. "After working with you these last couple of days, I know what Danny Martin meant to you. Today, at the cemetery, I saw what this case was doing to you. You have to solve it, Mike. If you don't solve it, it's going to eat a hole in your gut."

He paused long enough to gather his thoughts. When he began to speak again, he spoke louder, as if wanting the walls to hear what he was saying. "I knew we were sitting on the information that would break this case wide open, and I knew we would continue sitting on it until Washington gave us permission to take it to a grand jury. That's not right ... that isn't justice."

Now some things were beginning to make sense to me. Now I understood why Murphy, who I thought would fight me, gave in and let me pursue the case. Now I could see why he took over the first meeting we had with the FBI and interjected that I would work the case and that we would not hand it over to the Feds. Some things were clearer now. Others were still clouded.

"What will you do?" I asked out of genuine concern.

"Probably go back to Carbondale," he offered casually. "I shouldn't have any trouble getting in with the District Attorney's Office there. The FBI can have all this cloak-and-dagger stuff. I just want to work someplace where it's all laid out nice and neat. Do you know what I mean? Someplace where you know the bad guys from the good guys. There's too many fine lines here, too many shades of gray. I'm having trouble knowing who's on what team, much less what the score is. Like you said, we lose sight of the victim. We're so busy developing strategy that we forget all about the crime."

We smiled at each other, and then, quite spontaneously, shook hands. I muttered some things about hoping it all worked out for him. When the handshake was over, I said, "I'm going to ask you one question, and I want you to look me in the eye when you answer me."

"Ask," he responded.

"Regarding this audio tape I just listened to …"

"Was it doctored?" He smiled as he asked the question for me. "No way, Mike. The tape is only two days old. Even if we wanted to edit, we couldn't do it in that short of a time. The Bureau doesn't act that fast."

Again a smile crept over my face. That was the very first time I had heard Special Agent Bill Allen refer to his agency without an air of reverence.

We walked in silence out of the office and into the corridor. As we waiting for the elevator, Bill Allen asked me to keep his name, along with the fact that he had let me listen to the recording, out of my reports as long as I possibly could.

"I hear you're very creative when it comes to putting it all down on a report, Mike. Just do me that favor if you can. Keep me, and what we did here tonight, out of it. Okay? I mean, you know, if you can."

"If it goes down right, it won't have to be in a report," I assured him as the chrome doors slid shut.

* * *

A half-hour later I found myself sitting on the pier at Lake Ontario. I took nips out of the bottle of Scotch I had picked up on the way north and as I nipped, I smoked one cigarette after the other.

All kinds of thoughts ran through my head. The prevalent one was that I had been a sucker through the entire case. I had let emotions get in the way of me being a cop. One question I had for myself was if I was being set up. Maybe I was becoming too paranoid, but it was possible, I reasoned, that the recording could have been a phony, a mock up made out of bits and pieces of hundreds of yards of tape held by the Feds. They had all kinds of electronics, labs, technicians, resources, and means to make such a prop. Maybe I was giving the Feebs too much credit, but still …

Then, as a matter of practicality, there was the very probable scenario that the tape was real. The conversation I had listened to in the cramped, little, FBI audio room could very well have been — in fact it probably was — authentic. As hard as it was to admit that I had been given a snow job by Vinnie Ruggeri, it was obvious I had been snowed on like the many storms that hit Rochester throughout the winter. I was usually good at knowing when I was being bullshitted, but I sure as hell wasn't infallible.

One thing to my credit was that I had been somewhat accurate in assessing the conversation when I talked to the Old Man. He had, in fact, been fairly honest about not having ordered the hit, but not so honest about not knowing who did it.

The bottom line was that I was being played for a fool. I took a long pull on the pint bottle and reasoned with myself. If the FBI gave me a phony tape to listen to, what was their motive? Did they want me to go off half-cocked and confront Cavaluso or Ruggeri and tell one or both of them about the tape? What would that get them, a corruption case on a local cop? Ah! That could be. Nothing gave the Feds a big erection like having a local cop to wave in front of the press.

What if the tape was real? What would be the FBI's incentive in having me listen to it? Nothing. They would know I would take the information and try to use it to put a cap on the case. If I did that, then they wouldn't get the good press out of it, and they surely coveted good press.

Then there was another slant on the entire episode. There was always a chance that Bill Allen had been straight with me. Maybe he was just plain fed up with all the turmoil, just the way he told me. It might be the card got played exactly as it was dealt into the hand. Maybe the chameleon in Special Agent Allen had changed his colors from true-blue FBI to the hazy, grayish color of the real world. And, then again, it could be that Allen was using me to settle his scores with The Bureau.

I finished the bottle, screwed the cap back on, and threw it into the river. Standing up, I brushed off my pants, lit a cigarette, and walked back towards my car. Along the way I checked my automatic, made sure there was a round ready to go, and released the safety.

It was time to confront my friend Fast Eddy Cavaluso.

15

Sunday Morning:
The Last Ground Lion

After leaving the pier at Lake Ontario, I made one stop. Before doing what I had to do, there was one thing I *wanted* to do, and that was to call Diane. At first she was a little concerned about why I was calling her at almost 11 o'clock at night. It took some doing, but I finally convinced her that she had been on my mind, and on the spur of the moment I had decided to call her. Convinced that I wasn't calling her because I was drunk, she asked if I was okay. I told her everything was fine and that we were working late to put some finishing touches on the Martin case.

"Have you got the guy, or are you going out to pick him up?" she asked.

"We're picking him up in an hour or so," I said and tried to make it sound casual.

"Be careful, Michael. I don't know why, but you sound worried to me." She paused and then asked, "This isn't going to be a routine bust, is it?"

"They're all routine," I said casually. The tone of her voice finally reached me, and I had to ask, "When did you begin to worry about me, Diane?"

"Since when are any of the arrests routine?" she asked. Then she tagged on, "I always worried about you."

"Ah, but do you still care about me?" I teased with a hint of a smile in my voice.

"I never stopped caring, Michael," my ex-wife answered, without a smile in her voice.

* * *

It was just a matter of time before I found Eddy Cavaluso. After all, it was the shank of Saturday night, and he would surely be sitting in on some poker or craps game somewhere around the city. It was somewhat of a surprise, but the man wasn't at any of his usual haunts. The search to run down Fast Eddy took almost two hours, but I finally spotted his car outside a gambling joint on Ridge Road, on the city's far north side. Being well past midnight, the mob joints were hopping. I used the cell phone to make the call knowing it would take an Act of God to get him out of a good crap game, especially if fickle lady luck was running in his favor.

"Tell him it's Tommy Boy. I got me a problem over here," I said to the mutt who was taking the call. Eddy probably had fifty number runners throughout the city, and I knew most of them. Tommy Fiorro was one of Cavaluso's main men, so a call from him was sure to be accepted.

"Yo," Eddy finally said into the phone. "What's the problem?"

"Eddy, it's me," I said, not wanting to identify myself in case the middleman to the phone call was slow in hanging up his end of the line. "I'm in some deep shit out here. I need your help now!"

"You sound like it," he said in response to the urgency in my voice.

"I need something taken care of now, Eddy. Where can I meet you?"

He hesitated for almost a half a minute, then asked, "How's about on the island?"

"Okay with me, but make it fast, okay?" I responded.

"Give me a clue what you got going on," he requested. "It might take me an hour or so to get there."

"I don't have an hour, Eddy. I need you and I need you now. If you can't help me, just say so, but I don't have a frigging hour."

"I'll be there," he said and the phone went dead.

Only two things could shake Eddy away from a crap game. One was mob business, which included his personal gambling enterprise; the other thing, not necessarily in chronological order, was a friend in need. The latter was the card I had played.

I pulled away from the curb across the street from the alleged social club and pointed the car toward the city's heart. Eddy and I had only three places we used for our private meetings. We had just used The Box, so there was not much sense in returning to it so soon. Cobbs Hill was another meeting spot, but at this time of night, it would be closed to vehicles. That left Manhattan Square Park or, "The Island," as Eddy called it.

Large portions of the city had been torn down during the city's urban renewal efforts of the mid-1960s and early 1970s. Some portions of decayed city blocks had been rebuilt with homes and small apartment buildings. Other areas were not suitable for homes, so they were made into small recreational areas aimed at offering some ambiance of rural relaxation in the midst of the city's hustle. Manhattan Square Park, situated on the southeastern edge of the downtown business district, was one such place. It's a small city block with a few grass-covered, rolling hills and plenty of trees and benches. The hills and trees do a good job of cutting off some of the city noise. The design also offers the park some privacy from the passing motorists. That's a good thing for clandestine meetings, but not such a good thing for the elderly citizens who had been mugged in the park so many times. It was evident our City Fathers were eager to blame the street cops for the crime that happened, but they did nothing to make them part of the prevention or the solution.

The center area of the park was designed to be an ice skating rink, but not being one who does anything that would appear to be a sign of cooperation with winter, I can't say if it was still used for that purpose. A hundred or so feet from the rink are a sprinkling of park benches arranged around and below a two-story high, metal scaffold-like structure that's suppose to represent "Rochester's bridge with her sister cities", or some crap such as that. The city leaders say it's art, but it looks like scaffolding to me.

Taking advantage of the time it would take Cavaluso to show up, I walked around the park and was disappointed to find a small group of about ten or twelve kids hanging around the north side of the skating rink, right where I planned on meeting with my newest suspect. A small, blue cloud of sweet, burning herbal weed hung above the kids. I approached them with my badge held high, yelling I was a cop and ordering them not to move. That was all it took to clear the park of any possible interference with the privacy my appointment needed. Yelling, "Police! Don't move!" did wonders in clearing any gathering.

With the park to myself, my thoughts went to the future weeks and months after I made this arrest. For a few days I would be a hero, but after that I would be the Department's jackass. It would be divulged to the press that I used information from the secret FBI recording bugs to make the arrest. The FBI would cover for their guy, asserting that Special Agent Allen was trying to cooperate with the Rochester Police Department. I, in turn, would be offered up as the sacrificial goat. The newspapers would grab hold of the story through "highly placed sources in the investigation" and I would eventually face a Grand Jury, be indicted, fired in disgrace, and possibly be sitting next to Eddy Cavaluso in a prison cell.

A nagging thought prodded the back of my head. I had a feeling, a hunch, that my meeting with Fast Eddy Cavaluso would solve nothing and would probably point me in a new direction, toward a new suspect. The reason the thought tugged at my mind's sleeve was that I hoped it would be true. I was hoping Eddy would clear the air and show me how I had been misled. The case had done that to me. Here I was, wishing and hoping that the mob under-boss would be innocent and the FBI Agent would be guilty.

I took a cigarette out of a fresh pack, lit it, and blew the smoke into the still, warm, summer night's air. The words I used in confronting my suspect would be critical. He would have to know he was being nailed, but I would have to guard how I knew what I knew. He had to be hit with enough information to make him admit what he had done, but at almost all costs, the source of my information would have to be kept hidden.

For a second, the thought of not making the arrest was an attractive alternative. In reality, it was no alternative at all. The matter had to be settled. The victim and his family needed their peace. Skipping the arrest would be good for me and my few remaining years with the Police Department, but it would not be good for Kathy Martin. I was too far along in years to start worrying about my career. Besides, maybe I was getting too old and too soft for this job. The mistakes I had made in this case were evidence enough to substantiate that fact. Maybe I needed to be forced out of the way.

The spot for our meeting was secluded. The hill behind the benches would keep us out of view from cars passing along the northern edge of the park. The skating rink would protect us on the south side. To the east and west, the curving walkways and other small hills concealed the covey of benches where we would sit.

I was on my third cigarette when I saw the hunched man walking slowly in my direction. He was being led by the small, white, ever-sniffing dog. The sight brought a smile to my face, but I stiffened myself as I stood and erased any hint of pleasure from my mug and mind. Eddy took the long way around to reach me, looking right and left as he moved, ensuring we were alone. Max was in front of him by about four or five feet, his nose close to the sidewalk.

My eyes kept master and dog in sight, but my mind focused on the arrest. In a couple of minutes I was going to bust my long-time friendly enemy. He was an old man. Doing time in prison would probably kill him, and his few short years on this earth would be shortened even more. I was intent on getting a confession out of him, and then I was going to arrest him. I hated what I was going to do. I knew it was the right thing to do. It just felt wrong.

Usually, when I get this close to making an arrest, my mind and body are filled with excitement, anxiousness, and a sense of winning. None of those emotions entered my spirit this night. Some arrests are made with the SWAT team, and doors come crashing down. Others are made quietly, when the suspect is picked up as he leaves his house. And, often enough, an arrest comes as a result of a long, boring stakeout. Whatever the case, it's the time when juices flow and you feel the rush of adrenaline. However, this warm and breezy night, the high was absent. I sat there watching the man that I was going to arrest and I felt depressed.

As he moved toward me, I found myself wondering why I was feeling sorry for the dog that was going to be orphaned, so to speak. I told myself my feelings had to be with Danny Martin and his family, but my eyes trailed the dog and my mind wondered how he would do when he went to his animal prison after Eddy was incarcerated.

"What's the problem, kid?" Eddy asked as he extended his hand to me. "Sorry to get you out of the game, but I had to see you," I said as I stalled for time to assess the man who had gone from friend to killer.

"Forget about it," he said with a wave of his hand. With some physical discomfort, he sat on the bench. "I wasn't catching anything to be proud of."

Sitting down next to him I said, "There's some sad news floating around, Eddy," I said as Max inspected my shoes with his hyperactive nose. "I just heard you killed Danny Martin."

The old man sat motionless, expressionless, and silent. A minute went by, maybe two. Finally he asked, "Where'd you hear that?"

"It don't matter where I heard it or who I heard it from, Eddy. I know the information is good."

The old man got older, more bent as he sat next to me.

"And you believe this information, Mike?" It's difficult to describe, but the question wasn't a challenge to my statement. He was simply asking if I really and truly believed the information.

"It's good information, Eddy. It's backed up and it's solid."

He wiped his face with his right hand as his left hand patted the dog's head. "What can I say, Mike?" he asked almost as a plea.

"Well, you aren't denying it, so I guess it's true," I noted evenly.

The man sat silently as he leaned forward to stroke Max's back. I also think he wanted to gather his thoughts.

"It was an accident," he said more to Max than to me.

"An accident," I snorted. "You put three shots in the guy's back and you want me to believe it was an accident? Come on, Eddy! Do you really think I'm an idiot? Show me some respect. Don't treat me like a *cafone*."

"I mean ..." he started to say and then drifted off. The elderly man cleared his throat and began again. Max looked up at him as if sensing his master was in some type of pain. Eddy stroked the dog's head and started the sentence again. "I wasn't going to kill him. I just wanted to lean on him a little. And I swear to you, Mike, I didn't know he was no cop. I mean that. And, I didn't know he was your friend. I swear before all the saints in heaven, Mike, I would never have hurt him if I knew the kid was your friend."

"Why did you do it, Eddy?" I asked. "I heard your reason second-hand, but I want to hear it from you personally."

"I ... it don't make no sense now ... I thought, you know ..." He struggled with the words. "Remember back, when was it, maybe a year, a year and half ago? You and me was meeting in the Box, right after that jerk Frankie Lanovara got killed. You spotted something, somebody watching us, but you never said anything until after, maybe a day or so after. You was worried that maybe it was the Feds or somebody watching us. Remember?"

"Yeah," I said cautiously, wondering what that had to do with the present-day situation. "It was somebody in a blue pickup truck, if I recall correctly," I said as I barely remembered the incident in spite of what Danny had told me in his letter.

"Right, Mike. That was it," he said solemnly. "Well, I saw it too. I thought I knew who the truck belonged to, so when you asked me about it, I told you, 'Forget about it.' Right? Well, I knew it was Martin's truck. At the time, I thought maybe he was a cop and he was watching us meet. I always was suspicious of the kid. Like maybe he was a cop or a rat. Then, when you asked me about him, well I figures he ain't no cop, so he must be a snitch. I figures the kid was keeping tabs on me, or something like that. Then, after that, I began paying more attention to him, seeing what he was doing. Well, one thing and another, and I see the kid was always asking about this, that, and the other thing. Questions, too many questions. You know, like I told you the other night when me and you was meeting up on Cobbs Hill."

"You killed a guy because he asked too many questions, Eddy?" I asked in disbelief.

The man disregarded my sarcasm and continued. "I began to see he was trying to get close to Ruggeri. I figured the kid was looking to make points with Vinnie and was gonna tell him about me and you." Eddy Cavaluso rested for a second and drew a heavy breath. "I thought he was gonna snitch me out to

Vinnie, Mike. I had to get him away from us for good or I had to kill him."

"So you took him out, drove behind the school, and then you shot him, Eddy?"

"Kind of like that, Mike. It sounds like that but that ain't what I was gonna do." He looked at me to see if I was buying what he was selling. "I was gonna throw a little fear into him. I just wanted him to keep away from us. It's all confusing to me, Mike. It's like all rolled up in one big pot of sauce. At the time it was clear to me. I was clear about what I was doing. But now ... now I don't know. I was stupid to do what I did."

"But you knew he was a cop, right?" I pushed the broken man, who I wanted to hate but found I couldn't.

"No way, Mike! I never knew he was a cop. Forget about it! You know we don't kill cops. I thought he was a stoolie, a rat. All due respect my friend, but the kid was no good. I heard he was beating his wife, that he was *disgrazziato* as a husband, as a man. I was gonna take him out, rattle him a little, and, you know, do Vincent a favor." He looked at me and added, "Of course, I mean you no disrespect when I say these things. These things occurred before I knew he was your friend."

"What made you so sure he was a snitch?" I asked out of genuine curiosity.

"First, there was the thing when he saw me and you talking after Lanovara got whacked. Then, he started asking questions about me and that Fed, what's his name, Allen, talking together. Plain and simple, the kid was making me nervous, Mike." Again there was a pause and a deep sigh. "I tried to warn him to mind his own business. I was gonna scare him when I brought him behind the high school. I told him we had to talk. I was trying to tell him we didn't want him around anymore, but he was still asking questions. He was asking what me and some coppers talk about, and if Allen was crooked, and kinds of stuff like that. I told him to lay off his old lady, and that if he laid a hand on her again I was gonna break his friggin' legs. He started asking questions all over again, wanting to know who said he was slapping his old lady around. Finally, forget about it. I pulled out the gun and he grabbed for it. He missed it and I pulled back. The kid got outta the car and started running. I had half a thought he was gonna run back and tell Vincent I tried to whack him, so I popped him."

"And then you took his wallet," I said to see if he would correct me.

"I was gonna grab his wallet, Mike, but I never did. I grabbed a hold of his chain, the chain around his neck, and pulled it off. I thought maybe if yous guys found it gone, you know, that yous cops would figure it was a mugging or something like that. I was gonna put a snatch on his wallet too, but I heard some car came pulling in on the other side of the school so I split and took off out the other side of the parking lot. It was a stupid thing I did, Mike, and I beg your forgiveness."

We looked at each other in silence. The very few seconds lasted a lifetime. The little white dog stood up on his hind legs and put his paws on the old man's knees. When Eddy looked down at his dog and began to slowly rub behind both ears of the mutt, I shifted my gaze to the sidewalk and began sorting out my next move.

"I don't know, Mike," Cavaluso said before I could make up my mind. "My mother used to say, '*La giovenuto disordinata la vecchiezza tribulata!*' Do you understand that, Mike?"

"My Italian is a little rusty and very limited, Eddy, "I confessed. "It's something about when you mess around in your young life, you pay for it when you get older."

"Close enough, my friend," he acknowledged sadly. "It means, 'An ill-spent youth makes for a troubled old age.' That's what I have now, a troubled old age. I made a stupid mistake. I killed a young man who was no danger to me. He was a bother, like a pebble in my shoe, but I had no right to kill him. My judgment, my, what do you call them, my instincts, they're not what they use to be." He stopped and gave a long, moaning sigh.

He continued, "Like Vincent said, we're all chameleons, Mike. We do what we gotta do to survive. My wife, God rest her soul, is gone. My friends, the true friends of my youth, are all gone now. My only comfort is this dog. *Questo bello cane!*" Again, following his compliment to 'this beautiful dog," the old man reached down to scratch the dog's ear. Then, with another sigh, he lifted the Westie onto the park bench and seated Max next to him. "He's a beautiful dog, don't you think so, Mike?" With the question, the old man's eyes watered.

"He is, Eddy," I agreed, wanting to put off the inevitable action I knew I had to take. Again the thought struck me that once I arrested Eddy I would have to put the mutt in the animal shelter.

"You should have a dog, Mike," Fast Eddy suggested out of left field. "As we grow old, we need friends. You are like me, *compadre*. No wife. No interests. No friends. A dog would be good for you, my friend."

I wondered how this man, who I talked to only a few times a year, knew so much about my life and me. I also wondered why he kept referring to me as, 'my friend.' I let the former question go by, but asked the latter.

"You say we have no friends, but you keep calling me your friend. Why is that?" I asked.

"Does that make you uncomfortable?" he asked as he gave his full attention to the dog, stroking the long, silky back of the animal.

"Not really," I answered in a half-truth. The term was not making me feel uncomfortable, but it was making me reluctant to do that which I had to do. Switching the subject, I made a move to clear up questions that had been nagging me for the past few days.

"I know it was you who called Martin at his home before he left to meet with you," I lied. "What was he pissed off about?"

Cavaluso had to think before he answered. "Oh, oh that! I told him I had to see him, that his sister-in-law was concerned about him belting his old lady around, and that I wanted to talk to him, to see what his problem was."

Again, we lapsed into a silence. The news had hit me hard, and now that I knew that Phyllis had inadvertently prompted Danny's death, I wished I had never pushed Cavaluso for the information. I stood slowly as if to stretch my legs. It was going to be necessary to be in a position to make the arrest with as little confrontation as possible. The elderly man remained seated on the bench, petting his dog. I stood in front of him and looked at the dog that wore what appeared to be a big smile around his panting, pink tongue. Once again, it was Eddy who broke the silence.

"I call you my friend because I respect you, Mike. You do your business well, and you do it with honor. I respect that and I admire you for being that way. What else should I call you?" He let the question go unanswered and followed it with a second question. "Does it bother you that I call you my friend because you're gonna kill me?"

I started to answer, but Cavaluso cut me off with a wave of his hand.

"It shouldn't cause you trouble. You're entitled to kill me. In fact, it's your duty. I killed your friend. You must avenge what's been taken from you. Don't regret it, Mike. Do it. Shoot me, and you do me a favor." He looked up at me finally. "As a friend to Martin, and as a friend to me, you should kill me. I carry no grudges with me to the grave."

"I'm not going to kill you, Eddy. I'm not made like that. That part of my Sicilian heritage is gone from me." I took a deep breath, exhaled it, and said, "I'm going to arrest you."

Eddy Cavaluso looked up at me without an expression on his face. There was no surprise, no anger, nothing. His body gave a slight movement, as if he was prepared to shift his shoulders. The motion stopped when I asked the question that had been eating at me for the past several hours.

"Did someone in Martin's family pay you to whack the kid?"

"That's not true. Mike. There was no payment. It wasn't like that," he protested. I felt somewhat better knowing that Kathy or Phyllis had not paid for Danny's killing. I took some relief in knowing that part of the accusation was not true. The relief was short lived.

"It was as a favor Mike, not a contract."

The relief I had felt died instantly. "Tell me about it, Eddy. Let's clear the air on this thing!" I was getting angry and I didn't know why. "You tell me you were going to scare the kid, then you tell me you were doing the family a personal favor. Which is it?"

He offered a long, deep sigh into the night air before he answered.

"Mike, I swear to God, I was gonna scare the kid. That night, the night I whacked him, I was just gonna talk to him, scare him, you know, threaten him. It was, like I say, all rolled together. He was asking too damn many questions. I knew he must be a snitch to yous guys or the miserable FBI. Then too, the sister-in-law asking me to lean on Martin for smacking his wife around; it was all that together, Mike."

Cavaluso began to describe how he had called Danny on Tuesday evening and told him they had some serious business to discuss. He told me that even though he distrusted the kid, he had always been friendly toward him. I could understand his reasoning. The old Sicilians had a saying about holding your friends close and your enemies even closer. Consequently, when Eddy told Danny he had business to discuss, the kid may have thought he was on his way to a major break through in his investigation. Cavaluso described how they rode together and how he began to tell Danny he needed to change his ways, to mind his own business. Danny kind of threw off the suggestion, and told Eddy that was just the way he was, that he was an inquisitive person. Realizing that Martin wasn't going to heed the warning, Eddy told his passenger he had to take a leak. He drove behind Aquinas High School, got out of the car, and Danny joined him.

"I pulled the gun and told him in no uncertain terms that I didn't like him, didn't trust him, and didn't want him around no more," Eddy said. "I told him I knew he was beating up on his old lady, and that I was gonna blow his brains out unless he did a very good job of disappearing for the rest of his life and leaving his hands off the broad."

"And then you shot him?" I asked.

"No, Mike. I didn't want to shoot him. Forget about it! I had no intention of shooting him — if that makes any difference," he said with a shrug of resignation. "The kid got hot when I mentioned his wife and all. He wanted to know if it was his sister-in-law who was telling me that. He got rough and tried to grab the gun. I gave him a shove and he turned to run. Then, well then, I shot him. I was, I don't know, I guess I wasn't thinking clear." He took a long breath and let it out slowly. "I did it, my friend. I did it and I'm sorry to put you through this misery."

"Who, Eddy? Who in the family asked you to take care of Danny?"

"It's not important, Mike."

"It's important to me," I said angrily. I needed to know clearly, exactly, without any assumptions to be made on my part. "I'm not going to do anything about it, but I've got to know. Who was it?"

"I know a broad, Mike. She runs cocktails at a jazz place called Skelly's that I go to now and then. She's a nice kid, always has a smile for me along with a nice word. At my age, I guess that's important. She's the kid's sister-in-law."

"Phyllis?" I asked, hoping there was maybe another sister-in-law in the picture.

"Yeah, Phyllis," he confirmed. "She didn't want him whacked or anything, just scared. I figured I was doing her a favor, Mike.

You know? At my age, I still like to be useful. Maybe I was just trying to impress her. I don't know."

I felt like someone, something had deflated me. I was sick and just wanted the thing over with. I wanted to get this case closed and move on to something else.

"Stand up, Eddy," I said more as a request than a command as I stood in front of him. "I'm going to arrest you for the murder of Officer Danny Martin."

As I finished the last part of the last sentence, my right thumb began to push my sport coat aside so I could reach back, past my gun, and retrieve the handcuffs that swung from my belt. The movement caught the dog's attention and he got up to see what was going on. With my attention diverted to Max, I never saw Cavaluso's left hand come up. The thumb and forefinger of his beefy mitt circled my right wrist in a vise that was surprisingly strong for a man his age. The remaining three fingers did a nice job of locking my wrist in a death grip. Evidently, the arthritis that crippled his back and legs had not affected his hands.

My eyes penetrated Eddy's eyes. His eyes were locked on mine. I felt my right side being pulled down by his grip. For just a fleeting second, as I struggled to remain standing, I thought my captor was trying to pull me down to my knees.

I was wrong. Eddy was using his grip on my wrist as leverage to pull himself up to a standing position. As he was succeeding in doing so, the old Mafioso reached his right hand under his light windbreaker, pulled out a hand gun, and raised it to my face. Moving only my eyes, I looked down at the snub-nosed, .38 revolver that was resting against my cheek, below my left eye. Without a word, Eddy released his grip on my right wrist, reached inside my sport coat and pulled my 9mm out of the holster. Stepping back from me, he threw my gun into the bushes about ten yards behind me.

"Sit down. Mike," he said. Similar to my earlier statement, it was a request, more than a command. As he spoke the words, he pointed the barrel of the gun at a place on the bench next to

Max. I sat down and the dog stood on my left thigh with his front legs. Immediately he made the side of my face and neck the subject of his inquisitive nose before he planted a wet, sloppy kiss on my face.

I thought about rushing Cavaluso, about pushing myself up from the bench and throwing my shoulder into his mid-section hard enough to make him fall back and possibly lose the grip on his weapon. As I evaluated that thought in relation to the grip he had managed to put on my wrist, Eddy spoke.

"I can't go to jail, Mike. I'm too old for that. I'm too sick, too tired, too worn out for that."

My mind was formulating a small speech about the futility of running and hiding at his age, but my eyes were focused solely on the barrel of the .38 that was pointed squarely at my forehead. Gauging the three or four feet between us, I doubted I could rush him before he squeezed off the round. I decided to wait for a better opportunity, for his attention to be diverted, before I shoved him and pulled out the second gun I had stuffed in the small of my back.

"You ask me to kill you, but yet you fear prison," I commented. "You call me 'friend' and then point a gun at me. I don't understand your reasoning."

"There are some things worse than dying, *amico mio*, and living is sometimes one of them. There is nothing for me now, Michael. Forget about it! My wife is gone from me. I have embarrassed and troubled my good friend, Vincent. I have acted foolishly and killed a friend of my friend. Like a kid, I was gonna rough up Martin to impress a broad. I'm an old, crippled, foolish man who has no one, and I serve no function."

"Things have a way of working themselves out, Eddy," I offered in consolation.

"Forget about it," he said in that gruff, typical Fast Eddy fashion. "That night, the last time we talked up on Cobbs Hill, I knew it would come to this, Mike. I asked you to drop the matter, but I knew you wouldn't. So now ..."

In that moment I knew Eddy Cavaluso's plan. I started to push myself from the bench and cried, "Don't!"

The instant I began to make my move, the old man took one step back. "Take care of Max for me, my friend," he said. As he spoke, he put the gun to the right side of his head ... and pulled the trigger.

Before the pink cloud of mixed red blood and white brain matter could form completely, Max, who had laid down next to me, jumped upright on all fours. The dog barked once and then looked up at me, over to his falling master, and back at me. Then, in an attempt to resolve his confusion, the little white dog jumped from the bench and went to his master. He sniffed at Eddy's right hand, along his right arm and shoulder, up to his face, and he licked the cheeks and sealed lips that would no longer call him "my friend." Then, sitting down next to the lifeless body, little Max sent out a low, hushed, woo-woo-wooo, in three distinct syllables that are impossible to capture here in words, but will live in my mind and soul for eternity.

I used the cell phone to call for the necessary personnel to process the scene. When they arrived, Max and I were still seated on the park bench giving comfort to one another. The case had cost Max his dearest friend. It had cost me two of mine. The difference was that Max had known who were his friends. I had not.

This case, like many other cases, had taken its toll on me. Unlike the many other cases, it had left me sad and morose. I had spent very little time with Danny or Eddy. One I had known in my youth, the other came to me later in life. I had not perceived either of them as friends and had not sought their company, but without them I suddenly felt alone. Even though the early morning air was still warm and humid, a shudder spread through my shoulders, arms, and chest as I sat on the bench

petting the little dog and waiting. As the approaching sirens
pierced the quiet night, I found it necessary to wipe my eyes dry.

The scene was soon filled with uniformed cops, bosses,
Evidence Technicians, and Detectives. Questions were asked,
answers were given, and camera flashes lit the scene with
lightning-like bursts. Some of Eddy's blood had sprayed over on
my sport coat, so the crime scene technicians took it for
evidence. Max had tracked some of the blood as he sought to
make sense of his master's failure to hold him, so he, with his
bloody paws, was considered to be evidence also. They were
going to take the little mutt and put him in the dog pound, but I
told them to back off. The little guy had been through enough.
He wasn't going to sit in jail, not after everything else he had
been put through. Not for tonight anyway! I lifted the mutt and
tucked him under my right arm. He would stay with me for the
night, and in the morning I would dump him off at a friend's
house.

"You can't remove evidence from a crime scene, Lieutenant,"
a well-intentioned uniformed Sergeant called out to me as I
walked away.

I didn't stop walking, but merely slowed the pace a little as I
gave a half turn. Max was tucked firmly under my arm and used
the opportunity of me turning to get one last glimpse at the
motionless figure of the man who had been our friend.

"Forget about it," I said over my shoulder. The words were
the right words, but they failed to carry the meaning and flavor
they held when spoken by Fast Eddy Cavaluso.

Epilogue

The report I submitted on the case was concise, to the point, and mostly factual. Because the last minutes of Fast Eddy's life, along with his confession, were made while he was alone with the mutt and me, there were no witnesses to debate what might have been said or not said.

My report stated Eddy Cavaluso killed Officer Danny Martin because he suspected Martin was a cop. I took a little license there and added that Danny had, in fact, told Cavaluso he was a cop and that Danny was in the act of arresting Cavaluso for possession of the gun Cavaluso had drawn. The report offered some facts to bolster it, but it summed up by saying that the young cop was killed as he tried to make the arrest. It's not the truth, but at least it guaranteed that Kathy Martin would get Danny's death benefits for having been killed in the line of duty. It was my way of shooting back at the accountants, the MBAs, and the bookkeepers that were trying to run the Police Department. They were trying to worm their way out of taking care of the Martin family, and that didn't seem fair to me. Besides that, I'm damn sure Eddy wouldn't have minded being the fall guy in this particular case. In fact, I'm betting that Cavaluso would have gotten a kick out of the entire thing. After all, one of his favorite things was scamming, and scamming the government gave him added delight.

More license was taken when I skipped over the part about listening to the FBI tapes. I chalked up the arrest to information that came to me by way of an anonymous tip and let it go at that.

The official version reported that I had confronted Cavaluso with the information, and after a short discussion, he had shot and killed himself. There was no mention of Phyllis Conte's role in Danny's death.

The Internal Affairs cops came out and did their thing at the scene of the shooting and then afterwards in the cop shop. I gave them an honest and complete accounting of how I was going to arrest Eddy, and how he had gotten the better of me. Them finding my gun in the bushes where Eddy had tossed it helped support my story. The only thing I ended up with was an Official Letter of Reprimand for not advising the dispatcher I was going to attempt an arrest of a felony suspect.

Once I got clear of the Public Safety building, I stopped by Kathy Martin's home. It was very early Sunday morning, right about sunrise, when I gave her the news that Danny's killing had been solved. There were a few hugs shared by her, Phyllis, and me. And, with the news, came a flow of many tears, tears of sorrow and tears of relief. Phyllis didn't ask if Eddy Cavaluso told me about her, and I didn't volunteer the information. She and I exchanged some looks as I talked to Kathy, and I could read her guilt.

The Danny Martin case had brought some of us from the old neighborhood together, and when it was over, Phyllis, Kathy, Chrisy, and I all drifted apart again, each of us to his or her respective corner of the world. Homicides are like that. For one short moment in time, the case brings an assorted, random group of people together, to lean on each other and to depend on each other for the support brought forth by the other individuals in the group.

In that aspect, this case was just like a lot of other homicides I have been thrown into. On the other hand, because it dragged me into my past, it was different. What made the case so very different was that it made me take a closer look at what I believed, and who I was. As I sit alone in the apartment, with Joni James belting out some old songs, I realize my prejudices are not rooted in the color of people or in their ethnicity. My prejudices are rooted in what I, based on very little evidence other than my beliefs, *think* people are, and how *I think* they should behave. Having done that soul searching, I am not pleased by what I see, and I know I have to do things to change that picture.

I try to look back after each one of these cases and ask myself what I learned. This case had torn me up inside. I mourn the fact Danny was a friend that I really never got to know. I am saddened by the truth that I had used Eddy Cavaluso for information for many years, while he had seen more in our relationship than my prejudices allowed me to see.

Vincent Ruggeri taught me that all men are ground lions — chameleons that change colors, sides, and loyalties as the need strikes them. When he said it, I took it as a negative, but now I realize that men may change their colors, the side of the fence on which they sit, and their loyalties, for the good. I would like to think that Eddy Cavaluso, right there in the twilight days of his life, was a chameleon who changed for the better: from the thief and conniver he was during most of his life, to a stand-up guy. I think the same is true for Matt Murphy, who backed me when all the smart money was betting against me.

I learned not to be so hasty in my judgments and to wait and see the chameleons change color several times in order to learn their natural color. I had misjudged Bill Allen, Skip Winston, and Matt Murphy. None of them are exactly and exclusively what I thought them to be. Each of them, as they jumped from the fence post to the grass, changed their color. Sometimes I liked their new color, and sometimes I preferred the old one. I guess the bottom line is that appearances are in the eye of the beholder.

And I learned to look at people differently. Now, when I remember to do it — for old habits are hard to break — I try to look inside people, to see what's hidden inside, to see if there's a Danny Martin hidden somewhere in there, outside of my narrow point of view. And, most of all, I know that I, too, am a chameleon and that I change.

Max? Well, with my lifestyle, taking care of a mutt who needs to be walked, talked to, petted, and fed is kind of difficult. The little guy really needs all the attention he can get. There's a young detective who works in Checks and Frauds, and he's got a couple of kids around the house, so I figured that would make a good home for Max. But, I never got around to asking the copper if he wanted the dog. Consequently, Max is here sleeping under the desk as I finish this off. I get him out to the park at least once a week, and on times when I get called out late at night, there's a beautiful elderly lady who lives below me who is more than happy to spend time with my little buddy. The guys in the squad have taken to him, and the mutt has put on a few pounds. Diane says that taking in Max has shown her I'm becoming civilized, and that if I keep up this trend, I may actually be suitable for human companionship sometime in the future.

Besides, like Eddy Cavaluso had said, a guy like me kind of needs a dog.

The best thing about this case is that it closed with justice. Many times, in the total scheme of things, justice, because she's blindfolded, kind of takes it in the shorts. But this time, all things considered, justice was served. That's usually the way it works out ... justice isn't usually found in a courtroom. An old guy once told me, "If you want justice, go to a whorehouse. If you want a screwing, go to court!"

We had a case a few years ago that proved that point. Remember, I said earlier that a wife beater is the second-lowest form of the human species? Well, the lowest animal is the one that abuses kids. Justice hid from us in that case, and all we got in court was a screwing. Justice was delayed on those murders, but it was finally served. What happened was, there were young kids getting murdered, and we had a terrible time with it ... but hey, that's another story.

The author welcomes readers' comments by e-mail at: DetMikeAmato@aol.com.